A Case of Knives

JULIAN DE WETTE

A Case of Knives

UMUZI

Published in 2010 by Umuzi
an imprint of Random House Struik (Pty) Ltd
Company Reg No 1966/003153/07
80 McKenzie Street, Cape Town 8001, South Africa
PO Box 1144, Cape Town 8000, South Africa
umuzi@randomstruik.co.za
www.umuzi-randomhouse.co.za

First edition, first printing 2010
9 8 7 6 5 4 3 2 1

ISBN 978-1-4152-0118-3

Cover design by mallemeule
Text design by William Dicey
Set in Minion

Printed and bound by CTP Printers, Cape Town

In memory of Robert Sobukwe,
Rhodes Gcxoyiya, Mzonke Xusa & David Sibeko
who did not live to see the landscape change

    &

with appreciation and thanks
to my parents

DISCLAIMER

This story is not essentially about how things were, but about how they might have been. The views expressed by the characters are not necessarily those held by the author. Most names and settings in this work of fiction have been changed to protect the identities of persons dead or alive, or imagined. In the unlikely event that any person considers himself or herself aggrieved by the misuse of identity in terms of Section 5 of the Identity Registration Act, or if any person has any objection to the misuse of the identity of any other person in terms of the Act, he or she may at any time object in writing to the registrar.

Every such objection shall be lodged in triplicate and be accompanied by an affidavit in triplicate setting forth in detail the grounds upon which the objection is made. Any person or entity lodging an objection considered frivolous by the registrar will be prosecuted to the fullest extent of the law.

My thoughts are all a case of knives,
  Wounding my heart
  With scattered smart ...

– GEORGE HERBERT, 'Affliction IV'

In Africa, whenever an old man dies a library goes up in flames.

– AMADOU HAMPÂTÉ BÂ

The Devil Is a Meddler

Enoch's knowledge of his grandfather, Oupa Hans, was scant because his mother and father allowed the old man only brief and infrequent visits to their home. Grave reminders from his parents always accompanied these visits – Enoch was not to believe his grandfather's stories as they never amounted to more than a pack of lies.

Neither of them was sparing in their description of the eternal damnation he risked if he so much as believed anything Oupa Hans told him. Most children would have responded with even greater curiosity in light of such prohibition. However, Enoch needed no persuasion to accept his parents' point of view. While some babies are said to have been born with a silver spoon in the mouth, Enoch had inherited a delicate appreciation of the perils of damnation straight from the womb. Fear of retribution had become a constant companion and, just as a child jealously guards his playthings, he refused to share his days and nights of anguish with anyone.

An awareness of his predicament was sparked when a Malay friend, Ebrahim, invited him to a revival meeting in the company of Ebrahim's Christian mother. Her husband was away on a sales trip in Durban and knew nothing of the event. The crusade tent was smaller than the Boswell and Wilkie's tent that he and Oupa Hans had surreptitiously visited a few times when the circus came to town, although there were almost as many people squeezed inside. The tall, light-skinned evangelist from a place called Atlanta, Georgia, dabbed at his tears that flowed without stop. There was not a dry eye in the audience. With his persuasive voice ascending and descending, the evangelist whipped the congregation into a frenzy with a story of the personal hell he had created for himself – until the day he had stood in front of a mirror with a bottle of poison in his hand.

'My dear brothers and sisters, I hated myself so much, I wouldn't have missed my own execution. Like Socrates the Greek, I raised the poison to my mouth. I was filled with so much self-loathing that at first I did not see the angel standing behind me in the mirror. But, when the angel spoke, I listened.

' "Brother Michael," he asked, "how's it going?" '

These words made Enoch sit up and listen. What little he knew about angels was that they said things such as 'Glory to God in the highest', and would hardly ask a man how things were going. From the many Christmas pageants he had performed in, the angels spoke in the language of the King James Bible – not everyday, street language.

' "I'm just fine – can't you see?" '

' "It pleases me to hear that you're fine. But what are you up to?" '

'It's like, I'm standing there with a bottle of poison in my hand and this creature wants to know what I'm up to,' Brother Michael explained.

'Then the angel says, "A razor would be quicker and less painful."

' "Why should I leave a mess for somebody else to clean up?" I said, shocked by the angel's thoughtlessness.

' "I'm pleased to see you are a fastidious kind of man," the creature said. "Go ahead, exercise your free will – but don't forget I'm always there when people need help with cashing in."

'At that moment, my eyes were opened, my dear brothers and sisters, and just as clearly as I see you now, I turned around and saw the angel Lucifer standing behind me. If anyone had said "Satan" to me, I would have been looking for a serpent. Can you blame me for not recognising him first time round?

'An angel with the laughter of a demon … And as the devil laughed, I could feel the fires of hell as if I were inside a furnace. I realised then that I had a choice – and I chose life. My brothers and sisters, what will you choose?'

And then to cap it all the evangelist quoted from the book of the prophet Amos: 'Do horses run upon rock? Does one plough the sea with oxen? But you have turned justice into poison and the fruit of righteousness into wormwood.'

Enoch had never heard of anyone ploughing the sea with oxen, although the benefits of wormwood had been forced down his throat whenever he complained about an upset stomach. Brother Michael's words and the picture of him standing in front of a mirror surrounded by flames and clutching a bottle of poison, like the demon drink his parents always warned him about, were far more frightening than the stories Oupa Hans had told him. Since that day Enoch could never quite shake off the fear that committing a sin carried a punch as lethal as Brother Michael's bottle of poison.

Ebrahim and his mother wept without shame while Enoch never once took his eyes from Brother Michael's face. His first sighting of an American had brought him much unexpected anguish, and the only thing that had kept him glued to his seat was the damnation he could expect if he walked out in the middle of a revival meeting.

Smoking and wearing make-up were next on Brother Michael's list of sins – and he had sent ushers into the bleachers with huge baskets to collect cosmetics and jewellery and cigarettes from the congregation, which he then emptied onto the podium so that everyone could see what an unashamed tempter Satan was. Enoch had examined the growing pile on the stage, but Ebrahim's tobacco pouch filled with marbles, mostly won from him, evaded his scrutiny. It was probably at the bottom. Fortunately his yo-yo was still safely tucked away in his trouser pocket.

'Pride, my African brothers and sisters, pride and vanity are in that bitter bottle of poison I warned about. Praise the Lord – now you have been delivered. His yoke is easy, his burden is light …'

Later, when the ushers took around the baskets once more for the requested 'paper' offering, they reminded Enoch of the disciples gathering leftovers from the multitude after the miracle of the loaves and fish. Brother Michael had told them that he was on his way to the heart of Africa and needed every penny for the salvation of souls up there. Enoch wondered if he would melt down the jewellery like Aaron did – and what he would do with Ebrahim's marbles.

After school the following day, Enoch looked up the name Socrates in the library and discovered the statue of an ugly man holding a cup to his mouth. So the hemlock business was true after all. Below the illustration there was a quote he copied into his notebook: 'The unexamined life is not worth living.'

From then on Enoch only pretended to listen to what his grandfather told him, although always observing a level of polite behaviour. If he neglected to raise his school cap to him or stood absent-mindedly with his hands in his pockets, Oupa Hans – along with Enoch's parents, teachers, neighbours and other arbiters of good behaviour – had unrestricted licence to use the cane.

What little Enoch gathered from his half-hearted attention to Oupa Hans helped him to piece together details of his grandfather's life before he arrived in Cape Town. He had been born in Tarkastad, west of Queenstown, and as a young man moved to East London in search of work. His father, the brother of a famous Boer War general, had plunged the family into disgrace by marrying a Xhosa woman. This was considered even worse than the fact that he had been an unashamed proponent of negotiations with the British enemy, which made him a traitor to the blood twice over. However, what impressed Enoch most about his grandfather was that he could speak Afrikaans and Xhosa equally well.

Oupa Hans's occasional visits to Enoch's home usually coincided with pension day. It was Enoch's duty to meet the old man at the railway station on his way back from Cape Town where he went to pay his tailor's bill and to stroll from one stall to the next on the Grand Parade, buying fruit and chocolates. Oupa Hans had been paying off his tailor's bill for as long as Enoch could remember. Once he took the boy with him to visit Mr Salie, his tailor, but as far as Enoch could see, not a single penny exchanged hands between the two men. All they did was drink tea and eat small coconut pastries called herzoggies and talk endlessly. Mr Salie sat in front of his enormous sewing machine. In a corner near the window there were two tailor's dummies that looked as if they had not felt the weight of cloth in years.

Enoch was offered some pastries with a cooldrink, and afterwards he arranged Mr Salie's pins into an intricate pattern on a pincushion. Mrs Salie wrapped a few squares of green and pink coconut ice in a paper napkin when he and his grandfather left. On the train he asked Oupa Hans what a 'quinella' was. He told him that it was a Malay word for the kind of padding tailors used to build up the shoulders of a jacket.

'It's supposed to give me the look of a military gentleman,' Oupa Hans said, and with an impulsive gesture got up in the moving train and raised his shoulders to show the effect it would have. 'I'll also need a couple of medals. He's charging me twenty-one guineas – enough for the medals as well.'

The passengers seated in their compartment turned away. Enoch cringed and looked out of the window as the train raced past factories and belching chimneys. As soon as they arrived home, Enoch offered his mother some of his coconut ice and told her about the wonderful time he had had at Mr Salie's house. She took away the boy's little package, his barakat, and turned on Oupa Hans.

'How dare you drag the child to District Six, Pa,' she shouted.

'Not everyone in District Six is a skollie,' Oupa Hans replied defensively.

'Well, that's news to me, Pa.'

Enoch had rarely seen his mother so angry.

'I had to go for a fitting.'

'A fitting for what, Pa? Pa's been wearing that shabby suit for ages. Don't Pa dare do that again. The child's father will hear all about it.'

Enoch toyed with the idea of telling his mother about their visit to the museum, but he thought that that might cause even more trouble. She did not like him staring at the half-naked Bushmen in the diorama and, according to her, it was no place to take a child. He understood why she was upset with Oupa Hans, as he had not fitted on anything at Mr Salie's house.

Oupa Hans had to find his own way back to the bus stop – and he made sure to leave before Enoch's father got back from school. Like most parents, his father and mother understood their son's level of susceptibility and had raised him with a carefully instilled fear of District Six – that notorious patch of Cape Town they called 'Satan's own playground'.

On New Year's Day and especially the day after, menacing troops of minstrels from District Six, dressed up in satin like sunbirds, strutted about the streets of Cape Town playing banjos while Enoch's family religiously devoted the first day of the year to the church convention on Harrington Street. What his parents found even more menacing was that these thugs, without the slightest provocation, were known to fish out concealed flick knives whenever they saw anyone decent approach. Men from the District drank and smoked dagga, and whenever merchant ships docked in the harbour, they would send their loose women to consort with the sailors. On more than one occasion Enoch had heard his mother say, 'They are the scoundrels who have brought disgrace to our city.'

His mother had not given Oupa Hans the time to explain that he had taken every precaution to ensure their safety. Enoch and his grandfather had taken the Hanover Street tram that dropped them a few paces from Mr Salie's front door. While the boy had sat on the carpet in the comfortable living room, the dangers of District Six had seemed so remote that they had not even occurred to him.

Some time after his banishment, Oupa Hans sent a message that he wanted Enoch to meet him at the train station after school. The boy eyed the purchases in the carrier bag his grandfather had handed him as soon as his feet touched the platform and the train door slammed shut behind him. At the best of times, Oupa Hans was a slow walker and never missed an opportunity to engage strangers in conversation along the way. Their progress along the length of the railway platform was invariably stymied because a mere greeting to strangers never sufficed. Enoch was also obliged to listen to his long talks with the railway workers who leaned on their pickaxes or rested their chins on shovel handles and paid him little attention until this Coloured man started speaking Xhosa.

Oupa Hans used language as a kind of magic. It always amazed Enoch to see how quickly it brought about laughter and camaraderie between total strangers. Even the workers' boss at the station, pipe smouldering between his lips, strolled across the rails from where he had been supervising with folded arms, and leaned against the platform edge. At first Enoch suspected that he was going to order them to move along, but instead the man ran a hand through his thinning blond hair and threw in an occasional Xhosa phrase. Oupa Hans politely corrected his pronunciation.

Despite his preoccupation with the contents of the bag his grandfather had handed to him, Enoch managed to pick up a tolerable number of Xhosa words, which later he practised diligently in front of his bedroom mirror. The words came in handy the following morning when he attempted to greet the milkman and enquire after the well-being of his family. He was barely able to reply to the man; but it made Enoch think that if only he could pick up Latin that easily, he would be much further along in class.

It was not until the end of the following month that the boy let down his guard with his grandfather. Oupa Hans had spent the night in their servant's quarters and Enoch's father had asked him to accompany the old man to collect his pension at the post office in Cape Town the following day. Oupa Hans was becoming increasingly unsteady on his legs and quite forgetful. In fact, it wasn't unusual for him to be looking at goods on a shop counter one moment and asking the shopkeeper for the way home the next. Enoch's mother said that the old man had a problem with his nerves. However, as she too pleaded a case of nerves whenever she felt overwhelmed by too much aggravation about the house, Enoch was reluctant to accept her explanation.

What was important about the unexpected outing was that Enoch would have a legitimate excuse for a glorious day away from school, although he still had dozens of lines of Wordsworth to commit to memory. Enoch had chosen Wordsworth because the poet used simple language – whereas he felt that Coleridge went on a bit too much about the imagination. When he had raised this with his English teacher, he was told that Coleridge's opium pipe might have been the cause of this state of mind.

Enoch had begun to consider his choice of poem a serious mistake – as he ought to have realised from the length of the title, 'Composed a Few Miles Above Tintern Abbey on Revisiting the Banks of the Wye During a Tour. July 13, 1798'. At 150 lines the poem was considerably longer than the sonnets the rest of his classmates had undertaken to memorise. A trip to Cape Town was exactly what he needed to take his mind off this unfortunate blunder.

When they arrived at the train station, Enoch looked around for the railway workers, but the only people on the platform were Zwaanswyk pupils in their blue and black-striped school blazers. A few of his friends waved at him and must have wondered what he was doing out of school uniform. The boy and his grandfather waited in silence until the ten to eight slowly entered the station, allowing the train driver to slip his arm through the hoop of the signal key held out by the stationmaster.

After finding two unoccupied seats, and to distract Oupa Hans from speaking to other passengers, Enoch asked him how the signal key worked. His grandfather said he did not have a clue, which surprised Enoch because he normally had an answer for everything – but he didn't press the point: he realised that it was unlikely that he would ever become a train driver. He had something else planned. Besides, he was already thinking about the excitements of the Grand Parade.

Oupa Hans also had something else on his mind. 'You must stand up to your parents,' he told Enoch with surprising vehemence. 'You've got to stop being such a coward, you know. You're going to miss a lot in life, unless you do something about it now. Life's a challenge. Without challenges you won't survive ...'

What could Enoch say? It was not as if he held the balance of power at home. At breakfast that very morning, he had asked his father if he could join the lifesaving club. The club secretary had sent him a typewritten invitation a few weeks earlier, and with Oupa Hans seated at the table he had finally gathered the courage to raise the subject.

His father had a look of pained shock in his eyes. 'Don't talk to me about lifesaving – what you really should become is a soul saver! At least then you won't drown.'

Enoch was aware that Oupa Hans might come to his rescue, but all of a sudden the old man had a struggle with a bit of toast and he jumped up and slapped him on his back to help dislodge it. The force of his effort also dislodged his grandfather's dentures, which went flying across the floor. There was silence until Enoch retrieved and examined them – and announced that they had survived their excursion. Once assured that all was well, his father excused himself as he was late for school, and he left before there was any more unnecessary confrontation.

'At breakfast you let your father get away with his ridiculous nonsense. It almost killed me. Promise me that you will never become like him.'

To Enoch Oupa Hans's words were as good as sacrilege. 'But what about me? I'm a strong swimmer – and how am I to explain to the club that Dowa wants me to be a "soul saver" instead?'

But that wasn't Enoch's only concern. He had to come to terms with the prospect that his dreams of rescuing reckless girls from the grip of cruel waves and currents would never be realised. Once he had put in a modest request for a bicycle as a birthday present. He regarded a bicycle as a neutral thing – there was nothing about it that could even vaguely be construed as sinful or political – and his father acknowledged as much. But he had said 'no' with the kind of finality that had left the boy speechless.

'You'll just fall off and hurt yourself. And who would then be to blame?'

Finding himself up against such unyielding resistance, it seemed that Enoch's chances of ever gaining parental approval were extremely limited. And now his alliance with Oupa Hans also appeared to be on shaky grounds. It was difficult for the boy to hope to win the battles that stretched before him, especially since the battles chose him, rather than the other way round.

Fortunately, the ticket examiner came by and Oupa Hans began a frantic search through his pockets. Enoch had taken the tickets to avoid such a possibility and presented them to be punched. For the rest of the journey he stared out of the window, memorising the names of stations that remained on the route to Cape Town.

The two ambled across the Parade, which was not yet in full swing. Oupa Hans stopped a newspaper boy and bought the *Cape Times* as he expected a long wait at the post office. They joined the queue and he handed the newspaper to Enoch. He was more accustomed to getting his news from other people. He never stood in a queue without getting involved in heated conversations with the people around him.

'For book knowledge, you have to read,' Oupa Hans had told Enoch. 'But you'll never find out what real people are thinking with your flat nose stuck inside a book, my boy.'

About three years earlier Enoch's parents had forbidden him to read the morning papers and it had not taken him long to figure out why. When the papers began to disappear at home, he realised that there was something important afoot, something so dramatic that he was to be denied the facts. This was enough to goad him into a state of independence and he began to spend his paltry sum of pocket money on the *Cape Argus*, the evening paper – and not therefore subject to the strict banning order. The Afrikaans papers were unlikely to report anything of importance.

Day after day, in the privacy of his room, he became absorbed in the unravelling of the great story of the time – the sex and spying scandal that had brought down the Macmillan government in London – Christine Keeler, Dr John Profumo, Stephen Ward and Mandy Rice-Davies. The music of those names had once played constantly in his mind as the vowels and consonants skipped off his tongue. Enoch rapidly became the school expert on the 'Profumo Affair'. During the half hour before the school bell called for assembly and during break times he was in great demand in the quadrangle, and even those boys who professed a preference for the rugby ball or cricket bat were caught up in the intrigue of it all.

Such popularity was unparalleled in the history of a school where only academic prowess and achievement were accorded any significance. On the way home, boys and girls pressed around him, slowing down the walk to the train station. In fact, the money Enoch had invested in the purchase of newspapers showed considerable returns as his growing circle of friends generously parted with their tuck shop purchases in exchange for another twist of the story. For once in his life he was spoiled by success. This led to some dishonesty on his part as he was sorely tempted to embellish the previous day's events, adding even more tantalising detail as if he had been an invisible presence among those aristocrats cavorting in their country houses.

However, scandals of such magnitude were rare and Enoch's hard-earned popularity gradually waned, with even his few loyal hangers-on defecting to Solly Levin, who dealt out a seemingly inexhaustible collection of lewd schoolboy jokes. He could not compete with Solly's enviable scatological repertoire.

But there was worse to come. Quiet, superior Haima drove the final nail into his coffin. The Indian girl he had been trying to impress with an occasional invitation to the Little Theatre began to spread the word that Enoch was obsessed with things that had absolutely nothing to do with his life on the Cape Flats. She had shown no interest in joining him at a dramatisation of Herman Charles Bosman's stories, or the kabuki plays. Still, Enoch had the presence of mind to attribute her cruel words to immaturity and a philistine prejudice against theatre-going, rather than allowing them to become a blot on his character or a commentary on his humble circumstances at home.

While waiting in the pension line with his grandfather, Enoch was pleasantly surprised to see a photograph of the call girl, Mandy Rice-Davies, in the *Cape Times*. After such a lengthy absence, it was like renewing an acquaintance with a long-lost friend. Although it was a grainy black-and-white picture, it was not difficult to summon up the lush redness of her hair and her delicate complexion. In the past she had often appeared in colour on the cover of women's magazines. Enoch remembered Christine Keeler as the dark-haired, sultry one. She was what the Americans would call a 'classy broad'. Mandy had simply played second fiddle – the icing on the cake, so to speak.

The *Cape Times* report was rather detached, with only a passing reference to the scandal. Mandy had fled England to escape the fading spotlight. The whole episode seemed like ancient history now.

Enoch shuffled forward, a pace dictated by the slow progress of the queue. He looked over the newspaper to take his bearings. A group of pensioners surrounded Oupa Hans, hanging onto every word. How could a man with so much to say have so few friends, he wondered? His mother had a simple explanation: 'When the tongue wags uncontrollably, you are going to step on people's toes.' His father used the Bible as his point of reference, which carried more weight. He liked to quote: 'Man is defiled not by what goes into his mouth, but by what comes out of it. So guard your tongue, because the smallest member of the body can cause the greatest harm.' Enoch agreed with the biblical injunction and since he too had been guilty of not guarding his tongue, he was afraid that this lapse would haunt him in the future.

The editorial and letters page of the paper carried little of consequence, and the only other article of interest to Enoch was the story of squatters evicted a week earlier from Brown's Farm during a particularly drenching rainstorm. Their sparse possessions had been loaded onto a lorry and dumped beside them along the road. Except for the arrival of the SPCA to rescue the abandoned pets, chickens and cows from the elements, most of the families who had been living at Brown's Farm for generations were left to set up makeshift homes wherever they could find space.

Other than that, he considered the newspaper a complete waste of money. He folded it up and stuck it under his arm. The queue had made progress and some of the group around Oupa Hans had drifted away. The few who hung around appeared entranced by his stories. Enoch was conscious of the fact that he still wore short trousers – the only boy in his class to do so and, no doubt, another reason no one would take him seriously. At least this wrong was to be remedied at Christmas, as his parents had finally conceded that he was now old enough to wear long trousers.

'Please, meet my grandson,' Oupa Hans said as he introduced Enoch to the men and women.

'But this is a handsome young man, Mr Pretorius,' an elderly auntie said. She leaned back on her stick to take a good look at him. 'You better be careful of the girls.'

'Mrs Klaasen need new glasses, Mrs Klaasen,' one of the men remarked – and there was more laughter.

'I swear, I'm telling the truth,' Oupa Hans continued. Enoch could not help remembering his mother's admonition that he was to take great care of anyone who prefaced any utterance with those words. The bystanders had no such qualms as they turned to Oupa Hans.

'When the prime minister was still minister of native affairs, he was great pals with old Khotso, that stinking rich witchdoctor who lives in Cofimvaba – not far from where I was born. You must have read about Khotso, the inyanga.'

The people nodded their heads. They all knew about Khotso. Enoch assumed that they were loyal readers of the *Post* that thrived on tales of witchcraft, rape, drunkenness and murder with poster-sized headlines screaming from lampposts: 'Intimate Body Parts Sold for Love Potions.'

'Now don't go and get me wrong – both men benefited from their friendship,' Oupa Hans continued, 'but the day old Schoon became prime minister, his head grew a few sizes too large. When he was at Native Affairs, nobody asked questions about his meetings with the chiefs and healers – that was part of his job. But now he's afraid that people will start asking why the prime minister should be visiting a witchdoctor.

'Little do they know that the Boers would never have beaten General Smuts if it had not been for Khotso. The whole of the Broederbond ended up at the witchdoctor's compound, begging for his help against the traitor, Smuts. The Nationalist Party would never have come to power in '48 without Khotso's strong medicine.'

This was exactly the kind of talk that caused Enoch's parents a great deal of worry. Enoch wondered whether his grandfather had acquired his gift for storytelling from sitting around fires in the bush, somewhere in the Eastern Cape.

By this time they'd reached the Non-European service counter. Oupa Hans rummaged through his pockets, located his identity card and handed it to the pension clerk. His hands shook as he signed the receipt book and stuffed the proffered notes into his wallet without counting them. He took his leave from his new acquaintances with the promise that he would tell the rest of the story when he saw them again in the pension queue in a month's time. Enoch was beginning to question whether he had done the right thing by staying away from school. However, the prospect of a milkshake and a carefree stroll about town – away from the humiliations of the classroom – proved to be the winner.

It was apparent that this time there was to be no visit to Mr Salie's house. To make it a proper outing, Oupa Hans suggested they visit the museum. Enoch agreed, as there was an exhibit he was longing to see again – the Bushman diorama. There was also the stuffed whale. The tiny strips of whalebone that his mother used to stiffen his shirt collars had first piqued his curiosity about those giant seafaring mammals. Oupa Hans bought a bag of peanuts at the entrance to the Company Gardens and fed the squirrels on the way to the museum. This was something he enjoyed doing, but it also meant that Enoch could not race ahead. He ignored the boy's impatience and sat down on a bench to rest. Through the densely packed leaves of the oak trees that lined Government Avenue and the thicket of blue hydrangeas and agapanthus beneath, they could see the parliament buildings.

The old man shooed away the greedy pigeons and coaxed a squirrel onto his knee with a peanut. As if Enoch was ignorant of the fact, he pointed out parliament and said, 'That's the place of iniquity where the Boers bring their rubbish and put it into beautiful words. If only General Smuts was still around. I think it would be a great day if someone stuck a barrel of dynamite in the basement. That would make a lot more sense than blowing up stupid pylons where nobody can see them.'

Enoch looked around to see if anyone was listening and noticed that they were sitting on a 'Europeans Only' bench. He was relieved when Oupa Hans hauled himself up by the armrest and started walking. The squirrels scrambled for the peanuts scattered along the way. Enoch expected his grandfather to remark on the beauty of the mountains ahead, the glorious flowers and the trees from every part of the world. Oupa

Hans loved nothing better than dirtying his hands in the soil. He had worked as head gardener at the Wepener estate for years until his back gave in. Enoch's mother thought this weakness typical of the spineless Pretorius clan.

The prime minister and his wife had once lived at Wepener and Oupa Hans had retired soon after their son, Dries, had returned to South Africa with his English wife and had taken charge of the estate. Enoch wondered how much the old man really knew about Dries's father, Dr Schoon.

Oupa Hans handed his wallet to Enoch, who paid the entrance fee to the woman in the museum kiosk. Enoch handed Oupa Hans the change. 'No, you keep it, my boy,' he said.

The diorama was first on Enoch's list, because the figures behind the glass looked so lifelike. Against the back wall, under a starry sky, there was a cave painting of an eland hunt cut from the rock and brought down to Cape Town from the Maclear district. The delicate figures were elongated and, with the help of a translucent pigment, looked as though they were striding across the heavens. They had no need of wings to fly.

'You won't find a single Bushman up in the Drakensberg any longer. Nowadays it is Boer and native territory,' Oupa Hans said.

But Enoch knew what had happened to the Bushmen. He had heard the story often, but an outing with Oupa Hans would not have been complete, unless his grandfather had his say about things. Oupa Hans tapped on the written description.

'They should put the real story on here. When the hunter-gatherers were hunted, the few survivors were pushed into the barren Kalahari Desert. Don't you think that sounds more like the truth? The Bushmen did not come from the moon or the stars. They are people like us. I used to know a man called Veldkornet Stockenström near Prince Albert, who always boasted that he got a permit to shoot the last Bushman.'

As Enoch looked at the casts of men, women and children arranged around a pile of sticks that had been touched up with luminous paint to look like fire, he thought that this shooting business was perhaps another of his grandfather's stories. In the distance a hunting party stalked springbok with poisoned arrows, and in the foreground a family gathered in a primitive hut, an infant clutching her mother's dangling breast. A man carried a duiker across his shoulders, concealing parts of his body as though conscious of people staring at him through the plate glass.

The best part of the exhibit was the recording machine, which meant that Enoch could listen to the figures while looking at them. He searched around in his pocket for change, lifted the handset and listened to what sounded to his ears like a very strange language, spoken almost entirely in clicks. The figures in the diorama sprang to life with the laughter and songs of children. He imagined the hunters returning to their encampment with their prey and joining the dance.

'Those poor buggers were trapped in plaster of Paris from head to toe to create this diorama,' Oupa Hans said, tapping on the brass plaque. 'Bloody liars! They were wiped out like vermin.'

Enoch thought this remark a bit strong. For a while he listened to the animated singing after a successful hunt.

'Why does Oupa Hans always try to spoil things?'

'Look, even their toes and fingers are real. The bastards made holes for them to breathe through while the plaster dried, squashing and smothering them. The poor kids must have been petrified.'

Enoch was about to ask him how the veldkornet could have shot the last Bushman if there were survivors up in the Kalahari when a teacher led a bunch of rowdy pupils in front of them. No sooner had they arrived than they began to poke fun at the women's breasts and point at the naked children. The last time he had seen pupils behave like that was when they were teasing the animals at the Rhodes Memorial Zoo. His reveries were disturbed and he turned away. The pupils parted like the Red Sea to let them through.

'The Hotnots have come to check out their relations,' one of them sneered as they passed by. Although stung by the remark, Oupa Hans said nothing as their laughter followed them out. The old man looked tired. The walk up from the post office had been a strain.

'Why don't you go and have a look at the whale on your own? It's nice outside – I want to sit in the sun for a bit. Those barbarians spoilt it in there for me. I'll have the newspaper now. Take your time, my boy.'

There was nothing Enoch hated more than being called 'my boy' when he had a perfectly good name. He would be eighteen in just under a year and felt that he was no one's boy. Oupa Hans's name was Johannes

Frederik Pretorius, after his father – and Enoch's father had the same name. Although he did not mind his own name, it made no sense to him that he had ended up as 'Enoch'. Why had he been named after this ancestor of Noah? It seemed to have nothing to do with his family history.

When he had first been introduced to Mr Salie, he had grasped Enoch's hand and said, 'What a wonderful name. Enoch was the world's first tailor and he invented the sewing needle.'

'Did you hear that?' Oupa Hans had said, as if his grandson lacked the ability to take in the fancies of yet another storyteller.

'That's why my poor mother called me Idriss. It's the Malay name for Enoch. She must've been living in hope that a tailor would rescue the family from poverty. So, we have the same name. Isn't that something?'

'Yes, Mr Salie,' the boy answered, wondering why his namesake, Enoch the shepherd and prophet, had not invented the sewing machine instead. That might have made the world a much easier place.

As Enoch made his tour of the creatures of the deep, he could not help noticing that the whale had been clumsily stitched up. Why had he not noticed it before? It was so huge and daunting that the taxidermist had obviously not taken the trouble to do a good job. It looked as if the blubber scrapers had left huge gashes in the skin. Just because it was mounted yards above the viewers' heads did not justify the imperfections of its stretched skin, or make the coarse stitching invisible. A bunch of machinists from the Burlington Hosiery Mills could have done a better job.

Enoch began to feel restless and decided to join Oupa Hans in the fresh air, where he could look at things that were alive – the trees, the rose garden and the goldfish swimming in the pond. He walked out of the museum in time to see his grandfather hand a few notes to a boy and return his wallet to his back pocket. He rushed over, afraid that the old man had been robbed.

'Don't worry – Mr Salie sent him up here with a message,' Oupa Hans explained hastily as the boy swaggered off in the direction of the fishpond. 'I'm having something new cut for Christmas. Your mother is always complaining that I look like a tramp.' Then he laughed nervously. 'With my back, I'll probably be long gone before my new suit is paid off. That would teach old Idriss a lesson.'

He folded the newspaper. Enoch noticed that Oupa Hans had been going through the racing page – and had torn out the racing form, which he surmised must have accompanied Mr Salie's payment.

'I'm thinking of something in charcoal,' he said. 'Don't you think that would suit me?'

'Yes, Oupa Hans, perfect.'

Enoch sat down aghast. Gambling and betting on horses were strictly prohibited in the Pretorius household. Oupa Hans sensed that his grandson had not been deceived and went onto the offensive.

'Oh, come now, Enoch – stop being such a prig. There isn't enough of me left to entertain more than one vice – so I gave up drinking, which is just as well, because I've had more luck spinning the bottle than drinking from it. That's why Khotso helps me to choose the hot favourites.'

'But that's gambling, Oupa Hans!'

'So? We gamble every day. To win, we must choose the right thing.'

'But Oupa Hans, gambling is a grave sin. And that doesn't make Oupa any different to the people in District Six. Now I've got something else to hide from Mama and Dowa.'

Oupa Hans shook his head. He seemed tired, but it was obvious that he wasn't going to drop the conversation.

'This government is trussing us up just like they did with the Bushmen. Only now they don't need plaster of Paris. Your father is so busy doing his Christian duty, he doesn't see anything any more.'

'But, Oupa Hans, Dowa works hard and he's kind to poor people.'

'Poor people! Charity begins at home. And I'm not talking about what your father does or doesn't do – it's his blindness that bothers me.'

'Dowa is Oupa Hans's son …'

'What does that matter? Christ is supposed to open up our eyes so that we can look around and do something in this world. Instead we stare at our navels. If you want to go walking around like your father for the rest of your life, that's your own indaba. I can see that too much reason confuses you, my boy. You're the kind that likes to obey the strap – so don't come and blame me one day when you've missed out on life.'

Enoch felt deeply disappointed and did not know where he stood with his grandfather. One thing he did know was that for someone who understood how far and how fast gossip travelled, Oupa Hans should be more careful about the words he entrusted to strangers.

Fool's Gold

Oupa Hans lived in a cottage on the Wepener estate in Rondebosch. The Schoons had agreed that he could stay on after his retirement. Although he later rented a converted garage in Retreat, he continued to live at Wepener to ensure that none of the other staff got ideas about moving into the old gatekeeper's lodge. He visited his converted garage twice a month, mainly to let Trossie in to do the cleaning. His son and daughter-in-law considered this another of his extravagances, but Trossie, one of the kitchen maids at Wepener, lived nearby and was grateful for the extra money.

Enoch assumed that his grandfather needed another place to go to just in case somebody decided that his time at Wepener was up, but he doubted that there was any truth to the rumour that Oupa kept a woman in Retreat. Even his friends called his quarters a 'love nest', although it was clear to Enoch that there weren't many women around who would want such a shaky old man.

When Enoch was younger and he and his grandfather were out and about at Wepener admiring the estate gardens with the dogs walking to heel, Oupa Hans used to say to him, 'Just think, we could've been living in a house like this – if only our stupid ancestors had not hijacked Paul Kruger's will.' Now Enoch was old enough to realise that with the number of people who had staked their claim to that fabled gold, it would not have been worth anyone's while to get his hopes up.

Enoch couldn't understand why people lived in the past when they got old. To him the best thing about the past was that it was in the past. But there was nothing he loved more than going to the estate. His parents were happy for him to go there as he was out of harm's way. The elder Schoons spent part of the year in Pretoria where Dr Schoon attended to his duties as minister of native affairs. For the rest they lived at the ministerial residence in Cape Town. Their two sons, who were at a local boarding school at the time, spent their holidays at Wepener. Enoch often had the run of the place when, during the school term, he joined his grandfather for the weekend.

The housekeeper, Ou Mevrou Jansen, hardly let the boy out of her sight when he was there. She captivated him with her stories, which were far more lively and believable than anything his grandfather told him. He had his meals with the staff, with the exception of the strange butler, Mr Molinieux, who was served in his private quarters.

Enoch considered it fortunate that Mr Molinieux lived at the far end of the hall and he had no need to pass his door. The man in his black suit terrified him; it was the kind of suit men wore at funerals. He had invited the boy into his quarters once and had offered him a cooldrink. No sooner had Enoch sat down than he asked him if he knew what the word 'testify' meant. For a child Enoch had quite a good vocabulary and he was not going to allow Mr Molinieux to think that the Schoon boys, Dries and Fanus, were his 'intellectual superiors', as he had heard him say. They were much older than he was and he knew that Mr Molinieux tried to convince them that it was not a good idea to play with him, as it would give 'that jumped-up little Coloured ideas above his station'. Mr Molinieux had often belittled Enoch in their presence and poked fun at the way he spoke English. Oupa Hans called the butler an 'old-fashioned Scottish racialist', so it came as no surprise when Enoch later discovered that he was even worse.

Despite the dread he felt for Mr Molinieux, Enoch was determined not to be caught out. He stood up.

'*Testify* is when somebody gets up in church to tell all the people what the Lord has done for him,' he answered. 'Witnesses also *testify* before a judge in court.' Having demonstrated his grasp of the word, he sat down and finished his drink so that he could leave.

'I must go, Mr Molinieux, Ou Mevrou Jansen is waiting for me,' he stammered.

'Wait a minute, boy – manners, manners – no need to race anywhere. I am still waiting for your answer. I want you to tell me what the origins of the word are – where the word comes from, not what it means.'

'I don't know, Mr Molinieux,' he replied frantically, hoping to make his escape.

'So then, you see – you're not the bright spark Ou Mevrou Jansen makes you out to be. What do you think you're going to do with your life? Be a gardener like that broken-down old crock of a grandfather? He calls himself a horticulturist but I wonder if he even knows the meaning of the word …'

'Oupa Hans was trained as a horticulturalist, Mr Molinieux – and I'm going to be a doctor.'

'Oh, so you're going to be a doctor.'

Enoch was almost overcome by nausea when Mr Molinieux placed his hand on his shoulder and pushed him back onto the chair.

'Don't be in such a great hurry, Dr Pretorius. We've got plenty of time.'

Mr Molinieux usually had a rest after lunch and Mieta had already removed his tray. He sat down in front of Enoch and placed his hand on the boy's knee.

'Testify comes from the word testes or testicles. The word has a logical explanation, you see, Enoch. In the olden days Greek men used to – pardon the expression – bugger young boys. And they used to hold onto each other's testes like *this* when they pledged eternal allegiance or swore that they were telling the truth. Isn't that fascinating!'

As he said 'like this' Mr Molinieux squeezed Enoch between his legs. The boy leapt from the chair – the glass flying in one direction, and he in the other as he raced for the safety of the kitchen. His face was flushed and he could barely breathe.

'Now I'm going to die,' he said to himself. By the time he pushed open the kitchen door he was relieved to find that the tight band around his chest had loosened up.

'Enoch, why the hurry straight after eating? When will you ever listen?' Ou Mevrou Jansen said as he slumped down beside her at the table. 'Here – help me shell these peas. The girls always disappear after lunch. And I don't want to see you out in the hot sun without a hat.'

'Sorry, Ou Mevrou Jansen. My hat is down at Oupa Hans's house.'

'A lot of good it's doing down there. You look awful. I don't want you getting sunstroke.'

'No, Ou Mevrou Jansen.'

'Have you been crying?'

'Of course not, Ou Mevrou Jansen.' Now not only had Enoch done something bad, but he had also told a lie.

'Well, I hope you're not catching anything – and don't you "of course not" me.'

She then put her arms around Enoch and he could not hold back the tears. 'Has your Oupa Hans been nasty to you?'

He shook his head and thought, 'Am I going to die – am I going to die?'

'Whatever it is, I can tell you that there isn't much in this world that is worth crying about. How about a nice, cold glass of ginger beer?'

'No thank you, Ou Mevrou Jansen.'

'It'll make you feel better, my boy.'

'I'm not thirsty, Ou Mevrou Jansen.'

'Something must be wrong with you. You never turn down my ginger beer. Watch what you're doing with those peas.'

From that day Enoch stayed well out of Mr Molinieux's way. He restricted his visits to his grandfather at Wepener to the school holidays or at weekends when Dries and Fanus were at home. It made him feel safer. Although they were much older, the boys played with him and taught him to swim and play tennis. On a few occasions they even suggested smuggling Enoch into the European bioscope in town, but did not insist when he told them that his parents would not allow him into a cinema. They took him to the National Gallery instead, as Dries knew a lot about paintings.

They went to listen to a man called Dr Hugh Tracey, an expert on African music, and the boys paid close attention when he demonstrated the use of traditional instruments. As they left, Dries said to Enoch, 'If only that crowd in the museum showed as much interest in the indigenous people as they do in their musical instruments, this country would be quite a different place.'

When the brothers next tried to persuade Enoch to accompany them to the bioscope, Ou Mevrou Jansen overheard them and scolded them. Enoch told the boys that they should go on their own, but they would not hear of it.

'Look, you're only a shade darker than me, Pretorius,' Fanus said, 'and your father can't have anything against *Goodbye, Mr Chips*. It's not like it's a cowboy film, or something dirty.'

But the prohibitions of home were just as compelling for Enoch as those delineated by law – if not more so.

'Why don't you two go and tell me all about it afterwards,' he suggested. But Fanus would not listen.

'What a sorry life you lead, young Pretorius,' Fanus said in a patronising tone. 'I disagree with my father whenever I get to see him. What's so different about you?'

'How can you disagree with your father?'

'He's an extremely stupid man.'

When Fanus said that, it was as if someone had slammed a fist into Enoch's stomach. 'How can you say things like that about your father?'

'It's the truth. I see no use for a man who drives a wedge between black and white people. That is what Papa has done and I have rejected his politics.'

To Enoch's ears Fanus was beginning to sound like God. This was dangerous talk. Dries came to the boy's rescue. 'Don't listen to his pompous crap, Enoch. The last time we heard him defying Papa, Ou Mevrou Jansen gave him a good hiding. He jumped around and shrieked just like any other kid. Forget about the bioscope – why don't we ask Zachaeus to drive us up to Table Mountain? That's better than staying here and being bored stiff by pedantic old Fanus.'

But Enoch was to be disappointed. The southeaster had been blowing since just before lunch and by the time they reached the lower station the wind was at its fiercest and the cable car was not running. Instead the chauffeur, Zachaeus, suggested they cross the mountain over Kloof Nek and on to Camps Bay. They walked on the beach with their ice creams and Zachaeus sat on the running board of the car sucking at a strawberry milkshake.

Ou Mevrou Jansen was at her happiest when the boys were at Wepener. She occasionally allowed Enoch to spend the night up at the big house. As he was afraid to sleep on his own, Fanus invited him to share his bedroom. Ou Mevrou Jansen was proud of Dries and Fanus and told Enoch that no one would stand in his way if he worked hard and emulated them. At the beginning of the holidays she would demand to see his school report and, as if his parents starved him at home, piled his plate with food.

This provoked Mr Molinieux to say, 'Don't waste good food on the boy.'

'Come back the day you have an original thought in your head, Mr Molinieux,' Ou Mevrou Jansen replied, placing her arms around the boy. 'Just you wait, Enoch is going to be a doctor.'

During the school holidays Enoch would spend weeks in the company of the boys, until their parents arrived for Christmas or Easter. Even then the Schoons would stay at Wepener only for a few days before heading for their beach cottage at Pringle Bay, leaving their sons at home.

They had not been in Cape Town on the day Fanus died. It was the darkest day in Ou Mevrou Jansen's life – and she had seen many dark days. The headmaster of Bishops and the school doctor arrived at the front door, having phoned first. The doctor explained that Fanus had had a fatal asthma attack on the school's rugby field while the under-seventeen team had been preparing for the year's final match against Wynberg Boys' High. He had done everything possible to revive Fanus, but had failed.

This had happened just before the Settlers' Day weekend. Ou Mevrou Jansen and Enoch had been listening to the wireless while waiting for the boys to arrive for dinner. Enoch had been excited as Fanus had promised to show him how to use his camera so that he could take snaps of the garden. His last words to Enoch had been, 'It will be a damned good way to learn botany, Pretorius. And your father can't object, as it's one of the subjects for medicine. You can mount the snaps in one of my old stamp albums and I'll help you make a list of the Latin names.'

The week had dragged on – and suddenly he was gone. Enoch struggled with the tragedy, but he also worried about who would show him how to work the camera now that Fanus was no longer around. And what a shame that Fanus had died before he had been to university. Whenever challenged about what he would study, he would say, 'I'll be what I am going to be.' This casual approach to life used to annoy Ou Mevrou Jansen. According to her, clear ideas about the future were essential for the transition in this life as well as the next.

The doctor allowed Dries to accompany Fanus's body to the hospital. Enoch couldn't help wondering if it had been spooky sitting in the back of the ambulance, but had never had the guts to ask him. And there were also the harsh things he had heard Fanus say about his father. Could that have had anything to do with his death?

Ou Mevrou Jansen could not answer any of Enoch's questions. She simply clung to him and wept. Three days later, at the funeral, she was still weeping. The Schoons returned to Pretoria a few days after their son was laid to rest. They too were shocked and grief-stricken, but the minister of native affairs could hardly show his emotions in public.

It was some time before Dries spoke to Enoch, or even asked him onto the tennis court, but the boy understood his friend's grief. It was as if he too had lost a brother. Dries spent most of his weekends at school after that, and, according to Ou Mevrou Jansen, was working harder than ever for the matric exams.

But his mood did not last forever. On Enoch's birthday, Dries arrived at the Pretorius's front door in Lansdowne, bearing a fruit cake covered in marzipan and icing made by Ou Mevrou Jansen – as well as Fanus's camera and a brand new photograph album. And to celebrate Krugers Day he brought along a box of chocolates, each one in the shape of a coin and wrapped in gold foil. Enoch suspected that Oupa Hans must have told Dries the story about the family's stolen inheritance.

Dries was invited in for a cup of tea and scones. There was some debate as to whether the cake should be set aside for Christmas, but with Dries's encouragement Enoch managed to persuade his mother that his birthday was a good occasion for a decent slice and that Christmas deserved its own efforts. He blew out the ten candles one by one. Later Dries made Mr and Mrs Pretorius and Enoch pose beside the hibiscus bush, which was in full bloom, and took their photograph. Caesar, the neighbour's ridgeback, stuck his nose through the fence and Enoch took a photograph of him, despite the fact that the dog had charged him some time before and had brought him down. But he was now no longer afraid of dogs.

Dries showed him how to focus the lens and work the stops, as Fanus had promised to do – but to Enoch it hardly seemed possible that Fanus was gone. His mother and father had also been deeply distressed when Enoch had brought home the terrible news. Inevitably his mother had felt obliged to draw a lesson from the tragedy.

'That's what comes from playing rugby,' she had said. 'I'm warning you – don't you ever dare come and ask us if you can play that ruffian's game.'

Enoch fancied himself a swimmer and tennis player. His sporting heroes were Rod Laver and Frew McMillan. Well before Fanus's death he had already decided that rugby would be too rough for him. Despite his healthy appetite, he was a thin child and not very strong, and he would have hated being mauled in a scrum. And he had been warned that all kinds of rough stuff took place in the changing rooms.

The day of Fanus's funeral had marked the twelfth year that Hannes Pretorius had been working at Wepener. Ou Mevrou Jansen had kept her distance from him throughout that time. After the funeral, however, the two became fast friends. Enoch was allowed to spend even more time with her and the staff at the big house, and less with his grandfather down at the gate lodge. When Oupa Hans complained about this his parents replied that they did not mind, as long as Enoch said his prayers at night and Ou Mevrou Jansen took him along to church on Sundays.

But Enoch was discovered playing tennis the following Sunday morning, so his mother banished him from Wepener for quite some time. She only relented when Dries arrived with Zachaeus on a Friday afternoon and asked if Enoch could return with them.

'Ou Mevrou Jansen has been in a filthy mood for ages and she wants Enoch back for the weekend. And as I am sick and tired of Stellenbosch University, I'm leaving for England to finish my degree. I couldn't leave without saying goodbye,' Dries explained.

'Young man,' Mama said, 'you are privileged to do whatever you wish. You have my permission to say goodbye to Enoch right here. Nothing is stopping you.'

'With due respect, Mrs Pretorius, Enoch is good for Ou Mevrou Jansen, and the sooner he comes back, the sooner she'll stop treating me like a child.'

Mrs Pretorius came to her son's defence the way a lioness would protect her cub. 'He isn't a plaything, you know.'

'Mrs Pretorius, that's not what I meant. His grandfather hasn't seen him either in a while.'

Mr Pretorius was standing in the driveway, having a word with Zachaeus. He heard his wife giving Dries a hard time and Enoch was overjoyed when he said, 'Come on, Rachel, let the boy go. All he's been doing is sulking in his bedroom for months, anyway.'

'Well, all right – but don't blame me if something bad happens to the child.'

Enoch was over the moon and dashed to his bedroom to collect his things. Ebrahim's father had sent him to the madrasa to learn the Koran, so he rarely saw him any longer – and he had few other friends. Enoch was happy that his enforced loneliness was at an end.

That weekend turned into one of the most eventful of his life. With Oupa Hans looking on from the sidelines, Dries and Enoch spent hours playing tennis and, whenever they got too hot, they jumped into the pool. Zachaeus was to take Enoch home after tea on the Sunday afternoon. It was a sad occasion when Dries gathered everyone around him for his farewell. He was due to leave on the mailboat on the Wednesday. Ou Mevrou Jansen was not the only one who cried. She had tried to make him reconsider his rash decision and to give Stellenbosch a chance as he had only been there for a year. He had also disappointed his parents. But Dries was determined to leave. Other than to say that he found the atmosphere at the university stultifying, he offered no reasons for his decision. It was then that Dries made an important announcement.

'What I'd like to say is that, when we were hit by Fanus's tragedy last year, Enoch was the one who helped us with our grief. I was so upset and I didn't even want to have anything to do with him. But he persisted like the young hero he is.'

Just like the old men in parliament, everyone said, 'Hoor, hoor', and Enoch blushed.

'One fine day when you are ready for university, Enoch, I will send you to England and pay all your expenses. But don't worry, I will be back at Wepener well before then.'

Oupa Hans began to clap his hands – and everyone joined in. The clapping must have been quite loud, because Mr Molinieux came along to find out what was going on. When he learned what the commotion was about, he gave Enoch a filthy look and turned on his heels.

Enoch could not wait to get home to tell his parents the good news.

And then, when Dries returned from England with his wife Alison some years later, he insisted on seeing Enoch's school reports, and, impressed by the results, opened an account in Enoch's name at Barclays Bank, into which he deposited a large sum of money.

So there they were, Oupa Hans and his grandson, walking down Government Avenue towards the train station in silence, eight years after Dries had made his promise – and with only the final year at school before Enoch could be admitted to university. Enoch was still trying to gather the courage to tell everyone that he had changed his mind about being a doctor and that he now was serious about being an artist. Unbeknownst to his parents, he had been taking painting lessons on Saturday mornings at a community centre in Woodstock, but for the moment, he kept his plans to himself. Ou Mevrou Jansen had unwittingly been the inspiration when she had given him a box of watercolours and oil paints when he had presented her with his mid-year standard nine report.

Oupa Hans asked Enoch whether he would like to come back to Wepener to spend the weekend, as he did not want to go to Lansdowne to visit his son and daughter-in-law. They took the tram to Rondebosch and then walked to the gate lodge, where Enoch helped the old man out of his jacket, untied his shoelaces and made sure that he was comfortable on the couch. Enoch made a cup of tea and then walked across to the main house to greet his friends.

For some reason the kitchen was in an uproar and nobody noticed him standing in the doorway. Since Dries's return to South Africa, Ou Mevrou Jansen had seen his English wife turn every value she had tried to instil in the staff on its head. This had caused much friction in the house. For instance, Alison insisted that the staff call her and her husband by their Christian names, and she showed far too much familiarity with the servants for Ou Mevrou's liking. The ladies welcomed Enoch and kissed him – and Clara, the nanny, in a fit of excitement said, 'It's a good thing you came. There's going to be a big tea party on Sunday and the prime minister and Mrs Schoon will also be here.'

'Please don't mislead the child,' Ou Mevrou Jansen snapped.

'Alison said we can all go to the party,' Clara insisted, 'and that means him also.'

'Of course Enoch will be here. I'm going to need all the help I can get to keep order in this house,' Ou Mevrou Jansen replied, annoyed that Clara had taken it upon herself to extend the invitation.

Ukhanyo Lwabelungu: The Light Brought by Whites

Enoch woke up early on Sunday morning to the sound of Oupa Hans's snoring, which filtered in through the open bedroom door. The boy had helped his grandfather into bed the night before and had then gone up to the house to have dinner with Dries and Alison. On his return he found Oupa Hans stretched out on the sofa. There was a half-eaten bowl of porridge on a stool and the wireless was still on, but he was fast asleep. Over dinner Alison had remarked that she often visited Oupa Hans at the gate lodge and found him a remarkable man. This came as a bit of a shock to Enoch, especially as she described him as wise and knowledgeable. She sounded sincere and not patronising.

'I'm glad you think so,' Enoch had replied hesitantly, 'If only Mama and Dowa agreed with you, things would be easier for Oupa. Sometimes I think his mind is going.'

'I wouldn't worry too much, Enoch,' Dries replied. 'He is safe in the grounds and he can't wander very far.'

Enoch drew the blanket under his chin and listened to the rustle of the leaves of the oak trees bordering the driveway. The sound muffled Oupa Hans's snoring. In his half-wakeful state the boy ran through the events of the previous day, the tennis, the swimming, the meals and conversations with Dries and Alison. He adored Alison and thought her the perfect wife for Dries. She was clever and amusing, if somewhat unpredictable. He remembered the time when they had all gone to a performance of Handel's *Messiah* at the Drill Hall on Easter Saturday. Earlier that day they had collected him from home to accompany them on what Alison called 'our annual outing'. As they entered the beautifully lit hall, overflowing with regalia lilies, they discovered a rope running down the centre aisle. If anyone had a mistaken notion about the rope, there were ushers to show Europeans to one side of the hall and Non-Europeans to the other.

'What is going on here?' Alison asked the usher who had handed them the programmes. 'Last year there wasn't a rope down the middle.'

'It's something new, madam – like the queues in the post office.'

Neither Dries nor Enoch knew what to expect from Alison. She looked around the hall. 'Post office queues? My dear woman, do you realise that the *Messiah* premiered in Dublin on the 13th of April 1742 – that is 226 years ago to the day? If Catholics and Protestants could sit down together to hear this extraordinary piece of music, why can't we do the same tonight? This partition is an outrage! And I dare say, you must think so too!'

'It's none of my business, madam. I'm only doing my job. Why doesn't madam go and ask His Lordship, the Mayor?'

Alison unhooked the rope at the rear – all eyes turned on her as she walked towards the orchestra. She stared down at the mayor in his gold chains, cringing in his seat, picked up the front end of the rope, unhooked it from the stands and dragged it all the way to the back of the hall, where she dropped it into a snake-like heap. Not a sound was heard.

'There's enough rope here to hang the whole lot of you!' She called out as they walked out into a stormy night and returned to Wepener to listen to a recording of the *Messiah* on the gramophone. Alison's behaviour had shocked Enoch. And what about the audience?

In the early edition of the *Cape Argus*, Alison's photograph was on the front page, captioned: 'Outraged concert-goer tackles *Messiah* rope'. According to the review the atmosphere had been subdued throughout the performance and the audience had failed to rise for the Hallelujah chorus, as had become the custom 'since the 23rd day of March in the year 1743, when King George II rose to his feet during a performance of the *Messiah* to relieve a severe leg cramp.'

The editorial concluded that it might have been better 'had the irate concert-goer and her guests discreetly taken seats in the section reserved for Non-European members of the audience. But let posterity be the judge!' One of the Afrikaans papers, *Die Burger*, went to town about what it termed 'the scandalous behaviour of a foreign socialite who disrupted the annual performance of Handel's *Messiah*. Without regard to the laws and sensibilities of her adopted country or even the sacred nature of the music, she attempted to turn one of the city's premier cultural events into a political act.'

Although a number of journalists had telephoned the Schoon household for comment, not one of the ensuing articles mentioned Alison's relationship to the prime minister. Not all had been negative, however – many well-wishers, including people who had attended the concert, rang the Schoons or wrote to them in support of Alison's bold action.

From his bed Enoch could tell through the partially drawn curtains that it would be a perfect day. The punishing southeaster of the night before had exhausted itself, leaving a sky flecked with white clouds. Enoch hated the wind with a passion – particularly the southeaster, which would often blow for days – and the northwester that, in winter, brought weeks of constant rain and bitter cold. How often had he listened to their fury and wondered why meteorologists and writers had neglected to give them more original names. Whatever their destructive force, or their effect on mood, winds elsewhere were known by mysterious names such as the mistral, sirocco, harmattan, bora, or the poisonous wind of Arabia, the simoom. Even Canada had something called the chinook. While in this southernmost country on the African continent, no poetically named winds blew.

Enoch had a quick bath, put on his Sunday clothes, tiptoed past Oupa Hans on the sofa and headed to the big house for breakfast. The curtains had been drawn back and the windows opened to admit the fresh morning air. As Enoch passed by Dries's bedroom window in the north wing of the Cape Dutch manor house, the younger Schoon waved to him. He seemed oblivious to the upheaval that filled the rest of the house. The brass fittings and chandeliers gleamed and the servants were busy polishing the surfaces of glass and wood to prepare the house for the tea party that afternoon and the visit of Dr Sybrand Schoon, the prime minister, and Mrs Schoon.

Dries's daughter, Hanneli, hurried along the passage searching for her father, her soft footfalls finding the odd creaking board under the runners. The girl was distracted on hearing her name called and she ran into the east court. She rode her tricycle under the supervision of Clara, her nanny, and the shadows cast by the tall oaks and a leafy fig tree in the corner obviated the need for a bonnet.

It had not been easy for Dries to ensure the attendance of his parents at the party that afternoon. Whenever Dr Schoon managed to avoid an official duty, there was invariably some other function to take its place. However, Dries had persevered. Now that his father was prime minister, he wanted him to meet Chief Josias Nkosivile so that they could discuss the trouble in Pondoland before the situation got out of control. Enoch had overheard Dries's telephone conversation and gathered that Chief Josias had also been reluctant to attend the tea party and had tried to dissuade Dries from getting involved in such a delicate matter. However, the chief had agreed to attend as a social gathering was less likely to compromise the two leaders than were they to have an official meeting.

As Dries had not emerged for breakfast, Enoch sat down at the table on his own. He could hear Alison as she walked to her husband's room down the hall and scolded him for not helping with preparations. She appreciated the efforts of the staff, although she would not allow this to be an excuse for indolence on the part of her husband. Alison raised her voice whenever she was annoyed and even with the sounds of polishers, Enoch could hear her. It made him feel like an intruder, but the servants seemed to be used to it and usually just raised their eyebrows.

'What on earth's the matter? Hanneli has been looking for you everywhere. The very least you could do is keep her amused until your parents arrive. Clara is busy – and this party was your idea.'

'Hanneli will have more than enough attention later on,' Dries replied feebly.

Realising that she was having little effect in her attempt to rouse her husband, Alison went to inspect the drawing room where tea was to be served. A glance into the room assured her that Mr Molinieux and Clara had everything under control. They were reviewing the guest list as Enoch walked in.

Alison had previously asked the staff to join the guests at tea and this had caused quite a stir in the kitchen, where the atmosphere remained tense. With the exception of Clara, Mieta, the kitchen maid, and Mfilo – and, of course, Mr Molinieux, who would serve tea – most of the staff had decided to take the afternoon off, as they did not wish to annoy Ou Mevrou Jansen, who had expressed her misgivings when she heard that the staff had been invited.

'Madam is not supposed to entertain with the servants,' she had said to Alison in the kitchen, hoping that the staff would hear her and be dissuaded from attending – and a few of them had been. However, they had laughed at the housekeeper and called her 'old-fashioned'. They mostly approved of Alison's disregard for convention.

'Alison wants the staff to have tea with the guests,' Ou Mevrou Jansen complained to Dries, who was her only confidant in the household. 'You know, Dries, it isn't right – that overseas woman just does not understand our ways. Remember what was written in the newspapers that time.'

'But that's ancient history,' Dries said, making light of her concern. He told her that it had been a splendid idea that the staff had been invited, and that in future he would consider doing the same. But for Ou Mevrou Jansen, the tendency of Dries's English wife to subvert a domestic order carefully nurtured over the years – an order over which she had presided for so long – gave her little cause for amusement.

'It isn't fair on all the people who have worked here in the past without ever being allowed into the drawing room, except with pads under their knees and brushes in their hands. I know – I've been here at Wepener going on for almost eighty years. Who's the boss in this house anyway?'

'Things must change, Ou Mevrou Jansen; they have to get better. Excuses for holding people back can't be used any longer. Don't let that worry you. Not if you want to be here for another eighty years – don't you agree, Enoch?"

'Don't try to influence the boy. I've seen enough in my long life. Another eighty years? Not if I can help it.'

Dries kissed Ou Mevrou Jansen on her cheek.

'You think a kiss make things right?'

'It always has – and I don't want Enoch in the kitchen this afternoon hanging onto your apron strings. I'd like him to entertain some of the guests.'

Ou Mevrou Jansen sighed. 'Enoch I can understand – but the others … That Clara is a handful.'

'I'm going to drink tea with the prime minister and Madam Schoon this afternoon,' Clara sang as she chased Hanneli through the kitchen – more to reassure herself than to antagonise Ou Mevrou Jansen, who was annoyed at this unseemly display. Although she loved Clara and had watched her blossom into a beautiful young woman since her arrival at Wepener, she considered her manner immodest.

'I hear some educated natives also coming,' Clara persisted.

'Mfilo,' Clara called from the window, as the gardener positioned a stone along one of the borders, 'it's Sunday, hey, and you not supposed to work on the Lord's Day. You'll make that nice suit dirty. Why don't you come sit here in the kitchen and wait for the visitors – or go smoke your pipe in the shed?'

'Stop worrying about that blinking man,' snapped Ou Mevrou Jansen. 'Leave Mfilo alone. He's a grownup. If he wants to come in, he'll come in. Drinking tea with important guests – what next? Such things would never have happened at Wepener if the Schoons weren't always leaving the boys on their own when they were young – going here and going there. What will the prime minister say about all this madness?'

Further laughter erupted in the kitchen when Trossie, one of the kitchen maids, driven by unaccustomed daring, decided to remain at her post and watch the proceedings at a distance. She wanted to see how Clara would behave among the guests.

'Come on, Enoch,' Ou Mevrou Jansen called, 'let's go and see what I can find for you.'

Enoch followed her to her room, curious about what she had in mind. She opened the wardrobe in which Fanus's clothes were kept in mothballs and held out one of his suits. 'This was his best. By now you should have grown into it. Goodness only knows why you are still in short trousers. Your parents must really be daft.'

'Dowa says I'll get a proper suit for my next birthday.'

'You couldn't get a more proper suit than this one – here you are. When all of this party nonsense is over, I'll ask Mfilo to take the wardrobe down to your Oupa Hans's house – and you can wear whatever you want, whenever you want. And here's a tie to go with it.'

Enoch wondered what had made Ou Mevrou Jansen wait so long before permitting him to wear Fanus's clothes.

'But what will Dries say?' he asked.

'Who do you think suggested it? And he was right. Come and show me when you are ready.'

'And the prime minister – what will he say?'

'Do you think he even noticed what his children wore? Enoch, my boy, don't be proud – these are not cast-offs, they are gifts. Fanus is smiling on you.'

After Ou Mevrou Jansen left the room it took Enoch some time to gather the courage to slip on the long trousers, but when he did, he saw that they were the right length. He was instantly turned into a young man. He found the transformation almost frightening. He then knotted the tie – and slipped on the jacket. Enoch walked up to the mirror and was astonished at what he saw.

'Thank you, Jesus, thank you, Fanus,' he mumbled, and there were tears in his eyes. He could not remember what Fanus had looked like in the suit, but felt as if it had been made especially for him.

Ou Mevrou Jansen rapped on the door with her cane and walked in. 'Are you going to be all day? Here, let me have a look. Turn around. I thought that I'd have to get out the sewing machine, but it looks fine.'

She kissed Enoch, took his hand and led him into the kitchen. He was nervous about the reception that awaited him. With the exception of Dries and Alison, everyone was there and roundly congratulated the elegant young man who had emerged in their midst. They slapped Enoch on the back and kissed him.

'Sjoe! What will Oupa Hans have to say about his smart grandson now?' Clara asked. 'You've got to go and show him.'

'I'll go later,' Enoch replied. 'I want Dries to see me first.'

The bedroom door was ajar and he was about to enter when he heard Dries and Alison talking. He did not want to interrupt, but could see Dries lying on the bed.

'Really, Dries, you'll tempt me to hit you if you don't show some sign of life,' Alison scolded, though her voice was soft with an indulgent tone. He took her hand and drew her to sit beside him on the bed.

'No, definitely not now – mind my dress. Besides, the child might come in at any moment.'

Alison moved away from him, although not purposefully enough to escape his embrace. 'Mind my dress.'

'All I want is to hold you – to be held by you for a few minutes,' Dries said, 'and you make an awful fuss about your clothes. You've got other dresses, you know.'

'That's typical – everything is allowed when it suits you.'

'The point is, I have always been allowed before …'

Enoch had read, even imagined a great deal about, but he had never actually witnessed such intimacy between a man and a woman. He felt that it was wrong to spy and knew that he should leave, but something seemed to hold him back. It was Alison – she had parted her dark hair down the middle. Her simple hairstyle and her earrings, a single translucent, porcelain blossom set delicately on each lobe, showed off her beautiful features. Dries held her face gently, his hand under her chin; he kissed her eyes, then her lips. He undid the tiny ivory buttons, which passed easily through the eyelets of the lace bodice, and drew the top of her dress from her shoulders.

'Did you hear what I said?' Alison whispered. 'This is not the right time.' With a smile she got up from the bed. 'You know I don't like to be rushed; besides, someone is bound to arrive early.'

'Then we'll simply have to pardon their bad manners.'

'Polycarp's always the first to arrive. I'm not even sure why you invited him – he is only likely to aggravate your father.'

'Perhaps that's why I invited him. Actually, Pa has something to discuss with him – and don't forget Polycarp is an old friend.'

'I can't imagine what your father would have to say to an ex-jailbird,' she said. Her smile lingered before gradually fading from her face. 'Come, Dries, darling – enough self-indulgence. Why not go for a quick swim? It might have a salutary effect.'

Enoch hurried away to Ou Mevrou Jansen's room to collect his discarded clothes and went down to the gate lodge to show off his new suit to his grandfather. On the way he saw Dries dive in at the shallow end of the pool, touch the far end without surfacing and then swim back and forth with swift, powerful strokes. The speed with which he moved through water always amazed Enoch.

Oupa Hans had tidied up the cottage and was listening to the wireless when his grandson rushed in.

'Wait a minute. Go back to the door and walk in slowly. Make an entry like a gentleman.'

Enoch stood outside for a moment, knocked, opened the door again and entered.

'Now that's the ticket. If only your father could see you now. So, who was the tailor? Mr Salie couldn't do a job like that ... just look at you.' He rubbed the cloth between his fingers. 'This is top quality – must have cost at least fifty guineas. Just perfect for such a handsome young man.'

'It belonged to Fanus.'

'I can see that.'

'Is Oupa Hans coming up to the house?'

'No, my boy – I've got nothing to say to the prime minister. Here, let me straighten your tie … that's better. You can tell me all about the party before Zachaeus takes you home this evening.'

Enoch kissed his grandfather and returned to the house. He joined Clara, who was waiting for Dries. She held out a large towel as he hauled himself out of the pool.

'Ou Mevrou Jansen say she don't want Dries to make the floor wet inside and Alison say Dries mus' get dressed now before the people come.' Clara made little attempt to conceal her excitement. 'I wish Ou Mevrou Jansen was also coming to tea,' she said, hoping that Dries might still persuade the old woman to join them.

'From what I can tell, the two of you are always having tea. Anyway, Clara, you know she won't do anything of the sort. She is very set in her ways. Cheer up – Mr Molinieux and Mfilo will be there, as well as Mieta – and Trossie will be holding the fort in the kitchen.'

'I'm so nervous. Mus' I call your dad Mr Prime Minister, or is it all right to say Meneer?'

Dries took the towel from Clara. 'Look, he's no different now that he's prime minister. Call him anything you like – but for goodness' sake, don't call him "baas". Hey, now that's a very smart outfit you're wearing.'

His remark drew Enoch's attention to Clara. She looked stunning in an agapanthus blue frock she had bought for the occasion. The belt she had found to go with it diminished the size of her waist, and he marvelled at her trim figure silhouetted against the white wall of the house.

'It's my Christmas dress. I'll wear it to the service. All I need now is a hat and shoes and maybe gloves to match.'

Dries said, 'I can see that you're going to have to fight off your admirers.'

'What admirers, nogal?'

'Enoch, for one – he hasn't taken his eyes off you for a second.'

'Shame, Dries, don't make the poor boy blush.'

'Well, I do think it's a pity about you and Mr Molinieux …'

'I'm happy with what I got, thank you; and I think Mr Molinieux got a screw loose or something,' Clara replied. 'And Oupa Hans also thinks so.'

Dries was far too considerate to comment on Enoch's appearance and just smiled at him. Then he did something he had never done before. He put his arms around him and said, 'I hope we won't lose you now that you are a proper young man.'

'There you go and get his suit wet,' Clara protested as she took the towel from him and dabbed at Enoch's jacket.

Dries went indoors and left Clara and Enoch watching the road beyond the gate. Zachaeus waved at them as he drove down to the station to collect some guests arriving on the train from Simonstown.

Alison was in her bedroom at the far end of the passage nursing a large swelling on her shin, having walked into a pedal protruding from Hanneli's tricycle left outside her room. She asked Mieta, who was passing her bedroom, to find Clara.

'Clara,' she exclaimed in exasperation, 'Hanneli knows that her tricycle does not belong in the house. Just look at this bruise. What am I to do?'

'Haai shame, Alison, you mustn't be cross with Hanneli because why, I tell her to bring it in the house. I can't watch her outside when Mr Molinieux expect me to help get the tables ready inside.'

'No, of course not, Clara. I'm not blaming you. But what am I to do? I swear you spoil that child.'

'At least Hanneli didn't leave any tyre marks on the floors,' Clara said, searching for something to say in mitigation of the child's trespass.

Mieta, lurking close by with a duster, mumbled for them both to hear, 'I already polish over the tyre marks. I make right and then Clara go let the child scratch over.'

'Madam isn't talking to you, Mieta,' Clara snapped. 'Don't be so forward.' Then turning to Alison, she asked her to remove her stocking and studied the swelling.

'You like a peach,' she said, 'You bruise so easy. Maybe you mus' wear a longer dress. Anyway, this dress already looks creased. I don't know how – with all the ironing that goes on in the house.'

Clara helped Alison into a beige dress she had worn to a party in Cape Town just a few days earlier, and stood back to admire the effect.

'See, it comes nice over the bruise. Now you must sit careful so the dress don't pull up and show the mark.'

'I shall just have to be careful.' Alison got up and turned around. 'And what about the seams?'

'No – they alright. The stockings is fine.'

'Thank you. I hope you've asked Dries to use the side entrance. Mieta must be sick and tired of running after him and his daughter with her dustpan and broom.'

'It's her job – now don't worry about Mieta. She jus' like to make a fuss. Dries is already dressed and sitting by the piano like a perfect gentleman.'

'And Clara …'

'Yes, Alison?'

'You look absolutely fabulous. I wish I had your figure.'

'My figure comes from running after Hanneli.'

Dries looked refreshed; the swim seemed to have done him good. His hair was plastered down in curls as he had not bothered to brush it, and his head rested easily on his broad shoulders. He was sitting at the piano, playing a tune. Dries was much taller than his father, although his shy manner minimised what might otherwise have been an imposing presence. Enoch sat down in the drawing room and listened to the music. He noticed that the efforts of the staff at rearranging the room – as they had done recently by moving the armoire, or spiriting a Dresden figurine from the drawing room mantelpiece to a display cabinet – affected him deeply. No matter how trivial, such changes seemed to unsettle him. Enoch found this peculiar as he did not usually mind things being moved at his own home.

Dries stopped playing the piano when Alison entered the room and complimented her on her dress. 'I see you've decided to change after all. That dress really suits you.'

Although it was still early for the arrival of the guests, Mr Molinieux had taken up his position in the entrance hall. He appeared nervous and cast an occasional glance at Enoch, which caused him a reciprocal uneasiness.

'Now, Mr Molinieux,' Alison ventured with a smile, 'I hope you'll treat the prime minister with due respect.'

'Yes, madam.'

'He is the PM, you know – and I don't have to remind you that Mrs Schoon is still the owner of Wepener. I wouldn't put it past you to turn them away.'

'No, madam. You can rely on me to do my job.'

'I do wish everyone in this house would stop calling me "madam".'

Mr Molinieux disregarded Alison's remark. He thought she should appreciate that he had every reason to display only the utmost courtesy towards the prime minister who was, after all, the only person in a position to help him.

Mfilo sat on a bench in the potting shed hidden from the house behind a slight rise. He was dressed in a sharkskin suit rescued from the rag-and-bone heap in the garage. Only the trousers had needed altering, and Clara had lengthened them by letting out the turn-ups. When confronted with the invitation to join the Schoons at tea, Mfilo had expressed reluctance. However, Clara had eventually won him over. She thought Mfilo most ungrateful for saying that he did not want to have tea with abelungu as he would feel uncomfortable under the scornful gaze of Mr Molinieux who stalked about the house like a ghost in his starched white shirts, constantly brushing imaginary dust from his shiny lapels with a gloved hand. Of late, the butler barely greeted him and had all but forbidden him to enter the house. By being at the tea party, Clara had insisted, Mfilo would show Mr Molinieux that he was not to be bullied. As a further inducement, she suggested that Mfilo help Alison show the guests around the garden after tea.

When Mfilo's pipe went out for the second time, he wrapped it in a scrap of chamois leather, placed it in his pocket, drew a deep breath and entered the house by a side door.

'Look, Mfilo is already here,' Clara said in excitement as she spotted him in the hall, 'the first visitor. But no tea until the outside visitors come!'

Mfilo had hoped to avoid drawing attention to himself, but even Mr Molinieux managed a civil greeting before being called to the front door by the arrival of the prime minister and Mrs Schoon.

Dries took his mother's hand and sensed her nervousness. Arta Schoon's eyes were partially hidden under the brim of her hat and a net that accentuated the whiteness of her powdered skin. Dries kissed her cheek gently. She rested her hand on his arm, but the touch evoked little of the intimacy of her embrace when he was a boy, or when he and his brother had squirmed inside the towels she had draped around them so that they would not catch cold after a swim on a windy day.

'I haven't even been offered my first cup of tea and someone's already bothering me about a petition,' the prime minister protested as he greeted his son and daughter-in-law. Mr Molinieux had managed to detain him in the entrance hall to complain about a faulty identity card. Sybrand Schoon reached for his granddaughter, Hanneli, swept her up and kissed her on the nose. 'My little princess is growing so fast,' he said, holding her up so that she could give her grandmother a kiss.

'And I hope my princess is learning Afrikaans ...'

'Of course, Oupa – Enoch is teaching me.'

'Say compliments of the season to Oupa and Ouma,' Dries coaxed her, though realising that November was perhaps a bit early for holiday greetings.

Both out of courtesy and a fondness for showing that he had a firm command of the language, Sybrand Schoon made every effort to speak English when conversing with people such as Alison, who were not likely to understand Afrikaans. 'My dear daughter, you people must really come and spend Christmas with us. We are simple people – we don't send engraved cards. But I insist you come to Pringle Bay for Christmas lunch.'

For a moment Alison hesitated as they had made other plans for the holidays. The relationship between her and her in-laws, fraught at the best of times, had become even more strained after the Drill Hall incident. However, for the sake of harmony, Alison decided to accept.

'Why, thank you, Dr Schoon. We would be delighted.'

The prime minister could barely conceal his pleasure at being back at Wepener, the estate where his wife had spent her childhood and where they had lived as a couple until well after Malan had invited him into his cabinet as minister of native affairs. It had been with some hesitancy that they had deserted Wepener for the ministerial residence in Cape

Town, leaving their two young sons in the care of their nanny and Ou Mevrou Jansen.

It was generally known that Schoon had grown up in poverty on a sheep farm and that his childhood had been one long struggle. The family had lost most of their animals in the drought of 1923 and, although his father had not abandoned their farm at Zastron, he had never recovered from the loss. In those years there were no government subsidies or cooperatives, and farmers had to struggle as best they could.

It was only later in life, after his doctoral studies at universities in the Netherlands and Germany, and his marriage to Arta Lubbe, that Schoon had attained some status. Not that wealth had ever been the motive, but his marriage had made his life just that much easier and had catapulted him into a level of society to which it would have been difficult for him to gain entry without his wife's connections.

Dr Schoon looked about the drawing room, taking note of the furniture the staff had moved since his last visit. He rightly attributed a broken pane of glass on a display cabinet to Hanneli's tricycle. The piano had taken the place of a large stinkwood desk at which he had spent many solitary but rewarding hours working as a young government official. Even later, with his appointment to Native Affairs, he had drafted a number of important bills at that desk – and it had been there that the idea for the Bantu homelands had first occurred to him.

'You know, Alison, my dear, I hardly come in at the front door and that Molinieux chap confronts me about a reclassification thing – almost as if I can tackle his problem before I can get something into my stomach.'

'I'm terribly sorry, Dr Schoon. I'm afraid Mr Molinieux is rather preoccupied with the matter and he hasn't had much success with Pretoria. Perhaps you might suggest to him how best to sort this out.'

'Alison, even you must realise how bureaucracies work. After all, you British introduced the foot-dragging civil servant. Get Dries to call me in the morning – or he can have a word with my private secretary. I'll be in Cape Town for a few days.'

Alison smiled at the prime minister. 'That's very kind of you, sir. The civil service may present a problem – but it's the law itself ...'

'The law is the law, my dear – and it is up to us to obey it.'

Alison longed to reply, but she knew it a waste of breath to argue the

49

finer points of law with someone who would never be persuaded to see reason.

'May I offer you some tea?'

'Ag, Alison, what a short memory you've got. We Boers like our coffee.'

'Of course, Doctor. I'll have Trossie make a pot immediately. Please excuse me for not remembering. Mr Molinieux, would you mind asking Trossie for a pot of coffee.'

'Straight away, madam.'

Enoch had earlier noticed Mr Molinieux making some surreptitious moves to get himself standing close to the prime minister. Without taking his eye off the door, Molinieux listened to Schoon's remarks to Alison.

'Now don't go and make a big fuss over me, Alison, my dear. A little tea won't do any harm.' As an afterthought, the prime minister added, 'How is our Ou Mevrou Jansen? I miss her cooking. You must give her our best – or perhaps Arta and I will pop in for a minute to greet her before we leave.'

'She would be delighted. You will find her in her room, as she does rather need her afternoon rest. I've told her several times that she is well beyond working age, but I'm afraid I've not been very persuasive. I'm sure she would appreciate a visit from you.'

That very morning Enoch had heard Ou Mevrou Jansen distinctly tell Dries that she had no time for his parents and that she did not wish to see them – so he was surprised to hear Alison ignoring her wishes.

'I swear that woman will drop dead right in front of her cooking pots,' the prime minister remarked, shaking his head thoughtfully, 'but I suppose it isn't such a bad thing to leave this life in full swing.'

Enoch had met the Schoons on a few occasions, but that had not made him feel any less anxious in their presence. He never knew quite what to say to them, even though Dries had described them to him as 'normal but misguided people'. He noticed that Alison was trying to make her escape and was also about to move off when Schoon caught sight of him.

'Don't tell me this is the grandson of Hannes Pretorius?' he said and stretched out his hand.

'Yes, this is Enoch, Dr Schoon,' Alison replied.

'That's right – Enoch. I thought I recognised him – you're quite the young man now, aren't you?'

Before Enoch could reply, Alison presented Clara and Mfilo to the prime minister and his wife.

'So, here's the one who spoils my little princess, hey?' Dr Schoon said to Clara.

'Yes, Master Prime Minister.'

Schoon smiled and it seemed that Clara was about to faint. She swayed from side to side.

'Clara, man, it's nice to see you. As always, you do a jolly good job. If you were around when our boys were young, we wouldn't have had so much trouble with them.' Then turning to Mfilo, the prime minister said, 'And here's the man who's got green in his fingers. Later on you must take the oubaas and the ounooi for a walk and show us around your garden.'

'Yes, oubaas.'

'My husband,' Mrs Schoon said, 'can do anything with his head, but he can't plant a simple flower. When our newspapers write about him, you would swear that he could do anything. But flowers … you mention them and his eyes glaze over. Don't waste your time with the oubaas, Mfilo. I must say, with the exception of our Mr Pretorius, not a single gardener in the history of Wepener has done better than you.'

'Yes, Mfilo is an excellent gardener,' Alison said. 'It would be a great shame to lose him.'

'Surely he's not about to leave Wepener,' said Mrs Schoon.

'No, he's not,' said Alison. 'He's quite happy with us, but I'm afraid he is still an "illegal" in Cape Town and as it is I have to bail him out of jail constantly. If only Dr Schoon would scrap the Influx Control Act.'

'I'm sure they might consider an exception in this case. I can imagine it must cause you no end of bother – but it would be up to you to raise it with my husband.'

The prime minister chose to ignore his wife's remark. The amended Influx Control Act had been one of his proudest achievements; it had been a great success in preventing the swamping of white urban areas by natives. Without it the policy of separate development wouldn't have been possible. Mfilo fidgeted while Clara excused herself and walked away. She let her belt out a few notches and whispered 'die grootbaas' a few times until she regained her composure.

The prime minister touched Mfilo on the arm to get his attention. 'Yes, oubaas?'

'Without a word of a lie,' the prime minister said, 'Wepener is one of the finest gardens I've ever seen. It even beats Kirstenbosch. Like the English say, "It's tonic for the eyes." '

Over the years Mfilo had worked at many large estates in Johannesburg and Durban and could tell the potential of a garden simply by studying a handful of earth. That was one of the reasons Oupa Hans had recommended him ahead of the landscape gardeners and designers who had streamed to Wepener in response to the advertisement Mr Molinieux had placed in the newspapers. The botanical gardens at Kirstenbosch were another matter, and it was obvious to Mfilo that the prime minister was exaggerating.

'Thank you, oubaas,' Mfilo said. 'Oubaas mustn't say so.'

'Nonsense. So's true's God, Mfilo – but listen here, why don't you look me in the eye when I talk to you? Come on, a man isn't a man if he can't look another man in the eye.'

Had Mfilo had more sense he would have extricated himself from the conversation and gone to look for Clara. It was not as though he was ignorant of the fact that looking a white man in the eye was enough to earn a native three months in jail, with the bonus of a weekly flogging to help drive the lesson home. And yet, here was the prime minister telling him that he was not a man because he could not look umlungu in the eye.

Enoch wondered whether there was something he could say to rescue Mfilo from his predicament. However, to avoid being drawn into their conversation he turned to the wall to study a painting. Mfilo never stood up for himself when a misunderstanding arose in the kitchen, and it was hardly likely that he would be able to confront the prime minister. This was his first real party and already it had become an ordeal.

'Tell the oubaas, what is your tribe?' the prime minister persisted, trying to encourage Mfilo.

'Zulu, baas oubaas.'

'That's just what I was going to say. You must be very proud. A Zulu can look anyone in the eye. Hey, no wonder you get into trouble with the law – Cape Town is not a preference area for Zulus.'

'Excuse me, Dr Schoon,' Alison interrupted, having noticed Mfilo's discomfort. 'Allow me to introduce Polycarp van Wyk.'

'Alison, nobody needs an introduction to our poet. He's just the man I want to see. I was just telling Mfilo here that a Zulu can always look another man in the eye.'

Not expecting to be drawn into a discourse about the prime minister's perception of native lore, Polycarp appeared taken aback. 'Perhaps, sir, he's worried about showing disrespect. But I defer to your superior knowledge, Mr Prime Minister – I believe the native mind was the subject of one of your doctoral theses.'

'But what about us?' the prime minister persisted. 'When we speak, we always look each other in the eye.'

'We look and we don't see,' Polycarp responded. 'Besides, the Zulus might consider the custom disrespectful.'

This business about who looked at whom was dragging on far too long to Enoch's liking, and Mfilo looked mortified. Not only was he unable to look anyone in the eye – he appeared not to know where to look at all. Enoch, who was beginning to have second thoughts about the party, felt that perhaps Mfilo should have listened to Ou Mevrou Jansen.

Fortunately Polycarp came to the rescue. 'I'm sure, Mr Prime Minister, Mfilo is much in demand. We should allow him to share his gifts with the other guests – people always need gardening tips from an expert.'

'Of course, of course,' Sybrand Schoon said. 'How selfish of me.'

Mfilo heaved a sigh of relief and went off in search of Clara just as she returned bearing cakes and scones on a tray.

The prime minister turned his attention to Polycarp. 'Now, young man, I have a great favour to ask. My Dries tells me you've been having problems finding a job after your time in prison. It's news to me, but he says I'm responsible for putting you there. My son blames me for many things, but that's a father's burden – and just to show you that I'm a fair man, I have recommended you for a position where your views will be appreciated and not get you into trouble.'

'How is that possible, sir? The only place my views have ever got me is Caledon Square or Pretoria Central Prison,' Polycarp replied, 'and I'm not sure that I'm ready for either of those places at the moment.'

'Don't get me wrong, Mr van Wyk,' Schoon said, looking around to make sure that no one was listening, but ignoring the young Coloured boy who was hovering nearby, taking in every word.

'I know of a good job for you in the Transkei. I don't see eye to eye with an old friend, but I promised to help him. He needs a head teacher for his children and grandchildren. For some reason he wants them all to be teachers and university professors – so it will keep you busy. There's no better way to stay out of trouble. My friend will pay you a generous salary. Take down his telephone number and tell him you're the one I've recommended.'

As Polycarp had been thinking of leaving Cape Town, the prospect sounded interesting and, although apprehensive about the prime minister's recommendation, he took down the details. However, when he asked for the person's name, he found the prime minister reluctant to reveal it.

'Now don't you worry about who he is,' Dr Schoon said, looking around to make sure they were not being overheard. 'What I can tell you is that you won't be disappointed. And if you are, just pack your bags and leave. It is not a prison sentence. You and my friend should get along well – you are both of the same mind. But that's the end of our conversation, hey?'

'How can I possibly call someone without knowing his name, Dr Schoon?'

'Just call him Khotso,' the prime minister said and walked across the room, leaving behind a bemused Polycarp.

Enoch understood Schoon's disinclination to reveal further details about his friend. Khotso was the man Oupa Hans was always talking about and, as he was interested to find out more, he approached Polycarp.

'Did you hear that, Enoch?' Polycarp remarked. 'The prime minister and the witchdoctor.'

'What do you mean?'

'It's just typical – Schoon can't keep me in jail and now is trying to pack me off to the Transkei to this Khotso. I'm too subversive to teach at Stellenbosch, but he wants me to indoctrinate black kids in Cofimvaba instead, and he wants me there as soon as possible.'

Enoch liked Polycarp – he was an unusual man with red hair that always seemed to stand on end. No matter how much brilliantine he used, or how much he tried to flatten the spikes with his hands, he never managed to make it look like anything other than the bristles running down the spine of a ridgeback. He was a philosopher and a poet whose work never failed to catch the eye of the censors. Had he written in English, his work could, no doubt, have been published in England – but he insisted on writing in Afrikaans.

'Oupa Hans knows Khotso well,' ventured Enoch. 'Maybe you should talk to him.'

'That's a good idea. And you look great, Enoch. How's the studying coming along?'

'One more year, and then university.'

'Don't let these stupid bastards get into your head. They'll stick to you like lice. Believe me – it's hard to get rid of them.'

Enoch wasn't sure whether he should confide in Polycarp. He was sick and tired of his school. In fact, he had begun to hate it. Undeserved punishment and running battles with teachers and former friends had taken their toll – and no matter how hard he worked, the humiliations of the past year had convinced him that it was time to move on. He had suggested to his parents that he would do the matric year at his father and grandfather's old school in the Eastern Cape. However, his parents refused to consider sending him away to the Dominican Sisters at Tsomo. His father was adamant that he would never send his son to a Roman Catholic school, no matter how good its reputation.

'Come on, Enoch, be a man and stick it out where you are,' Polycarp insisted. 'And don't forget, Dries and Alison are expecting great things from you. When I was your age, I had to struggle to get ahead.'

'Nobody complained when Dries went off to England.'

'That's true, but Dries can find a soft landing wherever he goes.'

However, Enoch still had plans to move to another school, although he suspected that Dries would be disappointed. The bank account accruing interest and everyone's expectations had become a burden for him. Not that he was ungrateful, but the whole thing made him feel extremely uncomfortable.

'Let's go and get ourselves a cup of tea. You'd think that they'd be serving champagne.'

Polycarp and Enoch walked across to the table where Clara and Mfilo were in the middle of a squabble. 'You tell me lies, Clara,' Mfilo whispered. 'You tell me Nooi Schoon is a play-white – and she isn't. She got a white woman's skin.'

'Be quiet. What if Mrs Schoon hear you? She anyway got a powder puff and she use it plenty. Ou Mevrou Jansen told me.'

'I don't know why you listen to that old witch,' Mfilo replied, casting a glance in Mrs Schoon's direction. 'That Jansen woman always talk rubbish and the older she get, the bigger the rubbish. And why do you bob every time Nooi Schoon look over here?"

'It don't matter what colour she is – she's still the prime minister's wife and I can curtsy when I want to,' Clara replied.

In the presence of his daughter-in-law, the prime minister was reluctant to drink his coffee from a saucer. Besides, his wife had strictly forbid him such habits on the day he had first stepped across the threshold at Wepener. So he drank from his cup, holding the saucer firmly in his hand, which afforded him the opportunity to look around the room. He watched his wife engaged in conversation with Alison and Hanneli.

Enoch tried to keep a safe distance from the prime minister. From the look on Schoon's face, he could tell that between him and the staff there was a recognition of the position each of them occupied. Polycarp had told him that Dr Schoon considered society to be some vast machine in which each vital part was placed relative to the other. While such an assumption was by no means unique, it was the prime minister's theory that it was the position of the relevant parts that determined their function. With the wrong placement, a breakdown or disharmony was likely to occur. To avoid such a breakdown, Dr Schoon considered that a strict code of law governing race, behaviour and the social order was essential. This, apparently, was how he had arrived at his 'good neighbourliness policy', which he resorted to in order to counter the condemnation of what was wrongly perceived to be 'divide and rule' – which he insisted was actually the British way of doing things.

Polycarp's insight into the workings of the prime minister's mind had proved to have been a bit of an earful for Enoch, although it reminded him of Dr Schoon's repeated warnings on the wireless about communists being a threat to the government's carefully wrought balance.

'He was even banging that drum at last year's Battle of Blood River com-memoration, as if Dingane and his impis were in the communist advance guard. Just like Schoon – a red under every bed,' Polycarp said. 'I can only hope that the one under my bed will be a gorgeous brunette and not a frumpy Rosa Luxemburg look-alike in a red kappie and bloomers.'

Just then a large motorcycle with a sidecar came roaring up the gravel driveway, raising enough dust to obscure the rider and interrupting all conversation. Chief Josias Nkosivile got off the machine and handed his gloves, helmet and brown leather jacket to Mr Molinieux, who was wait-ing in the entrance hall. Two armed guards raced towards the house. Mr Molinieux intercepted them at the door and assured them that the prime minister would come to no harm. But before he could send the men back to their post at the gate, the one in command said, 'Now listen here, you moffie, you'll know all about it if you don't keep an eye on that skelm.'

Alison, who was greeting Josias in the front hall, enquired after the cause of the commotion.

'This obnoxious Boer insulted Chief Josias and me. And he threatened to assault me if there was any trouble!' Mr Molinieux blurted out.

'Who's your Boer? And assault is mild for what will happen. I promised you a regte nierhou,' the guard said, tapping his club across his palm for emphasis. 'It's our job to look after the prime minister; and if you try to stop us, this club will answer for it.' The man then turned to Alison, 'I ask your butler to please keep an eye on that native chap on the motorbike and he try to get clever with me.'

'What cheek,' Alison gasped.

'That's exactly what I say, madam. The prime minister is in madam's house and we got a job to do. His security is our responsibility – and when we request the guest list days ago, nobody sent it.'

With an abrupt salute, he turned on his heels and marched back to the gate, the sergeant close on his heels. At a distance Enoch could see his grandfather peering up the drive and then disappearing into his cottage.

'Animals …' was all Alison could say.

Unflustered by the drama, the prime minister nodded in Chief Josias's direction, hoping that this might be the only communication necessary between them. Realising that his presence was a cause of discomfort to the prime minister, Josias acknowledged his greeting – and then turned to embrace Alison and Hanneli.

'Last time you promised me a ride, Uncle,' Hanneli pleaded.

'That's why your uncle brought the sidecar today, my little princess. Be patient – we'll go for a ride just now.'

'Uncle, Oupa also calls me his little princess.'

'I see; now we can't have that. I will just have to call you Makhosazana.'

'What's it mean, Uncle?' asked Hanneli, attempting to raise her feet from the floor by hanging from Josias's arm.

'It means the very same thing – but in Zulu.'

'Ou Mevrou Jansen says she doesn't want people to talk native in the house.'

'Don't you worry – it's Zulu, not native. And I'll give Ou Mevrou Jansen a good talking-to.'

'Makhosazana, Makhosazana,' Hanneli repeated with the defiance of a child as she ran outdoors to inspect the motorcycle, with Clara hurrying after her.

Josias turned to Alison. 'You presume on my friendship to get me and the enemy under the same roof, hey? Your father-in-law and I have nothing to say to each other.'

'Come, Josias, a good part of the country is burning and the rest is in turmoil and all you can think of is your pride. You disappoint me. If anyone is responsible for this invitation it is your bosom friend, Dries. It was his idea.'

'Alison, you're very dear, but you don't really understand the situation ...' Josias hesitated.

'What absolute nonsense – and you accuse white people of being patronising!'

Chief Josias laughed. 'You're right, my dear – which reminds me, let me have some food. I haven't eaten since last night. And is there any coffee?'

Josias looked surprised as Polycarp approached him. 'What on earth are *you* doing here?'

'I should be the one to ask you, Josias. Why the hell are you here? Has the lion come to sup with the lambs?'

'Next time they ought to keep you behind lock and key for longer,' Josias said. 'Refusing to pay taxes and then having the gall to write a satire about the receiver of revenue. Thought you could get away with that, hey?'

'Anyway, it looks as though I shall be leaving town soon. To stop me from corrupting the Afrikaner youth, the prime minister recommended me for a job as head teacher to his friend, the witchdoctor. And if Khotso will have me, I'll go.'

'You mean Cofimvaba?'

'Do you know Khotso?'

'Of course – but I can't talk on an empty stomach.'

Mr Molinieux handed Chief Josias a large plate provisioned with a variety of sandwiches.

'Now that's better – as long as you don't mind me speaking with a full mouth. Where were we? Who doesn't know Khotso Sethuntsa, keeper of the magic wand? He's perhaps the only real friend Sybrand Schoon has. Those two are thick as thieves. Why do you think Schoon suddenly became prime minister? Good thing you aren't the superstitious type.'

'What on earth does Schoon's position as prime minister have to do with Khotso?'

'It's a good thing you're going to Cofimvaba. You'll find out soon enough.'

'By the way, Josias, have you met Enoch?' Polycarp said.

Enoch stood closer and they shook hands. He had met the chief before, and had read about him in the newspapers. Oupa Hans knew him well. The chief had risked coming to tea at Wepener despite his banning orders.

'So, who is this young man?'

'Mr Pretorius's grandson – and Ou Mevrou Jansen's new favourite.'

'Of course, I didn't recognise him all grown-up. You have a fine grandfather – and it's great to be in Ou Mevrou Jansen's good books. She used to be too quick with the stick. Is your oupa at home?'

'Yes, Chief Josias.'

'I'll pop in to see him when I leave. That will give those guys at the gate something to think about.

'Polycarp, my friend, you could do worse than Cofimvaba,' Chief Josias said. 'You'll enjoy your stay there. I'm sorry that I'm always at loggerheads with Khotso. We could learn a thing or two from each other. After all, he does have the prime minister eating out of his hand, which is more than either of us can say.

'Why don't you take this young man along with you? Not that you'd be lacking for company.'

'That's a great idea.' Polycarp turned to Enoch. 'So what do you say?'

'If only … but my parents won't let me. I've already asked them if I could do my matric at the Catholic school in Tsomo.'

'Well, we could always organise a protest march and twist your parents' arms,' Chief Josias suggested.

Dries approached with a teapot in hand. 'You'll do no such thing. Enoch has exams coming up and it's the wrong time to give him ideas.'

Polycarp put his arm around Dries's shoulder. 'It's the absolute height of luxury to have such a well-trained staff,' he said as Dries held the teapot over Clara's cup, 'and then to decry servitude. Putting ideas into Enoch's head? At least the inyanga's compound would be quite different to Wepener.'

'But everyone knows that Khotso lives in even greater luxury – with his fortune and band of merry wives,' replied Dries.

'Look at Clara – today she takes tea with the master, but tomorrow she'll be back with the pots and pans,' Polycarp countered.

'Sies, Polycarp. You know I don't work in the kitchen. It's Mieta and Trossie, not me!' Clara corrected him before walking off. 'What a nerve …'

'I suppose it calls for an apology …' Polycarp said.

'I would think so,' Dries replied.

'What I meant was an apology for inviting me and Josias when you knew your father would be here today. I don't suppose it's a liability for you – but what about us?'

'Why are you two always arguing?' Chief Josias wanted to know, attempting to restore peace. 'And you, Polycarp, are going to work for an inyanga, thanks to the very prime minister you claim to despise. Life is full of contradictions.'

The guests were spread around the room in clusters. The sound of cups and saucers lent a certain rhythm to the conversations. Alison appeared to be pleased with the gentle hum. She walked from group to group and, as the hostess, was spared from saying anything beyond a few well-chosen words.

The prime minister also appeared pleased, having fulfilled his old friend Khotso's request. He realised that although Polycarp had a great deal to learn, he had the makings of an excellent teacher; he was, after all, an intelligent man. There was also his background, which the prime minister admired. He was the only son of a poor railway worker from the Eastern Cape, yet the boy had distinguished himself in philosophy at Stellenbosch University where there had been much competition. He would be just the right man for Khotso.

Dr Schoon watched Josias in conversation with his son and appeared envious of the intimacy between the two men. His own relationship with his son had always been distant and exchanges between them formal. This had not been by design, but was simply the way things had turned out. Just as he had had an African friend during childhood, so too had Dries.

Josias's mother had been nanny to Dr Schoon's sons, and although the children had been inseparable throughout their teenage years, as he grew older, Josias had become an extremely difficult customer. No amount of solitary confinement had made him see reason. After frequent spells in prison, he came out looking for more trouble. Unless controlled, he was the kind of person who would stir up native sentiment against the government. And that had been the reason for his present house arrest, which he was now defying by his presence at Wepener. His banning orders forbade him to be in the company of more than one person at a time, and here he was holding court in a crowded room. Because Dr Schoon did not wish to be further alienated from his son, he had restrained himself from taking sterner measures against Josias.

The prime minister must have thought that by remaining in one spot he would not be obliged to speak to those guests with whom he was likely to disagree. However, he had not counted on the jostling that occurs at a party where, as if afloat on an ocean, one is carried along by the current. By turning to greet somebody, saying a word or two here or shaking a hand there, one may arrive in new surroundings. In this manner, Schoon found himself in the company of Josias, Polycarp, and his son.

'Dries,' he said, in an effort to find a neutral subject of conversation, 'how come I've never seen this painting before?'

'I'm sure you have, Papa,' Dries said, rather surprised as he had never discussed art with his father. 'Ma gave it on loan to the National Gallery years ago. I thought it would be nice to have it back in the house.'

'I see, and who is this Thomas Baines fellow – surely this isn't a very cheerful subject for a drawing room?'

Seeing no polite way of retreating, Polycarp tried to throw some light on the painting. It depicted a particularly gruesome slaughter by a party of hunters. 'It's one of Thomas Baines's most famous paintings – the 1860 *Antelope Hunt*. It shows Prince Alfred after his failed visit to Kaffraria, taking it out on the local fauna. It could be seen as a symbol for what might happen in our country if we continue to ignore the demands of our fellow Africans.'

'Young man, I've spent virtually my whole working life in Native Affairs and it is news to me that the demands of our "fellow Africans" are being ignored. Without our intervention the natives would have killed each other off a long time ago. This Baines chap is a fine artist.'

An embarrassed Dries interrupted his father. 'Don't you think it's terrible – the revolt that has been going on in Cato Manor and Pondoland?'

'That is exactly what I'm talking about – people trying to give tribal squabbles respectability by calling it a revolt. It's no more a revolt than a knobkierie jamboree.'

'Papa, I don't want to argue, but I do think you and Josias should get together and discuss the situation. Surely, there must be a solution.'

A troubled silence descended on the group. The prime minister and Josias stared at each other. Even though they stood close enough to touch, they were separated by an abyss of wariness – like Fontaine's goats, each jealously guarding his shaky precinct on a narrow bridge.

Dr Schoon knew that the situation in Pondoland had spun out of control, despite the fact that the minister of police had implemented the ninety-day detention law to control agitators. This law was having the desired effect in the cities; however, it had been less than successful in rural areas. He clasped his hands behind his back, his deep blue eyes greatly troubled. He seemed to sense that Chief Josias was after his job and would do anything to realise this goal. Suddenly it was as if Enoch could see right into the prime minister's thoughts. Josias had to be stopped at all costs if the country was not to be plunged into chaos – and to think that the man had spent much of his childhood in this very house!

'This is how the quagga became extinct,' Polycarp interjected, hoping to break the silence that had settled on the group. But no one turned to look at the painting again.

Dries glanced at his father and realised that expecting him and Chief Josias to discuss matters in this setting was unrealistic. However, Josias quickly recovered his wits. 'Don't worry, Dries – your father and I will meet across the table some day. No matter how congenial your home is, this is hardly the time or place for what we have to say to each other. But we must negotiate – whether we like it or not. And I will remember your good intentions.'

Kenny Parker approached Enoch. Kenny, a Shakespearian scholar with a doctorate, was another of Dries's close friends. He'd been invited to the tea to say farewell as he was soon to leave for England to take up a post at the University of Warwick. He would never have been offered a similar position in South Africa. He was remarkably cheerful for someone who had spent most of his adult life studying, only to discover that the colour of his skin excluded him from being a lecturer in the country of his birth.

'Let's hope by the time you graduate this madness may be over,' Kenny said to Enoch. 'Who knows? By then I might be back here lecturing at the University of Cape Town.'

He presented Enoch to a large woman who was standing by herself. 'Gladys, this is Enoch. He tells me that he would like to be an artist – perhaps you could show him the ropes.'

She laughed. 'What – this young man? I'm not so sure about ropes – pigments and brushes perhaps.'

'Whatever it is you artists do, it would be great if you could teach him.'

'But Kenny, Gladys is already my teacher at the community centre in Woodstock,' Enoch explained.

'Enoch has plenty of talent, Kenny – but he's got to put his mind to it. Let him finish his matric first, then I'll help him.'

Hanneli soon had everyone in good spirits. She insisted on leading Josias outdoors, scrambling into the sidecar of his bike. Her cries of excitement rose above the explosions of the powerful machine as Josias kicked it into life. He tied the strings of her bonnet under her chin and placed his helmet firmly on top, then steered a slow circle around the gravel drive. The child's shrieks and laughter brought some of the guests outdoors, and the guards, aroused at their post, came to attention, their eyes on the chief and their truncheons raised for any eventuality.

From an open window, Mfilo watched Josias, hoping that the chief would not flatten the borders that he had laid out with such meticulous care. As cigarette smoke drifted across the room, Mfilo nervously reached into a pocket for his pipe. He relished Ou Mevrou Jansen's absence. That woman would not even permit him to smoke his pipe in the courtyard because the smell of tobacco might waft in through an open window. Now, with the heel of his thumb, he tamped the Rum and Maple tobacco into the bowl and lit his pipe with a single match.

'Mfilo,' Clara cried aghast. 'Just now you stink up the whole house with your cheap tobacco. If Ou Mevrou Jansen was here, she would chuck you right out.'

With unaccustomed confidence he said, 'Well, she isn't here. I'm taking a smoke while I'm waiting to show the oubaas round the garden.'

'Now look here, Mfilo, you mustn't come and take advantage now,' Clara said nervously. 'We want to be invited again. Quick, put that thing out! You can't keep the prime minister waiting!'

'The oubaas must be patient,' Mfilo persisted with a show of stubbornness, 'because why, the flowers have their time – and the oubaas must jolly well wait his time also.'

'Sjoe! I don't know where all this rudeness come from. You so forward; Alison give you a finger and you take the whole hand.'

'The makhulu is only a man like me,' Mfilo replied. Nevertheless, a flush of excitement animated him as he made his way around the back of the house to meet up with the guests at the front door. As if reading from a seed catalogue, he stumbled over the names Enoch had come to know so well: the nicotiana, celosia, helianthus or Italian white sunflower, the globe echinops, blue thistles, springtime verbena, the white vinca with its red eyes, phlox, sun petunias, gazanias and the Barberton daisy – all these names and more had been crammed into their heads by Oupa Hans.

Polycarp stood at the edge of the great lawn, entranced by a fringe of light. Where the top of the mountain met the sky a line of silverleaf trees retreated along the face of the mountain. The roots of the trees grasped the rocks, leeching the stone for nourishment.

'When the settlers first came to these shores,' he said to Dries, 'they cut the silver trees down for stockades and firewood – the very trees that guided their vessels into sheltered harbours. Don't ask me where you plundered the remaining few for your garden.'

'Mr Pretorius got them – go and ask him. He's a genius.'

The prime minister, his wife and Mfilo walked at the head of the party. The late afternoon sun was still bright and warm with a few clouds scattered about the sky. Mrs Schoon asked Mfilo about the nierembergia. He spoke about the virtues of the purple cupflower he had planted in an encircling nest of white matricaria and marmalade-coloured rudbeckia. She told him that he had achieved a marvellous effect, even though to her it might have looked more like a park and less like the garden she remembered from her childhood.

When Mfilo realised that everyone was listening to him, he picked a mixed bunch of flowers and presented it to Mrs Schoon. He was thankful for the distraction caused by the prime minister who, when a flock of pelicans pumped their way across the sky, held his granddaughter aloft so that she could have an unobstructed view of the curious birds, probably on their way to Rondevlei.

The guests had been outside for no more than fifteen minutes when there was a sudden reversal in the direction of the breeze. The white cumulus was gradually obscured by grey cloud and it became a great deal cooler. The change in the weather was not noticed at first; however, the guests soon returned indoors where even the drawing room was becoming chilly. Some of them in their light summer clothes shivered visibly.

Mr Molinieux instructed Mieta to make a fire. He walked among the guests offering small glasses of sherry from a decanter. Polycarp hurried into a spare bedroom, drew a blanket from a bed and draped it around his shoulders. In the kitchen, Mieta perspired over a large Dover stove and then carried more wood through to the fireplace. Soon everybody was cosy again. Outside, the rain drummed onto the thatch and muffled the sound of the motorbike as Chief Josias took his leave. Witbooi, the prime minister's chauffeur, brought the Daimler to the front door while the prime minister and Mrs Schoon made their round of farewells and reminded Alison of the Christmas invitation. Witbooi had been silent since the day when, as an illegal diamond courier, his tongue was cut out over a dispute about some missing diamonds.

Darkness had fallen by the time Zachaeus took the last guests, Gladys Mgudlandlu and Kenny Parker, to their respective homes. While waiting at the gate lodge for Zachaeus to return, Enoch made a cup of tea for Oupa Hans and served him some of the cakes and pastries he had brought with him. He changed into his own clothes and told his grandfather about the afternoon's events.

Khotso: Man of Peace

That night Enoch wrote to thank Dries and Alison for inviting him to the party, and for his new wardrobe. He sealed the envelope and hid it in his satchel in case his mother went through his things before he could post it. The reply, delivered by Zachaeus a few days later, included an invitation to a performance of *Hamlet* at the Little Theatre. Alison suggested that he invite a friend along.

Enoch put his library books and sketch pad aside for two weeks to concentrate on his studies. It was important to get his father onto his side. He intended broaching the subject of attending the Catholic school at Tsomo once more when he produced his school report. Getting away from Cape Town had become an obsession, and planning his escape route was usually the last thought on his mind before he fell asleep. Dries agreed to postpone their theatre outing until after the exams and wished him success.

A week after the tea party, Enoch was dismayed to read in the *Cape Times* that the Special Branch had arrested Kenny Parker under the Suppression of Communism Act, hours before his departure for England, and had placed him in solitary confinement. Enoch assumed that this was the reason the letter he had written to Kenny had been returned to him. He read the article again, but no reasons were given for Kenny's imprisonment. Whatever his political views, and his friends considered them moderate, putting him behind bars was an extreme way of dealing with a Shakespearean scholar. Fortunately Kenny's wife and twin daughters were already sailing for Southampton on the *Pendennis Castle* with their belongings.

Enoch did not discuss this with his parents as he would only be told to mind his own business, as people were not imprisoned without good reason. These arrests were becoming more frequent and no longer sent shockwaves throughout the country. Some people may have been deprived of sleep, but for others these draconian laws worked as well as a sleeping pill. Enoch's mother's cousin had been placed under banning orders, but he had managed to escape across the border into Bechuanaland, and eventually found refuge in Holland. He was quickly forgotten at home, although the University of Leiden appointed him a professor of Ancient History, in the very same department that had granted the prime minister a doctorate some years earlier.

Coloured families that could afford it emigrated to Australia and Canada for the sake of their children; and men and women who opposed the government were deported. For the Non-Whites who chose not to leave, the Group Areas Act set in train a string of evictions. People were forced to move from where they had been living for generations, as these areas were now designated White. Many of the evicted Coloured and Indian families found themselves on the Cape Flats, their former houses and gardens either demolished or lived in by their paler relations. In some areas where the Slum Clearance Act had been enforced, church bells were rung in defiance, but there were no longer any congregants to fill the pews. At dawn the muezzin called out the adhaan from minarete but where were the faithful to heed the call to prayer?

As they increased, the arrests and detentions preoccupied Enoch and his friends at school – and because he was acquainted with a few of the detainees, his views were frequently sought. There was much talk about joining the struggle, but Enoch had no solution to offer as to how to subvert the enforced division of the country. These discussions upstaged the earlier interest in Christine Keeler and Profumo, actors in a play that had long since been forgotten. Whereas the pupils once talked openly, it now seemed to them that Special Branch policemen might be lurking behind every tree.

At most schools a playground is meant for recreation; however, play in any form was discouraged at Enoch's school. To tackle the virtually impossible task of making silk purses of the sows' ears entrusted to him, the principal thought it best to call the recreation area a quadrangle, which he hoped would encourage reading and sensible discussion. And often, during break, his brooding figure could be spotted behind one of the corridor windows, from where he could better monitor the activities of his charges. Any talk between pupils necessitated a book in hand. With consummate skill pupils voiced their newfound political awareness while appearing to recite poetry. Had the principal been able to lip-read, he would have realised that he was educating a group of would-be radicals who preferred Hansard to William Blake.

Enoch did his best to encourage his schoolmates not to be intimidated by Special Branch, which prompted most of them to laugh at him. However, recent events had opened his eyes and he had begun to see the country as a dangerous place to live, especially for the idealist he had become.

Debate in the quadrangle soon turned to outright enmity outside the school grounds. Political camps were formed – not based on friendship or the usual schoolboy interests. Enoch refused to join sides. This unleashed an avalanche of speculation about his allegiances, and whereas in the past his schoolmates had hung onto his every word, they now avoided him. Enoch was unaware of the rumours circulating about him, that he was spying on class members and squealing to the principal. Haima was the only one of his friends who dared stand up for him when Iqbal accused him of spying for the government. Such disloyalty may have stemmed from Enoch's refusal to allow his old friend to peer over his shoulder during the exams. With some apparent remorse Iqbal apologised for his behaviour the following morning. Enoch was surprised that he wanted to make peace and was not particularly keen to speak to him. However, he did not show himself averse to a modest reconciliation. He knew that, as it was exam time, Iqbal would soon be back asking for favours.

After assembly prayers the principal paused for a moment. 'I want all rumours about a police informant in our midst to be stopped immediately. And in the interest of a prompt and unbiased outcome, would all standard nine boys line up in front of my office. The rest of you can go back to your classrooms – quietly.'

Enoch was press-ganged into standing at the head of the queue. However, regardless of guilt or innocence, each boy was to get six of the best. The principal walked down the line to satisfy himself that he had a full complement of twenty-three pupils. 'I will entertain no excuses, boys – and if any are offered there will be an extra round of six. Right, Pretorius, you're up first!'

Each purposeful stroke reminded the waiting boys that none of them would be shown mercy. One after the other, they entered the office where, for the next half hour, the principal's energy did not flag. Those at the end of the line got as good as those in front – and there wasn't a single word of protest. The collective punishment was hardly likely to endear Iqbal to the others, and he was marked for later ambush. While Enoch would not permit himself to gloat, he decided not to interfere with their plans for revenge.

Two weeks later the exams passed without further incident. Enoch's efforts at peacemaking with Iqbal had met with some success, and he had even won back most of his friends. With the exception of Latin, he had done well in all his subjects. His parents seemed pleased, but kept on reminding him of the poor Latin results. 'How can you study medicine if you don't get an A in Latin?' Once again Enoch found himself under the magnifying glass.

Without considering the consequences, he replied, 'I'm going to be an artist.'

'And what about all that money for your university sitting in the bank? You have one more year at school – so don't do anything foolish.'

Enoch's parents became hysterical whenever he said anything that could be construed as a threat to the money, and in their opinion he was still young enough for the strap. Latin was really quite easy for him, but the teacher's bullying had made him panicky, and whenever he sat down to write a test his hands would begin to tremble, causing Caesar's careful planning for his military campaigns against the Gauls to vanish in a fog of anxiety.

'You think only of yourself. Nothing's ever good enough for you – you're always on the lookout for something extra ...'

His mother couldn't have flung a worse accusation at him. What was closer to the truth was that whenever Enoch got himself into trouble of any kind it was because he was either misunderstood, or because some good deed he had attempted had come back to haunt him. Latin wasn't the only thing to make him jumpy. And the more he became aware of how the government lined its own pockets and how its defenders went about with truncheons to beat up those who demanded their share, the more determined he was that he would not stay in the country.

Enoch made his escape to Wepener for the weekend, without mentioning to his parents his intention to study with the Catholic Sisters at Tsomo. He had already written to the principal, Sister Deduch, using Oupa Hans's address.

Although his grandfather was pleased to see him, he was less welcoming than Enoch had expected. He looked tired and asked the boy to make a cup of tea. While Enoch waited for the kettle to boil, Oupa Hans said, 'What's this I hear about the school in Tsomo? Everyone up at the house is talking about it.'

'Oh, it's just an idea. I thought it would be good to matriculate at the same school as Oupa Hans and Dowa.'

Enoch wondered what had crawled under his grandfather's skin. He was usually not this irritable.

'It's not at all the same school – nor the same teachers. My nuns are long dead.'

'But nuns are all the same. They teach the same stuff, wear the same clothes …'

'I sometimes wonder about you.'

'Dowa told me that the nuns treated him with respect and never beat him.'

'What's worse – a good caning, or writing a thousand Hail Marys? To me it sounds as if you want to run away from home. All I can say is, getting out of the line of fire turns you into a target.'

Enoch found a packet of biscuits in the kitchen and laid them out on a plate. The tea had the desired effect, and Oupa Hans cheered up. He did up his sandals and they went outdoors to sit in the shade of a tree.

'There's a letter for you on the sideboard. Don't worry – I haven't opened it.'

'It can wait, Oupa.'

'And before I forget, Mfilo and his men brought down that wardrobe of clothes for you and now your bedroom is more cramped than ever.'

'Let me go and have a quick look.'

'That can also wait. Sit down. You'll never guess where I was last week.'

'Oupa Hans spent the week in Retreat.'

'No. You're not even trying.'

'Oupa Hans never goes anywhere – except the pension office … What about Mr Salie's place?'

'I asked Zachaeus to drive me into town. I needed my pension money – and to collect my new charcoal suit. The suit was far from ready. Then I went on a long journey and that's why I'm so exhausted.'

'East London,' Enoch said, taking a wild guess.

'That's close. The prime minister wanted me to go up to Cofimvaba with him again. It's like a disease with that man. He doesn't want people to know that he sees Khotso so he takes me along to interpret for him as I keep his secrets. I've done it in the past, mind you, but he hadn't been for some time, and I was surprised when he sent Witbooi to fetch me. Schoon pays the rent on my place in Retreat. He even had it done up for me. Whenever I go to Cofimvaba, I must tell everyone up at the house that I am at my other residence.'

Enoch sat open-mouthed. To him this sounded like another of Oupa Hans's tall stories.

'You don't believe me.'

'It's not that …'

'Do you think I could actually afford to pay rent on my pension?'

'Why would the prime minister take Oupa Hans with him when he has the pick of so many interpreters? And if he doesn't want anyone to know of his visits, why is he sending Polycarp up there?'

'Those are good questions, my boy. What you don't realise is that I know the witchdoctor, Khotso. I know his wives – and I know all about him. Khotso would not allow any old Xhosa interpreter into his house. Those inyangas have their reputations. I don't know why Schoon wants Polycarp there. I'm not a mind reader. But with this new Bantu Education thing, Khotso is desperate for someone to teach his children.

'Do you remember that story in the *Post* about a year ago – about his visit to the Queen? Everything in it was rubbish. "Her Majesty snubs Witchdoctor" – can you imagine that?'

'No, Oupa Hans.'

'Maybe the *Post* is too lowbrow for you. Khotso may have power, but he also has his pride, so he asked me to go and set the story straight. People are afraid of getting on the wrong side of Khotso and the editor actually listened to me. But maybe now is not the right time to tell you about Cofimvaba.'

'Please, Oupa, I want to hear about it now.'

'This is not to be repeated. Get me another cup of tea first – and one for yourself.'

Enoch suggested borrowing Dries's tape recorder, but Oupa Hans would not let him.

'Do you think the Apostles stood around with tape recorders and took down what Jesus said? You've got to train your ear to listen and your mind to remember. When you tell a story, you will find your own words for it.'

'How will anyone know it's true?'

'That's your problem. You've got to convince them. Do you doubt the Gospels?'

The question shocked Enoch. 'Of course not, Oupa Hans.'

'So there … Write your own tale, whatever it is, and don't wrap it up in fancy words. Use words we can all understand. Otherwise, who would want to read it? Make the story yours. I taught Mfilo everything I knew about gardening. What he does now is his own business. I am the teacher and you are the apprentice.'

'Oupa Hans doesn't need to tell me everything. I can read Oupa Hans's mind.'

'It's one thing reading other people's minds – it's something else trying to understand your own.'

When Enoch sat down over the summer holidays to write about his grandfather's visit to Cofimvaba, he did not attempt to reconstruct the story. He set down whatever he could recall and embellished those parts of which he had scant knowledge. Oupa Hans did not help him, or provide any further information, and when the boy asked him to read passages he had completed, the old man refused.

'I will read it when you are finished and I'll tell you if what you have written is any good. Then you can put the book away until the right time comes. You don't want to upset Khotso; he's a very powerful man.'

'Who says it will ever be a book?'

'It will have to be. It's all I have to leave you.'

'And when is the right time?'

'Maybe after Schoon and I are dead.'

'Thank you, Oupa Hans.'

'Who says your oupa isn't a generous man? Enoch Pretorius's name might be remembered if you write this book. And it would be a good way of honouring your family.'

The Inyanga's Craft

Hannes Pretorius was still in bed when Trossie woke him with his breakfast. He had set his alarm for eight, as Zachaeus was to take him to his place in Retreat, from where Witbooi, the prime minister's chauffeur, would collect him and drive him to George to meet up with the prime minister who was attending a by-election function. They would then drive on to Cofimvaba. Pretorius was not looking forward to the journey. The last time he had been there, he and the prime minister had returned exhausted.

Khotso adjusted his tie and bent down with some difficulty to straighten the creases in his grey flannel trousers. A woman stood at the far end of the brightly lit passage; he called her to him and she slipped the brown tweed jacket over her husband's shoulders. He buttoned his jacket and pinned on the Victoria Cross awarded him for valour as a member of the South African Native Labour Corps. The woman's bare feet raised not a sound on the wood floor as she returned to the stoep to resume her place as Khotso's fifth wife in the waiting line of thirty women, each one dressed according to her own taste and clan. Most preferred the texture of cotton and linen to the coarse weave of kaffir sheeting purchased in bright orange bolts at Fraser's Scottish Trading Store on the Cofimvaba road.

At the first sight of dust a lookout raced to the house on horseback to bring word of the prime minister's arrival at the farm gate, about half a mile away from the house. Khotso looked into the mirror once more and smoothed down the narrow lapels of his jacket. His gentle face and stooped bearing belied his agility, although a back injury continued to cause him pain. This injury was sustained almost thirty years earlier when a bus from his fleet, reversing out of the garage, sideswiped his lumbering old Mercury. However, since his arrival at Cofimvaba a few years later, he had yet to miss a morning when he did not have the pleasure of riding on his horse along the many miles of fencing which surrounded his land, admittedly of modest size when compared with a white man's farm.

Khotso's pleasant manner, his confidence and calm nature reassured all who came to seek his help. He drew his inner strength from the wisdom of his ancestors, as no empty display of ritual would have satisfied the people who approached him for comfort and guidance. If there were only a few people who could divine the elusive distinction between the natural and supernatural, Khotso was one of them – although he never belittled others who claimed this ability.

He welcomed any gift as tribute, and this, as well as wise investment, formed the basis of his enormous, though by no means conspicuous, wealth. Local people brought humble gifts, often animals that may have become burdensome to keep, or chickens that had spent their brief lives scratching in muck to dislodge a seed or morsel. The poor brought these offerings in exchange for help, and they left the compound restored with promises of wealth and sexual prowess.

Men and women from distant parts of the world also brought gifts from which they no longer derived pleasure: ingots of gold, which lined the walls of a special safe sent to Khotso from an admirer in Minnesota – in addition to the jewels, watches, and money they left at his feet. Whether they were rich or poor, simple or sophisticated, when people left the compound at Cofimvaba for their respective kraals, villages, towns or countries, it was clear that they had been touched by a presence for which no goat or chicken (whatever the possibilities of later adding flesh to sternum and thigh or, for that matter, even the costliest jewel in the most extravagant setting) could compensate.

There were rumours that Khotso had even managed to get his hands onto Kruger's gold. Whether true or not, in the middle of the compound there was a plinth reserved for the statue of Paul Kruger the Boers had erected in Pretoria. Khotso looked forward to the day when the statue would no longer be revered. He would then transport it to Cofimvaba and finally set the man in his place of honour.

It was, however, the adulation of his followers that Khotso found most difficult to accept. He took pains to explain to them that he too was only human. Talk of his visit to Buckingham Palace over a year earlier was still making the rounds of the kraals and caused him much embarrassment. Her Majesty the Queen and the Queen Mother had received him graciously. His people loved and respected the Queen Mother, and when they heard that he was going to London to receive the Victoria Cross years after his display of valour, they had asked Khotso to present to her their petitions concerning the wrongs suffered at the hands of the Union government. Upon his return home, the tale of his royal visit unfolded in hut after hut.

Praise singers, frustrated and rendered inarticulate by a singular lack of achievement by their chiefs, appropriated the choicest morsels from the stories doing the rounds of the kraals and substituted the name of their chief for that of Khotso. But the people could not be fooled. While they understood the deception of the praise singers, they sympathised with the predicament of their chiefs; it was the white man who had made it difficult for a chief to distinguish himself in battle or wise counsel. And where would their own chiefs have found precious jewels to take to London? Broken bits of coloured glass perhaps, disgorged from the gizzards of scrawny chickens. They would certainly not have had the guts to obtain stones from the illegal diamond-buying syndicate. One just could not tell with some chiefs, nor with their imbongi who would distort any facts to embellish their own wretched accomplishments.

The truth was that during Khotso's audience with the Queen, Her Majesty had offended him in a manner he had never encountered before. She had presented him a gift of an exquisite cut-glass decanter (for which he had yet to find a use), but she had then hesitated to accept a gift he had brought all the way from Cofimvaba. In a pouch of soft kid leather, he had presented to her a black diamond disparaged by the uniniti-ated as the costliest lump of coal ever found outside India, and several pigeon's blood rubies, in addition to a choice selection of emeralds and Kimberley diamonds.

Her Majesty the Queen had suggested that perhaps Khotso might place the jewels at auction in London and donate the undoubtedly rich proceeds from the sale to the betterment of his brethren in the Transkei. She had even offered to afford him every assistance in this regard. This had infuriated Khotso; such ingratitude had not been evident when King Edward vii had been presented with the Cullinan diamond. It had been named the Great Star of Africa and mounted on the cross of the corona-tion crown, just under the Black Prince's ruby.

Later, in a fit of pique, Khotso sent the black diamond as a gift to

Emperor Hirohito of Japan, who named it the Black Star of Africa. A senior courtier wrote to Mr Khotso Sethuntsa to inform him that His Imperial Majesty derived great contentment from meditating on an object of such rare beauty.

According to the people, Khotso had breathed a curse on the House of Windsor as he was led from the Queen's presence. Few others had done as much as he in the interests of his people; however, for the sake of the Queen Mother who was much loved in the Transkei, he had taken great pains to undo the curse. What was true was that he had resolved to do everything in his power to ensure that the Union of South Africa would bow out of the Commonwealth. He had not changed his resolve, and that was why he had summoned the prime minister to Cofimvaba. He was adamant to secure a South Africa free of any ties to the Crown.

With the red dust settling in the wake of the Daimler as it came to a halt at the front door, Khotso knew that the time had come for him to convince Schoon that his was the right course of action. His senior wife, Nohlwandle, had a final look into the kitchen to see if everything was ready. The cooking, brewing and baking were timed to coincide with the expected arrival of guests, although unannounced visitors never left the compound on empty stomachs. The scones had been taken from the oven, milk tarts placed on a windowsill for cooling, and the kettles put on to boil. She then joined her co-wives on the stoep.

Witbooi, the mute chauffeur, opened the car door and Dr Schoon and Pretorius emerged, looking stiff. They walked slowly up the path towards the silent reception of women. Pretorius alerted the prime minister to the eighth woman in line with her shaved head. Schoon stopped to enquire about the bereavement in her family. Pretorius conveyed his sympathies in Xhosa. She thanked the prime minister for his kind words, and assured him that she would inform her family. Dr Schoon asked Nohlwandle to write down the address of the post office closest to the woman's ancestral kraal and promised to send a telegram of condolence to her mother.

By the time the prime minister reached Khotso's youngest wife, Witbooi had moved the car to a garage adjoining the stables where boys waited eagerly with pails of hot water, rags and polish to wash away the red dust accumulated over the miles of road and bring the duco and chrome back to a full shine. The chauffeur was shown to a rondawel where a table had been set and where he could rest before making the return journey.

Sybrand Schoon marvelled at the vast openness of the landscape in front of him and wondered when Khotso would have a runway put in. The drive from George had proved exhausting (a few times in the past he had been obliged to make the even longer journey from Pretoria) and, however smooth and comfortable the ride, he was finding it increasingly difficult to sleep in the car. He knew that an aeroplane would be just the thing, although filing flight plans could prove difficult.

Schoon embraced Nohlwandle and she took him by the arm and led him around the garden to allow him to stretch his legs. When they returned to the stoep, Khotso's tenth wife stepped forward and held out a porcelain basin filled with water in which the prime minister dipped his hands. He removed his glasses then splashed the water on his face, reached for the proffered towel and gently dried his hands and face. The women addressed Pretorius as Bawomkhulu, the Xhosa word for grandfather. Nohlwandle signalled the junior wives to withdraw. They walked off in silence, each to her respective quarters.

Nohlwandle guided the prime minister into the reception room where Khotso was waiting. The two men greeted each other. This was their first meeting since Sybrand Schoon had taken the oath as prime minister, and both men betrayed a slight nervousness as they sat facing each other. Khotso greeted Pretorius and showed him to a chair. 'Good to see you, Johannes. You look younger than ever. Your tailor is quite an expert.'

'Thank you, Khotso. But the man is a dawdler – and he demands payment up front.'

'You and I know where his money goes.'

Sybrand Schoon was distracted by an array of scones and melktert. He reached for a steaming scone, halved it and spread it with butter. He remembered the delicious scones he had eaten on a previous visit to Cofimvaba during his tenure as minister of native affairs, and was reminded of the discomfort caused him at the time and the way he had skilfully avoided a crisis for the government. Without warning, Khotso had brought in at least twenty Pondo chiefs to press him on the question of native education. The chiefs had been concerned that their sons would be deprived of learning and not be able to develop the skills and character necessary to lead their people. On that day Schoon had been in top form, persuading the chiefs that their sons would be even more demanding and restless than was usual if their minds were to be crammed with white man's knowledge, and that it would only cause the natives to neglect and ultimately forget the distinctive values of their own culture.

It was uncertain whether the chiefs had listened to Schoon's lecture, or the old man's interpretation, because the Pondos had departed with the idea that the white man's way was the way of the future and that the minister of native affairs intended to condemn their sons to the status of wood-hewers and water-drawers. Whatever Schoon's intention, he had failed to convince the chiefs of the richness of their own pastures. He later blamed Pretorius for all these misunderstandings.

The prime minister was fastidious about his first cup of coffee. He had travelled a great distance and needed tranquillity to collect his thoughts. The coffee was to his liking, and as he was in the company of old friends, he disregarded convention and poured the coffee into his saucer to cool. Khotso found it peculiar that his Boer guests and their Coloured relations would persist in drinking tea or coffee from saucers when they held perfectly good cups in their hands, but he dismissed the idea that they did it out of fear that a black man's lips may have previously touched the cup. It amused Khotso, but what mattered most to him was that his guests were comfortable (although it had occurred to him when he had first observed the decanting from cup to saucer that it might spare much trouble if the tea or coffee were poured directly from the pot into the saucer).

The prime minister reached for a second cup of coffee and edged a slice of melktert onto his plate. The egg-yellow custard, dusted with cinnamon and cast in a mould of flaky pastry, was his favourite. Nohlwandle had employed a special cook to bake this, as none of the other cooks had the patience or expertise to get the recipe right. If it was not the pastry, it was the filling – if it was not the filling, it was the oven temperature. He removed a cinnamon stick embedded in his slice and smoothed over the surface with a fork.

'You know, Khotso,' he ventured, his first attempt at conversation that afternoon, 'this is just as good as my Arta makes it.'

'That should hardly surprise you,' Khotso replied. 'The recipe comes from your wife.'

This left Sybrand to wonder what form of magic Nohlwandle had employed to lay hands on his wife's special recipe.

'Is nothing sacred any more?' he asked.

'Not since you've joined forces with the devil. So – what does it feel like to be prime minister?'

'Ag, go on now man, Khotso; let me tell you, only God underwrites the risks of the white man in Africa.'

'But the devil has clout too, my friend. Surely you would not have taken the risk without raising the odds in your favour.'

'Don't forget, Khotso, you are the man who got me into this fix. How was I to know that your muti would work so quickly on Strijdom – and leave the door open for me?'

'I warned you. From the day Strijdom got native women to carry the dompas, he was doomed. He could mess with the men, but the women had it in for him and you can be sure they gave him bad medicine. Anyway, you could at least have worn some smarter clothes, Sybrand. Black is for the grave.'

'Don't be daft. Do you think we all dress like you? You wear your grand medals like that Sap Smuts – even though you almost lost your life for him up there in the desert. Thank God you stopped Smuts just in time – before he gave it all away to the English. I heard that Her Majesty would not accept your presents. That's not the way to treat a brave man. But it was fine when you put your life on the line for her. And what does it matter if I'm a bit shabby? Let me tell you, I would be much happier with your life here in Cofimvaba. I have nothing but worries in Cape Town and Pretoria.'

'There must be something we can do about that. I'm sure we can arrange a swap,' Khotso offered. 'You can dole out platitudes here to my wives and I will go to Cape Town in grand style with a big wooden spoon to stir up parliament. Of course, I'll miss my wives, but the white man's ways are not without benefits. So what do you say – swap?'

'Even the sun agrees.' Sybrand Schoon sighed as he watched the lengthening rays break through the leaves outside and light up the particles of dust suspended in the air.

'I'd like to see the look on Mr Speaker's face when I walk into parliament. It would be worth it just for that. But I would need all the protection I can get. Inyangas are not much good when it comes to their own safety.'

'I suppose that's why you have those lions guarding your gate – they weren't there when I last came.'

'They are modelled on the lions in Trafalgar Square. Mine are in bronze. They will remind people that our republic will survive long after we're gone.'

'I'm not here to talk about bronze lions or brass monkeys, Khotso.'

The prime minister's smile faded as he remembered the real reason for his visit. He raised himself reluctantly from his chair and followed Khotso, who strode ahead down the long hall to the divining room. Pretorius trailed behind them. It had taken many years, almost as long as he had served as minister of native affairs, for Schoon to accept the wisdom of the bones. And although he now acknowledged their message, Schoon was afraid to provoke the displeasure of God by communicating with the spirit world.

'A man must do what a man must do,' Schoon said aloud, hoping that the Lord would turn a blind eye to the proceedings.

Among Khotso's three new apprentices, Redemptus – who at first had been reluctant to have anything to do with divination – had proved to be the most accomplished. But he could not help feeling that the bones were simply a trick devised to prey on the weak. Khotso had been kind to him, treating him like his own son. Redemptus had told him that God had placed him at Cofimvaba for a purpose of which he was as yet unaware. Khotso rang a silver bell to summon the boy.

'So, Bawomkhulu, this is the white man who has come to taste the medicine of the ancestors,' Redemptus murmured to Pretorius, waiting at the door. The boy squinted into the darkness to get a glimpse of the men sitting in silence. The prime minister looked smaller than he had imagined him to be.

Redemptus later told Pretorius that, in his opinion, the umlungu should not be permitted the protection of the ancestors, some of whom may have been killed at the white man's hands. But Redemptus explained that as a Zulu, he was not going to be held accountable for the promiscuity of the Xhosa ancestors. He did as he was asked. Khotso had tried to convince him that the Boers were a simple people in need of protection against the power of evil, like everyone else.

'So why were the Xhosa ancestors hiding in the holes of jackals when their people needed them to drive the white man into the sea?

'And what about God, who is greater than all the ancestors?' Redemptus asked. He wondered why the Almighty would turn his back on the Boers, who were known to spend a lot of time on their knees. 'But God maybe is tired of their proud ways.'

At a sign from Khotso, Redemptus entered the divining room, followed by Pretorius, whose job was to interpret. The boy pounded his bare feet on the polished yellowwood floor. Except for the low benches, the room had no other furnishings. It was shaped like a rondawel, its walls faced with polished tiger's eye transported all the way from Kuruman by lorry. The light of a single candle drew out the patterns peculiar to wood and stone and outlined the figures of three men perched on a bench with bowed heads – and that of a young boy poised to shake the bones from a horn cup.

Redemptus had a skirt of monkey tails around his waist and a leopard skin strapped securely across his chest. He danced about the room, creating a rhythm that grew louder and more insistent with the steady pounding of his feet on the hardwood floor. The rattles of shells and seeds tied around his wrists and ankles resonated as his feet hit the ground. He danced to the rhythm of the yellowwood tree, his toes slamming down on the grain arranged in an elaborate pattern on the floor.

Khotso spoke his instructions to the boy in Zulu. Despite his considerable experience in native affairs, Schoon could not follow the exchange. He had not learned any of the tribal languages and had always relied on the services of an interpreter. Once, when challenged by the paramount chief in Umtata about what he called an oversight, Schoon had replied that there were too many tribal languages to learn them all with any degree of fluency and that he did not wish to be seen to show a preference by learning the language of any one tribe. However much he felt excluded, he had Pretorius with him to reveal the secrets of native lore that lay outside his own field of experience.

To observe a measure of confidentiality, Khotso had instructed Redemptus not to set eyes on the configuration and to leave the room as soon as he

83

had thrown the bones. With an almost inaudible chant, Redemptus called on Khotso's ancestors and, as if caught in a game of chance, he scattered the tiny knucklebones from the cup onto the floor. Pretorius could tell from Redemptus's face that he understood the message of the bones; however, without betraying a sign, the boy withdrew silently from the room.

Although no more than a few minutes of silence elapsed after Redemptus left the divining room, time seemed to weigh heavily on Schoon, as did the sight of Khotso's brooding face. In the distance a woman's voice could be heard, calling over the sounds of children playing. Schoon shut his eyes and waited. Khotso had been born barely a year after him in a mountain village near the border of Basutoland. His mother had brought the boy to live at the Schoon farm at Zastron a few months after his birth. Could it have been Khotso's black skin, darker than any he had ever seen before, or the depth of his eyes that had first fascinated the impressionable young Oybrand?

By the dim light of the candle Schoon looked at Khotso's face. All the time he had known Khotso, he had acted like a free man. But why were the other natives so threateningly shut off to him – the millions, no less ordinary than pavement? Now, in his hour of reckoning, he realised that he had seen something in all those black faces encountered throughout his life, something he was struggling to understand from the scant evidence offered on their faces.

'You go out of your way to make enemies, don't you?' Khotso said, hesitant to break the silence.

'It doesn't matter what I do, Khotso. There's always someone trying to get at me. Every native wants to get me like the women got Strijdom. I don't even know about my own people. Everywhere I look there are enemies. I don't have to search under my bed any more. Even you act as if you are no longer my friend.'

'I'm sorry that you doubt my friendship. But it must mean something if you come all this way to see me.'

'You think you control me. You think it's a joke to ask if I have sold my soul to the devil.'

'As long as you don't think I'm the devil.'

'Then how did you fix it that I ended up as prime minister?'

'It was ambition, my friend. Yours – not mine.'

Schoon took his handkerchief from his pocket and wiped his glasses. 'I can't help it, Khotso. I sit in church on Sundays and I can't keep my mind on the Lord. You are the one I see hovering over the pulpit. God ignores me – and now I must grovel in front of your ancestors. Who can I trust? I can't talk to my wife because she'll only get upset.

'And those Pondo chiefs you paraded in front of me when I was last here? Do you think I couldn't see you showing off in front of them – like you had me in the palm of your hand? They are the ones who say they'll kill the elephant that tramples the grass on which their cattle feed. Who is that elephant? It's me, I'm telling you; it's me.'

'Well, if you're so certain – you should know what to do about it. I have asked you many times to sit in this room on your own to fight your demons.'

'See what I mean? Now you are trying to frighten me by leaving me on my own. It won't be that easy to lure the next prime minister into your chamber of horrors.'

'I wouldn't be so sure – anyway, all I am asking is that you stay here to confront your fears of the Pondo chiefs, the Zulu chiefs, and any other chief. Look them in the eye – and then you can undo the fingers clasped around the knife.'

'What knife are you talking about? Don't speak to me in riddles. You are the one who can undo those fingers for me. I came to you for help and instead all I will take away are more fears because you want to lock me in this room with your ancestors … It's like we exist only in each other's dreams.'

'We confront each other in our dreams because we deny each other in real life,' Khotso replied. 'When the dreams of Europeans are handed down to us, they become nightmares.'

Sybrand Schoon glared at Pretorius to make sure that he was inter-preting Khotso's words accurately. 'How can he say that to me, when I'm sitting here in his house?'

He turned back to Khotso, 'You think you've got a hold on me because we inhabit each other's sleep, but all I want to know is what the bones say so that I can get on with my life. But no; as usual you want to be clever and make jokes and when I leave I won't know anything more.'

Having said that, Schoon knew that he was the cause of the dependency that existed between them. Khotso had never proposed anything to him that might have promoted his own interests and really did not need him. He had more than enough money and power. This inequality disturbed the prime minister.

'Why don't we get Redemptus back to throw the bones again? Give the boy another chance. If I can trust him, why can't you? He may even show you why we inhabit each other's dreams – even though we have less than squatting rights.'

'I insist that the answer comes from you, Khotso. You don't think I came all this way to consult a boy still wet behind the ears. Give me something to protect me from my enemies. I've had to lock up more than twenty thousand people already.'

These visits always had about them an uncomfortable intimacy and ended up with neither man being satisfied. Pretorius was becoming adept at interpreting what Khotso had told Schoon so many times. But he knew that on their return journey, Schoon would hold him responsible for Khotso's words.

'Do me a favour, Sybrand,' Khotso continued. 'Locking up people goes nowhere. It is time to set people free – give them their freedom. What I am telling you is that by locking up thousands over strikes, pass protests, liquor riots or that kind of nonsense, you are just driving them to martyrdom. There are people out there ready to self-destruct and your government seems hellbent on encouraging them.'

Khotso walked around the room, running his hand along the cool surface of the wall. He stared at the candle burning slowly.

'Please sit down, Khotso. You make me nervous.'

Despite the chill in the room, the prime minister was perspiring. He removed his jacket and placed it beside him on the bench.

'How can I help you when you won't trust me?' asked Khotso. 'Death is waiting for you – just like it's waiting for me. There's nothing profound about that. It's a simple fact; but there will be no freedom for my people in your death. Why would your death benefit us? The natives' demands have nothing to do with that. You have surrounded yourself with lapdogs. Their mouths are full of flattery.'

The prime minister listened in silence. He looked at the candle sputtering in the molten wax. In the flame he could distinguish many faces.

He recognised those who had transferred their hatred from Strijdom to himself; he saw the faces of people behind bars, men chipping stone on Robben Island, children playing along dusty paths. Never before had he been able to recall actual faces; but there they were: his wife Arta, as well as his dead son Fanus – faces whirring through his mind like a film slipping on sprockets.

'I can't leave until I know more about those who plan to assassinate me,' the prime minister insisted as he rubbed the scar on his cheek from an earlier attempt on his life.

'Now I'm a magician as well? It wasn't enough that I saved your life once when that madman came after you? Give Redemptus one last chance to throw the bones.'

'Redemptus is only a boy – why don't you throw the bones yourself?' Schoon pleaded. 'Please man, Khotso, do it for me, hey?'

Khotso gathered the bones and rang the bell.

Redemptus must have been expecting to be called again. Despite the sound of the boy's feet on the floor, Schoon failed to notice him enter the room. He was still preoccupied with the inventory of faces, of people known and unknown.

'Look, Khotso, they're as vivid as holiday snaps – my wife, my boys, and even my granddaughter.'

The tiny bones fell louder than before. Redemptus shut the door quietly. Schoon stared at the bones intently while Pretorius scratched his head, wondering what he was doing there.

'Khotso, look man – the bones fell the same way.'

'Forget the bones,' Khotso replied. He too appeared drained, yet he could not allow his friend to leave without some reassurance.

'Sybrand, you have a long drive ahead of you. You will sleep peacefully on your journey. Here's a special amulet. You must wear it all the time; it will protect you. Explain to your wife that it is for the rheumatism. And here is some impepho for you to burn in your office. For now, that's all I can do. Go in peace, my friend. I'll be here whenever you need me.'

Witbooi placed the replenished picnic hamper in the boot of the Daimler while the prime minister wound down the window and waved at the women assembled on the stoep. The two men shook hands and Khotso said firmly, 'I think it's high time we left the Queen and her dominions, don't you, Mr Prime Minister? Before the Africans and Asians get us kicked out. Leave the Commonwealth and set up a republic.'

'Don't worry. Nobody will kick us out – least of all Nehru and his pal Nkrumah,' Schoon replied. 'But I've been thinking along the same lines myself and I'll see what can be done about it.'

'I've had a call from a young man called Polycarp van Wyk,' Khotso said while Witbooi nursed the engine. 'He sounds just like the kind of man I need for a head teacher. I've decided to take my children out of government schools and set up a new place for them on the compound. Thank you for recommending a decent teacher – I hope he's not coming to spy on me.'

'I can't guarantee anything; with his background he might not be suitable,' the prime minister replied.

'Nothing is ever guaranteed, but I am deeply grateful.'

'It's actually I who am grateful, Khotso. Perhaps you are just the man to run the country. It isn't as if you aren't doing so already, hey?'

'Off with you, Sybrand, the engine is beginning to sound impatient. And goodbye Johannes – thanks for your help.'

Khotso stood watching the Daimler depart in the red dust of the evening. He called to a couple of boys who followed him to the garage where Witbooi had off-loaded two cases of fine brandy. Khotso instructed the boys to carry the boxes to a stream that flowed down past the back of the stables. He watched them break the seals and pour the oak-brown liquor into the water.

Reflections

Although it had been difficult for Enoch to write about the prime minister's visit to Cofimvaba, Oupa Hans had made it come alive by telling him a story full of bizarre and vivid details. It was all so strange and Enoch had been surprised by how much he could recall. It had provided him some insight into people like Schoon, for whom respectability and the law hid a deep insecurity. When Enoch raised this dichotomy at dinner one evening, his mother warned him that politics and religion were private matters and not fit subjects for conversation. She said that people did not like to have their beliefs questioned, especially not by an opinionated young boy. He had surprised himself with the progress he had made on a piece that was not the usual school composition at which he excelled. He had never written anything like it.

Enoch hid the pages in his satchel's secret compartment. His father had made a fuss about his using the Underwood typewriter, which Enoch had monopolised for days. But the typewriter, on which virtually every second key required attention, was hardly conducive to fast progress.

After twelve years on the waiting list, the post office had finally allowed the Pretorius family the privilege of having a telephone installed. As his mother now telephoned the meat order through, it meant an end to Enoch's weekly visits to the butchery. It also meant that Oupa Hans could telephone the family at any time and Zachaeus no longer needed to deliver his messages.

Enoch telephoned Oupa Hans to ask whether he could spend the night at the gate lodge as he had a theatre date with Dries and Alison. He was still embarrassed about the Iqbal incident and had decided not to extend the invitation to Haima. He was also deterred from calling her by the risk of having one of her parents answering the telephone. However, his friendship with Iqbal had been restored to the extent that Enoch had allowed him to look over his shoulder during the exams. It had been quite a feat for Iqbal to manage under the hawk eye of the invigilator.

That afternoon Zachaeus turned up to collect Enoch for the theatre and broke the news that the Coloured people were to be evicted from their homes in Simonstown, as well as the Indians, who were to be dumped in a dreadful place called Rylands Estate. As if Enoch had some control over the matter, Zachaeus asked him what those people would do. Enoch knew that Haima would be devastated as her family lived in Simonstown. She had told him how much she loved the view across the bay from their balcony; on clear days she could see Hangklip in the distance. In a month or so, she may well be living in a grubby housing estate near Athlone and looking at a few scraggly Port Jackson and eucalyptus trees. He hoped that this setback would not affect her or her ambition to become a doctor.

It was the final performance of *Hamlet* that night. Dries, Alison and Enoch had an early dinner. Mr Molinieux served it and then retired to his rooms after cheese and coffee. The Schuuns were too discreet to ask Enoch about Haima (they'd been expecting him to bring her along) and he was too upset to tell them about her family's predicament. They would read about the threatened evictions in the newspapers. Zachaeus had told Enoch that many recent white immigrants and others who could smell a bargain had already snapped up the houses in advance of the evictions. Enoch imagined the priest at the Church of St Francis counting on a more generous congregation. On their return to Wepener after the play Alison asked Enoch why he was so subdued and what had dampened his usual enthusiasm for the theatre.

Enoch was apprehensive about seeing his grandfather in the morning. Would he criticise his amateurish attempt at writing the story when he showed it to him? However, Oupa Hans was waiting up for him when he arrived back at the cottage.

'I thought you people would never get back.'

'I'm sorry, Oupa Hans. The play went on for ages – and Zachaeus was a bit late. I didn't expect Oupa Hans to be here.'

'Well, it's my home. I had no reason to sleep in Retreat when I have a comfortable bed waiting for me. I don't like staying there. It gives me nightmares. And besides, I want to see what you've written.'

Enoch retrieved the typescript from his satchel and handed it to Oupa

Hans. He removed his jacket and tie, made tea and prepared for a long wait. Oupa Hans was the kind of reader who went back and forth over the lines with his finger. Enoch looked at his grandfather from time to time. Oupa Hans's cup of tea remained untouched and the changes of expression on his face did not seem to bode well for his grandson. When the old man finally blew his nose and poured the cold tea down his throat, Enoch knew he had come to the end of the story.

'Where did you get this nonsense about the Cullinan diamond and the Japanese emperor?'

'Everyone knows that, Oupa Hans. And Oupa told me to add my own interpretation.'

'Yes, but you're making a stew. What does the Cullinan diamond have to do with the story?'

'It's just a little detail for colour.'

'So, there's not enough colour? I should've known better than to trust a boy.'

'When I looked up pigeon's blood rubies in the encyclopaedia, Oupa Hans, I found a reference to the British royal crown – and when I looked that up, I found the Star of Africa.'

'If only you had found the Star of Africa!'

Enoch asked his grandfather why he was getting all worked up about a few details. 'I can change it if Oupa Hans likes.'

'That's not the point – what's written is written. When Jesus turned water into wine, the Gospel only says that he did this and called for that. It was at a wedding, but there's nothing about what the bride and bridegroom wore – or about what presents the guests brought. It's a simple story people could remember and retell. Do you think readers will want to know all this stuff about diamonds and rubies?'

'Well, it's all fact.'

'Enoch, I'm a simple man with no university education, but that doesn't mean you can impress me with a lot of mumbo jumbo. Get straight to the point. All these twists and turns bore people and they stop reading. It sounds just like another fairy tale.'

'At least Oupa Hans has matric ...'

'Don't try to confuse me. People will say that I twisted Schoon's words and that the Nats had been working on leaving the Commonwealth for years. They'll probably also say that by the time Khotso got the idea, plans for the republic were already under way.'

'But Oupa ...'

'You've had your say – now listen to me. You've made the prime minister look like an idiot and on top of it, got the Pondo chiefs to disrespect him. That wasn't what happened. Do you realise what the consequences could be?'

'If I got the meeting wrong I could always redo that bit?'

'It is your story now. But I just hope that this won't end up in Khotso's hands.'

'Sorry, Oupa Hans.'

'You'll be a whole lot sorrier if he gets hold of it. You think an old man can't tell stories. Book learning isn't everything, you know. When I'm out in the garden, all sorts of things come into my head.'

'I said I'm sorry, Oupa ... I don't know the rules of writing and who will read this story anyway?'

'That's not the point. You should try and do a good job. Now it's time for bed. You look tired. We can talk some more in the morning.'

Enoch knew that he ought to have been more careful about what he had written and that he had underestimated his grandfather's intelligence. He reread the story but decided not to change anything. He eventually fell asleep.

The first thing that struck him the next morning was that Oupa Hans was singing. He had never heard him sing before – not even when they had been to church together. He could hear the clatter of crockery as his grandfather brought breakfast through to him on a tray.

'Good morning, Enoch. Aren't you going to get up? Trossie's away, so I made something.'

'Yes, Oupa Hans – thank you very much,' the boy said, confused by this show of good spirits. He could see lumps in the porridge, but he swallowed them down with the help of a cup of sweet tea.

'I've been thinking – if you fiddle around too much with that story, you will just throw it off balance. It's true about the Cullinan diamond. I was just upset that you had taken over the story.'

Enoch gulped and narrowly avoided choking.

'If Oupa will excuse me, I must go up and thank Dries and Alison for last night.'

Dries wanted to hear a full critique of the play from Enoch. Alison reminded him that he had patients waiting at the SHAWCO clinic. It was one of the Cape Flats health and welfare centres Dries ran for the university.

'You do little enough for the great unwashed!' Alison told him.

Enoch was relieved that Dries would soon be on his way as he had been so preoccupied by Haima's predicament that he had actually missed most of the play and in consequence did not have much to say about it.

Dries took his bag from Mr Molinieux and said to Alison, 'If only you knew how many people walk into the clinic after a night of non-stop drink and dagga. Many of them have been turned away from emergency rooms at the hospitals as they can't cope.'

'Dries is right – the doctors can't deal with the pressure,' Enoch added.

'Thank you, Enoch. My darling wife thinks my life is a picnic.' Dries kissed Alison and said that he would see her at dinner. Hanneli got into the car beside her father and Zachaeus dropped her off at the gate lodge. She got out of the car, greeted Oupa Hans and then ran back along the drive to where Clara stood waiting for her.

The Immorality Act

A few months after Clara had begun work at Wepener, Cyprian Molinieux noticed how readily she responded to his instructions regarding her duties in the house. She had more to do than just care for the expectant Alison. He had familiarised her with every corner of the house – what belonged where, as well as the origin of each piece of furniture and every painting. Clara had impressed him with her rapid assimilation to the ways of the household, considering that her prior service in an assortment of Non-European homes around the Peninsula had not afforded her much experience.

Not that Wepener was by any means a conventional household, although hard work and loyalty were highly prized. And as a teacher takes pride in the achievements of his pupils, Mr Molinieux was pleased to see his efforts well reflected in Clara's diligence. One of his achievements had been to persuade Clara, within a few days of her arrival, to address the Schoons by their first names, as they had requested – even though this contradicted his training and inclination. In fact, Mr Molinieux heartily disapproved of the practice. He was careful not to criticise Clara's occasional 'master' or 'madam'. What had also impressed him was her command of the English language, which had improved remarkably and shown very little of the ineptitude he had expected from a girl who had previously spoken only Afrikaans.

Clara's eagerness to learn never flagged. After a period of time, this had led him to consider that the situation might be further enhanced between them, were a more personal element introduced. Originally when the thought of marriage occurred, it had frightened him. However, as the months progressed, he began to feel more comfortable with the idea. Of course this would mean circumventing the Mixed Marriages Act. But Clara's attractions helped him resolve any qualms he might have had, including the fact that such a step would violate certain principles he stood for. Clara was a beautiful and desirable woman, and her readiness to please outweighed the disadvantage of her skin colour.

Although Mr Molinieux had received no legal training, he was an avid reader of the *Government Gazette*, delivered at regular intervals by the postman. With the keenness of a scholar, he studied the new laws, the amendments, as well as the repeal of old laws. Having committed the relevant details to memory, he deposited the unwanted documents in the dustbin or the newspaper pile beside the wood stove. When serving breakfast, Mr Molinieux and Dries frequently discussed parliament's most recent enactments. The two men scorned the government, although for different reasons – Mr Molinieux because it was composed almost entirely of Dutchmen, and Dries because of the unjust laws it promulgated. They fed their scorn on the rich fare provided in the pages of the *Gazette*, relishing the inordinate details and convolutions contained within the language of the law. Mr Molinieux had come to believe himself quite an expert.

Only a few people would pursue such a subject for pleasure. Who, for example, other than officials of the Meat Board, would have cared that animals, as defined by the law, were more than simply four-footed or cloven-hoofed creatures? Their welfare was provided for under the Abattoir Act, or the Consumption Of Meat Based On The Animal Products Act, which defined an animal as 'any member of the following kinds of animals, namely, cattle, sheep, goats, horses, pigs, mules, or donkeys of any age; or any member of any other kinds of animals to which the Queen's Most Excellent Majesty, the Senate and the House of Assembly of the Union of South Africa may, by proclamation in the *Gazette*, apply the provisions of the Abattoir Act; provided that a karakul lamb which is slaughtered mainly to obtain the pelt thereof, shall not be deemed to be an animal for the purposes of the Act'.

The latter clause was to protect farmers who, to obtain the highest prices for the karakul pelts, dragged the lamb from the belly of the ewe before it could be born naturally.

'And a calf – according to the law what is a calf, Dr Schoon?'

'Don't ask me. Do I look like a farmer?'

'It is most unlikely that any farmer in the Union would know. You are a doctor though, and a doctor should know zoology.'

'What you're talking about is animal husbandry – anyway, go ahead, enlighten me,' Dries said, knowing that it gave Mr Molinieux pleasure to show off this peculiar pastime.

'It is a bovine animal of which no portion of the backmost components of the fourth molar in the upper jaw has penetrated the gum.'

It was, however, not on the strength of farmyard arcana that Mr Molinieux had gathered the information to tackle the predicament that now confronted him. Over the years the *Gazette* had revealed to him the basis for classification of each racial grouping: European, Native, Cape Malay, Asian, with the definitions gradually being modified to allow for greater ease of interpretation. He had even come across a group from Natal classified as Lost Tribe. Then there were the Cape Coloureds and Other Coloureds, previously known as Non-European, or Mixed.

No longer was a White person simply 'one who in appearance obviously was White, or one who was generally accepted as a White person – not including a person, who, although in appearance obviously a White person, was generally accepted as a Coloured person; the latter being neither a White person nor a Native'.

With later amendments to the Population Registration Act, perceptions of personal habits and general demeanour were taken into account when a determination was to be made as to the reclassification of an individual.

While Mr Molinieux was both by appearance and origin obviously a White person, his parents having immigrated to the Union from the north of Scotland, he had discovered sufficient flexibility in the law to make an application to the secretary for the interior for reclassification as a Coloured person on the grounds that he had generally been accepted as such. He managed to obtain an affidavit from a building contractor who had done some renovation work at Wepener and two others from his labourers. These testified that Mr Molinieux had shown distinct Coloured traits, that many of his friends were Coloured and that he worshipped as a member of a Coloured Seventh Day Adventist church in Athlone. A magistrate had cursorily examined Mr Molinieux and with his findings supported by the affidavits, the secretary for the interior had authorised a new identity document with his racial grouping as Other Coloured.

With this prized document in hand, Mr Molinieux decided to propose marriage to Clara, knowing that she would take into account the sacrifice he had made to win her hand. He had waited patiently for some days until he could approach Clara away from the other staff. When Ou

Mevrou Jansen sent Clara down to the cellar to get some vegetables that Mieta had neglected to take up to the kitchen, Mr Molinieux followed her and shut the cellar door to ensure that their voices would not be heard upstairs.

Clara noticed an approaching shadow on the wall and was surprised to find Mr Molinieux, but took the opportunity to weigh down his arms with potatoes and onions. As he stood there, his face lit by a bare electric bulb, he asked Clara, in a gentle but firm voice, if she would be his wife. Although Mr Molinieux had anticipated a positive response, he was thoughtful enough to ask her to consider his proposal carefully before making such an important decision.

However, Clara replied that she could give him an answer straight away. 'It's nice and polite of Mr Molinieux to offer me time to think about his proposal, but it isn't necessary. I'm already engaged to Mfilo.'

She showed him the ring she wore on a chain around her neck. 'I'm surprised Mr Molinieux don't know – what with all the talk in the kitchen. But thank you – it was nice of Mr Molinieux to ask. I never knew Mr Molinieux think like that about me.'

At first Mr Molinieux could not understand, much less forgive, such temerity. His arms collapsed at his sides, the potatoes scattered around him on the tiled floor and the onions lay in knotted bunches at his feet. He reached into his breast pocket for his new identity card.

'But look – I'm Coloured now, just like you,' he protested, showing her the card. 'I did it for you. Do you have any idea of the sacrifice I've made? Not only do you reject my proposal, but you insult me by telling me that you are engaged to a Native – which is against the law!'

'Mfilo is waiting for reclassification and he's going to be a Coloured too. That's the truth, Mr Molinieux, and I wish you would believe me.'

Clara set the pocket of oranges aside and placed her hand on Mr Molinieux's arm, realising that he had gone to a lot of trouble in order to win her affection. He brushed her aside and fled up the stairs.

Mr Molinieux's mind, however, was set on marriage. Scarcely a few months later, he turned his attention to a parishioner of the Calvary Presbyterian Church in Mowbray and proposed marriage again – this time to Miss Jennifer Aspeling, a woman of British ancestry and a spinster. Without hesitation she accepted his proposal. Mr Molinieux slipped the ring onto Miss Aspeling's finger.

He'd decided to take her into his confidence because he did not wish to appear to have deceived her if word of his temporary identity should become known. He advised her that a wait of a few months might be prudent before informing her family of their engagement. Still on bended knee, he begged her to be patient while his application for reclassification as White was under way. Because of an unfortunate misunderstanding, he told her, his classification had been changed from European to Other Coloured.

In all his life Mr Molinieux had never seen blood drain from a face so precipitously. He began to fear for Miss Aspeling's health as the sudden loss of blood revealed the ravages of horror on her face.

'How the devil, when you are European, can you become Coloured – and then, all of a sudden, European again?' Miss Aspeling demanded, spitting out the word 'Coloured' as if she had swallowed a dose of cod-liver oil. A resident in the country for forty years, she had lived there long enough to grasp its peculiarities and laws. Mr Molinieux, aghast at the mixture of anger and resentment on her face, saw the promise of this marriage crumbling. She wrung her hands, as if the warmth kindled in her palms would somehow cleanse her of being associated, however briefly, with a Coloured man.

Mr Molinieux, who moments earlier had turned around Clara's rejection by gaining Miss Aspeling's consent, now stood by helplessly as she slumped on the couch.

'But you will see for yourself, Miss Aspeling,' Mr Molinieux implored, hoping that the fear of spinsterhood might be greater than the shock of his identity. 'Pretoria is fully conversant with the story. As we speak they are attending to my petition. I would be pleased to share the relevant correspondence with you.'

Observing that his words were having little effect, Mr Molinieux had the presence of mind to realise that a further clarification of laws relevant to his case might only make matters worse. In desperation he again showed her his identity card; 'Look, it's only a piece of card after all. For God's sake, look at me, Miss Aspeling. Can't you see they've made a mistake?'

It was imperative for him to reassure her, but the despair on her face distressed him.

'I received this identity card in the post and was deeply shocked by the error. Honestly, Miss Aspeling, I've got pure Scots blood in my veins – one hundred per cent,' Mr Molinieux told her.

'Don't you dare come near me – and I don't care what blood you've got in your veins – just keep it to yourself!' Miss Aspeling shrieked.

In a futile appeal to her vanity, he persisted. 'But just look at me, Miss Aspeling – after all, you are a high school teacher – surely you can tell that I am European. The law says that a person is White when his habits, education, speech, deportment and demeanour show him to be such.'

However, Miss Aspeling had no ear for the letter of the law. She knew about play-whites and marginals who could be whiter than white in their behaviour and speech. She now sat rigid and unheeding on the couch where she had earlier accepted his proposal. Eventually she managed to regain enough composure to demand that Mr Molinieux leave her house immediately, otherwise she would be obliged to call the police. He left the house in a state of utter dejection.

'Don't talk to me about the law,' she shouted, flinging his hat after him. 'You'll hear all about it. And take this wretched ring with you.' Her hand shook as she struggled to remove the ring from her finger.

Mr Molinieux found himself on his knees once again, this time to retrieve the ring from under a shrub where it had been flung. He would later return it to the jeweller. And Miss Aspeling, who sometimes found her devotion to the Scriptures flagging, thanked God with a renewed zeal that Mr Molinieux had only ever held her hand.

As their duties compelled Mr Molinieux and Clara to communicate with each other daily, he found it hard to conceal his continuing frustration from her. He blamed her for just about everything that went wrong in the house, including the fact that he was no closer to having a positive determination on the matter of his identity. Clara avoided being provoked. And she did not allow Mr Molinieux to forget his predicament. She was resourceful at finding ways to taunt him – not because she was spiteful, but to deflect the increasing number of barbs he directed at her. He once overheard her telling Ou Mevrou Jansen that he had a fine cheek to make the wedding arrangements before he had even proposed to her.

'That big wedding cake Trossie says he's hiding at the bottom of his cupboard must be stale by now. Next thing we know, there'll be mice in the house. Mr Molinieux thinks just because I'm Coloured I will say, "Ja, baas; Nee, baas". But he got another think coming.'

When Clara realised that her remarks had been overheard by Mr Molinieux, she tried to find something nice to say: 'Shame, but Mr Molinieux did help me a lot in the house.'

Ou Mevrou Jansen, who resorted to English only in moments of extreme excitement, remarked, 'What do you mean *shame*, hey? Serves him jolly well right. He just thinks because he wears a black suit and white gloves, he's ready to get married any time, hey? Just like that.'

The old woman tried to get some sound from her rheumatoid fingers. 'I'm fed up with that nasty piece of work – sick and tired. He thinks he can have his way with the girls. Just let that Mr Molinieux call me a Bushman again and I'll wring his bladdie neck and remind him he's a Coloured.'

The fact that Clara had recently taught Hanneli to recite 'Apple tart, lemon tart, tell me the name of your sweetheart ...' was hardly calculated to help. While this may not have been intended for Mr Molinieux's ears, it found a ready mark. His preoccupation caused him to look in the mirror constantly to see if perhaps, inadvertently, he might have acquired the demeanour of a Coloured person. The greater his determination to cast off his burdensome identity, the more obsessed he became. Although despondent with the lack of response from officials at the Population Register, he continued almost daily to correspond with them. However, in Pretoria a pair of naked statues the director general had commissioned to provide a more classical appearance for the building's entrance garnered more interest among the taxpaying public.

In the most recent communication he had received, an official sent a cyclostyled form with the pertinent paragraphs outlined in red ink, advising Mr Cyprian Bannister Molinieux that reclassification was not a matter the registrar took lightly. Mr Molinieux's original application for reclassification as Other Coloured appeared from the record to have been an entirely voluntary matter, and the supporting documents submitted by him had left no doubt in the registrar's mind that he was entitled to be reclassified as Coloured. The official gratuitously added that, had Mr Molinieux been a Jew, he would have known that circumcision was irreversible.

Steamed Ginger Pudding

There was so much going on in the big wide world that Enoch found he could barely cope with the unravelling of the lives of those with whom he came into contact. How could he make sense of all these divergent stories – least of all, his own? He was worried about Kenny Parker and would have liked to discuss his concerns with Dries. He tried once, but Dries told him that something was being arranged and would not elaborate. And then there was Oupa Hans who appeared, like Khotso, to have a strange influence on the prime minister. Enoch was discovering that all these people seemed to have hidden areas of their lives from scrutiny.

He began to wonder whether Mr Molinieux's predicament was a punishment from God for what he had once done to him. He felt little compassion for this man who knew that the colour of his skin gave him power over others now that power had been denied him through his own stupidity. He considered telling Oupa Hans about what had happened in Mr Molinieux's rooms. But what point would there be to that? Much worse could have happened.

'What's eating you now?' Oupa Hans asked.

'Oh, nothing. I was thinking about Kenny Parker. Doesn't Oupa Hans think it's funny that Dries and Alison haven't helped him?'

'I wouldn't worry about Mr Parker. I'm sure Dries can handle it.'

'I hope so. And what about Mr Molinieux? Ou Mevrou Jansen says that Aspeling woman has it in for him – she's really spiteful. I can't understand why the prime minister can't go over the heads of the bureaucrats and get his old identity reinstated.'

Oupa Hans took some time to reply. 'I think Miss Aspeling should've climbed into the bugger with a sjambok. That man is really off his head. He's seen Mfilo and Clara together and suddenly he goes and falls in love with her. Miss Aspeling has had a lucky escape. How many other people's lives has that man messed up? Mr Molinieux thought he would take advantage of the law to marry a very pretty girl, but the law came back to bite him. Now he's squealing like a pig. No, my boy, don't feel sorry for a man like that. There are millions of real people out there whose lives have been ruined by these laws. He made a silly mistake.'

'But Oupa Hans, if the law hadn't existed he wouldn't have these problems.'

'When you grow up, Enoch, you will discover that some people like playing games.'

'Was Clara wise to turn him down? I think she would have been more comfortable in his quarters, instead of living with Mfilo in a leaky old shack.'

'What has comfort got to do with it? My father grew up on a farm, but took a Xhosa woman for his wife when he could have chosen a farmer's daughter. His family disinherited him. But now my sisters even pretend not to speak Afrikaans and one day they hope that their children will be accepted as White.'

'But I wonder why the prime minister doesn't help Mr Molinieux ...' Enoch persisted.

'What does Schoon care? The very first day Mr Molinieux walked into Wepener, his attitude made Schoon feel inferior and he's still at it.'

'How old is Mr Molinieux?'

'In his mid-fifties. A cup of tea would be nice, my boy, and we'll sit outside for a bit.'

Enoch filled the kettle. Oupa Hans liked three teaspoons to the pot and hot milk with his tea. He wondered why Mr Molinieux had taken such a long time to decide that he wanted to get married.

'You know, Enoch, once when Trossie came to clean my place in Retreat she told me that Mr Molinieux has some very strange habits. But it's not the kind of story you'd tell a boy.'

'I've heard lots of things, Oupa Hans.'

'He also gave her a pot of Mum and demanded that she put the stuff under her arms while he watched her. And she did it because she was frightened of losing her job. How's the tea coming along?'

'It will be ready in a minute, Oupa. Trossie would never say voertsek to a dog, so she was probably afraid to tell Mr Molinieux to get on with his own business.'

When Enoch went through with the tray, his grandfather was fast asleep. He went up to the house for a swim. Alison came out to the pool to keep him company. She told him that one of the benefits of marrying Dries and moving to South Africa was the glorious, golden tan she had got.

'It cheers me up no end,' she said. 'I can't understand why you should want to go to England. It's so dreary – and it's not only the weather. You can go to so many other places. Have you thought about America? It's such an exciting country.'

Enoch had recently been talking to Dries and Alison about his dreams of travelling abroad. It was a subject that much occupied his thoughts.

'I wouldn't mind seeing the prairies and the Rockies some day,' Enoch replied. 'But I've been thinking about India.'

'America is a great deal more than just mountains and grassland – you don't know what you're missing. Perhaps you could convince Dries and we'll all go to India together. No reason we couldn't visit China as well … if they'd let us in.'

'What about his job?'

'You know about Dries and his jobs … He works because it makes him feel good and he thinks inherited money is a curse and that sort of thing. But don't copy him. You often seem quite courageous, but then your head disappears inside your shell like a tortoise. You remind me of Dries. When we first met he told me that I was the greatest thing ever to walk into his life and then he'd push me away. But don't worry – he's sorting himself out.'

Mr Molinieux arrived at the poolside with the drinks tray and mixed a gin and tonic for Alison. Enoch asked for a juice and Mr Molinieux glared at him.

'I've also been thinking about India,' Alison said. 'It would be a great place for Dries to work – and I could help him. But don't expect too much. Dries is accustomed to the good life and trifles with politics – just enough to convince himself that he cares.'

Enoch had always known Dries as hardworking and conscientious and he was not quite sure what to make of this.

'However much he denies it, he's under his father's thumb. I believe the old man goes to see a witchdoctor. At least, so I've heard. Don't you think that's odd?'

Enoch could tell that Alison was prying. 'Dries is kind and generous,' he said.

'Don't get me wrong. He has his good points – and they're not inconsiderable.'

Whatever Alison's views, Enoch had no doubt that they were very much in love and they complemented each other well.

'I would strongly discourage you from going to England. I am not entirely unpatriotic, but I find the British a peculiar race – and don't even think about Biafra. Dries told me that you read that Mitford woman's book about West Africa and went on about going to Biafra. The British used to call the delta region the Oil Rivers Protectorate. Everything revolves around money and the British are particularly talented at smelling it out. I don't want to sound too gloomy, but my father told me that civil war is not very far off. But India sounds perfect – and you can learn all you want about Eastern religions.'

Enoch was pleased that Alison had taken his dreams to heart. Before she could continue Mieta came out to tell him that Oupa Hans's lunch was ready. He excused himself and carried the tray down to the gate lodge. He returned to join Alison and Hanneli, who were seated at a table by the pool. Hanneli wanted Enoch to take her to the tennis court after lunch, but Clara insisted that she have a nap first.

'Where's my daddy?' she whined.

'If he were at home, he would also make you have a nap,' her mother replied.

Then she asked, 'Why don't we have your parents over to lunch or dinner some day soon, Enoch?'

'They'd be thrilled.'

'Good, I'll give your mother a call. Maybe we can discuss this trip to India then. And surprise Dries at the same time.'

'I don't think that would be a good idea, Alison. You see, my parents are ...'

'Conventional?'

'Well, yes.'

'Just like the Schoons. Dries says your parents are charming. I've only met them briefly. I think it would be a super idea to discuss your future with them. I'll give them a call.'

Enoch knew that his parents could turn on the charm when they wanted to, but he did not think an invitation to Wepener a good idea. For one thing, he had not produced his school report and had been relieved that Dries had not asked to see it. Nor did he want Dries to see his Latin teacher's ridiculous comment: 'When Ovid wrote "dripping water hollows out a stone," he had Enoch's brain in mind. Don't be disappointed if he does not measure up to expectations!'

He hoped that his grandfather would dissuade Alison. It was one thing having a decent dinner, but talking about his future with his parents at the same time would not be a good idea. It was this kind of tribal suffocation, also evident among his friends and their families, that Enoch was trying to escape.

'Shall I invite Haima to dinner as well?' Alison asked. 'It was such a pity that she could not come along to the theatre. You would've been much more cheerful had she been there. Be more persistent next time.'

'Haima is a vegetarian.'

'I think our kitchen could run to vegetarian fare. I'll let Ou Mevrou Jansen know.'

'She's a Hindu. Mama and Dowa will not approve.'

'Dear Enoch, there are few things parents do approve of. I'm sure Haima's parents can be just as difficult.'

Enoch saw a way out of his dilemma. 'I very much doubt that she will be able to come, especially now her parents are being kicked out.'

'What do you mean?'

'Simonstown has been declared White and they have to move to a dump called Rylands Estate.'

'I could wring the neck of every stupid Nat ...'

'That's what Oupa Hans says – but he thinks there are too many of them.'

'You've got to think of the long term, Enoch. You're far too meek for a young man. By the way, I don't wish to raise your hopes, but Dries has been on the telephone to London and it seems my father might be able to help Kenny Parker.'

Alison expressed her distaste for the dessert and asked Mr Molinieux to bring out the cheese board. Ou Mevrou Jansen knew that Enoch liked steamed puddings, however hot the weather, and he and Hanneli scoffed down the pudding. He thought it superb – rich and dark, with a fragrance of Jamaica ginger and smothered in custard.

Clara arrived to take Hanneli for her nap.

'Why is Mr Molinieux in such a state again?' Enoch asked.

'I think you'd be upset if you were rejected by a beauty like Clara ... and then on the rebound proposed to a frumpish school mistress. A few weeks ago Miss Aspeling came to see me and demanded that I dismiss "your manservant" for impropriety. She is set on revenge because she discovered that, for some complicated reason, Cyprian had been reclassified as Coloured. She came to warn me that she had lodged a serious complaint against Cyprian with the Department of Interior. Fortunately it was his day off. Goodness knows what would've happened had they run into each other. Miss Aspeling was really seedy-looking, but she had beautiful blue eyes. Forty, maybe fifty, and never been kissed ...' She paused and looked at Enoch. 'I don't suppose you have ever kissed Haima ...'

'Enoch would be too frightened to kiss a girl – even if she stuck out her lips at him,' Clara said cheekily and took Hanneli indoors.

'So, have you?' Alison asked again.

'Excuse me?'

'Has she ever kissed you?'

'No – I've barely even spoken to her,' Enoch answered to forestall any further questions.

'Had you had brothers and sisters you would have been more daring. There's nothing like a bit of sibling rivalry to liven things up. But I left home as soon as I was allowed to put a signature to my trust account. Awfully mercenary, don't you think?'

No one had ever been so candid with Enoch before – nor were they the kind of questions he thought Alison should have asked him. There had always been boasting about girlfriends at school and he had felt compelled to concoct a story about Gloria, a Xhosa girl, whom he supposedly escorted to the theatre and museums from time to time, but she had returned to the Eastern Cape. This story had earned him the scorn of his friends who swore that he had become so desperate that he had to go for a native girl. But that was the whole idea: Enoch provided just enough detail to interest them, without fear that anyone would demand proof. That way, he could string them along.

Gloria had been a mere contrivance, allowing him to while away endless hours in the library taking notes to impress an imaginary girl with a profound knowledge of art and literature. He had not yet gone to the extent of inventing a passionate embrace – that was still to come. So there was no clear answer to Alison's question.

Alison was talking again. 'I've got to warn you that in return for getting Kenny Parker out of the country, my father made us promise that we would have my niece to stay for a few months. She's been sent down from school again and she's an absolute pest. My sister really needs a break from her daughter and at the moment the girl is tormenting my parents. They had never guessed that their darling granddaughter would turn out to be such a terror. So be warned.'

'But what has your niece got to do with me?' Enoch asked.

'Don't be so naïve. For a young man, you are very old-fashioned. Should this exchange of prisoners be effected, I am sure she'll make a play for you. Please don't think me imprudent, Enoch, but I advise you to keep your distance from Caroline and spare yourself and us a lot of trouble.'

To Enoch this came across as an uneven swap – a spoiled, wayward girl in exchange for a top-class Shakespearian scholar. Alison must have read his thoughts.

'Of course, you might see this as a purely opportunistic affair, frivolous in the extreme. But Daddy is like that – no matter what the situation, he tries to squeeze maximum benefit out of it. Perhaps that's why he's so good at what he does.' She heard a voice. 'Is that your grandfather trying to get your attention?' she asked.

'He may need me down at the cottage,' Enoch said, relieved to make his departure.

'We'll expect you at dinner. Polycarp might be here as well. Bring your grandfather up for drinks.'

On the walk down to the gate lodge Enoch tried to fight off an unexplained sense of excitement in the pit of his stomach. When he got there, he found that Oupa Hans had eaten his salad and pudding and had left the main course untouched. 'I'll have the rest for supper. Make sure you cover the plate and leave it in the pantry.'

'Alison invited us over for drinks.'

'I'll see how I feel later.'

The Nature of Identity

Mr Molinieux had his day off on Wednesdays. He had chosen this day as the break as midweek gave him the necessary rest for a job that demanded more strength and presence of mind than might be supposed. He could lay aside his black suit and gloves and dress more casually, if only until the following morning.

His appointment in town, by a fortunate coincidence, had fallen on a Wednesday, although Alison would have allowed him to take off any other day had he asked. However, he rarely requested a change as he felt this would undermine his authority with the rest of the staff. Reasons for their absences, excused and unexcused, ran the usual gamut of family sickness and death – and at least twice, imprisonment, when Mfilo had been arrested under the pass laws and Zachaeus had to drive Mr Molinieux all the way to the squalid police station in Elsies River to post bail for him. Everyone, from the humble Trossie to Ou Mevrou Jansen, knew that Mr Molinieux had Wednesdays off, and the staff arranged their work around that.

He had kept his business in town to himself. Thanks to the eventual intervention of the prime minister the Population Register of the Department of Interior had at last made a determination as to the nature of his racial identity. The only procedure that remained for him to regain his former identity was the application of the magistrate's official stamp on the document.

Mr Molinieux's appointment at court was scheduled for four o'clock, which would leave sufficient time afterwards for tea at the Mount Nelson Hotel – and for the evening he had decided to see a rerun of *The Man in the White Suit* at the Labia with Alec Guinness in the leading role. For the first time since his rejection by Clara and the subsequent humiliation by Miss Aspeling, he felt ready for a pleasant afternoon in town.

Having earlier supervised breakfast for the family, he now dropped his gloves and shirt into the laundry basket and ran a hot bath. With a towel knotted around his waist, he laid out his clothes for the afternoon.

The pleasant smell of herbal bath salts drifted through the open bathroom door.

'Nothing,' he said, as he caught a glimpse of himself in the mirror, 'will ruin my afternoon.' He had obtained the good wishes of the Schoons when, during a quiet moment at breakfast, he had informed them of his business at court that afternoon. Dr Schoon had mapped out the directions he was to follow from the car park on the Grand Parade to the magistrate's court, and assured him that on his return they would be waiting at Wepener to toast his good fortune. Mr Molinieux, who seldom went into town, ignored Clara's polite enquiries when she caught sight of the map.

'Please mind your own business,' he snapped.

While shaving, he reflected on the consequences of his ill-conceived actions and the abuse he had suffered from the authorities. In only a few hours he would assume his identity again and forget that the Department of Interior had deliberately employed every conceivable delay to thwart his petition – despite his repeated assurance that, in the event of his rightful identity being restored, he would never again bring the laws of his adopted country into disrepute. He had ignored Mrs Schoon's advice and had kept the whole matter from the press. Such publicity would have caused him immense embarrassment. The whole experience had reminded him in no uncertain terms that being a European was not only a privilege, but also a responsibility.

This was something he had tried to instil in Dr and Mrs Schoon. What baffled him most at Wepener was the almost obsessive manner in which the young couple proceeded to turn a traditional household into an experiment for their liberal inclinations. It was all very well for them to profess the coming of a golden age of equality as, after all, it would be their sort of people whose comfortable lifestyles were at stake. All in all he found the pair much too eager to sympathise with Non-Europeans, whatever their background.

Although Mr Molinieux did not see eye to eye with Ou Mevrou Jansen, there was one matter on which they were in full agreement: no matter how inarticulate her attempts, she too had tried to tell Dr Schoon that this attitude undermined the proper running of the household. The Schoons had never made it clear to the staff that he, Mr Molinieux, was responsible for the management of Wepener, and this had encouraged

Ou Mevrou Jansen to act as though she was in charge. He also strongly disapproved of the way everyone had indulged the boy, Enoch, since his first arrival at Wepener.

When Dr Schoon, recently married, had returned to South Africa, Mr Molinieux had been impressed with the informality he and his wife had introduced; but later the behaviour of the servants and subsequent improprieties had confirmed to him that this was wrong. Take the case of Clara: in which other household would one find a nursemaid who had the effrontery to ridicule the well-intentioned reprimands of her superior? He had not been granted the authority to employ or dismiss staff, and neither Dr Schoon nor his wife could understand how difficult his job had become as a result. Admittedly, they were his employers and he owed them his unquestioning loyalty, but Mr Molinieux felt strongly that it would have made his job easier had they left the running of the house entirely in his hands.

When he finally lowered his body under the foaming surface of the bath and reached for the hot tap with his toe, he did not hear the timid knock at the door. Trossie entered the bathroom intent on the morning's cleaning. He had given her permission to clean his rooms, but she usually waited for him to hand her the keys before she ventured in with mop, pail, polish and fresh linen. Mr Molinieux sat up, aghast at her presence. Although he was partially submerged under a generous layer of foam, this was the first time his adult body had ever been exposed to the gaze of a woman.

'Of all the nerve, Trossie!' he shouted over the sound of running water. 'What are you doing in here?'

Trossie stood frozen over the lavatory pan, with the brush and cleanser in her hands.

'Get out immediately! Scram, you blithering idiot!'

Trossie's arms and legs refused to budge – she was rooted to the spot. The sudden confusion, horror and shame had rendered her immobile. Only moments before her whole body had been primed for the morning's work. She had badly wanted to please Mr Molinieux, upon his return from town, with a job well done. His body glistening with foam and water, he tied a towel around his waist, snatched the Vim and toilet brush from her hands and escorted her from his bathroom.

'Now listen, you fool – just you wait for me in here,' he shouted while returning to the bathroom to dry himself. This was exactly the sort of behaviour he had so often cautioned against. Since the Schoons had chosen to be remiss in their responsibility towards the servants, it had become his sacred duty to impose discipline. Dressed in his royal blue bathrobe, Mr Molinieux seated himself at the dressing table, his back to the mirror, and assessed the situation.

Trossie was an extremely timid woman, and he realised that she was by no means the worst offender. However, this sort of behaviour had to be nipped in the bud. He was determined to show her that he was in charge.

'Now listen to me, Trossie.'

'Yes, master,' she sobbed.

'I want you to stop this childish snivelling right away – do you understand?' He crossed his legs and clasped his hands over his knee. 'And get my slippers from the stand. I'm sick and tired – fed up with the way things are done in this house. Who's in charge here, anyway? Tell me, child, is it me, or that Bushman in the kitchen?'

'Sorry, master?' she murmured, not understanding his tirade.

'What did I bloody well ask you? You people never listen. Who is in charge here?'

'Master is, master,' she replied, drying her tears on her apron, although unable to suppress her sobs.

'I demand an apology,' Mr Molinieux said, reluctant to describe her presence in the bathroom.

'Sorry, master.'

'At last. Now was that so difficult?' From the tone of his voice it appeared that he was appeased by Trossie's contrition. 'You know how people talk. What would the chatter be if the other servants knew about your rudeness?'

'So's true's God, master, I won't say anything.'

'These things have the habit of getting out, you know, child,' he said firmly. 'What you did in there wasn't nice. What with the law, those people in the kitchen can say just about anything happened.' He tugged at his moustache and cleared his throat, 'The master in the bath and you right beside him?'

It was unnecessary for him to continue because at that moment the full implication of her actions dawned on Trossie. Both hands flew to her mouth to smother the fresh sobs as she fell to her knees at Mr Molinieux's feet and begged for forgiveness. However, he decided that a further prodding would not be amiss.

'But, my dear girl, how can you expect the master to forgive you when the law of the land is so unforgiving?' He placed a hand on her shoulder. 'Just think, right now I can hear the police say that I, as a white man, have led you astray. But come, girl; it isn't necessary to make so much noise. Somebody might walk down the hall and hear you.' He handed her a handkerchief. 'This experience will remain our secret. Listen, it's all right; I won't tell the police what happened.'

'But master, what will the police do, master?' she asked in terror. Trying to find an explanation for the guilt and shame massed on her shoulders she glimpsed some light through the darkness. She tried to reassure Mr Molinieux that his reputation would remain intact – that nobody would ever point a finger at him. 'Because why, master, master and me didn't do nothing wrong.'

'It's not that,' he said, 'it's what the police will say we've done.'

Out of desperation, Trossie blurted out, 'But master and me didn't make rude, master.'

Mr Molinieux leapt from his chair in a show of horror. 'What on earth do you mean?' He shouted at her. 'Of all the nerve! No, Trossie, you simply don't understand. Master in his bathrobe, with you right beside him. You had better go and lock the door just in case someone walks in and gets the wrong idea.'

Trossie locked the door, then whispered, 'Nobody can say anything because they know I do the turning-out for master on Wednesdays.'

Mr Molinieux looked at his clock and decided that enough time remained for him to continue. He was beginning to enjoy the power he had over the girl.

'You're right, Trossie. But what really bothers me is what the police would think – you know what they are like,' he said as he beckoned her closer.

Trossie stared at the floor, unable to account for the filth the police carried around in their minds.

'Trossie,' he said, placing his hand on her shoulder again. 'It's all right – nobody can walk in now.'

Trossie collapsed once again onto her knees, wringing her hands in self-recrimination. The gesture reminded him of Miss Aspeling. 'Hang, girl, you know, you could be in real trouble.'

'Shame, master – sorry, master,' she cried.

Her tiny voice sounded so pathetic that it evoked some sympathy in him – however, he refused to heed caution. 'Even master can make a mistake once in a while.'

He placed his hand on her neck and felt the warmth of her skin. She had pulled her hair severely back to hide any indication of its natural spring. He looked at her features, a strange admixture of European and Bushman, her sad, green eyes embedded in a wrinkled face. Her forehead and cheeks looked pinched. He gazed at her frightened eyes in the ancient face and looked down at her tiny porcelain hands. Mr Molinieux realised that he had captured Trossie in his hands like a bird.

'Had you not been such a big girl, I'd have given you a thrashing,' he said, with an indulgent anger. 'You know, girl, you deserve a good hiding.'

Trossie was exhausted. 'Ja, baas,' was all she could mutter.

'Imagine if anyone saw my hand here,' he said, placing his hand on her breast. Then finding the buttons on her uniform, he undid them and slipped his hand inside. 'What do you think they would say?'

Mr Molinieux helped her to her feet. 'That was very naughty of you, Trossie,' he said as he removed her apron and unbuttoned her uniform.

'Sorry, master,' she whispered. His hands explored every part of her body almost dispassionately while continuing to caution her about the shame she had brought on him. He had never before experienced the effect a woman's body could have on him. He reassured her by telling her that she was a much better girl than Clara.

'Thank you, master; she's forward, master,' Trossie answered. 'Clara even think she's white, master.'

Mr Molinieux took her hand and guided it under his robe, where he helped her pick up the rhythm of his increasing desire. He led her onto the Persian rug – the one she took into the courtyard every Wednesday and pounded vigorously with the carpet beater, helped her onto her knees, removed his robe and crouched over her.

'I have a good mind to give you a thrashing,' he repeated, slurring his words. Unfettered by the identity of a European until later that afternoon, Mr Molinieux moulded himself to the arc of Trossie's back. When finally his breathing slowed down he became aware of the smell of poverty on her skin – wood smoke and damp. He saw her fingers spread out against the rich colours of the rug, her face a crude mask. He shrank from her.

Trossie appeared unable to move. He tapped her on her shoulder; with the intimacy gone, he surprised himself by being able to touch her at all.

'Now please, get up, girl; come on now. Put on your clothes and leave me in peace.'

Trossie crawled across the rug to reach her uniform. He observed her slow movements, raising first one arm and then the other – and the clumsy trail of buttons up the front of her uniform. He firmly secured his own robe. Finding his voice again, he asked, 'Trossie, you're all right, aren't you?'

'Yes, master.'

'The next time master will definitely not be so lenient, understand?'

'Sorry, master,' she stuttered. She tied on her headscarf and took up the rug.

'You can return to do the cleaning after I've left. You know how to get master's rooms spick and span, don't you?'

Mr Molinieux wondered whether it would be appropriate to offer her money. He unlocked his desk. 'Before you go, Trossie …'

She waited, the rug tucked under her arm and her hand on the door-knob. He counted out four ten-shilling notes, and put the money into her pocket.

'But master, master did already pay me my wages.'

'It's just a little extra. Get something for the children.'

He recorded the gratuity in the accounts book as Trossie shut the door quietly. She left the rug in the courtyard and locked herself in the staff toilet. She began to cry and, as she could not face the other staff in the kitchen, she stayed there, waiting for the sounds of Mr Molinieux's departure.

Mr Molinieux moved within range of the mirror. In the looking glass there appeared what he had come to accept as his face: the thin, greying hair, prominent nose, moustache, receding chin and opaque brown eyes. His appearance had undergone many changes since the day his parents had first brought him to these shores by cargo vessel to escape the persecution attendant on their class in Britain – a ten-year-old boy, watching the giant ropes let out to moor the vessel to bollards on the wharf. Now he was unable to recognise himself.

As he peered deeper into the mirror, he was shocked by his jaundiced look. He was especially yellow about the eyes. He felt the eight pints of his Scottish blood swirling about inside him, the contaminated parts infecting the healthy parts. Then his whole body began to shake.

'Take hold of yourself!' he shouted; but the command had no effect as a shock engulfed him. Mr Molinieux marched about the room, his arms and legs commanded by unseen voices. When a sudden and even more violent seizure came upon him, he fell onto his bed. He saw on the ceiling a sea of yolk spreading towards him.

With equal suddenness, he was restored; his body no longer shook and he regained the use of his limbs. Reunited with a welcoming world, the familiar walls of his room and the view from the open window, he hurriedly bathed in the tepid water and put on his best suit, ready to face the afternoon's prospects.

It Was No Deed of Mine

With less time available to reach the court than he had planned, Cyprian Molinieux drove his grey Prefect along Liesbeeck Parkway faster than it had ever been driven. He advanced steadily along the Heerengracht where the statue of Bartholomeu Dias brooded like a bronzed malignancy over the Foreshore. He turned left onto Buitenkant Street where the houses gave way to office buildings, shops, hotels and wholesale establishments.

The southeaster whipped up the red brick dust and sand, thrashing it against the exposed faces of pedestrians who retreated from the high wind through every available door. He turned left onto Caledon Street, but there was parking for officials only. He eventually found a vacant spot on the Grand Parade, opposite the City Hall, where Dries had advised him to park. The severity of the wind kept customers away from the rows of fruit and flower sellers who had taken up defensive positions around their displays.

At the entrance to Caledon Square, he was stopped by a policeman dressed in regulation khaki with a revolver in a holster at his waist. Molinieux explained that he had an appointment. The policeman waved him through. He had twenty minutes to spare. However, a sergeant looking at his papers informed him that he was at the wrong place. The Race Tribunal sat in a building adjacent to the Supreme Court on Queen Victoria Street, some distance away. His mistake angered him. He hurried past St George's Cathedral, turned into Queen Victoria Street, and eventually found the entrance.

The rotunda over the bench gave the interior the atmosphere of a church. Several people were seated in the public gallery and a woman moved to make room for him in the front row. Looking around, Molinieux recalled the minister of interior being asked by an opposition member to explain why there were increasing numbers of people from all population groups seeking reclassification. The minister had dismissed her question as unpatriotic, and commended the law for its positive achievements:

'To many, a certainty has now been granted that they have never had before.'

As members of the tribunal took their seats after a break, it was as if Cyprian Molinieux's transgression against Trossie eclipsed his obsession with race and colour. He kept his eyes focused on the huge display of proteas on the stenographer's desk. However, the flowers failed to hold his attention as he struggled to subdue his rising guilt. His actions were not deserving of the favourable judgement he expected the court to hand down later that afternoon.

Nor could he find reassurance in the sombre portraits of the judges president going back to the time when laws were first introduced to the Cape Colony. The men sitting in their black robes could just as easily have gathered to pronounce the death sentence in the Supreme Court next door. The fact that so many supplicants were assembled showed Mr Molinieux the lengths to which people would go to establish their identity. It was as elementary as naming a child.

Where better to demonstrate the workings of racial classification than in the Cape with its diversity of races and groups? Not that the Population Registration Act of 1950 was unknown in other parts, but it was unlikely that a Coloured person plagued by contrary genes in a remote town such as Prieska would petition to be reclassified as White – and no Coloured or European living anywhere would ever have approached the Race Tribunal to be classified as Native.

As if the magistrate's court recognised the crepuscular nature of those gathered in the public gallery, the petitioners were not assigned seats according to their present classifications. That would be a privilege accorded them when they took their first steps as reincarnated men and women and exited the court to assume their new lives. Almost an hour later, when the Race Tribunal had duly examined and approved the new identities of some five petitioners, Mr Molinieux, who was now acutely aware of the time, became concerned as his case had not yet been called. He no longer entertained thoughts of tea at the Mount Nelson. Teatime had come and gone.

The grave voice of the magistrate reverberated around the rotunda as he informed an African woman that her application for reclassification as Coloured had been approved – and, mindful of her status as the wife of a lecturer in Bantu languages at the University of Cape Town, the authority had been vested in him to impart the Department's findings to her. Nothing stood in her way as she had satisfied all the requirements of the Population Registration Act, although he would advise her and her husband, an earlier beneficiary of the Act, to change their names to something more acceptable to the Coloured community to which they now aspired.

However, when he handed her the final document, signed and approved with the seal of the Cape Town Race Tribunal, the woman betrayed herself with a simple gesture. She reached out to receive the document with both hands in the African way, rather than reaching for it with one hand as a Coloured person might have done. The magistrate withheld the document. She had come so close and yet, at the very last moment, had failed at something so simple.

Mr Molinieux was shocked to hear the magistrate inform the woman that he could not allow her to assume a new identity until all traces of her previous self had been done away with. However, a date was to be set for a new hearing at which time she would have the opportunity to approach the court once again for a determination in respect of identity.

He saw the woman reach into her handbag for a handkerchief and raise it to her eyes. She rushed from the court, unable to hide her humiliation. From the gallery audible sighs of disappointment escaped the lips of those continuing to wait. Anyone among them could so easily have been in her position.

Mr Molinieux recalled the many times he had lain awake at night, unsure of his own identity. He had developed a real dread of being Coloured and having all trace of his previous existence erased. A wave of revulsion overwhelmed him and he was afraid that this new mountain of degradation would follow him as he approached the bench. He thought of the boy who had arrived in Cape Town, having set sail from Tilbury forty years earlier – and now being pitied by others as confused by their identities as he was.

He would have been closer to leaving the court with the proper documents in hand had the clerk of the court summoned people to the bench in alphabetical order, rather than in order of arrival. Around him the other petitioners were also beset by anxiety, and there was an unspoken empathy among them.

'Cyprian Bannister Molinieux,' the clerk of the court called out through the echoing chamber. It was already half-past five, long past normal working hours, and he could not believe his good fortune when the clerk announced that his would be the last case the tribunal would consider that day. The remaining petitioners would be notified by post as to when they could return and it would not be before the New Year. The clock on the distant wall was ten minutes slow – he could so easily have been dismissed along with the others.

The clerk showed Mr Molinieux to a seat in front of the tribunal. The members regarded him from their bench with the authority vested in them by their office. As he was so obviously a European, not only in looks, but also in bearing, the magistrate examined him less critically. He flipped through the pages of the file before him. The magistrate could quite clearly make an accurate assessment of the man's identity and he even managed a smile, which served to encourage an anxious Molinieux.

'Mr Cyprian Bannister Molinieux,' the magistrate addressed him, 'Anglo-French to my ear, not so!'

'I beg Your Honour's pardon, but the name is Scottish.'

'Aha, very interesting – it just so happens that Robbie Burns is one of my favourite poets.' He held forth in a stentorian voice:

Of all the numerous ills that hurt our peace,
That press the soul, or wring the mind with anguish
Beyond comparison the worst are those
By our own folly, or our guilt brought on:
In ev'ry other circumstance, the mind
Has this to say, "It was no deed of mine:"

'You must be familiar with those lines, Mr Molinieux.'

'I'm afraid not, Your Honour.'

Mr Molinieux noted that the tribunal found the magistrate's recitation amusing. The stenographer appeared to have kept pace, ensuring that the words of the poet appeared in the official record.

'Now Mr Molinieux, if the decision on your identity was up to me, I'd say here and now that you are a European male. It is unmistakeable. Not to speak of your name – which you inform me is of Scottish derivation.

Judging by the size of the file, I gather there has been extensive correspondence relating to your case.'

'Yes, Your Honour,' Mr Molinieux replied, apprehensive of the bulky file on which the magistrate tapped with his gold fountain pen.

'I must submit, Mr Molinieux, that I find it extremely irregular that there is a "File Incomplete" stamp on it.'

Mr Molinieux stammered, 'I beg your pardon, Your Honour, but there must be some misunderstanding. I have a letter from the Population Register right here. It confirms that everything is in order – and that Your Honour is required to make a final determination as to appearance.'

He walked up to the bench and placed the letter before the tribunal.

'No need for that, Mr Molinieux. I have a copy in your file,' the magistrate said, handing the letter back to him. There was some hesitation in his voice. 'This could only be the registrar's doings. "File Incomplete" on a copy of a letter informing you that everything is in order. Had it been up to me, I would have passed you with flying colours. The registrar must feel that the matter has not been satisfactorily concluded.'

'But how could that be, Your Honour?' Mr Molinieux asked.

'It appears they have decided to give serious consideration to a counter-petition submitted by a certain Miss Aspeling, spinster of Olieboom Road in Mowbray. Are you acquainted with an individual by that name, sir?'

'Yes, Your Honour,' he said firmly, having regained his composure. 'But this is impossible. The law states explicitly that no frivolous petition, counter or otherwise, would be entertained.'

'Your knowledge of our law is to be commended, Mr Molinieux, but the file distinctly says that Miss Aspeling has lodged all manner of complaints against you. The best you can hope for is that these will prove scurrilous and not lead to an official investigation. At this point the court would like to remind the petitioner to restrict his replies to the questions put to him by the bench.'

Mr Molinieux was furious that an official dressed in black robes could, in the name of Her Majesty the Queen, deny him his identity; but because of the degradation he had so recently fallen into, he felt he could hardly argue the case. Had details about the incident with Trossie appeared in his file, he would have been behind bars rather than appealing a case of identity.

Then came the bombshell. 'Following official pressure to finalise the matter, the court has exceptionally invited the counter-petitioner, Miss Jennifer Aspeling to present her complaints in person. Would the clerk of the court show Miss Aspeling in.'

Cyprian Molinieux's face was ashen. He had not seen Miss Aspeling since his proposal. She was led from an antechamber and sat down some distance away from him. She looked gaunt and was dressed as though she were in mourning.

'Miss Aspeling, you will not be required to take an oath in view of the informal nature of this enquiry, but please note that you will address yourself to the questions put to you by this court as though you were under oath. So the court would caution you to tell the truth. Is that clear?'

'Yes, Your Honour,' Miss Aspeling replied without looking at Mr Molinieux.

'Miss Aspeling, the tribunal would like you to confirm orally what you have set down in writing.'

'Yes, Your Honour – I confirm that what I have written in my counter-petition is the whole truth.'

'Did Mr Molinieux admit to the nature of his racial classification before or after his proposal of marriage?'

'After the proposal, Your Honour.'

'Would you consider this concealment an unintended omission or a wilful act?'

'A wilful act, Your Honour.'

'In view of the complications for the petitioner occasioned by your counter-petition, would you have any clarifications to offer in mitigation of his claim for reclassification?'

'I have nothing further to say, Your Honour.'

Mr Molinieux found it difficult to tell from the magistrate's quizzical look whether he thought that the case resulted from any injustice inherent in the law, or from Miss Aspeling's allegations. Although Cyprian was neither plaintiff nor defendant, he felt that his appearance before the Race Classification Board had earned him the taint of an accused man.

The magistrate quietly conferred with members of the tribunal before he spoke again. 'Miss Aspeling, a final question – I would like you to cast your mind back to what you have referred to in your counter-petition as "the incident". To the best of your knowledge, was the submission of your counter-petition occasioned by your emotional state at the time or was it a response to the legal implications had you proceeded with the proposed marriage in contravention of the Mixed Marriages Act?'

Molinieux could tell that the magistrate's question had upset Miss Aspeling and it surprised him that she could pull herself together enough to reply. 'Your Honour, the counter-petition has nothing to do with my emotional state at the time, which I recall fully, nor was it a response to possible legal implications. I did only what was to be expected from any law-abiding citizen of our country and reported a premeditated contravention of our race laws.'

'The Race Tribunal would like to express its gratitude to the counter-petitioner for her assistance to bring this matter to a conclusion. She may now be excused.'

The pallor of Molinieux's face worried the magistrate. 'It must be a bitter pill,' he said, 'but did Job ever question the ways of God? And he was a man tested like few of us will ever be.'

Molinieux clenched his teeth as he stumbled over his words. 'This injustice does no honour to the name of God.'

'Oh, it can't be all that bad now,' the magistrate intoned reassuringly.

'Your Honour, as this marriage was planned to take place after my reclassification, legal ramifications do not enter into the matter. The petition for reclassification had been lodged prior to the proposal of marriage – and well before my introduction to the complainant. There was no intention of deceiving her or contravening the law. In the absence of any impropriety, I would submit that in filing a counter-petition after the submission of my appeal to the Population Register, Miss Aspeling had been swayed by revenge. The Race Court is therefore bound to consider this step as frivolous.'

The magistrate raised his hand to silence him. 'It sounds as though you are in the wrong profession, Mr Molinieux. It is conceivable that a misunderstanding has crept in and that is why Miss Aspeling's allegations will be thoroughly investigated. I give you my word. And, Mr Molinieux, I hope you will consider my suggestion. You would be well advised to go to Pretoria in person. Demand an immediate appearance before the registrar. He is authorised to make a determination on the spot. I have absolutely no doubt as to the true nature of your identity. I am an old hand at this sort of thing.

'Should you, for whatever reason, decide not to take that route, you may approach this court once more for a determination in respect of identity. Thank you.'

The magistrate looked at the clock on the wall and turned his gaze on the departing throng. 'At least you have some certainty. Just look at those poor souls; what a miserable Christmas it will be for them – the infernal waiting.'

The open door admitted a blast of the southeaster, accompanied by the sound of the groaning oak trees that lined the Company Gardens. With a measure of authority he held in reserve for difficult cases, the magistrate briskly shut the file in front of him. 'You must not allow us to detain you, Mr Molinieux. Good fellow ...'

Only then did Mr Molinieux realise that the laws he had read and committed to memory had become devoid of the amusement they had once afforded him. How could the magistrate have dared boast an acquaintance with the works of Robert Burns? How could such a man have any opinion at all about poetry?

As Mr Molinieux walked down to the Foreshore, he looked impassively at the OK Bazaars' window display of wind-up toys, dolls, lead soldiers, matchbox cars, lucky dips, teasels – and at the entrance, Father Christmas sitting on a chair, in earnest conversation with a child on his knee. He stopped at a stall on the Parade to quench his thirst with a milkshake, choosing his flavour from the cordial bottles arrayed on a shelf. The fruit hawkers were still in fine voice, shouting the merits of fragrant white peaches, mounds of strawberries, apricots, pineapples and bananas. After the subdued lighting of the court, the array of colours was blinding.

The streets leading to the docks were deserted. The wind had dropped somewhat, but sudden gusts swirled refuse along Adderley Street. He was indifferent to the plight of the office workers battling to get home. The protection of the city had deserted him. His hopes had been crushed. With all thoughts of the evening's entertainment dismissed, he wandered down to the Foreshore enveloped in a cloud of dust. To shelter from the wind, he leaned against the pedestal from which the Portuguese explorer Dias, the tall, broad-shouldered seafarer, gazed out over the Cape of Storms. The cruel waves had claimed his life so far from home almost five hundred years earlier. Mr Molinieux circled the statue and then headed for Duncan Dock. The sky was darkening as he walked swiftly for the last half-mile or so. Before he could deliver himself to his folly and fling himself over the edge of the dock, he reconsidered his decision, saw an empty crate and sat down on it to plan a course of action.

It was from the edge of one of these wharves forty years earlier, his mother by his side, that he had had his first view of Table Mountain. But the mountain no longer held any attraction. In the distance he could see a late shift of stevedores, their mouths covered with handkerchiefs against the dust, move deftly against the wind, making relays between the tall cranes and lorries, unloading bolts of cotton from Egypt.

The Union Castle mailboat was no longer in sight; it had departed for Southampton at four in the afternoon – about the time the Race Tribunal was to have restored his identity. In the distance several ships lay at anchor. Mr Molinieux decided that he would not punish himself for the short-sightedness and cruelty of the authorities. In time he would devise a plan that would shake the country to its foundations. It would require a calm, single-minded approach. Sitting on the crate, looking out at the distant waves crashing against the breakwater, he planned his revenge, however long it might take him to carry it out.

The Black Hole

There was a knock at the door of the gate lodge. Enoch jumped up from the sofa to see who it was.

'Hope I'm not disturbing you – I thought I heard voices.'

'Of course not, Polycarp,' Oupa Hans said. 'I've been expecting you.'

'Mr Pretorius, I wondered if I could have a word with you ...'

'Is it private?'

'I'd like Enoch to stay. It concerns him too.'

'Please sit down. We were just about to have a cup of tea – right, Enoch?'

'Don't go to any trouble.'

'Nonsense. Enoch's been basking in the sun all morning with the lady of the house. What can I do for you?'

'I'm leaving for Cofimvaba in a few days and wondered if Mr Pretorius had any advice for me. It's about Khotso and his family. What can I expect from them?'

'Johannes Pretorius is the last person to be giving advice.'

'That's not true, Mr Pretorius. Dries told me that Mr Pretorius has often gone along with his father to Cofimvaba.'

Enoch stood in the doorway. He wondered why Oupa Hans had tried to make a secret of these visits to Cofimvaba – it sounded as if Dries knew all about them.

'I hope you've got the kettle on, Enoch.'

'Yes, Oupa.'

'Polycarp, I encourage you to go and see Cofimvaba for yourself and make up your own mind. I think you'll find it interesting.'

'I agree, Mr Pretorius, but I'd like to make a sensible decision. I don't want to find myself in another fix.'

'Enoch, please shut the door.'

'But Polycarp said it wasn't private, Oupa Hans.'

'I have something private to say to him.'

Enoch shut the kitchen door and got the tea ready. He was not pleased with his grandfather's sudden need for secrecy, especially with matters that interested him. What could they possibly have to say to each other that Enoch couldn't hear? He arranged some of Ou Mevrou Jansen's pre-Christmas batch of allspice biscuits on a plate.

He's been basking in the sun all morning with the lady of the house! Enoch thought if only Oupa Hans knew what he and Alison had been discussing, he would not have made that remark so lightly. He had learned a lot in a short time.

'You can come through now,' Oupa Hans called.

Polycarp held the door for him as he walked in with the tray. 'Here, let me pour,' he offered. 'You've never told me that you were a writer, Enoch. What other secrets have you been hiding? Sugar, Mr Pretorius?'

'One teaspoon, please.'

'Now we have something in common, my friend, but don't breathe a word about this to Dries. He's always going on about what a great doctor you'd make. Don't worry, writers and journalists are just as important.'

'Are these Ou Mevrou Jansen's biscuits?'

'Yes, Oupa Hans. Who else makes them like this?'

'I've given Polycarp permission to read the piece about Khotso. I can save my breath and it will give him some idea about Cofimvaba. He can fill in the details for himself when he gets there. He's also interested in the Pretorius family. Polycarp and I plan to visit your parents tomorrow morning. You can stay here and catch up with the writing. Borrow one of Dries's typewriters. And don't let me catch you up at the pool, or on the tennis court. You can warm up my plate of leftovers, so you won't need to go up to the house for lunch. Do you understand me?'

'Yes, Oupa Hans. But why are Oupa Hans and Polycarp going to see Mama and Dowa? Is anything the matter?'

Polycarp answered, 'I want to ask them if you can come along with me to Cofimvaba. Your grandfather thinks it's a good idea. Would you like to do that?"

Enoch was thrilled with the prospect of such an adventure. The visit would be just what he needed to get a better insight into what he had learned from his grandfather, and he could have a look at the school at Tsomo while he was there.

'I can't think of anything I'd like to do more.'

However, Oupa Hans was more cautious. 'Let's see if your parents agree – you know what they're like. But I want you to understand that there will be no visit to Cofimvaba unless you start writing down what I have already told you. By the time you get back to Wepener with all that new stuff in your head, you will have forgotten everything I've just told you.'

'Oupa Hans, please make them say yes.'

'I can't promise anything. I might tell them that Polycarp has offered to give you Latin practice along the way. But don't worry, my boy. I'll think of something to pull the wool over your Mama's eyes. I could, of course, tell them that you are writing about the Pretorius family. As long as you keep your part of the bargain, I'll try to arrange it. Now, Enoch, where are those pages? And Polycarp, I'll have a heart attack if you say anything about Enoch's writing.'

'You have my word, Mr Pretorius.'

Enoch gave his grandfather a hug, then fished out the folder from his satchel and handed it to Polycarp.

'You know how stubborn your parents are. I'll have another one of Ou Mevrou Jansen's biscuits. Enoch, why don't you have your bath while Polycarp starts reading and then you should get dressed for dinner.'

Enoch settled himself into a deep bath and thought about these new developments. He fervently hoped his parents would agree to the journey. He knew his school friends would not believe him when he told them about his visit to a witchdoctor.

A knock at the bathroom door startled him.

'Are you going to be all day?'

'I'm almost ready, Oupa – who's going to interpret for us at Cofimvaba? Why can't Oupa come with us too?'

'Not so fast. Nothing's certain until I discuss this with your parents. Polycarp speaks Xhosa perfectly well. Please, I've got to get in there. That tea ran right through me.'

Enoch chose one of Fanus's lighter summer suits for dinner and then rummaged through the wardrobe to choose some clothes for the journey. He made a list of the things he would need from home. Polycarp was sure to be warned that they wanted their son back in one piece, and his mother would also insist on seeing his driving licence. And there would be the inevitable prayers for travel mercies.

Polycarp had finished reading Enoch's manuscript. 'I don't mean to sound patronising, Enoch,' he said, looking up. 'But your command of English is outstanding and your choice of language very mature for a young man. I especially like the way you explore the relationship between Khotso and the prime minister.'

Enoch respected Polycarp's political views – but he had not expected him to be so enthusiastic. Enoch considered himself no more than a transcriber.

'Actually, Afrikaans is my home language, but Oupa told me to write this in English.'

'Your oupa told you a simple story, and you have turned it into something captivating. It makes me want to take off for the Eastern Cape right away.'

'Nothing is stopping us – I've already packed my things.'

'Goodness me, you even look like a writer in that smart get-up.'

Enoch was not sure what writers were meant to look like. Whether it was summer or winter, Kenny Parker always wore the same old tweed jacket and grey flannels. Polycarp never wore anything special. In fact, had it not been for his startling red hair and freckles, he would have looked like a policeman in his safari outfit.

'This is one of Fanus's suits,' he said with pride.

'It looks like it was made especially for you. Where is Mr Pretorius?'

'Oupa will be out in a minute.'

'Did I hear my name?'

'Yes, Mr Pretorius. I think you have every reason to be proud of your grandson. This is an excellent piece of writing and I can't wait to see the rest. But I must warn you. If anyone gets their hands on these pages, you can kiss Wepener goodbye. Special Branch will see it as a plot to subvert the authority of the prime minister and it is likely to earn you both a holiday in solitary confinement ...'

Enoch cut Polycarp short. 'Don't forget we are expected for a drink tonight, Oupa.'

'What's wrong with that English woman? She knows I can't go near the bottle. Why don't the two of you go and leave me in peace. We'll see each other tomorrow.'

Enoch and Polycarp made a tour of the house to greet the staff before joining Dries and Alison for drinks in the drawing room. Mr Molinieux looked anguished and ignored Polycarp's outstretched hand. Enoch had previously overheard him say that Polycarp represented the worst of the poor whites. Mr Molinieux did, however, greet Enoch – with his usual cold manner. But a warm welcome and an appetising smell of roast lamb awaited the two in the kitchen. Clara held onto Hanneli as she tried to slip off her chair.

'Supper first – and then it's time for your bath. Maybe Enoch will read you a story later on.'

'Where were you this afternoon?' Hanneli asked. 'You promised me to play tennis.'

'Sorry, Hanneli, I was busy. I'll come and read to you after your dinner.'

'Don't make promises to the child if you don't intend keeping them,' Ou Mevrou Jansen admonished. 'And give me a kiss. You look handsome, my boy – it's the first time someone is wearing that suit.'

Ou Mevrou Jansen's eyes misted over, and Enoch knew that she was thinking about Fanus. She sat in her easy chair, sipping at her drink. Wiry, grey waves of hair held down by hairpins and a hairnet framed her brown face. Her neck and the folds of her breast were wrinkled in the manner of the Bushmen – although she frequently asserted, 'Ek is nie 'n Boesman nie,' swearing that she didn't have a single drop of that lazy blood in her veins.

Dries and Alison fell silent when Enoch and Polycarp walked into the drawing room. It appeared that they had been arguing. Alison waited for Mr Molinieux to leave the room before she spoke.

'I would like you two to talk some sense into Dries. He wants to leave for London tomorrow on a mission of mercy and refuses to listen to me.'

'Darling, I said we should both go. That would make more sense.'

Enoch wondered if talk of going to London would dominate the evening's conversation, and he hoped that it would not jeopardise the prospects of his journey to Cofimvaba.

'We'd only be gone for a week. You must see your father so we can get to the bottom of this Caroline thing. Don't you think we should know what we're letting ourselves in for?'

'I don't see why Polycarp can't go with you,' Alison said. 'I need to be here. It is just before Christmas and I've got things to do.'

'Enoch and I are off to see the witchdoctor in a few days, so I can't go. Anyway, my passport has been withdrawn. You can always shop at Harrods, Alison, and see your family.'

Alison frowned at Polycarp. 'Surely you're not taking Enoch to see that wicked man? If Dries goes to London, I insist that Enoch stays here to keep us company. It's nonsense dragging him off to some godforsaken place. Hanneli and I are not going to be abandoned by you men. And I'm sure Mr Pretorius needs him here to help him – that's why Enoch is at Wepener, after all. Isn't that right, Enoch?'

Enoch was struck dumb. But Alison soon enough betrayed the cause of her mood. 'I'm not going to stay here on my own with Molinieux dragging his feet around the house. He gives me the creeps. He's been in a funk ever since he got back from court and refuses to say a word about it. I can only assume he didn't succeed – first it's Kenny and Caroline, and now Molinieux. He may be an excellent butler, but he is a most peculiar person. Just the other day Ou Mevrou Jansen told me that he had Trossie in floods of tears – poor girl.'

'Well, I've got to go whether you come or not, Alison,' said Dries. 'Your father's in a position to do something about Kenny Parker. We need help from London and he can organise that. Special Branch searched Kenny's house the day before yesterday and discovered a manuscript hidden behind a wood panel. The rumour I heard is that it's a detailed plot for the overthrow of the government. If we don't get him away he will be tried for treason – and that could get him years behind bars, or his life. For God's sake, Kenny's not even a communist.'

'By the time they are finished with him, he will be.' Polycarp drained his glass of wine. 'Dries, why don't you go on your own to see Alison's father? I have a copy of Kenny's manuscript you must take to London. It's not what Special Branch makes it out to be. He hid the manuscript because he did not want his wife to find it. It's actually a novel, *The Essential Nature of Grammar* it's called, a love story, really. He was afraid his wife would find it and think he was having an affair – though I suppose writing a book is a bit like having an affair. Little did he know that the cops would get to it first and apply their analytical skills to his literary efforts. Our Special

Branch friends are no connoisseurs of literature – for them writing any book is bound to be a subversive act. You should try to find a publisher for Kenny's book while you're over there. I'll put off my trip to Cofimvaba for a week – and Enoch can stay here and help keep an eye on Wepener.'

Clara knocked. 'Excuse me please for interrupting. Enoch, Hanneli is waiting for her story.'

'Don't stay too long – we have other things to discuss,' Alison said.

Hanneli was bouncing around on her bed when Enoch walked into the nursery. 'I know what story I want best.'

'I'm sure you do, but tonight I'm telling you one from my head.'

She placed her hands on his face and looked into his eyes. 'I can't see it … where's the story?'

'Why don't you shut your eyes and listen, and then you'll see the pictures too. The story is called "The House that Jack Built".'

Hanneli obediently shut her eyes. 'I can see the little house. It's like Oupa Hans's house.'

'How did you guess? Now listen – and don't open your eyes. Do you see a cow, a dog, a cat and a rat?'

'I can see them all – and there's a pig too.'

Hanneli had a peaceful look on her face. Enoch lowered his voice when he reached the last verse.

> This is the priest all shaven and shorn,
> That married the man all tattered and torn,
> That kissed the maiden all forlorn,
> That milked the cow with the crumpled horn,
> That tossed the dog,
> That worried the cat,
> That killed the rat,
> That ate the malt
> That lay in the house that Jack built.

Hanneli was fast asleep.

'Haai, the child didn't even say her prayers yet,' murmured Clara.

'Don't worry, Clara,' Enoch whispered. 'I'm sure the Lord will forgive her this time.'

'Don't come and blame me if Ou Mevrou Jansen asks. You know what she's like.'

When Enoch returned to the drawing room Mr Molinieux was pouring another round of drinks and announced that dinner would be served in a few minutes.

'We've sorted it out, Enoch,' Dries announced. 'You'll be pleased to hear that Alison, Hanneli and I will go to London for a week – and by the time we get back, you and Polycarp will have returned from Cofimvaba. Sorry for all the confusion.'

They walked into the dining room as Mr Molinieux removed Oupa Hans's place setting. Enoch said grace.

Dinner was a desultory affair. Alison suddenly said, 'But why can't Enoch come with us? I'm sure he'd love to see London and he can make up his mind about England.'

'I don't have a passport either,' Enoch replied. 'Oupa Hans has family near Cofimvaba. He would like me to meet them before they all die off, isn't that so, Polycarp?'

'That's right. Enoch is writing a family history about the Boer general and his tanned relatives.'

'There are a few family members left and I've got to interview them before they ...'

'That could be interesting,' said Dries. 'Why don't you take along my typewriter? Take the portable one and your camera. That's such a great idea, Enoch.'

'Oupa Hans has got plenty of photographs in his album.'

'Let me show Enoch where to find the typewriter,' Alison said, and accompanied him to the study.

'Perhaps it was not such a good idea for you to go to London anyway,' she said to him. 'What with this Kenny Parker business – and I've got to sort Caroline out as well. I'm sure there'll be many other opportunities. You should apply for a passport soon.'

A Teacher Is Welcomed

Two weeks later, when he returned to the gate lodge, Enoch was surprised that Dries and Alison had not yet returned from London. Alison had telephoned Ou Mevrou Jansen to say that they had been delayed, but had not explained why. Enoch sat down at his grandfather's table with a Xhosa dictionary he'd found up at the house and the typewriter. Oupa Hans wanted him to go outdoors and find a shady spot in the garden, but Enoch knew that he would need the old man's help with the Xhosa, so he stayed indoors with his grandfather.

On their arrival at Cofimvaba, Enoch noticed that Khotso seemed fascinated by Polycarp van Wyk and the rich colour of his hair. It was as if Khotso had never seen anything like it. Enoch wondered whether he was considering using some red clippings for his divinations. Khotso and Polycarp shook hands.

'May I present Mr Pretorius's grandson … Enoch Pretorius.'

'Pleased to meet you, umfaan. I am a friend of your grandfather. I was wondering if Mr van Wyk had brought you along as an assistant teacher. We could use another teacher around here.'

Although Khotso's compound was pretty much as Oupa Hans had described it, it did not live up to Enoch's expectations – there were no witches groaning incantations over a bubbling pot. He saw only a tranquil and well-ordered setting far removed from dark images of magic that had often played havoc with his imagination. He also looked around for Redemptus, Khotso's apprentice. And where were Khotso's numerous wives?

During their journey Polycarp had warned him not to expect too much. 'Even though you may have heard all sorts of stories, things are rarely what they appear to be. But keep your eyes open.'

Khotso invited them into his study and introduced his guests to Andrew Gumede, his adviser. Khotso had asked Gumede at short notice to abandon his interests in Cato Manor and come to Cofimvaba to attend to the formal details of Polycarp's teaching contract. It became apparent that Gumede had been reluctant to make the journey, and that he thought the business of a new school and a Boer teacher to be merely one of Khotso's whims. Enoch was delighted to hear Gumede say that there was nothing wrong with the mission schools in Tsomo and Queenstown, and that these schools still maintained some independence from the government. His sons had received an excellent education at a Catholic school and he would never have considered sending them elsewhere, he told them.

But Khotso wanted his own school. It was obvious too that this venture would require school buildings and the awarding of contracts for plans, bricks, cement, paint, windows and roofing materials, and that Gumede was beginning to see potential benefits for himself in all of this. Then school benches, slates, chalk, inkwells, dipping pens, drawing paper and books would also be required – and that would only be the beginning. Gumede even mentioned the necessity of a uniform for the children. If he could convince Khotso to employ this white teacher, then the long journey down from Cato Manor would have been worthwhile.

It was now Polycarp's turn to look puzzled. Most people would have supposed Andrew Gumede – swathed in a blanket and clutching a knob-kierie – to be the witchdoctor and the stooped, well-dressed Khotso a businessman, or possibly a teacher. His imagination had not prepared Polycarp for the man he saw in front of him, dressed in a tweed jacket, grey flannels and starched shirt.

Following his conversation with the prime minister at the tea party, Polycarp had put through a couple of trunk calls to Khotso before agreeing to go for an interview. He was still ambivalent about the job, although the long journey had left him plenty of time for reflection. The meandering route he had chosen allowed him to stop at his parents' home in Fort Beaufort, a crumbling town situated between the Keiskamma and the Great Fish rivers. Polycarp told Enoch that it was near the site of many frontier battles between the Xhosas and settlers.

Polycarp had not visited his parents since his release from prison. They had virtually gone into hiding after their son's imprisonment was reported in the *Kokstad Advertiser*, especially as the appalling conduct of the Van Wyk boy had been ascribed to the fact that he came from an

Afrikaner family that by some quirk of fate happened to be Catholic. No one understood how something so bizarre could have come about, but the Van Wyk family had inherited their faith from an earlier generation.

In the way a single cancerous cell proliferates to corrupt the whole body, so a single ancestor had been the family's undoing. An Irish great-grandmother had brought her Roman proclivities along with her. It had taken the grafting of the O'Rourke woman onto the Van Wyk family tree that had started her descendants' slide from a modest farm and trading post on the outskirts of Grahamstown to the obscurity of a railway siding in the Eastern Cape. But nothing in the lives of the Van Wyks was now appreciably different from that of any other ordinary Afrikaner family – with the exception of Polycarp's behaviour, possibly caused by this ancestor from whom he had inherited Catholicism and his red hair.

Polycarp's parents were overjoyed to welcome their only child home, if only for a brief visit. With Enoch's encouragement, he told them that he was on his way to Cofimvaba to teach the children of a rich Xhosa chief. Having told them this, he realised that this was exactly what he wanted to do.

'Are you talking about that witchdoctor, Khotso?' his father asked, removing his railway cap and scratching his head. 'That shrewd millionaire?'

'He's the one, Pa,' Polycarp confessed.

His father laughed. 'That will give those bastards at Railways and Harbours who want to chuck me and your ma out of our house a fright. Khotso is not Xhosa or a chief – he's from up high in the mountains of Basutoland. Ask him about Oom Paul and all that gold. They say he had something to do with that Irish gangster Kelly who grabbed Oom Paul's train when he tried to escape – and got the gold. But Khotso was still a child then, I think.'

Although Mr van Wyk had retired from his position as stationmaster at Fort Beaufort some years earlier, he continued to wear his uniform and to appear on the platform twice a day when the trains stopped. He had attained the position of stationmaster, having first worked as a porter at De Aar and later as a clerk in the ticket box. Fifty years of dedicated service had meant little to the South African Railways and Harbours hierarchy, which had been trying for some time to evict him and his wife from their tiny railway cottage.

'They think because I do native work, they can treat me like one. They want to throw your ma and me into the street because they found another Boer to do their dirty work. Call this place a house? It's got a zinc roof and mud walls. Just wait for the big flood and we will wash away into the Great Fish River, house and all.'

Because of these and other long-held resentments, Mr van Wyk did not question his son's choice of employer. Khotso was wealthy. Van Wyk knew that most natives had honoured the commitments made to him over the years – as opposed to his fellow Afrikaners, who always tried to get the better of him.

Polycarp was sitting in the study at Cofimvaba, sipping coffee poured by the man his father had described as a 'shrewd millionaire'. Enoch was struck by the rapidity with which Andrew Gumede devoured a peach and then hobbled from his chair to fling the stone from the window, reminding him of Polycarp's father squeezing the large, brown pips of a loquat from a tree growing beside the station platform, forcing them into the hard soil with the heel of his boot and saying, 'Another tree will grow here, just you watch.'

Gumede settled back comfortably in an armchair to study Polycarp's curriculum vitae and testimonials.

'So, Mr van Wyk, do you really think you can handle my lot? Their present teachers tell me that they are a spoilt and unruly bunch,' Khotso said.

'Most children can be difficult. I'll try my best,' Polycarp replied.

'I lose count, but according to the latest compound census one hundred and five of them will be starting school with you. I think there are about nine others who will continue at the Catholic school to finish their matric. But they are all now at home for the Christmas holidays, children, grandchildren – the lot. As for the others, they are too young, too lazy, or too old for school.'

'That sounds fine to me, sir, but I'll need two or three assistants, especially for the younger children.'

'Of course, Mr van Wyk, you don't think I brought you all the way out here to teach on your own? Is this young man going to be your assistant? You will be the head teacher, and there will be at least two or three others. You may get some help from my wives, who spend long days in their so-called parliament, finding ways to dish out my money. School will not begin until the middle of January and I'll have plenty of time to find some assistant teachers before then. Elizabeth is an excellent teacher, but she's expecting a child. There are still classrooms to be built, but I wouldn't know about that. I've never seen the inside of a classroom.'

Polycarp was apprehensive as Andrew Gumede scrutinised his curriculum vitae, which Alison had meticulously typed.

'You're a man of thought, Mr van Wyk,' Khotso observed, 'although I hope you will teach my boys and girls more than just silence.'

The men broke into uneasy laughter.

'Well, actually, sir,' Polycarp ventured, 'I have these ideas about teaching.'

'I would be very pleased to hear them.'

'But first I would like to know what it is that you would like me to teach your children?'

Khotso assumed a stern look. 'Please, Mr van Wyk,' he said, 'Gumede here is my lawyer, an accountant and a businessman. I am a simple inyanga. Would I ask Gumede how to interpret the bones – even though he would like to? You are the teacher and it is not my job to tell you what to teach. But if I can offer you any advice, I would say take everything you have learned and try your best to cram it into my children's heads. If you have to, force-feed them.'

'With respect, sir, education is not that simple. I don't want to turn your children into bastard Europeans. There's a lot that is valuable and good in African culture and traditions.'

'You are talking to someone who knows all about our culture and traditions. I would be no good at my job if I did not. Do you consider yourself a bastard African?' Khotso asked.

'I hadn't really thought about it, sir …'

'Then maybe it's time you did, Mr van Wyk. But I think our young friend Pretorius is a good mixture of Xhosa and European – maybe he could explain it to us.'

Enoch was tongue-tied as he had never given this much thought.

Even though Oupa Hans was always talking about his Xhosa family, the connection seemed very remote. He struggled to come up with a clever answer, but Khotso continued …

'You, Mr van Wyk, are just as much a bastard African as we are bastard Europeans. Enoch's grandfather always tells me that we are like branches grafted onto the same tree. However, the mother, our land, was already here. Your ancestors came here to barter their wares while we were still living off the land. Then they took our land. I'm hoping that some of my children will learn how to remedy that. That is what I'll be educating them for. Only by exercising their brains can my children grow.

'As for my children's traditions, Mr van Wyk, I don't expect you to teach us our culture. My children should know their own culture from their mothers – all the good stuff and the bad. And if they become bastard Europeans as well, that can only be to their benefit.

'What I want them to do is to go far in this country of ours. The prime minister tells me that you are a bit of a rebel. So do your best and leave the culture to us. My children should be able to compete in this new world of ours. I've already told them that. We can't all be cattle herders; there isn't enough pasture to go around, what with Schoon telling the chiefs that he doesn't want us casting longing looks at the green pastures of the Europeans.

'My medicine for creating wealth is powerful. I also make amazing muti for healing – but unfortunately I have not found a remedy for stupidity. And if I did, I wouldn't hand it out to all those politicians who visit me under cover of darkness to beg for love potions.'

Polycarp laughed. Andrew Gumede drew the richly provisioned platter of cold meats closer and helped himself, while Khotso poured another round of coffee.

'There's a serious gap here,' Gumede interrupted, pointing at Polycarp's cv. 'No work. Maybe a long holiday, Mr van Wyk?'

Khotso noticed Polycarp's embarrassment. 'I'm glad you raised that, Andrew. Mr van Wyk was in jail then. If you listened to the wireless, you would know that he's a famous man. Don't forget that you've also been locked up a few times.'

Then, turning to Polycarp, Khotso said, 'You've got many things in common with the black man – even his experience. Where was I before

Gumede interrupted? Oh yes, our friend, the prime minister – what's your connection with him? Why is he recommending someone as a teacher who he's put in prison?'

Polycarp sounded defensive. 'I can't answer for him. In any case, Dr Schoon's recommendation doesn't mean that I have any connection with him or his government. His son, Dries, is a close friend from university days, but I hardly know his father.'

'Mr van Wyk,' Khotso replied, 'I've known Sybrand Schoon since our days together on his father's farm in the Free State. I cannot tell you how thankful I was for the drought that drove his father off the farm, as my family was forced to leave too. Even as a child I knew that I had to move on with my life.

'I've known Schoon for as long as I can remember and I've never felt the need to apologise for our friendship. But the prime minister is now trying to force on us this business of educating the native to prepare him for his position in society. We live in different worlds. There is a telephone in my house. If I wish to speak to someone, I ring up and the lady at the exchange puts a call through for me. I reach for a switch and a light goes on. Voices speak to me on the wireless. I don't want my children to go through life believing these things to be the white man's magic.

'What good is a chief with all the cattle in the world if his children do not have opportunities? Mr van Wyk, your job will be to help my children explore things outside the limits of this kraal. We human beings always need someone to blame for our misfortunes. It could be witchcraft … or the government. If you or I were to obey our own stubborn cultures and traditions, we wouldn't be sitting here having this conversation. I want my children to be fully accountable for their own successes and failures – nobody to blame.'

'I think that's reasonable.'

Khotso hesitated, then continued. 'Every time I have even the smallest business matter to attend to, this Zulu has to come down from Cato Manor – or from wherever his interests have taken him. Gumede may be covered with a blanket, but he has made more money for me than I could ever hope to spend. Without him, I would have been travelling from kraal to kraal throwing old chicken bones. Gumede has served me well for almost thirty years.

'I want you to know something none of my wives nor even Schoon knows – I can neither read nor write. Just like Paul Kruger – but that did not stop him from being president of the Transvaal.'

Khotso's admission shocked Polycarp as it seemed to contradict his whole demeanour. Gumede was becoming impatient with all this talk, and Khotso's rash disclosure clearly annoyed him. Over the years he had covered up Khotso's inability to read or write, but now his friend had revealed this to two strangers.

In the uncomfortable silence that followed, Polycarp's interview appeared to have come to an end. Enoch noticed the carved busts of Paul Kruger and former prime ministers on the mantelpiece – there was Hertzog, Jan Smuts, Malan and Strijdom. In a corner on a workbench another bust was taking shape. Although there was not as yet a likeness, Enoch was sure that Khotso was working on Sybrand Schoon. The carving tools were lined up in a neat row like scalpels on a surgeon's tray, and there was no sign of wood shavings.

Khotso continued. 'Mr van Wyk, during your stay at Cofimvaba you will meet many of the local chiefs – they have already started clamouring to send their children to my school. Gumede calls them traitors and thieves, but I would like you to consider their requests. Tell me, Polycarp, what did you expect to find here?'

'To be quite honest, I really didn't know what to expect. I have a much better idea now. Besides, my old father was very pleased that I'll be working for you.'

'Good, we'll get along splendidly. Let's shake hands on that.'

'I'd be honoured to work here at Cofimvaba.'

'Come, Gumede, where are the papers, quick, get an inkwell so Mr van Wyk can sign before he changes his mind.'

To Enoch it appeared that Andrew Gumede was an impatient man, but he took his time spreading a sheaf of papers on Khotso's desk and leafing through them until he found the contract he had prepared in triplicate. He motioned Polycarp to a chair beside the desk. Without bothering to read the terms of the contract, Polycarp signed his name with a flourish.

'You will bring much progress to this compound, Mr van Wyk – just you wait and see. But there are a few things I must tell you. Number one, my wives are the ones who run this compound. They will have to approve plans for a schoolhouse and the same goes for orders of books and other equipment. Gumede knows the ropes. I can already see him ringing up the cash register. Maybe you could ask young Enoch's advice about school uniforms.

'The school is something my wives have begged for, so I would be surprised if they caused you any problems. We will need a permit from Bantu Education – Schoon can organise that. Gumede will deal with the other permits; he'll know how to arrange it with the clerks for a few sacks of sugar and mealie meal. The native commissioner has agreed to the school in principle.

'I hope you will like your living quarters – they are private and comfortable. There is, however, one more thing I'd like to mention.'

'Yes, sir?'

'I cannot allow any alcohol in my compound. I'm sorry, but I insist on that. I recently discovered that it disturbs the ancestors who help me in my divinations. If you need to drink, there is a bottle store and bar in Tsomo. The store was rebuilt after the Pondo fires – the off-sales is always the first building to go up in flames and the first to be rebuilt.'

Polycarp agreed to respect Khotso's wishes, although Enoch knew that Dries and Alison had given him a case of Meerlust and another of dry sherry as parting gifts. Khotso rang a bell for his senior wife, Nohlwandle, who arrived to show them to Polycarp's quarters: two adjoining rondawels with whitewashed walls, apricot pip floors and large windows with mesh to keep out insects. As Khotso had promised, the rooms were quiet and well away from the main house.

Polycarp asked Nohlwandle when he could approach her parliament with the requirements for the school. She expressed a warm welcome on behalf of all the women and children at Cofimvaba.

'We will invite you to the bhunga at our next sitting and you can tell us all about your plans then.'

'I look forward to that,' Polycarp replied.

A large steamer trunk which Polycarp had borrowed from Dries and two suitcases crammed with his books and clothes had been removed from his car and placed on the floor. Enoch's suitcase stood beside them. The cases of wine had been left in the boot.

'You can see how much we appreciate your being here. We took the liberty of getting your trunk and cases into your rooms, knowing you will stay, Mr van Wyk. Thank you for coming to Cofimvaba.'

As he looked about him, Enoch realised that he had entered a world quite different to any he had known before. Oupa Hans had told him about his childhood. His grandfather had grown up around a hundred miles west of Cofimvaba and had spent most of his early days surrounded by black people, many of whom he still counted as friends. In this inyanga's kraal, Enoch had finally entered their world, a world that for many people was unknown and frightening. His thoughts were interrupted by Gumede driving his Austin Princess hearse up to the rondawel door.

Andrew Gumede entered the room, leaning heavily on a cane. He was in a hurry to return to Cato Manor. He told Enoch that he had just heard on the wireless that a number of policemen had ransacked one of his beer halls and had overturned the barrels of utywala that now flooded the township's streets. A crowd of angry women who brewed the traditional beer had attacked nine of the policemen. There would be hell to pay, Gumede assured him.

Gumede made no secret of the reason for his visit. He drew a wallet from the pocket of his shorts and offered to buy any available drink. He took the Meerlust and sherry off Polycarp's hands at two guineas per case.

'Sorry to have to put your good wine into this old crock. The police never bother me when I drive a hearse – and most people are too super-stitious to think of stealing it. The Cadillac is only for Sundays.'

A satisfied Gumede sped off a few minutes later, leaving a cloud of exhaust fumes in Polycarp's room.

Traditional Medicine

Over the next several days Polycarp spent a great deal of time with Khotso's wives, working out plans for the school. Because there were only six weeks before the new term began, they decided on prefabricated buildings. Later, with planning permission, Khotso hoped to replace these with permanent structures similar to the houses in the compound. Enoch, with a camera and notebook, was left to his own devices. Elizabeth, Khotso's youngest wife, took him around and introduced him to everyone. He was keen to meet Redemptus, Khotso's apprentice, who, although a year older than him, had never been to school. Despite their lack of a common language, Enoch's time with Redemptus proved to be one of the most extraordinary experiences of his young life.

Polycarp was busy from morning till night, and was pleased when Enoch told him that Redemptus had invited him to share his rondawel. Enoch was happy even though he had to get used to the discomfort of sleeping on a mat spread out on the mud floor. Redemptus rarely woke early, which left Enoch plenty of time to think about all he had seen and heard and review his notes.

He found it peculiar that Khotso seemed to be using former prime ministers as fetishes. Of the wood carvings only the one of Paul Kruger did not look dead. And what about Sybrand Schoon, whose bust still remained unfinished? He wondered when Khotso would whittle down the wood and shape his face – and then make room for him alongside the others.

Later Enoch would slip out to have breakfast with Polycarp and be brought up to date on what he and Khotso's wives were planning. He then returned to the rondawel and prodded his new friend. Redemptus was a heavy sleeper; however, when awake, his actions were charged with an energy that conveyed itself to those around him. Elizabeth told Enoch that since Redemptus's arrival Khotso and his wives had come to love him as a son.

Redemptus was especially dear to Khotso – not as an acquisition, but as someone whom he had been called upon to protect, despite the boy's insistence that he had all the protection he needed from the Lord Jesus Christ. Although Khotso had never felt drawn to Christianity, he admired Redemptus's faith. Whatever the case, Redemptus's unassuming manner and his willingness to interpret the bones in the way of the Xhosa ancestors brought him close to the people who came to Khotso for help. Since their chiefs devoted most of their time to devising ways of acquiring the white man's goods – a preoccupation so encompassing that they could not find time to listen to the problems of their own subjects – the people streamed to Cofimvaba.

When the muti of their local inyanga or the pills of doctors proved useless, the people knew where to go. This pleased the chiefs, who then had more time to increase their herds and line their pockets. So appreciative were the local chiefs that, overlooking the fact that Redemptus was an uncircumcised Zulu boy, they made him a member of the amaphakathi, an inner circle of Xhosa elders.

Redemptus had just turned eighteen. As he had not applied for permission to be in the Transkei and because he wished to travel to East London and Cape Town, Khotso had advised him to apply for a dompas. Despite repeated reminders from Andrew Gumede, Redemptus told Enoch that, since he had been able to travel freely without the benefit of a pass for the past eighteen years, there was a good chance of negotiating the next few years without one. He would keep his distance if the police kept theirs.

But it was the distressing memory of two brief spells in prison and his reluctance to repeat the experience that convinced Redemptus to take the bus to the pass office in Tsomo, a dusty town some twenty miles from Cofimvaba. The prospect of seeing a photograph of himself, the attractions of which had been extravagantly described by Gumede, was another factor that persuaded him. Khotso suggested that Enoch accompany Redemptus because he did not trust the clerks at Native Affairs who, on the lookout for bribes, took advantage of new applicants. With only a smattering of the language acquired from his grandfather, Enoch was not sure how he could help Redemptus, but he saw it as an opportunity to visit the Catholic school.

He soon realised that Khotso had been right – it was not going to be easy. At first the clerk told Redemptus to return to Zululand, where by law he should have submitted his application. He had no business being in the Transkei. Their attempts to convince the clerk to issue the document were dismissed with contempt. In fact, the clerk even threatened to call the police.

'Look, Zulu boy, you don't speak English and you also deaf,' the clerk raged. 'Can't you hear the tea bell ringing – and what's that camera doing around your neck? Here – let me look at it.'

Enoch told the clerk that it was his camera.

'And what are you doing in here? This isn't Coloured Affairs. I'll put the police on you too.'

'Give me back my camera, or I'll report *you* to the police,' Enoch warned.

The clerk handed the camera to Enoch, and, seeing no point in further argument, he and Redemptus walked down to the post office and telephoned Khotso from a tickey box. Khotso was furious and told them to go directly to the commissioner's office.

The clerk's face was pale as Enoch and Redemptus walked into the building. He showed them to an office down the hall. Commissioner Brownlee was still talking to Khotso on the phone as they entered.

'Please take a seat and accept my apologies for my clerk's behaviour. Which of you is Redemptus? You must understand, we can't just dish out passbooks to all and sundry – there are procedures we have to follow. I'll make sure that you get yours immediately.'

'Siyabonga kakhulu, nkosi.'

'Don't mention it.'

Enoch concluded that, in his own interest, the commissioner could not refuse a request from Khotso, who had great influence on the chiefs and elders in the region. Commissioner Brownlee reached for a copy of the *Illustrated London News* on his desk. However, before dismissing them he summoned the obstinate clerk and informed him that he held him personally responsible for offending Khotso. The clerk, who had earlier wielded such power, heard that his pay would be docked at the end of the month, a customary punishment for insubordination. The man fell to his knees before Brownlee, swearing that in future he would not overstep the bounds of his authority.

As soon as he opened the doors after the tea break, the clerk gestured to Redemptus and Enoch and asked them to move to the front of the queue.

'Why don't you first tell me that Khotso send you? Then there would be no problem,' said the worried-looking clerk. 'Thanks to you, I now got it coming from two sides.'

'What does it matter who sent me? I could have said the Lord sent me – but would that have made any difference?'

'Don't come and bring the Lord into this. It's who you know that will unlock doors.'

'All I want is a dompas – what's that got to do with unlocking doors?'

The clerk begged Redemptus to make sure that the misunderstanding was cleared up with Khotso. The pass would be issued later that afternoon so that Redemptus would not be obliged to return for it in two weeks, as was the usual procedure.

The clerk gave them directions to St Dominic's School and they set off to find it on the outskirts of town. Enoch was to be disappointed as the nuns were in silent retreat at a convent near Queenstown. The janitor offered to show them around the school, but Enoch decided to return in a few days.

The dompas was ready and waiting when the two got back to the Native Affairs building. As they were hungry, they crossed the street to sit in the shade of a tall syringa tree at a Portuguese tearoom. While Redemptus could not read the words inscribed in his crisp, new passbook, he could recognise his name. But it was the photograph that fascinated him. It was like a mirror in which his image had been frozen. The look of astonishment showed the apprehension he had felt when the clerk had pressed a button and a misty blue light had exploded before his eyes.

Redemptus was spelling out his name to Enoch by pointing at each letter in turn when they became aware of a woman looking at them. They greeted her and she went back to eating from a bowl of putu, washing it down with mouthfuls of amasi from a jam tin. The baby on her back was held in place by a blanket tied across her chest. The child's head was huge and thrown backwards – its eyes shut in sleep. Enoch asked the woman if he could take her photograph.

She struck a pose and her baby woke up – beating its head frantically against its mother's back. The child's pitiful howls sent a group of young men seated around the table scampering for the shade of a distant tree. Enoch assumed they were youths who had come from surrounding villages to find work through the Government Labour Bureau.

The mother put the screaming baby to her breast, but the child could not be induced to suck. By this time the objections raised against the mother and her child from the distant table reached a crescendo. She drew a jam tin filled with sugar closer, in which she dipped her nipple. The child, consoled, sucked hungrily until the sweetness on the nipple ran out. The woman did not seem to notice Enoch photographing her while her breast went back and forth between the baby's mouth and the jam tin. Sensing that the young men were approachable, the woman told them that Ntombi was her youngest child. Her own name, she told them, was Charity Ntuli.

'I haven't seen my husband, her father, since this child is born,' she confided. 'When that good-for-nothing see her with a big head, he think it's because his enemy put bad medicine on the horn of his cow.

'I tell him it's all rubbish,' she said, looking at Enoch. 'He won't listen to me. But that bastard go run away and sign up by the Labour Bureau. The white baas send him to the mines. Now I only got the Lord to look after my five children.'

'Your man sounds a bit like bad medicine,' Redemptus said, offering her a piece of his bread. 'I hope he sends you money.'

'Why do you think I spend my last sixpence on a bus, hey? I come to see the baas commissioner – if he know anything about my husband. But the clerk in there tell me the baas don't have time to waste. He said it's us women who chase the men away to the mines.

'So I come out here and the Portuguese baas give me putu and amasi for free. I ask those boys over there if they see my husband in the mines, but they too busy asking for jobs. All they say is, "Hard lines you witch, a man is after a new wife when he leave his village." We got no men around here any more – only tsotsis who fight women.'

Redemptus reached into his pocket and pulled out a ten-shilling note. 'Buy some food for the children,' he said. 'Be glad your husband got work and maybe he send you something.'

'What do I do with such a stupid husband?' she asked. 'For the last few months he don't send me a single postal order. Last year I get something every month,' she said, counting off the good months on her fingers.

She told the strangers that her daughter should have been walking by now. 'Ntombi,' she said, stroking the child's head, 'she crawls everywhere. The child is naughty – the child pick up ringworm just like that. She likes red clay and when I'm not there to smack her hands, she eat it.'

Charity Ntuli lifted Ntombi onto the table and showed Redemptus the child's head and her body covered with gentian violet, which the district nurse applied generously every week.

'The ringworm is alive and move around her body,' Charity said, 'and it find places everywhere – look at this new one,' she said, placing her hand on Ntombi's protruding stomach.

She told them that the district nurse blamed Ntombi's fingernails for the spread of the ringworm, and when she took the child to the clinic the nurse tied a sock around each of the child's hands.

'Nurse Elizabeth tell me her brain isn't growing normal because the water push down on it. But look, you can see she's clever.'

Redemptus had previously seen children with water on the brain and knew that no amount of care could reduce the size of Ntombi's head, as might have been possible with a baby's stomach distended by lack of food. Years ago children such as Ntombi would have been flung from the nearest cliff or left to the hyenas. Clearly, Charity loved her daughter. He talked to Ntombi whose bright eyes responded to the uneven timbre of his voice.

If Redemptus had doubts about his own abilities, he had none about the power of the Lord Jesus Christ who worked through him.

Redemptus pushed the jam tins out of the way and asked Charity if he could lay Ntombi on the table. He then passed his hands over Ntombi's body and turned her onto her stomach. He shut his eyes to pray, and when Ntombi turned herself onto her back again, laughing and kicking, her skin was clear and healthy – not a sign of ringworm or scab, only the vivid gentian violet remained. Charity was struck dumb with amazement – and so was Enoch.

Redemptus cradled Ntombi in his hands. He held her gently, while Enoch and the mother watched him shape Ntombi's forehead, the back of her skull and her nose; he then brought her eyes closer together. Enoch was terrified, but continued to photograph what he saw.

'Now take her,' he said to Charity Ntuli, who was slumped in a state of shock. 'Wash off this blue ointment stuff in the river. In a week you will see she will walk.'

It dawned on Charity that the mighty Lord of Zion was at work through the hands of the boy. She fell to her knees weeping, holding Ntombi to her breast. By this time the young men who had deserted the table had come back to see what the fuss was about, as the child was now silent and the woman had begun to howl. They approached the table brandishing their sticks. Enoch and Redemptus hurried away in the direction of the Tsomo bus depot. Redemptus wiped away his tears on his sleeve and Enoch could not believe what he had just seen.

On the bus back to Cofimvaba, Redemptus reached into his pocket to study his photograph, but could not find his dompas. He turned out each of his pockets, but all he found was a bus ticket and a crumpled pound note. Enoch remembered that Redemptus had left the passbook on the table, next to the jam tin. They had both been so absorbed with Charity Ntuli and her baby that the document had been forgotten.

Because of the trouble the clerk had caused him, Redemptus was reluctant to return to Tsomo for another pass. Had he been intent on securing a replacement, he would have been compelled to travel all the way to Queenstown – because, barely a week later, on a Saturday night, the fires of the amaPondo, the people of the elephant's tooth, had spread to Tsomo, leaving the Labour Bureau, pass office and the Portuguese tearoom in ruins. Only Fraser's Scottish Trading Store remained unscathed, although the *Kokstad Advertiser* reported that the store had been liberated of its entire supply of Parker fountain pens and bottles of blue ink.

Following Enoch's return to Cape Town, Polycarp wrote to him that Redemptus had discovered that he had no cause to make the journey to Queenstown. His passbook had been in safe hands all along. After the boys' departure Charity Ntuli noticed the document on the table. She rushed in hot pursuit of Redemptus, but the Cofimvaba bus had already left. That was when she decided to return the passbook to its owner.

Dear Enoch

I very much enjoyed your company on the journey from Cape Town. My apologies for neglecting you during your last week at Cofimvaba, although I was pleased that you and Redemptus got on so well. He left here rather abruptly in the company of a strange man called Apostle Zebulon Mtetwa, who told us that Redemptus performed a miracle in Tsomo. You didn't tell me about it and you know how we Catholics love miracles.

Speaking of which, I went to see Sister Deduch at the school and put in a word for you. She said that they would be delighted to have you at St Dominic's, although she would first like to have a look at your last school report – so send her a copy if you haven't changed your mind. It would be great to have you nearby. I could see you in Tsomo whenever I need a break. Don't allow Dries or your parents to dissuade you. Had I listened to my parents, I would've been punching tickets on a train. Don't forget that hiding behind the walls of Wepener and sticking to the Cape Flats can really limit the view. It's only for a year and will give you a wider view of South Africa. However, what you do with your life is your decision. As for your writing, I wish you the best.

You're lucky not to be trying to write here at the moment – a huge crew of workmen have descended on the compound and all I hear is sawing, hammering, cement mixers and loud voices from early morning until sunset. (Even Khotso has abandoned his house for the peace of a hut some distance away.) I envy you and your grandfather sitting in the cool silence of Wepener. Dries and Alison must be back by now – what news of Kenny Parker? Please let me know. Since you missed the whole Apostle and Redemptus saga, I have attached a piece I have written about it and hope you will find it of interest. But don't judge it too harshly – remember, I'm a poet. Give my best to Oupa Hans and to the rest of our friends at Wepener.

Your friend,
Polycarp

The first Redemptus knew of the whereabouts of his dompas came barely a week after the events in Tsomo when the Chief Apostle of the Church of King George Save Zion for the Master ordered a few of his most trusted followers to join him and Charity Ntuli on a pilgrimage to Khotso's compound, at the address inscribed on the flyleaf of Redemptus's passbook. Chief Apostle Zebulon Mtetwa, a Zulu who had come to the Transkei to reap a rich harvest of souls among his Xhosa brothers, had learned about the healing of Mrs Ntuli's daughter, for whom he had offered up prayers in the past. There was no doubt in his mind that a miracle had taken place, for Ntombi had suddenly become a beautiful baby.

The district nurse, however, held other views. Sister Patience Tsele had always insisted that it would only be a matter of time before Ntombi died. She was proved wrong when Charity Ntuli turned up at the clinic two days before her usual weekly appointment with a healthy child who could not be restrained from crawling around the waiting room. The nurse said that Redemptus was a sorcerer, while the district surgeon in Kokstad, well acquainted with native superstitions, in public agreed with the nurse's claims of sorcery, but in private declared the business a miracle. He dismissed the nurse's accusation that Ntombi had died and Mrs Ntuli had stolen somebody else's child. Traces of gentian violet were still visible on her body. The doctor decided to forget the matter. Not so with the district nurse.

'Sorcery and witchcraft must be stamped out if my people are going to prosper.'

Charity insisted that she had witnessed the miracle. She said that the Spirit of the Lord Jesus worked through the hands of Redemptus, and that her little girl had been healed. Every Zionist now knew the name of Redemptus as the members of the Apostle's congregation had spread the word of the healing throughout the Transkei.

It was for this reason that Apostle Zebulon Mtetwa had walked thirty-five miles across hills and erosion gullies in his flaming robes, wearing on his back the mane of a lion killed by five men and carrying a caged dove signifying the Holy Spirit on his way to Khotso's compound. His purpose was to order the young prophet to leave the heathen kraal and share his medicine with God's chosen people. Four seamstresses, who in the course of their journey had shifted the weight of the Singer sewing machine from one head to another, accompanied the Apostle. They brought with them bolts of taffeta, satin, muslin and orange sheeting. The Apostle was in no doubt that he was to return with the boy, Redemptus. However, he had taken precautions and had brought along his isanusi, a frail old woman trained in the art of smelling out witches.

Despite her astonishment at the arrival of such an unusual and colourful party, Nohlwandle directed the seamstresses to a rondawel where they set up their sewing machine. Redemptus's presence was required so that the women could measure him for a coat fit for a prophet. He came running from his room, his eyes darting from one person to the other. Charity Ntuli threw her arms around him and told him she had found his passbook.

'The Lord tell me to bring it back to you.'

'Hawu Bantu!' Redemptus exclaimed. 'It took a lot of people to carry such a small book.'

Redemptus was bewildered when Charity took out a tape measure. He stood by while she called out the measurements to a woman who wrote them down on a sheet of paper.

'A prophet must wear sandals with his coat of many colours,' Charity announced when she saw his polished shoes and bright green socks. 'Otherwise he don't look like a man of God.'

A bemused Redemptus told her that he was not a prophet, but no one would listen to him. The seamstresses chalked a pattern on brown paper and the women produced a rough garment, while Charity kept the bobbin supplied with thread.

When it dawned on Redemptus that he was being prepared for yet another role, he began to despair. Even though he was an orphan from a minor Zulu clan, Khotso had welcomed him and took him on as his main apprentice. Because the chiefs appreciated his interpretation of their ancestors' wishes, Redemptus had prospered in a remarkably short time and his herd of cattle had increased to the extent that Khotso had advised him to sell some to conserve the pasture.

The needle ploughed on through the material, shifting from one seam to another and only halting when Charity changed the colour of the thread on the bobbin. The isanusi had not taken her eyes off Redemptus for a moment, while the mountain of food delivered on trays lay uneaten on a table.

Having accosted Nohlwandle near the main house, the Apostle demanded an immediate audience with Khotso.

'I must see your husband now, now,' he insisted, 'to discuss the terms of Redemptus joining my people.'

'Khotso is in a meeting, Apostle Mtetwa. He will see you just now.' Nohlwandle told him that Khotso was shortly expecting two other guests. 'Please be patient,' she pleaded. 'He won't be a minute.'

Zebulon Mtetwa strode about with the impatience of a man kept waiting. He had brought along Redemptus's passbook, to which people had already attributed magical qualities. The Apostle had received many offers of money for the document, and he planned to use it to bargain with Khotso. While he waited, he could not help noticing the splendour of his surroundings and the strange buildings and sculptures in the compound. Though he had lived in a simple hut all his life, he had learned to accept the idea that God could shower his blessings on sinner and believer alike. Mtetwa had never before seen a house like Khotso's with its rough-hewn beams, large windows and white exterior walls, which provided a canvas for the shadows cast by the jacaranda and frangipani trees. The Apostle found a bench in the shade and consoled himself with the thought that it would not profit a man to gain the most beautiful compound in the world if he was certain to lose his soul.

A door opened and Khotso emerged in the company of an old man. The Apostle recognised Ganyile, a Pondo whose hair had been white for so many years that it had begun to turn brown. He had driven the Apostle out of Pondoland on several occasions, saying that Zionism was undermining the struggle against the white oppressor. As the two men walked down the steps, Ganyile wagged a thin finger under Khotso's nose.

'White men?' he said angrily. 'The only thing my people know about them is the boot and the sjambok.'

When the two men unexpectedly came upon the Apostle, Khotso reached out a hand in greeting. Ganyile, however, refused to greet Zebulon Mtetwa. He drew his blanket tightly around him and with a scowl turned away from the Apostle.

'It's because of cowards like you, Mtetwa, that the black man will always walk in the white man's shadow.'

'When you come to stand in front of God and his angels, you won't have any shadow at all. If I were you, chief of Pondos, I'd worry about my soul and not about the white man.'

'Get rid of that traitor, Khotso,' Ganyile shrieked. 'What's all this talk about God in an inyanga's kraal? Have you gone soft in the head?'

Khotso placed his arm around Ganyile's shoulder and, to avert further argument, escorted the Pondo chief to his cart. The dust raised by the wheels of the cart and the hooves of the horses enveloped Ganyile as he rode off, hunched on the seat, his hands on the reins and his mind on the long journey ahead.

Khotso was troubled by his talk with Ganyile, who had told him about the chaos the police had caused in Pondoland and the subsequent riots. Khotso warned Ganyile that the authorities were planning to declare a state of emergency in Pondoland, the Ciskei and the Transkei. Commissioner Brownlee had telephoned Khotso several times to tell him that he had already demanded the assistance of the chiefs in the maintenance of law and order. The news of the commissioner's interference had infuriated Ganyile, who was counting on the uprising to undermine the government.

Khotso had no reason to doubt Ganyile. The old man's passions ran hot, but his facts were accurate and his perception on target. Khotso knew that it would take very little to ignite the situation. He decided to talk to Schoon urgently.

All concern, however, had disappeared from his face by the time he welcomed his new guest.

'Apostle Mtetwa,' he said, 'what a joy to see you. It is a privilege – I can't imagine what has brought you to my kraal. Is your flock hungry? I will see to it that they are fed.'

'Thank you for your generosity, but my flock is hungry for the word of the Lord. That's why I'm here.'

'I regard it as a privilege that you come to my home to hear the word of the Lord. Not everyone who visits me knows the reason. I wish things were as straightforward for my old friend, Ganyile. I was telling him that the white man walks in the black man's shadow and not the other way round; but do you think he listens?'

'You're a busy man, Khotso, and I'm not here to talk about Ganyile.

I'm here about Redemptus. The boy is ready for ministry. He must come labour in the vineyard. It's the Lord's will.'

'Aha, I see you have a vineyard now.'

'I'm not making jokes, Khotso. There's a spirit around,' he said searching the room with his eyes, 'that must always twist and turn words.'

'It takes some doing to know the will of the Lord. What, may I ask, do you want with Redemptus?'

'Right now he's with my handmaidens who are sewing him a prophet's coat even better than my own robe.' The Apostle drew himself up so that Khotso could gain the full effect of his red cloak.

'Well, the boy must have agreed,' said Khotso. 'Apostle, you go into battle well armed with your handmaidens. I can't hold Redemptus here against his will. But when he decides to return, my door will be open for him.'

'I've come to rescue the boy. He will not be a backslider.'

Khotso knew better than to argue with a man dressed in flaming robes. He wasn't pleased about losing Redemptus, but he was sure that the boy would return to Cofimvaba as soon as he discovered the truth about the Zionists.

'Why Redemptus?' he asked.

'You have eyes and ears everywhere and you don't know about the miracle in Tsomo?'

'Apostle,' Khotso answered, 'the boy had nothing to do with the fires.'

'Who said anything about fires? I'm talking about a healing by the Holy Spirit. Charity Ntuli's little girl. Redemptus took the child's head and shaped it like a lump of clay. Even the district surgeon said it was a miracle.'

'No, Redemptus didn't tell me about it. He told me that he had lost his passbook.'

'Here, I brought you his dompas. Lock it away in your safe, because someone will steal it for magic. People think his dompas will heal anyone.'

'And what do you think, Apostle?'

'I tell you it's the Lord that heals. People find it hard to believe in God. They need useless objects to put their faith in.'

The Apostle could barely conceal his delight when Khotso said, 'The boy can go with you. It would give me great pleasure if you and your people would stay the night. That way we can do our part and send Redemptus off with a feast. You must all be hungry and tired. I can arrange for one of my buses to drive you and your women back tomorrow morning. Nohlwandle will see that you are all comfortable. Don't be surprised if she is upset – she loves the boy and I know she will not be happy to see him go. I must go and take care of my other guests.'

Nohlwandle led Mtetwa to one of the rondawels furnished with a comfortable bed made up with clean linen, but she had little to say to the man who had invaded her compound. She encouraged the Apostle to rest until sunset.

She issued instructions about the feast. She loved Redemptus and was worried that the Apostle would exploit him. She felt only sadness when she retired to her own quarters to pray for God's blessing on the boy.

A Most Disobliging Boy

While waiting for Zachaeus, Enoch reviewed the paragraphs he had written. Oupa Hans was in bed, listening to the wireless. He was upset that Polycarp had been meddling with Enoch's writing. Enoch had been barely able to concentrate and he could not suppress his excitement about Dries and Alison's return that evening. However, when Zachaeus stopped the car outside the gate lodge, he told Enoch that, at the last moment, Alison's niece had decided to accompany the family to South Africa and that there would be no room in the car for Enoch.

The flight must have been delayed as it was just before midnight when Enoch heard the car turning up the driveway. He was disappointed that it was too late to greet them. The next morning Oupa Hans told him not to disturb the Schoons and to wait until lunchtime before he went up to the house.

'You've got plenty to keep you busy. What about that landscape sitting in the corner? Gladys came all the way from Gugulethu to give you a painting lesson. The least you can do is finish it.'

'But I've been writing all week, Oupa Hans.'

'So, work on more than one thing at a time. I can't wait for you to go to university.'

For Enoch the morning was turning out to be a nightmare. It was as bad as being at home. He had visited his parents a few days earlier. Initially they had been interested in his visit to Cofimvaba. His father had expressed some regret that he had not gone to Tarkastad, but Enoch had been pleased when he suggested that they go there together during his furlough.

Enoch's mother wanted to look at the photographs and he eagerly spread them out on the table and pointed out who was who. She was curious about Khotso and his wives, and with a disapproving look counted the number of women who surrounded him.

'Khotso's planning to marry another woman. He says it will be his last. Oupa Hans has been invited – and maybe he'll take me along.'

'I should think not,' his mother said. 'Your grandfather can do what he likes, but he's not dragging you along.'

She then saw the photographs of St Dominic's School and things went downhill from there. His mother accused Enoch of going behind her back – and he replied it had been a good enough school for both his father and grandfather. Her eyes then fell on the photograph of Charity Ntuli dipping her breast into the sugar pot.

'What the devil is going on here?'

Enoch didn't even try to explain, but showed her the photographs of Redemptus and Ntombi. He hoped to deflect his mother's attention by telling her about the miracle he had witnessed. She said there were no miracles – although they might have happened in the time of Jesus. All these apparitions and things were just a Catholic plot. Enoch realised that he was getting nowhere, and decided to return to Wepener.

When Enoch joined the family around the swimming pool before lunch, Dries enquired how his writing was getting along.

'Given enough time, even a monkey on a typewriter could turn out a Shakespearean play,' Alison quipped.

'That old chestnut about random theory, darling ...' Dries responded gingerly.

'I am aware of that, silly.' She suddenly got up and left.

'I'm sorry, Enoch – you are going to have to be patient with Alison. She's upset about her niece being here. Caroline is a rather disagreeable girl and it's not going to be easy for any of us. I suppose we'll just have to cope. She hasn't stirred yet – which could be considered a blessing.

'Alison found a great publisher for Kenny Parker's book and, thanks to her father's intervention, Kenny will be released from detention and expelled from South Africa in a few days time. We met up with Mrs Parker and the twins in London and she's thrilled that Kenny will be joining them soon.'

'That's wonderful news. Your trip to London sounds like a real success.'

'It was better than not doing anything at all.'

'But you took a big risk. What a pity Kenny couldn't leave of his own free will.'

'I agree, but he is in no position to pick and choose.'

'What did Alison's father do to convince them?'

'I'm not sure. All I did was to describe the situation to him – then, I suppose, he made a few telephone calls. It's better not to ask. Don't you worry. You'll find out soon enough. I thought you and Polycarp were coming back together.'

'So did I, but he wanted to stay and get things organised; you know what he's like. Khotso is relying on him to do everything. Gumede, his manager, is only interested in making a profit for himself out of the school. I got a lift back with his bank manager who drove over 100 miles per hour all the way to Cape Town without saying a word.'

'I suppose he was one of Khotso's clients.'

'He looks after Khotso's investments. Polycarp wrote to me – he's getting to know more of the local customs. Would you like to read his letter? I've also had the photos developed.'

'Bring them when you come to dinner. There is something I've been meaning to say to you, Enoch, before Alison gets back. The money in the bank belongs to you – no strings attached. When you turn eighteen, you can spend it on going to university or however else you please. I want you to understand that. I have no claim on the money. It was Fanus's inheritance from grandfather Lubbe and now it is yours. So, whatever anybody else says, just ignore them.'

But it was difficult for Enoch to ignore the pressure his mother and father piled on him. If anything, he had begun to feel that he would be much better off without the money. He once heard Mama telling Dowa, 'It's that darned money that gives him a hold over us – it's truly the root of all evil.'

Little did she know that Enoch had been thinking of buying Dowa a brand new Nash – although he feared that the car would probably spend all its time in the garage. For Mama, he had a holiday in Spain in mind. She often said how wonderful it would be to ride on a donkey through the Pyrenees – and with an additional excursion to Barcelona. She had not been on horseback in years. It was something she hankered after.

As Alison and Caroline walked across the lawn to join them at the pool, Enoch was struck by the girl's appearance – short dark hair, her eyes heavily made up and her mouth covered in red lipstick. She was barefoot and wore a mini-skirt and bikini top.

'Caroline, this is Enoch Pretorius, a friend of the family. Enoch, this is my niece, Caroline Fuller,' Alison said.

Enoch got up, but Caroline ignored his hand, fumbled around in a tobacco tin and proceeded to roll a cigarette. Mr Molinieux seemed taken aback when she offered to roll one for him, declining politely. He did not seem pleased either when Caroline called him 'Charlie' and asked for a Bloody Mary with lots of vodka and a splash of Worcestershire sauce.

She blew a cloud of smoke in Enoch's direction and said, 'So you are the boy who can do no wrong. Life must be pretty exciting for you. And what's this "Enoch Pretorius"? A bit of a mouthful, don't you think?'

Enoch was about to say that his namesake had invented the sewing needle and that Pretorius had been pretty hot stuff during the Boer War when Dries intervened and said, 'I think we should go in for some lunch now.'

He took Enoch's arm and led him to the house. Enoch first went into the kitchen to greet the staff and Ou Mevrou Jansen. Hanneli was thrilled to see him and insisted on having her lunch with the grownups, a privilege she had enjoyed at her grandparents' house in England.

'Did you meet the girl?' Clara asked. 'Ou Mevrou Jansen thinks she's going to be a handful.'

Ou Mevrou Jansen just shook her head and gave Enoch a kiss. 'Be careful, my boy,' she said as Mr Molinieux rang the lunch bell. 'Don't let her mislead you.'

'Why is everyone trying to warn me off?' Enoch asked. 'I can look after myself.'

Clara rolled her eyes.

Dries was the only one who seemed lively at the table. Alison had a headache and excused herself halfway through lunch, saying she needed a rest. She took Hanneli along with her. Caroline had a hearty appetite and asked Mr Molinieux for a second helping – although she too excused herself before dessert and said that she was going to catch up on lost sleep. Dries and Enoch finished their lunch in silence. Enoch wanted to ask him about Caroline, but waited for Mr Molinieux to leave the dining room.

'Has Caroline seen a doctor about this mood thing you told me about?'

'She's been seeing one off and on since she was fifteen. Normally this thing does not show until late adolescence. I think it runs in the family – but let's not talk about it. How about a game of tennis?'

'Great idea, Dries, but I'm out of practice,' Enoch replied, grateful for the opportunity to get out into the fresh air. 'But only for an hour. Oupa Hans wants to see me back at the typewriter – and Polycarp sent a quote to inspire me – the words of a woman called Abbess Hildegard von Bingen: "Oh, fragile child of earth, ash of ash, dust of dust, express and write that which thou seest and hearest."

'By the way, Gladys came around and gave me my first private lesson in oils.'

'I'm very pleased to hear that – it will be hard to find a better teacher. I've been collecting her work for years,' Dries replied.

In the thicket beyond the tennis courts, Mfilo threw a stick into the air for Byron and Augusta Leigh, the two ageing cocker spaniels, but the dogs seemed uninterested and came tearing in Enoch's direction as he returned to the gate lodge to change into his tennis clothes.

There was a beautiful, cream-coloured envelope on Oupa Hans's sideboard. It was addressed to Enoch. He turned it over and saw the name 'Mrs Dries Schoon' embossed on the back. He ran his thumb over the letters and immediately felt a sense of foreboding, but there was no need for it. The sheet bore a single quotation from Virginia Woolf: 'If you do not tell the truth about yourself, you cannot tell it about other people.'

'Anything interesting?' Oupa Hans asked as he came in.

'Not really, Oupa. Just a quotation Alison left for me.'

'How strange – now all of a sudden everyone is sending you quotations. First your father, then that Parker man, Polycarp and now Alison. They obviously don't think you can improve your mind on your own. When Alison came around earlier with the dogs she wanted to know if you would like to go for a walk in the woods. I don't know why she left you a note if it was something she could've said to you. And here I thought she was bringing you an invitation to one of those smart parties.

'Don't forget, you've got plenty of work to do. And don't be out on the tennis courts all afternoon – you can do some writing before dinner.'

'I know, Oupa. I'll see Oupa later. Have a look at the last bit I wrote from Polycarp's notes.'

'Wait a minute – what does Polycarp have to do with our story?'

'It's just a little bit of local colour – things I missed seeing.'

'The day that scoundrel teaches you anything about local colour …
You mustn't let him come and interfere. In the end they'll all claim that
it's their story.'

Enoch could sense that Oupa Hans was jealous. Some days it was
Enoch's story, and on other days it was his story.

Hanneli had managed to evade her afternoon nap and was perched
on top of the umpire's chair so that she could get a good view, well out
of the way of the balls. Enoch served a number of aces, but Dries said
his return strokes were at best unpredictable. Byron and Augusta Leigh
were lying in a safe spot in the shade of an overhanging tree.

'Alison sends apologies for leaving the table. She can only take Caroline
in small doses.'

'Oh, it doesn't matter – but thanks, anyway. I missed her when she
came round with the dogs.'

'The dogs can go for a walk whenever they want to. Alison was just
trying to get out of the house for a bit. That girl is a real pest. She's even
scared off all her boyfriends.'

Enoch wondered whether Dries and Alison were going to do something
about Caroline's moods. He could recommend Dr Curry, the man his
mother had taken him to when she got the idea into her head that something was seriously wrong with him and that he needed to have his head
examined. His mother had been threatening to do so for years, but it
was only after she had laid hands on the Cofimvaba photographs and
deemed them sufficient proof of Enoch's affliction that she telephoned
Dr Curry for an urgent appointment.

Enoch had no choice in the matter. He felt embarrassed as Dr Curry
fired indiscreet questions at him in front of his mother. The doctor came
up with an innocuous diagnosis for Enoch: a mild case of anxiety; he
offered to prescribe pills for the boy. His mother stopped the doctor as
he drew his prescription pad nearer.

'Since when can you treat a personality disorder with pills, Dr Curry?
It's not like it's the flu, or something. The real trouble is that Enoch thinks
he's too big for the strap. He goes to the Transkei for a few weeks and

suddenly he starts talking about miracles and taking snaps of a naked woman. Just look at these … I warned his grandfather.'

Enoch had been answering inane questions all afternoon, and only near the end did Dr Curry ask him whether he preferred to be addressed in English or Afrikaans.

'English would be fine, doctor,' his mother replied for him.

'I'd prefer Afrikaans, Dr Curry.'

'Very well, Enoch. It is good to hear that people still enjoy speaking Afrikaans.'

Having said that, the doctor continued to discuss Enoch's situation in English, as though he were not present. Enoch had done everything possible to put off the appointment with the psychiatrist. However, when his father told him that a talk with Dr Curry could do him no harm, he'd consented.

From Dr Curry's window, Enoch could see the white walls of the Valkenberg mental hospital shimmering in the afternoon sun.

'Enoch says he will only go to church when he feels like it, doctor.'

'Mrs Pretorius, there's nothing wrong with your son's personality. He suffers from a common anxiety disorder – and I can give him some treatment for it. As for the photographs, to me they appear to be perfectly innocent. And no one should make him go to church. Some day he may change his mind.'

'Yes, when it's too blinking late!'

Enoch had not heard his mother use such language before. Why couldn't Dr Curry analyse Mama and Dowa instead, he wondered? Then the doctor would realise that Enoch was not the one who needed pills. There was nothing the matter with him.

'Neither does your son suffer from obsessions or delusions. He seems to be a perfectly healthy boy. Do you have any strong feelings about anything in particular, Enoch?'

'What about all the pedagogues, parents, politicians, police and perverts who pretend they have the God-given right to run our lives? There's no getting away from any of them. Isn't there a pill for their disease? That would do us all a world of good.'

Enoch had knocked the wind out of his mother's sails and she gasped feebly, 'Did you hear what the child just said, Dr Curry?'

'I certainly did.'

'That's what we have to endure day after day. His poor father works his hands to the bone and then the child has the audacity to tell his friends, "Dowa doesn't work – he's a teacher." He likes to wind us up – talking nonsense about the Hindu religion …'

What Enoch's mother really meant was that she had come upon the Bhagavad Gita on his bookshelf when she had no business being in his room. On more than one occasion Enoch had seen her nosing about under the pretext of tidying up.

'He's a most disobliging boy.'

'This is what we call "growing up", Mrs Pretorius. In our jargon, we call it a "process of individuation". And Enoch is right, you know – had there been a pill I could prescribe for the insanity of our country, I would gladly have done so.'

'Please don't encourage the boy, Dr Curry. Things are bad enough as it is.'

Enoch's mother could see that she was not getting anywhere with the doctor. Not once had she convinced him to agree with her. Enoch sensed that the session was drifting into dangerous waters when she suddenly got up and said, 'If this conversation goes on for much longer, doctor, we'll all end up in Valkenberg.'

'With respect, I think you are wrong, Mrs Pretorius. I am a parent myself and would be proud to have a son like yours. He is a well-balanced and capable young man. If you want me to prescribe anything for his anxiety disorder, please let me know.'

'*Anxiety disorder*, my foot! Enoch, if you are not prepared to take our advice, there is nothing your father or I can do.' With a determined look his mother turned to Dr Curry. 'Enoch's not the one who needs the pills around here!'

Lobola Causes Many Lawsuits

Dear Enoch

I've spoken to Dries on the telephone, and it seems as if he's had some success with Kenny Parker's problem. Even the *Kokstad Advertiser* ran an article on his expulsion from the country. Whatever Dries managed to do is a mystery to me, as it must be to you – although I think Alison's father might have some influence. The important thing is that it has worked for Kenny, which is great. I read Kenny's manuscript and it has inspired me to write some prose – not for publication, of course. I don't want to put my oar in your boat, but I would appreciate your comments on my efforts.

A few days after you left Cofimvaba in a hurry, Andrew Gumede turned up in a huff. He told me that Khotso treats him worse than a slave and warned me to stand up for my rights. He asked me to accompany him to the kraal of a local chief where he was to conclude bride price negotiations for Khotso's wife-to-be. These negotiations had already been dragging on for months as the chief would not agree to a price for his daughter.

As I feel responsible for sending you home early and depriving you of the experience, I am sending you a description of a very interesting visit to Chief Letlaka's kraal. By all means, adapt it for your book, although you might consider it a digression from what you have set out to do. I look forward to reading your completed manuscript some time in the future and will write again if anything interesting crops up here. Give my best regards to your Oupa Hans.

Your friend,
Polycarp

Andrew Gumede's left leg was a full two inches shorter than his right, but he refused to wear an orthopaedic shoe with a built-up sole to compensate for this discrepancy. Instead, he had developed a gait that caused his body to swing from side to side, as this attracted the eye to his immense torso. Under his arms he invariably carried a two-volume compendium of the *Laws of the Union of South Africa*, published long before the profusion of amendments, of which he could not be bothered to keep track.

Business at his funeral parlour had improved greatly since he had purchased the second-hand Austin Princess hearse from a white competitor. The silver-grey hearse, a 1956 model, had been well cared for and polished daily to maintain its high gloss. Continuing riots in Cato Manor had allowed Andrew to travel south to Cofimvaba, as the authorities had suspended weekend funerals for an indefinite period to prevent mourners from turning these occasions into political rallies.

It was during one of these weekends that he had responded yet again to Khotso's summons to come to the Transkei to conclude negotiations with Chief Letlaka, whose eldest daughter Khotso proposed to marry. Upon arrival at Cofimvaba, Gumede was taken to a rondawel to wash off the dust after his journey. While drying his hands he noticed the form of a man clothed in scarlet asleep on the bed. On the floor was a lion skin and a caged dove. He hurried off to see Khotso. Nohlwandle opened the door and laughed with pleasure to see Khotso's old friend. She showed him into her husband's study.

'Last night, my dear Khotso, I slept in the kraal of the Pope. And what is the first thing I find on my bed when I arrive here? A woman? No, your hospitality has never extended that far. I find a man in red petticoats sprawled across my bed. Could he be our old friend, Zebulon Mtetwa, who fled his clan in disgrace and then moved south to pull a fast one on the Xhosas? He might be one of us, but we Zulus are far too clever for his kind.'

'You can never be too clever to avoid being conned, my friend.'

In addition to the marriage negotiations, Khotso wanted Gumede to finalise Polycarp's contract. The bhunga had decided that he merited a higher salary and the necessary amendments to the contract had to be made.

'I really don't understand you, Khotso,' Andrew began. 'Forgive me if I offend you. You want to educate your children, yet Nohlwandle tells me that you have allowed Redemptus to join that madman who calls himself an apostle. And it was me,' Gumede continued, thumping his chest for emphasis, 'who brought that boy to your attention. He's worth quite a bit.'

'Redemptus is not a child. I let him go because he needs to learn a few things. Let the boy find out for himself about the Apostle ...'

'That man is a fraud who preys on the people. At least tell him about Mtetwa,' Gumede pleaded.

'Perhaps it is the will of the Lord, as the Apostle said. I can't stand in the boy's way.'

'You must be going mental – and what's all this I hear about miracles? If there is any truth to it, the boy should be kept here. All I'm saying is that a man must look after his investments with care.'

'The boy isn't an investment. Let's discuss what you came for. Is the lobola contract ready?'

'Everything is in order.'

'Excellent. Then go and see Chief Letlaka straight away and get his thumbprint on the contract. Why don't you take Polycarp along with you and introduce him to the chief? He might make an impression on that snake. Meantime, I'll ask the herdsmen to separate the lobola cattle so that the vet can inspect them. I don't want any talk about my beasts being diseased.'

'I can't hang around long – I have to get back to Cato Manor. On Friday night I'm judging this year's ballroom competition.'

'Just make the arrangements.'

Andrew Gumede gathered the legal documents together into a folder. 'I hope the negotiations with Letlaka are not going to drag on. I can't stand the man. Some chiefs think because the government spoils them with white bread and sugar they can get any price for their daughters. I've only got one wife – and yet, all these years I have cast nets only for you.'

Khotso laughed heartily and placed his arm around his friend's shoulders. 'You cast my nets wide enough for yourself also.'

'You and your many wives – you should take a rest, my friend.'

'I will, in good time. But tell me, how can you organise ballroom competitions when people are being shot in the township? I heard that fourteen more have been killed.'

'Khotso, my brother, you are beginning to think like a white man. In Cato Manor we bury people every day – when the government allows us – and a ballroom competition comes only once a year. Do you think a few policemen are going to stop us? If you want to see real rioting, just get that prime minister friend of yours to ban our temperance ballroom competition. Dancing is a good thing. You should know, you were once an Arthur Murray champion.'

Khotso did not like being reminded of the old days. 'Ah well, Andrew, maybe I'm becoming a little old-fashioned. My dancing days are long gone.'

'Not until the coffin lid comes down.'

'Be off to Letlaka. Later we'll be giving Polycarp an official welcome, so make sure you two are back in time.'

With Polycarp in the passenger seat, Andrew Gumede departed to conclude the business of adding yet another woman to Khotso's growing clan. He parked the Austin Princess as close as possible to the spot where he had hidden the Oude Meester bottle – had he gone for a drink to Beki's shebeen at the edge of Cofimvaba, Khotso would certainly have heard about it. Gumede decided to leave the hearse at the side of the road and the two walked the remaining mile or so to Chief Letlaka's kraal.

Letlaka had been converted to Christianity in his youth and was proving to be a difficult customer. Although he had agreed in principle, he was reluctant to give his daughter in marriage to Khotso. He was married to only one wife and she had presented him with several beautiful daughters, and now the Anglican priest had taken to warning the chief about eternal damnation should he allow even one of his daughters to be married into Khotso's family of heathens.

Gumede was not surprised that a Christian chief would consider giving his daughter in marriage to a heathen, especially in view of the material benefits that would accrue to the family of Khotso's bride. What he knew was that Letlaka was in the government's pocket; even the newspapers were onto him. Perhaps it was for this reason that Letlaka maintained that he had no need to marry off one of his daughters to Khotso. However, with the help of some skilful negotiations, Andrew had persuaded him to see the benefits of such a match. But the last minute interference by the priest, as well as greed, had thrown the negotiations off track.

As they walked along the dusty cattle path, Gumede hoped that he could reason with Letlaka, or at the very least appeal to his vanity. He did not know any chief who was proud of being in the government's pay. When a chief returned to his kraal with sacks of government sugar and samp and a few head of cattle on the back of a rickety lorry, it was hard to pretend that he had earned these things with his own hands. More often than not, his people would wonder what he had pledged to the abelungu in return. Gumede hoped to convince Letlaka that acceptance of Khotso's offer was preferable to competing with other chiefs for the scraps tossed at their feet by the government.

At every two hundred paces Polycarp was bemused to see Gumede revive his spirits with a gulp from the Oude Meester bottle. In fact, Gumede was quite inebriated by the time they crossed the last hill and the chief's kraal came into view. The sight of Letlaka's paltry herd reassured Gumede that he should be able to make the owner see reason. The flags encircling the kraal proclaimed to the visitors that Letlaka's wife and daughters had harvested the mealies and brewed the new utywala. Looking out across a deep-green stand of mealies, Gumede deduced that the chief must own a water pump. The tall stalks, large ears of corn and the deep-red tassels attested to the fecundity of the soil. But what he saw led him to fear that Letlaka might not be persuaded by a sweetener, and as he came closer even the herd of oxen appeared considerably larger and healthier than at a distance. Gumede steadied himself with a last gulp of brandy.

The chief sat under a bluegum tree, gazing out over his fields. Late blossoms of the wild peach trees lent their subtle fragrance to the air, and tall hedges around the kraal kept the breeze from the curling flames over which the women stirred huge pots.

'How is it possible to charm a despicable snake like Letlaka?' Gumede asked Polycarp, after which he flung the empty brandy bottle into a mealie field. 'What does Khotso know? The man sits in his dispensary all day long and gets us to do the dirty work.'

As they entered the enclosure, they heard the singing of timorous children's voices. The elders sat around Chief Letlaka in a semicircle and passed a calabash to him when he indicated his thirst. Gumede did not immediately approach the chief; instead, placing the two-volume law books on the ground at his feet, he reached under his blanket into the pocket of his khaki shorts and drew out a pair of spectacles. He beckoned to an elder and handed the glasses to him, telling him that they were a gift to Letlaka from Khotso that would bring wisdom to the chief as their former owner had been a lawyer. Chief Letlaka had spent most of the afternoon drinking the freshly brewed utywala, and in a friendly manner he suggested that the Zulu approach him for discussions.

Chairs were ordered for Gumede and Polycarp, and they sat down at the edge of the circle. Gumede perceived that Khotso's name had made the usual impression on the chief, and he confidently got up to join the inner circle. Rumour had it that Letlaka had been about to send his daughter off to work as a maid in East London when the prospect of marriage to Khotso had presented itself. Andrew Gumede knelt and was then invited to sit down and address the chief, who was adamant that he would conduct his own negotiations rather than leave them in the hands of some untrustworthy relation.

'The government,' Andrew said in greeting, 'they look good after the chief, hey?' The elders readily agreed with the Zulu's assessment of their benefactor's largesse. Having obtained this acknowledgement, Andrew manoeuvred himself behind the chief, took hold of a roll of fat at the nape of his neck and repeated, 'The government, they look good after your chief, hey?' The elders nodded their heads, although they became increasingly suspicious of this line of cross-examination. By what authority did the Zulu grab hold of the neck of their chief as though he were a dog? Weren't the lobola negotiations the purpose of his visit?

Emboldened by his success, Andrew walked around to face the chief and pushed his forefinger into Letlaka's midriff. 'Look at this impressive stomach. It must've taken the harvests of ten mealie fields for the chief to grow such a stomach.'

Chief Letlaka could not contain his pleasure. Not even his imbongi had admired him in this fashion before. He encouraged the children to sing a song of welcome and ordered the calabash passed to the Zulu, who drank deeply. When the people saw their chief laughing because he was proud of the legend of his stomach, they joined him in his mirth. Letlaka's entire body trembled in waves and the false teeth given to him by Andrew on a previous visit clattered over his short bursts of breath.

All laughter stopped, however, when Andrew reached for the roll of fat behind the chief's neck and attempted to hoist him from the seat. 'It must've taken the hindquarters of at least six beasts,' he called bravely into the shocked silence, 'to grow the neck of your chief as thick as a bull's.'

To avert any further praise of the chief's body, the elders rose and led Andrew Gumede to the women's quarters to introduce him to Khotso's bride-to-be. As he left the circle, he repeated, 'The government looks good after the chief – but Khotso can do much more to help Letlaka and his people.'

Her father's claim had not been without foundation; the young girl presented to Gumede was beautiful beyond expectation. He saw before him a modest young woman able to meet her responsibilities as one of Khotso's wives. Bongiwe's beauty reassured him that he would leave Cofimvaba with a sizeable reward, and this engendered a spirit of generosity when he approached the chief to finalise the delicate matter of lobola.

The chief and his elders sat in silence as the calabash was passed from hand to hand. Letlaka's praise singer, seething at Gumede for having charmed the chief so agreeably, came forward to recite his chief's praises. But before he could begin, the Zulu jumped in ahead of him with unexpected agility and announced to the startled gathering that he, Gumede of the Nkandla forest, the son of a long line of praise singers, would laud the accomplishments of so noble a chief as Letlaka. The chief perched his new spectacles on the edge of his nose to gain a better view.

Chief Letlaka will devour the white man's fields
and drink his brandy; his seed will be so plentiful
that the Great Bull will supplant the white man.
When he is old – and has nothing but a kaross for warmth –
his many daughters will honour him and provide for their father.
Chief Letlaka, great chief, who can stop a thousand
assegais with his bare chest,
eagle that soars skywards to talk with the ancestors,
whose wisdom tells him to use the four wheels of the government
to save the tyres of his own lorry,
bull that fills the bellies of the poor with milk,
son of mighty Xhosa chiefs

whose faithful wife grinds the mealies,
roasts his meat and works his fields,
maker of beautiful daughters –
one day he will sit in heaven with his Creator.

Andrew Gumede bowed low before him, and Chief Letlaka called for a freshly provisioned calabash.

'How is it possible,' he demanded of his elders, 'tell me, how is it possible for a stranger to know all these things about a chief?'

They shrugged their shoulders and maintained an insolent silence. Letlaka raised himself from his chair and stood before them. 'How is it that my elders know nothing? How is it that the thing they do best is empty the chief's calabash and eat the fat parts of his meat?' He dismissed their replies with an impatient hand and thanked the stranger, who knew without having known, and had given his existence substance.

Chief Letlaka enquired after Khotso's health. Gumede was prepared for this and read to him the certificate of good health issued by the district surgeon in Kokstad. Letlaka had heard that Redemptus, a favourite among his people, had been replaced by a white teacher who knew nothing about the people's medicine, and asked for an explanation.

'Honoured chief,' Gumede responded, still breathless after the effort of recitation, 'this man, Van Wyk, has come to us as a teacher. Here he is. But Redemptus will not be far away. The Apostle does not own him. Your people can take a bus or walk when they want to go and see him.'

'Why does Khotso need a white man for a teacher?'

This question had been on Gumede's mind for some days. 'Khotso is taking his children out of the government schools and he needs a first-class teacher for his children, the grandchildren of chiefs, so that they can become university professors.'

'And what about the children of my clan? I also want a teacher,' Letlaka demanded.

'That will be up to the chief's daughter. If the chief will allow her to marry Khotso, she will have the opportunity to put his request to the bhunga of the abafazi.'

Chief Letlaka then reminded Gumede that he had been raised a simple Christian. 'Like all God-fearing Christians, I married only one wife and

God has blessed this marriage with beautiful daughters. Giving away one of his daughters is a painful thing for a chief to do.'

'It is a painful thing to do, nkosi yam,' Gumede agreed, and added (while wondering what he could offer as imvulamlomo, a little something to grease the wheels), 'but there is medicine for such pain.'

'Father Shepstone has been to my kraal to warn me against such a sinful match. He says that the lobola cows will fall sick or walk back to their old kraal.'

'That too, is painful, nkosi, but it is a lie.'

'God in his wisdom showed me that I must sacrifice my beloved daughter in marriage to a heathen. If a Christian woman joins Khotso's kraal, he and his family will be saved from the devil's hell.'

These considerations had helped shape Letlaka's decision. 'For my beautiful, eldest daughter, Bongiwe, I will ask for fifty of Khotso's beasts – the dairy kind, each one in milk and certified by the Boer vet from the Transvaal. The cattle will stay here to make sure she is happy and well treated in Khotso's kraal. Fifty isn't a lot to ask from a rich man like Khotso – a man who got his money from Oom Paul with the deep pockets.'

Gumede, who had previously decided on fifty head, felt obliged to bring the chief down to forty-five, and the chief, who had said fifty in order to obtain forty, consulted with his elders.

Chief Letlaka returned to Gumede with an agreement for forty-five head of cattle before the Zulu could trick him. However, something positive had emerged from the negotiations. With the excitement of the occasion, Letlaka had forgotten about the new lorry promised by Khotso and not one of the elders dared raise the subject for fear of upsetting the chief and losing his privileged place around the fire.

Andrew produced a bottle of India ink from the pocket of his shorts so that he could return to the compound with a firm promise and a thumbprint appended to the antenuptial contract. He searched through one of the law books to find the contract he had previously drawn up, unfolded the sheet and read the document to Letlaka in both English and Xhosa. He explained to the chief and his elders the finer legal points of customary law, and then entered the number of cattle agreed upon.

Letlaka called his imbongi over, showed him the contract and asked him to verify the number and type of cattle on which they had agreed.

The imbongi reluctantly assured Letlaka that everything in the contract was just as the Zulu had explained. The chief pressed his thumb onto the inkpad and, with Gumede's help, affixed his print to the bottom of the page. Gumede signed the document on behalf of Khotso and then asked a woman to bring some beef fat. Dipping Letlaka's inked thumb into the rendered suet he cleaned the chief's finger of all traces of India ink with his handkerchief.

The Eviction Notice

It was one of the most glorious days of summer. Wepener sat like a jewel in a setting of lawns, gardens and trees. The wind was calm, and Enoch had decided to take the easel outdoors to work in the shade when Oupa Hans stopped him.

'And where do you think you're going?'

'Outside, Oupa Hans – to work out there.'

'Not so fast, my boy. You stay right here. I have never seen anyone so easily distracted. That Caroline girl will come down and disturb you – just like she did yesterday. Next she'll also demand to have a look at what you're writing. And I don't like her rolling those cigarettes and smoking around here. Before we know it, you'll be doing the same thing.'

Oupa Hans whistled for the dogs and took them off in the direction of the woods. Enoch watched him walk briskly towards the rocky path beyond the woods, despite his unsteady legs. Byron and Augusta Leigh knew that the holes and crevices up there hid an array of smells and secrets. He was walking towards the part of the estate that backed onto the mountain where he had once seen a secretary bird making short shrift of a cobra. Oupa had once also found a bruinkapel which one of the dogs must have killed and left on his front door mat. This had caused consternation at Wepener, as the staff knew that the cobra's mate would be drawn to the mat to keep vigil and take revenge on anyone who approached. It had taken Dries some time to persuade them that this was a myth, but not before each room and piece of furniture at the gate lodge had been inspected. Oupa often joked that his cottage had never had such a thorough cleaning.

Enoch was sure that Oupa Hans was right about Caroline coming by. Oupa thought that she was making a nuisance of herself, and perhaps he was right. She had been there the day before, wearing hotpants, and neither he nor his grandfather had quite known where to look as she stretched herself out on the couch and filled the ashtray with cigarette butts. While she rolled another cigarette, she had casually asked, 'How many children do you think this Khotso man has?'

'More than a hundred – that's the count for the new school,' Enoch replied, having told her about Polycarp's latest preoccupation.

'Gosh, Khotso must be a hard worker – that's many more than the number of kids old Charles I had, even with the scandalous goings-on at his court.'

Enoch had forced himself not to think about Caroline all morning; even the mention of her name distracted him. He had promised his grandfather that he would complete the next chapter before he went home. His mother was waiting to take him to Stuttafords the following day to buy the long-awaited suit for Christmas. She had mentioned putting the whole thing off until Enoch's birthday, but he thought this to be an idle threat aimed at making him toe the line. Not that this was likely to scare him, as he had his own secret store of well-tailored suits.

What if Caroline really wanted to read what he had written? Enoch thought that he might allow her to persuade him. She may have been kicked out of school, but she was a very clever girl. And who knows? Her grandfather got Kenny Parker's book to a publisher, so there might be hope for his. Oupa was right, Enoch thought, it required discipline to keep sitting in front of the typewriter, and at that moment he found it virtually impossible to fix his mind on the writing. No sooner had he sat down than he imagined a gentle knock at the door. Once or twice he actually got up to look, but soon realised that he was fooling himself.

He tried to concentrate on the life Redemptus had ahead of him as a disciple of the Apostle – and tried to picture Khotso's marriage ceremony at Cofimvaba, to which Oupa had been invited.

Enoch had still not given up hope of attending the Catholic school at Tsomo. He had sent off his school report and was waiting to hear from Sister Deduch, who would only consider his admission once she received the 'full blessing' of his parents. In his most recent letter to Enoch, Polycarp had said that he had gone back to see Sister Deduch about him, but she had shown more interest in offering Polycarp a teaching post.

Whatever his religious inheritance may have been, Polycarp did not impress Enoch as someone who would attend mass regularly. His Catholicism seemed to Enoch no more than an accident of birth, something he might return to later in life once his restlessness and rebellion had deserted him.

Eventually there was a timid knock at the door. To hide his eagerness, Enoch took his time to gather the completed pages and put them out of sight before opening the door. It was not Caroline. Oupa Hans had a surprise visitor. It took Enoch a moment to recognise Idriss Salie, the tailor, looking like a broken old man.

'Is Mr Pretorius home?' he asked – Enoch could barely hear his voice.

'I beg Mr Salie's pardon … Is there anything I can do?'

'I have to see Mr Pretorius now, now.'

'Oupa Hans is somewhere out there in the woods with the dogs. Please have a seat and I'll go and find him.'

Enoch eventually spotted Oupa with the dogs. 'Is there no peace for an old man? I go out for a few minutes and you take the opportunity to jump up from the table. Get your work done.'

'Oupa Hans is worse than my teachers.'

'Someone has to be.'

'Oupa's got a visitor – Mr Salie. He doesn't look too happy.'

Oupa Hans took Enoch's arm. He was breathless and struggled along. 'Well, let's get back then. These dogs are going to be the death of me.'

Oupa had been horrified at the foreign names Alison had given the dogs, and had simply called them 'honde'. Oupa used to say, 'The English treat human beings like dogs and dogs like human beings.' He undoubtedly loved Enoch, but Hond 1 and Hond 2 were high on his list of favourites. They were from the same litter. The vet had neutered Byron some time ago and there had been no puppies. Augusta Leigh had been spayed soon after she had come into heat for the first time and packs of marauding dogs had stood baying outside the walls of Wepener.

'Can't think what the hang Idriss Salie wants. He hasn't come here before.'

'Maybe he has a Christmas present for Oupa Hans.'

'Do you think so? Was he carrying anything?'

'Not that I saw, Oupa Hans. He just looked upset.'

'Well, with that new girl around, who isn't upset these days? Strange – I'm not expecting him. Don't go so fast, my boy. Idriss Salie is an easy-going kind of person. He's funny and makes me laugh – nobody tells him what to do. Maybe the bookies are after him. People get jealous when they see others making money. Look at Khotso – if his enemies were not so afraid of him, they would have run him out of business long ago. They know the white man is under his thumb and that's terrifying magic …'

'Maybe Mr Salie needs a loan.'

'He's never asked me for money before. Maybe it's that university thing.'

With all the exciting events in Enoch's life, he had forgotten about the incident. Oupa Hans had shown him an article in the *Post* about a Fakir and Kalifa display the tailor had helped the poet I.D. du Plessis organise at the University of Cape Town. What had started out as a demonstration of traditional Malay culture had ended up as the first ever happening in South Africa. On a stage smouldering coals had been poured into a sandpit and levelled with a rake; men in red fezzes and robes walked on the coals, while others pierced their half-naked bodies with swords. Even before the cultural display had ended, rock bands performing under strobe lights had taken over the stage. As a member of the organising committee Mr Salie was held at least partly to blame for the wave of immorality that had subsequently swept the campus. The student leader responsible for subverting the event in Jameson Hall had fled the country to find refuge at an Oxford college.

Mr Salie was now in hot water with the university authorities and the Muslim Judicial Council. He had even had a lengthy visit from Special Branch. Such accusations against an old man were likely to set anyone's nerves on edge. Du Plessis, the poet, denied any knowledge of the affair.

'Idriss, what a pleasure to see you – what a surprise.'

'I'm sorry always to be a nuisance, Hannes …'

'Enoch, a pot of tea please. What do you mean a nuisance, Idriss? You're not here for the names of the …?'

'What names?'

'You know … Khotso hasn't sent them yet.'

'Horse racing is the last thing on my mind.'

'Then this must be serious. What's the matter?'

'Curse the Boer!'

'Not so fast – the Boer will be his own undoing.'

'I will curse evil wherever it hides and I will curse it a thousand times.'

'Hey, Enoch, Mr Salie won't eat those biscuits – they're not halal.'

'I'm sorry, Mr Salie.'

'Your grandfather is full of nonsense. A biscuit or two won't make any difference.'

'Maybe Mr Salie would like something more filling?'

'With my stomach, Enoch? You must be joking. Lucky for me I can alter my clothes when necessary – if I can find a matching bit of cloth. All day long, that woman of mine really spoils me; she brings me koeksisters and samoosas. Nice cup of tea, Enoch. Your oupa tells me what a good tea boy you are.'

Enoch winced. 'It's not as though I hope to make a career of it, Mr Salie.'

'You never know, my boy, you never know. It might come in handy one day.'

'The boy is sensitive, Idriss'

'Well, Hannes, I didn't mean any harm. There was that line I learned in school: "They also serve who only stand and wait." It was our school motto and after all those years it just came back to me like a flash as a lesson for Enoch. Your Mr Salie does have a brain, you know.'

'I don't think Milton was speaking about being a waiter, Mr Salie,' Enoch replied, aghast that anyone would confuse the acceptance of an inner tranquillity with the clatter of a tearoom.

'You see, you're a clever boy. There are many jobs you can choose if you want to earn money sitting on your backside – you can be a jockey, a writer, a tailor or a chauffeur. The colour of the money depends on what's under your bum.'

Oupa turned to Enoch, 'Did Khotso send anything back with you?'

It had been Khotso's idea that he should travel back to Cape Town with the bank manager and, as the man was in a hurry, Enoch only had minutes to cram his things into a suitcase, grab the typewriter and camera and hop into the car. He could vaguely recall Khotso asking Polycarp to write something down for Oupa Hans. Khotso had given him a sheet of paper as they shook hands.

'Yes, I almost forgot, Oupa Hans. I've got something for you in my satchel.'

'That's not the kind of thing you forget, Enoch. It could have been life or death. You must learn not to be so careless.'

Mr Salie relaxed. 'Don't tell me you are also taking some of Khotso's medicine, my boy. I'm warning you – they tell me it can make you forget all your misdeeds.'

He even began to smile, showing the discolouration of his teeth caused by his pipe.

'Where's the envelope, my boy?'

'It's not in an envelope, Mr Salie.' Enoch handed the folded sheet of paper to him. He smelled of extra-strong mints, which meant that he had had a drink. Enoch did not recognise the names he read out: Java Head and Sea Cottage. To him it sounded like a secret code. Mr Salie heaved a sigh of relief – and so did Oupa Hans.

'Thanks to our messenger I can already smell the money, Hannes,' Mr Salie said as he pressed his lips to the paper, folded it and put it in his wallet. 'And here I was ready to go with Pale Lagoon, that colt Mrs Oppenheimer bought in Kentucky. I thought the colt was going to be God's work of art, but Enoch, it looks like you brought home the real winners.'

'Good,' Oupa Hans said, 'now that we've settled the important matters, we can relax.'

'But that's not why I came, Hannes. Yesterday the Boere came to give me an eviction order. District Six is going to be cleaned out, top to bottom, starting with our road first. Look, it says here that the minister of community development, the Honourable P.W. Botha, is going to destroy our homes – the bulldozers are coming, Johannes.'

Oupa Hans scanned the eviction order. 'Doesn't look like there's anything honourable about the bastard. He doesn't mince his words.'

'But why mince words when you've got people to put through the grinder? Our old kasbah will be turned into a fancy white suburb in no time. Where can we go? I don't want to leave our home. I want to die there. My family has been living in that house for over a hundred years, and now they want to knock it down. I'm telling you, it's worse than cutting off my leg. Slum clearance, nogal – they're going to pull down every single building and no one will remember who lived there. I swear, every family will come back to haunt any whitey that dares to build on top of the rubble.'

'More than a century of history and architecture gone at the stroke of a pen,' said Oupa Hans.

'I couldn't have said it better, my friend – and where do we go now? I don't want to be dumped in a township.'

'I've got a good idea, Oupa Hans,' said Enoch.

'Your good ideas always land us in trouble, but let's hear it.'

'I think Mr Salie and Mochie Salie should move into Oupa's other place. There's plenty of room for the tailoring stuff and he'll find new customers in Retreat. There's even a mosque nearby.'

Mr Salie would not hear of it. 'No, my boy – we wouldn't dream of taking advantage of your poor grandfather. That's not a good idea. We want this eviction order overturned. We're not the only people they go-ing to chuck out.'

Enoch thought of his mother's cousin, Tannie Marie, and had another idea. 'The only people who have eviction orders overturned are those who become White. There might be some hope for Mochie Salie, but maybe Mr Salie is a little too dark. What does Oupa Hans think?'

'They are getting rid of everyone – even our Jewish neighbours – and since when will my Amiena want to become a White woman? We haven't got time for silly ideas,' Mr Salie said dismissively.

'I think the boy's idea about my house is good, Idriss. I don't think I will ever move there, and you can pay me a small rent. The place has a decent little garden; it is safe, and Enoch is right, you'll find plenty of new customers. The boy is not as stupid as his parents make him out to be. You and your wife have some good years left – go and live there in peace. It will make me happy to know that you are there. And it's nearer to the stables in Steenberg.'

'Do you think there's anything Khotso can do for all of us in District Six? That's what I came to ask you about.'

'I'll call him tonight; Khotso will do his best, I'm sure. In the meantime, you and Amiena must move to Retreat. Let me go and get the keys. Please write down the address for Mr Salie, Enoch. There is furniture, but you might want to move your own things.'

Zachaeus stood at the door and cleared his throat to get their atten-tion. The dogs were at his side and were hoping that they could slip in unnoticed. Zachaeus told them that Ou Mevrou Jansen had felt quite ill in the morning and had not gone to communion. But she was feeling better now and wanted to attend evensong at the cathedral.

'Enoch, the old lady says she will be ready in twenty minutes, okay, and Alison is going too.'

'You better get ready for church, my boy,' Oupa Hans suggested.

Enoch sat in front of the car next to Zachaeus, anticipating Mr Salie's promise of a present for his bright idea. He was going to ask his wife to cook a crayfish curry for Oupa Hans and Enoch.

'Caroline not coming along?' Enoch asked, curious that Alison had taken up churchgoing.

'Thank heavens, no,' Alison replied. 'All we want is a bit of peace.'

Ou Mevrou Jansen and Alison spoke non-stop about plans for Christmas Eve, until Zachaeus dropped them off at the cathedral doors and went to find a parking space.

With her stick tapping out each step on the flagstones, Ou Mevrou Jansen walked to the front of the cathedral so that she would not have any distance to go for the holy sacrament. As it happened to be Solemn Advent Vespers, there was to be no sacrament. Enoch would have preferred sitting in a back pew with Zachaeus, but as Alison seemed pleased to accompany Ou Mevrou Jansen, he followed and sat between the two of them. They listened in awe to the choirboys singing the invocation: 'Deus in auditorium meum intende. Domine, audiuvandum me festina. Gloria Patri, et Filius, et Spiritu Sancto. Sicut erat in principio, et nunc et semper, et in sacula saeculorum. Amen.'

The youthful voices filled the cathedral, almost bringing tears to Enoch's eyes. The only time Latin did not give him pain was when he heard it being sung. However, he soon began to struggle with a coughing fit when the dean censed the Bible before and after the Gospel reading. Enoch was allergic to incense.

Nothing the dean said in his unctuous voice bore any relation to the coming season – but then it would have been difficult for him to compete with the choirboy singing the words of Mary in the *Magnificat*: 'My soul proclaims the greatness of the Lord: my spirit rejoices in God my Saviour. For he has looked with favour on his lowly servant: from this day all generations shall call me blessed.'

183

After the service Alison drew Enoch aside. 'It would be remiss of me not to warn you, Enoch. I wouldn't ignore Caroline, but you must be careful. She's a flirt and tries to prove how irresistible she is. She's been kicked out of two of the most liberal schools – so that must tell you something. She always seems to be down at the cottage. Oupa Hans must be really fed up. Please be careful.'

The Metropolitan Handicap

Be it enacted by the King's Most Excellent Majesty, the Senate and House of Assembly of the Union of South Africa: 'Coloured person' means a person who is not a White person or a Native; 'Native' means a person who in fact is, or is generally accepted as a member of any aboriginal race or tribe of Africa; 'White person' means a person who in appearance obviously is, or who is generally accepted as a White person, but does not include a person who, although in appearance obviously a White person, is generally accepted as a Coloured person.

Any person who considers himself aggrieved by his classification by the director in terms of Section 5, and any person who has any objection to the classification of any other person in terms of the said section, may at any time object in writing to the director against that classification.

Mr Molinieux pored over the wording in the statute book. While the Act had little bearing on his actual colour or appearance, it had proved sufficient grounds for the predicament that both Clara and Miss Aspeling had caused him. He used the ancient typewriter on which he normally struggled with the household accounts to set the words on paper. He planned to form a scroll for the centrepiece of the Christmas wreath he was making, and which he would hang in protest on the gates of parliament.

Every such objection shall be lodged in duplicate and shall be accompanied by an affidavit in duplicate setting forth fully the grounds upon which the objection is made; and if the objection relates to the classification of a person other than the objector, a copy of the objection and the affidavit shall be transmitted by the director to the person to whose classification the objection relates.

In this respect, the director of classification had observed the law scrupulously, and had sent Mr Molinieux by registered post a copy of the objection lodged by Miss Jennifer Aspeling of Mowbray. This had prompted

Mr Molinieux to send her an early Christmas card in which he had written: 'I pray that you may never find a husband after you so cruelly rejected the hand of an honourable man.'

For the hundredth time, he reflected on the details of Miss Aspeling's baseless accusation that, while in theory he might have the appearance of a white man, his actions had betrayed the behaviour typical of a Coloured.

Mr Molinieux had even failed to cancel the initial wedding arrangements made with the Presbyterian minister in Athlone. At that time he had acted on the firm conviction that Clara would accept his marriage proposal. The minister had first insisted on seeing the prospective bride and groom together; however, he had displayed an understanding for the delicacy of the situation and had foregone this requirement.

So much of what had happened to him during the past months could be traced back to that morning when he had written down for the minister's information Clara's personal details from her domestic service file, which he had delivered to him along with references from her previous employers. The Reverend Malgas had understood Mr Molinieux's need for secrecy and, having satisfied himself as to the honourable nature of his intentions, had declared his support for the proposed marriage between Miss Clara Gous, spinster of Steenberg, and Mr Cyprian Bannister Molinieux, bachelor of Rondebosch. Reverend Malgas had asked only that Mr Molinieux present to him the document issued by the Race Reclassification Board as soon as he received it. In an unaccustomed moment of excitement, Mr Molinieux had rushed to Cape Town to place an order at Stuttafords for a four-tier wedding cake, which he had concealed at the bottom of his wardrobe. He had also bought the engagement and wedding rings, the former of which he had later tried to press on Miss Aspeling.

Following his rejection by Clara, Mr Molinieux had tried to telephone Reverend Malgas, but his hand trembled so much that he had replaced the receiver in its cradle. He then decided that the embarrassment of the marriage banns being read publicly for the third and final time would certainly be no worse than the betrayal he had already suffered at Clara's hands. Had she not been the one to lead him on? Once, while they had stood together on the stoep listening to Hanneli's chatter, she had expressed a desire to have her own children. Wasn't that just the sort of thing to awaken a man's interest? For this and other reasons, the wedding had appeared to him to be a foregone conclusion.

Cyprian pushed these thoughts from his mind and settled down to the task at hand.

Every person who lodges an objection with the director in terms of sub-section (2) against the classification of any other person shall deposit with the director an amount of 10 guineas which amount shall: (a) If the objection is sustained by the board (of three persons) to which it has been referred for decision in terms of sub-section (3) be refunded to the objector; or (b) if the objection is rejected by the board, be forfeited to the State; and should the objections be unfounded, frivolous or vexatious, there could be recourse to the aggrieved within thirty days of the board's findings.

At the bottom of the page Cyprian typed the concluding paragraph in capital letters: A PERSON WHO IN APPEARANCE OBVIOUSLY IS A WHITE PERSON SHALL, FOR THE PURPOSE OF THE ACT (POPULATION REGISTRATION NO 30/1950), BE PRESUMED TO BE A WHITE PERSON UNTIL THE CONTRARY IS PROVED.

Cyprian knew the last clause to be a complete travesty of justice – because the magistrate himself, well acquainted with the letter of the law, had stated that he was in appearance obviously a white man, but had failed to make a final determination.

The house bore the customary silence of a Sunday morning. Everyone was out, including Ou Mevrou Jansen, who had gone to the morning service at St Saviour's in Claremont. The quick whistle of a dove's wings and the sound of a door swinging lightly on oiled hinges drew him to the trap he had set up in a remote corner of the back garden. Over the years this area had been filled in and raised against the slope of the mountain, and now was indistinguishable from the surrounding vegetation. Proteas and ericas flourished under the tall shrubs. By his last count, Mr Molinieux had trapped ten turtledoves, and there were now two more in the trap. According to the rough design he had sketched out, he needed twelve to decorate the circumference of the wreath. He drew on a pair of gloves and took one of the doves from the box at his feet, placed the neck between his fingers and with his thumb applied pressure to the jugular vein. He swung the flapping bird above his head until he felt its neck snap.

The idea of a wreath had first occurred to him when he discovered a wheel at the bottom of the debris in the gardening shed while searching for an old pair of Wellington boots. He had painted the rusty spokes and rim in gold. He positioned the doves on the spokes, and between each dove a pinecone complemented the design. The doves and pinecones were attached to the wheel with a red velvet ribbon. In the centre of the wheel he placed the scroll on which he had typed the extracts from the Population Registration Act. Around the rim he wound supple branches snipped from a fir tree in the wood, and wove the strips of velvet ribbon in and out around the spokes which held the greenery in place and supported the limp necks of the doves. This would be his Advent wreath. Mr Molinieux concealed it in the boot of his car.

That night, after he had poured the last cup of coffee and glass of port and had supervised the completion of all household duties, he drove into Cape Town, following De Waal Drive along the mountainside. He found a parking spot under a palm tree near the entrance to the Mount Nelson Hotel, across the road from the Company Gardens. As he walked past the entrance gate to parliament he noted two guards on duty – one apparently asleep, the other pacing back and forth.

Mr Molinieux turned past St George's Cathedral and made his way back up Queen Victoria Street, entering the Gardens once more by the Museum entrance. And, as he anticipated a long wait, he sat down on a bench near the foot of a statue. He felt feverish and his palms perspired far in excess of the possible effect of the warm summer's night. The rising moon concealed behind a cloud gave the statue in front of him a look of malevolence; the burnished skin of the man's face sported a bushy moustache, while his eyes focused on the distant sea. In the dim light an outstretched arm, more in an attitude of resignation than of victory, remained steady. Mr Molinieux read the inscription mounted on the plinth – the statue was that of Cecil John Rhodes.

No sooner had he sat down than he caught sight of the lone figure of a man scurrying along a path in the rose garden. The man waved at him and approached while unbuttoning his fly. Mr Molinieux removed a dagger from his jacket pocket and, detecting a seriousness of intent he had not counted on, the stranger moved off to continue his quest for more amenable quarry.

Mr Molinieux sat down again, waiting for the guard at the entrance to parliament to relax his vigilance. He waited for about an hour before he considered he had a chance of approaching the gates unobserved. He hurried back to the car and stealthily removed the wreath. As both of the guards now appeared to be asleep, he attached the wreath to the wrought iron gates of parliament. Anyone passing by, or even the guards entering to take the next watch, would at first not have thought anything out of place. The wreath appeared to be the heraldic emblem of the coming republic.

The sound of the cathedral bells chiming the hour of eleven reached him as he wiped his perspiring hands on a towel, engaged the Prefect's first gear and released its clutch. Shortly afterwards he brought the car to a halt in a lay-by off De Waal Drive. The evening's events had exhausted him and he fell into a deep sleep. Had he been conscious, he would have seen the city bejewelled with Christmas lights, the moon-bleached sands of the bay, the gentle waves and pinpricks of light on the ocean indicating the presence of ships at anchor. It was the sun at daybreak that eventually woke him.

Because of the hour, Mr Molinieux decided that he might usefully employ the time remaining before he need return to Wepener. Mfilo's passbook had still not been endorsed for work in the Cape. Mr Molinieux decided, there and then, that he would find out where the boy lived, and he would report him to the authorities. He had never been to the shack where Mfilo and Clara lived together, but he knew that it was situated somewhere off Prince George's Drive on the way to Muizenberg. While in the past he had tried to spare Clara the embarrassment of a visit to her humble home, he was now determined to discover where she sheltered Mfilo against the law. He decided he would tell her that he was returning to Wepener after an early morning walk on the beach – and that he had stopped by to collect them for work and spare them a tiresome bus and train ride to Rondebosch. He would make sure that he was back in time to supervise breakfast.

Mr Molinieux was afraid that it might be unsafe to enter a township on his own, so he stopped at the gate lodge to see if he could convince Oupa Hans to accompany him, on the pretext of taking the dogs for a walk on the beach. Enoch was up writing when he knocked – and so was Oupa Hans, who had had a restless night. It was an extremely rare occurrence for Mr Molinieux to be calling on him, and Oupa Hans only agreed to go on condition Enoch went as well to take care of the dogs. At first Mr Molinieux balked at the idea of having to take one of the larger cars, but if they were going to drive Clara and Mfilo to Wepener, he needed to.

It was too early to knock at Clara's door, so he suggested stopping at the Kleyweg Hotel for a cup of coffee. This was the hotel where Enoch's father used to work during his student years, so it had been pointed out to him on innumerable occasions. Although he spotted some activity and the smell of frying bacon reached them, the dining room was locked and the irritable clerk at the desk informed Mr Molinieux that breakfast would not be served for at least half an hour. The dogs were driven to distraction by the smell, and rather than wait, he drove along Prince George's Drive and parked on the gravel strip at Sunrise Beach.

Only Byron and Augusta Leigh knew for certain what they wanted to do. As Enoch walked across a dune, they headed directly for the water's edge, barking at the incoming waves. Enoch studied the mountains and the curve of Simonstown across the bay through a pair of binoculars he had found in the car. Haima had told him that her father had refused to abandon his shop and had dared the authorities to throw him and his family out.

Mr Molinieux sat in the car, even though he had been the one to suggest taking the dogs for a walk along the beach. Oupa Hans looked somewhat revived as he whistled for the dogs and walked towards Enoch.

'Get the dogs on the leads,' he shouted. Enoch did as he asked, but wondered why he had wanted to bring the dogs along without allowing them to run freely.

'Look at the horses,' Oupa Hans said as he took Augusta Leigh's lead from Enoch, and smiled as the first rider came over the brow of a sand dune.

The stable hands rode the horses bareback towards the beach. The animals, picking up the smell of salt and seaweed, strained at their bits, anxious for the morning canter on the tide-hardened sand. This appeared to be the most enjoyable part of their exercise regime. Impatient with the slow pace set by Java Head, the horses cantered past the leader of the string, free of the accustomed whips and saddles.

During the season satin-clad jockeys rode the thoroughbreds; but they now carried their grooms dressed in soiled overalls and balaclavas, despite the prospect of warm weather later in the day. The beach was clear – an hour or more remained before the first surfers and bathers would appear. At certain spots solitary anglers clung stubbornly to the rocks exposed by the receding tide, but they were merely part of the landscape. Oupa Hans made Enoch hold the dogs, took the binoculars from him and pointed out the horses he recognised.

The riders guided the animals along the beach in the direction of Strandfontein, Colorado King in the lead, closely followed by Mr Salie's favourite, Pale Lagoon.

'There's almost half a million guineas worth of horseflesh out there,' Oupa Hans remarked in awe.

He explained that most mornings the grooms at the Muizenberg stables were up well before dawn to pamper their charges; the horses were fed and curried and their legs massaged. The smell of arnica worked into the powerful flanks of the twenty thoroughbred horses permeated the air. Oupa told Enoch that once the chores were done, the stalls mucked out and the manure piled by the willow tree, the grooms helped each other mount the horses. He had often been there when he was still head gardener at Wepener to collect manure directly from the stables – not that horse manure was the best thing going, but it added something to the compost heap.

On their return, the grooms' voices and the thud of hooves carried over the sound of the waves to reach them standing next to the car. The riders, many clenching long-stemmed pipes between their teeth, conversed among themselves. Oupa Hans greeted some of them as they reined in their horses on the gravel. The horses and riders then cantered past the car, and Oupa Hans asked Mr Molinieux if he could follow them at a discreet distance so that he could study their form.

To Oupa's surprise, they did not turn into the entrance to the stables;

instead the horses, with Java Head back in the lead, continued for a further half-mile along the road and turned into Steenberg Estate where Clara lived. To Enoch this seemed a misnomer, as the only structure vaguely reminiscent of an estate was a large general store and an adjoining house with curious wrought-iron trellises over which, despite the early hour, washing hung.

Mr Molinieux slowed the car down as several children appeared from nowhere to welcome the riders and horses and accompany them to a large clearing bordered by wind-stunted Port Jackson trees. The riders paraded the horses in a circle, while the excited residents of Steenberg Estate gathered around. Enoch immediately recognised Mr Salie, looking much more cheerful than when he had last seen him. Enoch glanced at Oupa Hans, who did not seem to be surprised, although he gestured to him to keep quiet.

From the car he could see Mr Salie lining up strips of coloured paper on a battered deal table. With a thump to the withers as the horse paraded past him on their exhibition trot, and a sniff of the air for arnica that might betray a stiff limb or sore muscle, Mr Salie wrote the odds on a blackboard, having ascertained the condition of each horse with a trained eye. Like a professional, he called out the odds and issued betting slips. Oupa Hans got out of the car and, out of Mr Molinieux's hearing, explained to Enoch that Mr Salie was in the business of making money.

The curtain raiser Mr Salie had organised would be a carthorse race, because he wished to give the local boy riders some practice and a sense of ambition – and to flatten the course for the thoroughbreds.

The Steenberg Estate was where Red Hunter, the paragon of the African Breeders Association, had sustained a disastrous injury two years earlier. The stallion had put his foreleg into a molehill and torn a ligament barely days before the Metropolitan Handicap, the most important fixture on the racing calendar of the country. According to Oupa, only the action of the quick-witted Mr Salie had saved the stable hands from serious consequences. Realising the predicament of the grooms and the prospects for his own business should the truth become known, he'd decided that a well-aimed shot would put everyone off the track. Following Mr Salie's instructions, the grooms had led the horses back along Prince George's Drive, where he had shot Red Hunter in the hindquarters.

It had been a healthy dose of prejudice that had saved the grooms – and the fact that horses do not talk. The head groom had raced back to the stables and alerted the trainer that, on his return to the stables, directly after morning exercise on the beach, Red Hunter had been shot by a white man. The owner, trainer, Criminal Investigations Department and the newspapers implicitly believed the story related by the grooms. The incident had even received coverage abroad. In London, the *Times* reported: 'At that early hour there was clearly nothing the shocked native grooms could do to ward off a determined gunman whose purpose had been the removal of the favourite from the Metropolitan Handicap, the main seasonal fixture in the Cape.'

As the type of bullet drawn from Red Hunter's quarters had not been encountered in South Africa before – despite the abundance and variety of firearms in private hands – it confirmed the suspicions of the police that they were searching for a professional.

The grooms, who had emerged as heroes from this episode, were now more cautious. In fact, they had waited until well after Red Hunter's first successful attempt at stud before they risked the resumption of their informal fixtures at the Steenberg Estate. Mr Salie, who had planned to place a hefty bet on Red Hunter, had also learned an invaluable lesson, and determined that in future he would not take unnecessary risks with the delicate legs of the racehorses. It was not until much later that he managed to convince the grooms with the usual sacks of mealie meal and sugar to resume the illicit races.

A cursory inspection of the course satisfied the grooms that it looked safe enough. Mr Salie had been living in Retreat for little over a week, but already the proximity of his living quarters to the Steenberg Estate had delivered unanticipated benefits. One problem remained, however – the white man seated in the parked car at the side of Patel's grocery shop. Mr Salie walked over, ignored Oupa Hans and spoke to Mr Molinieux. However, Mr Molinieux was so intrigued with the spectacle that Mr Salie was obliged to address him twice.

'Can I help the master with anything, master?' he enquired in an obsequious manner that he hoped would appeal. 'Does master want anything?'

'Oh, I beg your pardon, no. We had just driven down to the beach to watch the sun come up and I saw the horses. We followed them back here.'

Enoch did not let on that he and Oupa Hans knew Mr Salie. But there was plenty he wanted to ask him.

'Sorry master, I'm just checking for safety's sake, because why – shame, only las' year, there was a bad accident nearby when a person shot Red Hunter in the bum. Master knows, a man can't be too careful. It was even in the overseas papers.'

'You're so right; one can't be too careful with such beautiful creatures.'

'I can see master is a gentleman with good taste.' Mr Salie may not have liked the looks of Mr Molinieux, but as he was with Oupa Hans, he decided that the white man probably liked a good race as much as the next man, and was not the type who would get the police involved.

'Master's right. Can I sell master a ticket for the race, master? We trying them out for the Metropolitan.'

'I wan wondering what you were up to, you scoundrel,' Mr Molinieux replied – the first time in days Enoch had seen him laughing. 'No, sir, unfortunately I'm not a betting man. But don't let me keep you from your business; by the way, would you know where Miss Clara Gous lives?'

'Is she the lady who lives with that native, master?'

'As a matter of fact, I came to collect her for work,' he said curtly, upset by the reference to Mfilo.

'Ja, that lady is too good to live around here. Master mos' definitely come to the right place, just over there by the pondok with the garden. I'm sure the black man must steal his madam's plants. A person can't trust anyone any more. There it is, over there by the blue door – master can't miss it. Mus' I send a boy to go fetch her for master?'

'No. I will go.'

Mr Molinieux watched the bookmaker return to the betting table. Enoch overheard Mr Salie tell the grooms that he had just received the largest bet ever – a record for Steenberg.

'Steenberg is getting grand these days with white people coming. You'll see, just now they come here instead of going to Kenilworth – and old Salie's pockets will be bursting full. And yours. Just you watch.

'Listen now. The Englishman is okay. If he make trouble for us, he'll get the same treatment like Red Hunter. Come now; make the race a good one for Salie. What's good for Salie is good for you. Jus' let him go to the police and I tell them he's the one that shot Red Hunter.'

The grooms appeared to be satisfied with the bookmaker's explanation. He had jotted down the number of the Mercedes, along with a brief description of the driver. While he had been talking with Mr Molinieux, a large group of squatters and Estate dwellers had gathered around to place their bets. Some knew by instinct which horse would perform best on the sandy track, while others waited until after the exhibition trot before they risked their money. They listened to Mr Salie shouting the odds on the runners. The bookmaker accepted bets for as little as a shilling, although a few of the punters, whose weekly pay packet had survived the worst ravages of the local shebeen, wagered as much as a guinea.

Mr Salie called the jockeys around him and allocated their starting positions with a toss of a coin. The men appeared anxious to get going, and Mr Salie must have sensed their unease.

'We want to get this race over and done, chop-chop and get the horses back to the stables.'

When Enoch turned around he saw Mr Molinieux walking off in the direction of the shack Mr Salie had earlier pointed out to him. He knocked a few times, but no one answered the door.

Mr Salie rang the saddling bell, salvaged from the local primary school, and, as there were neither starting stalls nor gates, the horses were lined up behind a length of rope that was dropped at a signal from him. Then they were off, to cover the full eight furlongs that had been agreed. The horses started out gingerly, but once they had negotiated the first bend where there was some bunching, they began to show their mastery as if they were thundering down the green turf of the Kenilworth course. The horses raced each other, turning the earlier canter on the beach into a prelude for the rough-going gallop of the Cape Flats.

The riders, some still clenching pipes between their teeth, tested the strength and skill of their charges in ways that punters at Kenilworth or Durban would never get to see. There were no quinellas, jackpots or sweepstakes – nothing that would complicate the quick exchange of money – only the used bus tickets with their known cash values. Nor did the bookmaker seem to risk unreasonable odds. For the grooms, too, the race held the prospect of a profitable venture. Oupa Hans told Enoch that they could earn more money here than in two weeks of hard work at the stables, and they enjoyed the praises showered on them by the betting enthusiasts of Steenberg.

The outcome of the race did not interest Mr Molinieux when he returned to join Enoch and Oupa Hans. This was the first time he had visited a squatter camp, and it was obvious that he was ill at ease in the place.

'I'll deal with Mfilo later today,' he threatened as he looked at his watch. 'We must just have missed them. Let's get out of this confounded place.'

He was visibly anxious to return to the comfort and security of his household duties at Wepener. Oupa Hans looked disappointed when Mr Molinieux reversed the car, thereby cutting short his pleasure.

'Java Head is the one,' he said to no one in particular. 'Khotso is never wrong.'

'A merry Christmas, master,' the bookmaker called after them as the wheels of the car spun in the sand and they drove back to their familiar world.

Ex Unitate Vires

History is a matter of flair rather than of facts.
– HILAIRE BELLOC

Dear Polycarp

Thank you for keeping me up to date with events at Cofimvaba.
I had heard about the wedding as Khotso has invited Oupa Hans.
I've asked if I can go with him. It would be great to see you and
Redemptus – if he's back at Cof. Thank you also for your advice
about historical perspective. What I neglected to say when we
discussed this on our journey is that, to my mind, memory is a
clutter of happenings, past and present. Does it really matter which
preceded which? Not as long as actual events are remembered. If
time is a mere human construct, as my teachers keep saying – then
what of chronology? What difference do a few years here and there
make in the recounting of events? It's not as though I'm recording
the order of discovery of artefacts in an archaeological dig. I'm
writing a simple story.

Mama often exasperated me with tales of her hard life that
changed for the better on the day she married Dowa. She would
commence one story – then draw on her stock of memories and
often introduce a third, maybe even a fourth strand which bore little apparent relation to the first one. However, at its conclusion the
tale would coalesce with its own clarity. To me it has always been
strange to see how her disordered mind shaped its memories, but
as long as the story amounted to the sum of its parts, it ultimately
made perfect sense to me. It must have been something I inherited
from her. Fond greetings to you and Khotso's multitudes.

If taking tea with the staff had caused an upheaval at Wepener barely a
month earlier, Dr Schoon's request to Dries and Alison sparked what was
tantamount to a domestic explosion. The prime minister had asked if he

could treat members of his cabinet and their spouses to a pre-Christmas dinner at his wife's family home. He considered the official residence far too formal for the kind of atmosphere he wanted for the occasion. For days, the arguments that ensued – behind closed doors, but within hearing of the staff – drew comment in the kitchen. Because of his contempt for the prime minister, even Mr Molinieux made his disapproval known, and once again found an unlikely ally in Ou Mevrou Jansen.

'We've got to draw the line somewhere,' Alison argued. 'It would be a disgrace to have that bunch of hoodlums at Wepener. They represent everything I despise.'

'I agree, but this has come at such short notice and the invitations have to go out,' Dries reasoned.

'I've made my decision. What on earth is wrong with your father hosting it at Groote Schuur?'

'You know how much Ma hates that place.'

'She's just going to have to put up with it.'

'It's only for one evening – and surely, this is my parents' house as much as it is ours. Let's take Caroline away for a day or two. It might do her good to see some of the country.'

'So now you're using Caroline as an excuse. If we go anywhere, the only sensible thing would be to leave her at home to terrorise that crowd. Too scared to stick out your neck. There are some things you do – others you don't, but you always do as you please. And what about the staff and their well-being?'

'Ma has asked for Molinieux's help, but for the rest, she'll make do with staff from Groote Schuur.'

'What absolute cheek – and don't blame me if we have a riot on our hands here.'

'Look, darling, either you or I will have to climb down.'

This exchange was followed by silence and the sound of footsteps coming down the hall.

Caroline had arrived in her bathrobe demanding breakfast. Ou Mevrou Jansen, who had succeeded in banning her from smoking anywhere near the kitchen, told her that, as it was well beyond breakfast time, she could have what Enoch and Hanneli were having for morning tea. It surprised everyone that she did not make a fuss. Soon they were all tucking into brawn sandwiches and Milo when Dries walked in, looking upset. He and Alison were always careful of what was said in Hanneli's presence, and Enoch had tried to divert the child's attention from her parents' quarrel by teaching her the words to a Sesotho wedding song Elizabeth had taught him at Cofimvaba: Fiela, fiela, fiela …

When she caught sight of her father, Hanneli leaped from her chair and threw her arms around his legs. Dries picked up his daughter and stroked her hair. 'It looks like Oupa and Ouma are coming to stay and they're having some friends over for a party.'

Hanneli escaped from her father's arms and ran around the kitchen. 'Oupa and Ouma are coming – *hooray!* When, Daddy, when?'

'In a few days, my darling.'

'Can I sit next to Enoch?'

'We'll be here to greet Oupa and Ouma when they arrive – but you, Mummy, Daddy and Caroline will then go on a little holiday.'

'And what about Enoch? He's coming on holiday too?' She sat down beside Enoch. 'Daddy says we all going on a holiday. Let's sing him our song …'

'Enoch will be staying here with Ou Mevrou Jansen.'

'Then I want to stay too. Come on, Enoch – let's sing.'

'Fiela, fiela, fiela ngwan-ya-na, Fiela ngwan-ya-na o se je-le mat-lak-a-leng.

'Fiela, fiela, fiela ngwan-ya-na, Fiela ngwan-ya-na o se je-le mat-lak-a-leng.'

Ou Mevrou Jansen glowered from the end of the kitchen table. She got up to confront Dries. 'If I had any say, I wouldn't allow a government chef or his potato peelers to set foot in this house, including those stupid ministers and their wives. You can forget that idea, my boy.'

'It was Ma's idea.'

'I don't care whose darned idea it was. I agree with Alison. Nobody touches my pots and pans. And don't you worry about it; I'll speak to your darling mother.' She left the kitchen in unaccustomed haste and Hanneli dashed to get her walking stick that was leaning against the draining board. They heard Ou Mevrou Jansen slam the door to her quarters with such ferocity that everyone jumped. Hanneli howled and rushed to Clara for comfort. Trossie was also in tears. For want of anything better to do,

Mieta made a pot of rooibos tea and asked Enoch to take it down the hall to Ou Mevrou Jansen, while Clara took the child to the nursery.

'The rooibos will be good for the old lady's nerves. You know mos, Enoch – she will take it from you.'

Enoch was less sanguine about entering the lion's den and felt he needed a nerve tonic himself. His hands shook and the tea lapped onto the tray. He wiped it up with his handkerchief and placed the tray on the floor so that he could knock at her door.

'Who's there?' She demanded, her voice quivering with suppressed fury.

'It's only me, Ou Mevrou Jansen.'

'Go away! You knew about this all along.'

'It's me – Enoch, Ou Mevrou Jansen.'

'Don't be such a nuisance. I'm on the phone.'

'Mieta made a pot of rooibos tea for Ou Mevrou Jansen.'

'Then come inside. Shut that door. I've never been so angry. Look at my hands; I can't stop them shaking. Ah, tea ... would you also like a cup? Sorry, Enoch, sometimes I just wish the Lord would come and take me away. At least I gave that Arta Schoon a good piece of my mind. And in the end we agreed that I will be in charge of the banquet. I hope you will give me a hand, my boy. At my age I'll need plenty of help in the kitchen. I'd like to tell you a secret, Enoch ...'

'Of course, Ou Mevrou Jansen.'

'But maybe this is not the right time. It's very complicated – I'll tell it to you some other time, before the Lord comes to take me away.'

There was nothing Enoch liked better than a secret, and he felt bitterly disappointed. For a moment he thought of encouraging her. Eventually she did speak to him and he left even more bewildered than when he had entered her room.

Later that evening, while Enoch and Dries had drinks after a game of tennis, Dries explained that his father had made a promise to Khotso on his last trip to Cofimvaba, but first he had to get his cabinet's support. Oupa Hans had mentioned this to him – and Enoch had written about it – although he listened carefully because his grandfather was likely to have left out important details. According to Dries this promise had become an obsession for the prime minister. For him the declaration of a republic would be the beginning of the undoing of the Union and a decisive farewell to the Commonwealth. It would represent nothing less than a bold scuttling of the old British order.

'After he saw Khotso, my father seemed to stop thinking that the Crown – an easy paregoric for the sentimental – could play any part in what he considered had already become "Our Republic". Of course, this had been Khotso's plan all along.'

Dries said that Alison had jumped to conclusions when she had heard this and had confronted her father-in-law. She was certain that it was just another ploy to bring about the complete disenfranchisement of the natives. There had long been rumours that Coloureds were to be struck off the common voters' roll and Indians returned to their homeland. The 'Republic' was to be the prize Dr Schoon hoped to bequeath to the nation, and for which he would always want to be remembered. However, Dries was convinced that his father's ambitions for white supremacy would fail and instead unite the majority against racial segregation.

'To me, that's the true meaning of "Ex Unitate Vires", the motto for the new republic, Enoch. It's a huge risk, I know, but I'm sure racial unity is what Khotso had in mind all along. So it's a risk worth taking. That's how I convinced Alison that this banquet should go ahead. But I must admit she was sceptical about Khotso's motives for the republic.'

'But don't you see, Alison is right. It's all spite – it's all to do with Khotso's visit to England.'

'Never listen to rumours, my friend.'

There was a glint of excitement in Dries's eyes. Enoch was baffled by all of this – the government wilfully manipulating the future of the country for the benefit of white people and thereby inadvertently sowing the seeds of its own destruction.

'This is going to make history, I'm telling you, Enoch. I'd like you to stay here and give Ou Mevrou Jansen and Molinieux a hand. And keep your eyes and ears open,' Dries said, slapping him on the back.

However, Alison remained unconvinced, and for once Oupa Hans agreed with her when Enoch later told him what she thought of the whole idea. Was it really true what Oupa Hans had said that time, Enoch wondered, that Dries had the inclination of a moth for its own extinction?

Much had happened since the prime minister's last visit to Cofimvaba, but the unrest in Pondoland and particularly in townships around Durban had not been stamped out as successfully as he might have wished. Although native protests against his plans to establish a republic had become widespread, his minister of police had assured him that there was no immediate cause for concern. In Schoon's mind only a few formalities remained before the Union Jack would finally be lowered over parliament, and, with the hoisting of the new flag, the apron strings to the Crown would be cut, placing the actions of his government beyond the meddlesome reach of Her Majesty's government forever.

Not least among matters now awaiting the prime minister's attention was the referendum on the republic. *Die Landstem* concurred with his certainty that the majority of the white population was firmly behind it. The government printing office already had the forms available for distribution to polling centres around the country. The design and colours for the republic flag, as well as heraldic emblems and a new currency were likely to have widespread interest, although many of his supporters thought these were minor matters when compared with plans to celebrate the new republic in towns, villages and even on remote farms. Judging by the wave of public enthusiasm, Dr Schoon could only anticipate a successful outcome.

There was also talk of drafting a new constitution. He had been planning to invite the members of his cabinet and a few special friends to a banquet at his official residence to canvass their views. However, it had been Arta's idea to host the event at Wepener, her family home, and he had readily agreed as this was a more intimate venue. And Dr Schoon understood that, no matter how hard she tried, his wife was unable to shake off the ghost of Cecil John Rhodes that stalked the precincts of Groote Schuur.

Even though he had a clearly defined course of action, Dr Schoon was aware that, for the most part, his ministers understood the thoughts and feelings of the voters in their constituencies. The prime minister knew how to listen and how to lead. As there was nothing as good as fine Cape wines and generous helpings of meat and fresh garden vegetables to coax the best from his cabinet, Dr Schoon had asked his wife to plan a banquet for the men and their wives – and where better to have it than at Wepener? A congenial atmosphere, stripped of the sparring that was inevitable when the cabinet met in chambers, would prompt some of their best thinking.

He was confident of his ministers' support. And since the whole matter would have serious financial implications, he had also invited the receiver of revenue. Like him, these men had been incensed by the words of that old fool, Macmillan, who had droned on about *winds of change* heralding a new African order. Fortunately the good old southeaster had blown that pompous Englishman out to sea, even though some newspaper editors had taken Macmillan's words as prophetic. However, the susceptibility of the English press would be put to good use when the time came. Those winds were undoubtedly blowing – but what was less certain was what they would leave in their wake.

Dr Schoon was convinced that the proposed referendum set out what most European voters wanted – independence from Britain with constitutional guarantees for white supremacy. While this may have appeared a narrow path to certain people of British ancestry, Dr Schoon felt that it was time that their views be suppressed. The Afrikaner was now ready, and if the truth were known, had always been ready to walk his own spoor.

On this beautiful summer's evening, waiting for the arrival of his guests, the prime minister was pleased that it was now too late to change course or redirect his bold plans. He leaned back comfortably in an armchair to discern if he had neglected any eventualities. But as far as he could see, there were none. In fact, the republic had become a reality for him on the very day he had given his word to Khotso, finish and klaar.

Still, it was important to distinguish between the founding of a republic on the one hand and disengagement from the Commonwealth on the other. Once the republic and its status within the Commonwealth had been confirmed, South Africa would show its independence by walking out – and, if necessary, leaving the United Nations as well, especially since the traitor Smuts was long gone, dead and buried a mere two years after his defeat at the polls.

The prime minister found it of great benefit to work within the law, and for this reason he was adept at crafting new decrees for public security and combating political upheaval. In the event that the ninety-day detention clause proved inadequate, it could be amended to 180 days of solitary confinement. Later, if necessary, it could be changed to 365 days and, in the long run, indefinite incommunicado detention. These laws would undermine the position of people such as Josias Nkosivile who inflamed anti-white sentiment, spurred on by liberal English swine who did everything possible to hang on to the Union Jack as though their very lives depended on it. At this very moment Special Branch were following up leads that would ensure that Josias would spend the rest of his life in prison.

If the press were to be believed, Josias had appealed to the Commonwealth to jettison the Union and at the same time had contradicted himself by calling on the Crown not to abandon its sovereign responsibilities. This was the sort of mumbo jumbo at which Macmillan had excelled. The tantrums in London, Delhi and Accra served as a smokescreen, as far as Schoon was concerned, and U Thant's reign at the United Nations would soon come to an end. Concerns about the boycott of oranges, apples, sherry and the loss of Commonwealth membership occupied the liberals and diverted attention from the issue of the republic. To the prime minister it was evident that the natives and their liberal friends could not effectively grapple with two issues at the same time. The trick, he discovered, was to stay just one step ahead of them.

Dr Schoon tried to ignore his own inner turmoil. It was as if he accepted that there was to be no escape from his fate. But he hoped that if he could prove his loyalty to Khotso, the witchdoctor might neutralise the threats against him. Dr Schoon had recently turned sixty and was obliged to exercise care in the choice of what he ate. As he was a cautious man, he listened to the advice of his doctors to observe a sensible diet. Throughout the past thirty years, his weight had remained more or less constant, and since he had a hearty appetite he felt that he was not being indulgent or imprudent when on occasion he would have the extra chop or second helping of pudding.

Dries and his family had gone to spend a few days at the beach cottage, and Dr Schoon now sat awaiting his guests in pleasant anticipation of the dinner and subsequent discussions. This was, after all, not your usual protocol affair with someone or other presenting his credentials.

During her telephone conversation with Ou Mevrou Jansen, Mrs Schoon had dispensed with her husband's original idea of an informal braai and had asked the irascible, elderly cook and the butler to choose a suitable menu. Mrs Schoon did not want to be seen to be meddling in the affairs of the kitchen, nor did she wish to run foul of Ou Mevrou Jansen. She had previously discussed the guest list with Mr Molinieux to reassure herself that the dinner was in capable hands.

Mr Molinieux suggested that roast lamb and vegetables would be a sensible choice for the main course, and with Ou Mevrou Jansen's approval wasted no time in placing an order with Shapiro's Butchery on the Main Road. Taking into consideration the occasion, Mr Molinieux was adamant that the butcher send only the finest quality meat. This put the blockman on the defensive. He retorted that he could not recall an occasion when he had not sent top-grade meat to Wepener.

Later that day, after supervising the polishing of the family silver, including a dozen candlesticks, Mr Molinieux instructed Enoch in the duties of a footman. Clara was also to assist at the table and, as she had done this before, Enoch was to watch her and Mr Molinieux closely throughout the meal. Enoch familiarised himself with the guest list, holding it up next to the front page of an old issue of *Die Landstem* which bore a photograph of each cabinet member – unfortunately without their wives.

The guests arrived within a few minutes of each other. Mr Molinieux told Enoch that the punctuality of the ministers could be ascribed to their obedience to the division bell at parliament and their eagerness to make their voices heard on the floor. He then instructed Enoch to take their hats and coats and, offering the guests a glass of sherry, showed them into the parlour.

When all the guests were assembled and the greetings attended to, Dr Schoon addressed them. 'Ladies, Ministers, Receiver of Revenue – as we are all friends and colleagues, let us not stand on ceremony. Mrs Schoon and I simply wish you a hearty welcome to our home. So please let us raise our glasses to the coming republic. And also, here's to a happy and blessed Christmas.'

The prime minister and Mrs Schoon regarded cocktails merely as a convenient interlude to accommodate the late arrival of guests and last-minute preparations in the kitchen. As they were now all present,

Dr Schoon led everyone into the dining room. Enoch managed a level of politeness, but refused to imitate Mr Molinieux's 'Honourable Minister' this, and 'Honourable Minister' that … He had discovered some time ago that protocol would never be one of his strengths, and besides, it was difficult to remember the ministers' names from the photograph he had previously studied.

Kleinhans of Foreign Affairs and Mrs Kleinhans were present, as were Dr Schoon's successor at Bantu Affairs, the affable Gawie Pienaar and his fiancée, Devora Myburgh. Mr and Mrs Schoeman – Railways and Harbours – were there, as was Interior Minister Marius Venter, whose wife, Marietjie, was indisposed due to a summer cold. Her absence was a disappointment to Mrs Schoon, as she brought a natural sparkle to any dinner table. The justice minister and Mrs Byleveld were present, as were the education minister, Dirkie Mulder and his wife Emmerentia, who, because of her husband's inability to put thought into words, was reputed to be the one actually running the ministry. Minister Mulder did, however, have a reputation for compassion. He had contested a by-election and had won the prestigious Gardens seat from a formidable opponent who, although no less committed to white ascendancy, had the advantage of a fortune and a hereditary title. The victory had been a considerable feat for Mulder, especially in view of malicious speculation as to his racial pedigree. Enoch recognised Mulder immediately, and his predicament caused him to feel a guarded sympathy, even kinship towards him.

Minister of defence and confirmed bachelor, Johannes Kowie Brink was there, or Kowie Johannes Brink, depending on which newspaper one read, as were Wynand Moerenhout and his wife Orna Groskopf who, although married to the receiver of revenue for some twenty years, had retained her maiden name in honour of her sister, a famous writer and broadcaster. Seated next to them were minister of sport and culture, Wynand "Sprikkies" Bouwer and his wife Mienie. With his good-natured insistence that sport was culture and culture sport, Bouwer was the only leftover from the Strijdom era. After culture came Coloured Affairs, Dr Wessel de Bruin and Patricia, his English wife. Known in society as a trendsetter, Mrs de Bruin had introduced Empress Farah Diba's hairstyle, the beehive, to the country – the startling success of which was clearly evident among the women. Minister of community development,

P.W. Botha, turned to greet Mr Molinieux. This afforded Enoch his first look at the man who had signed off on the destruction of District Six. When Mrs Schoon asked after Minister Botha's wife, he replied grumpily that he had no idea that she had been included in the invitation.

Mr Molinieux and Enoch showed the guests to their appointed places at the table. They appeared well fortified by the sherry and the prime minister's toast to the new republic. Not present was the minister of manpower and development, who had accompanied the governor of the reserve bank and the minister of finance to an important meeting in London to represent South Africa. The creditworthiness of the future republic was to be discussed with city bankers and representatives of the Bretton Woods institutions. An invitation had, however, been extended to the finance minister's wife, Sussie van Zyl, one of Arta's closest friends. They were both members of the Afrikaner Women's Circle, whose charitable works among the unfortunate were almost as well known, and even said to rival the efforts of the various 1820 settlers groups. Enoch showed Mrs van Zyl to her place between the minister of defence and Piet Greyling, minister of police and security.

Klaas Rijpma, minister of agriculture, and his second wife Mrs Mienie Rijpma were the last to arrive, having just returned from Prieska aboard an air force plane. The Rijpmas had been visiting that Godforsaken part of the country where people carried their umbrellas as a token of faith that God would send rain. The farmers were in despair as they had suffered crippling losses caused by persistent drought and locusts – and America continued to flood world markets with huge surpluses of mealies, which had left them at a distinct disadvantage. They demanded a discussion of their difficulties with the minister as the Prieska dam would soon run dry. Klaas Rijpma was a popular man and, in a country where the ability to speak English in a clear and concise fashion was considered a mark of intelligence, he had attained the reputation of a genius.

'I won't make another long speech,' the prime minister began. 'But all I want to say is both Mrs Schoon and I are happy to have you with us this evening, although we are disappointed that some of our colleagues could not be here. Thank you, Minister Rijpma and Mrs Rijpma for stepping in at such short notice – and I would like to commend our air force at Ysterplaat for providing transport. I must tell you that Minister van Zyl is having great success with the bankers in London, although no less so with Mrs van Zyl's Christmas shopping. I put through a trunk call to him this afternoon and he assured me that our discussions have his full support. We are all in this together. But it's a well-known fact that there's only one woman in this country who likes to talk politics – so after dinner the ladies will accompany my wife to the drawing room and the ministers will join me in the study.'

There were a few anxious glances and in some cases traces of horror were visible on the faces of the guests when Ou Mevrou Jansen's notion of a festive banquet was placed on the table. Minister Rijpma and his wife were the only ones who looked on the spread with any semblance of pleasure and, as he devoted much effort to the supply of government subsidies to the farmers, it could be said that he was responsible for placing meat, vegetables and fruit on every table throughout the country.

The prime minister sat at the head of the table and his wife took her seat at the far end. Despite Mr Molinieux's watchful presence, Mrs Schoon rang a tiny silver bell and summoned the wine steward, having noticed that one or two of the ladies and a few of the ministers appeared to be in need of replenishment. Many of them required rather more than the earlier glasses of sherry to face what had been placed before them. On the long mahogany dining table, amidst the maze of crystal, silver, china and candlesticks, were placed twenty-five perfectly roasted sheep's heads arranged on enormous Limoges platters and surrounded by prodigious quantities of fresh parsley and rosemary.

Dr Schoon expressed his approval at the unexpected sight of his favourite dish, and he reached out to pat the back of the minister of agriculture. 'My goodness, Klaas, so many sheep, hey, and look at today's price of a chop. This must be a great day for my wife to indulge me with a little luxury from my childhood.'

The wine was poured and Minister Rijpma insisted on drinking to Mrs Schoon's splendid choice.

'I, for one, haven't had a good skaapkop since university days. Mrs Schoon, to your very good health and to our republic.'

The ministers and their wives could have been mistaken for feudal lords sitting down to a lavish medieval repast provided by their peasants. Such a conclusion, however, would have been entirely erroneous, as the sheep's heads had been ordered from Shapiro's Butchery on the Main Road in Rosebank only a few days earlier. This being the first time that Mr Shapiro had received an order for sheep's heads from Wepener, he suspected that the Schoons might be away on holiday and that the staff had placed the order for their own consumption. Just because they worked at Wepener did not mean that they were exempt from the suspicions generally harboured against most servants. The butcher telephoned the house and spoke to Ou Mevrou Jansen to inform her that Mr Molinieux had cancelled the original order. She curtly told him that Mr Molinieux had telephoned the new order through at her express instructions. She thanked Mr Shapiro for his concern, although she reminded him that there were several competitors along the Main Road who would be more than happy to supply provisions for the Wepener Estate without casting aspersions on the integrity of the staff. Mr Shapiro apologised profusely as he did not wish to risk losing an account of long standing.

To ensure freshness and quality, the chastened butcher had raced down to the abattoir at Philippi where, under the curious and envious gaze of the workers, he selected only the choicest sheep's heads. He later supervised his blockman as he dressed each one with a razor so that they would be perfect, like everything else he delivered to Wepener, for the table of one of his most prestigious customers.

The minister of agriculture admired the doltish look of the ewes and the budding horns on the ram heads. Although he had not been trained as an economist, he knew that the farmer must have realised a handsome profit from the wool, legs and shoulders, loin chops, kidneys and lungs and all the unmentionable bits between the extremities of head and tail. He could think of many things more delectable, but there was no greater bargain than a good old sheep's head. Minister Rijpma approved of Mrs Schoon's sense of economy, and declared to the assembled guests, 'Yes, the merino certainly provides a handsome income for our farmers. We have done well in that department, and there can be no greater tribute to our industrious farmers than the feast we see so generously displayed before us.

'Mr Prime Minister, with your kind permission I would like to propose a toast to the proud achievements of our farmers – and may they achieve even greater success in the coming republic.'

The prime minister clapped his hands in appreciation and the other diners followed suit. He shut his eyes and led the table in grace, which allowed some of the ministers and their wives to cast imploring looks at each other from opposite sides of the vast table. Mr Molinieux indicated to Clara and Enoch to place a head on each dinner plate and the wine steward followed, bearing two decanters. Mr Molinieux took around the huge platter of vegetables. Enoch envied him the task, although the platter may have been a bit heavy for him.

Gawie Pienaar, who had been chosen for Bantu Affairs as much for his adaptability as for his intelligence, began to show his fiancée, next to whom he had been placed, the proper way to tackle a sheep's head. While he may have been the youngest and the least experienced among the members of Dr Schoon's cabinet, ambition and common sense had taught him never to decline hospitality, however humble, especially in his frequent contact with chiefs and headmen. He ate and drank whatever was placed in front of him.

Little conversation ensued around the table as the guests proceeded, in as graceful a manner as possible, to deal with the dish set before them. Enoch noticed the discomfort of the diners and he was certain that many of them had never tackled a sheep's head, although Mrs Schoon savoured the tender jowl meat as if she were an old hand at it. Mr Molinieux's face bore no sign of complicity.

Miss Devora Myburgh prised open the jawbone cautiously, moved it onto her side plate, beckoned to Enoch for it to be removed and whispered to Minister Pienaar that she found herself incapable of looking at the uninviting teeth. The prime minister announced to his guests, 'The success of our republic demands that a person must go to the depths to come out at the heights. Once we are on our way up, nothing, not even the Crown, will turn us back.'

Enoch noticed Mr Molinieux cringing at Dr Schoon's inane remark, as though the last thing he wished was to be serving his tormentors. Just two days earlier, in a rare display of candour, Mr Molinieux had admitted to Ou Mevrou Jansen that had it not been for his loyalty to Mrs Schoon, he would not have agreed to officiate at the banquet. It was the prime minister and not his wife who was responsible for the difficulties he had encountered during the past year. However, Mr Molinieux's initial refusal to make common cause with Ou Mevrou Jansen's attempt to sabotage the banquet had later given way to admiration for the old woman's guile in indulging the inordinate meat cravings of the Dutchmen, and encouraged him to relish the opportunity to eavesdrop on such an unusual gathering. Before their departure, Dries had advised Mr Molinieux to make sure that the minister of interior's glass was topped up throughout, as it might prove useful to have a brief word with him at an appropriate moment.

At a nod from Mr Molinieux the wine steward replenished Mrs van Zyl's glass. She dislodged the sheep's eyes from their sockets and concealed them under the jawbone; however, another glass of wine left her wondering if perhaps the scrutiny of the eyes had not been preferable to the empty sockets now staring back at her. Mrs van Zyl excused herself from the table, while Schoon tried to bring life to the half-hearted attempts of his cabinet colleagues and their wives. He complimented Minister Pienaar on his dexterity. 'Now there's a young man after my own heart,' Dr Schoon remarked. 'I didn't appoint Pienaar to Bantu Affairs for no reason.'

The prime minister could not help entertaining a fleeting thought that his wife's menu, delectable as he may have found it, may have reflected her feelings about certain people she considered her social inferiors. No sooner had Mrs van Zyl returned to resume her seat at the table, than both Minister Marius Venter and Mrs Byleveld excused themselves. Many of the guests, however, including Minister Brink, the Rijpmas, and Miss Devora Myburgh ate with relish and appeared for the most part oblivious to the discomfort of the others. Mr Molinieux took the opportunity to exchange some hurried words with Minister Venter when he emerged from the cloakroom, and the minister agreed to review his case the moment he returned to his office in the New Year.

When the laden cheese board was carried in, Mr Molinieux perceived that perhaps the unsanctioned plot hatched in the kitchen by Ou Mevrou Jansen might have been taken too far. The centrepiece, an enormous cheddar, had been chiselled into the shape of a sheep's head. Everyone admired the dexterity of the carver as well as the arrangement of soft fruits, placed in tiers around the centrepiece.

Dr Schoon helped himself to a bunch of grapes and said, 'I know you will find this hard to believe, but I too was once a boy. Take it from me –

I know what we have to do to get support for our very own republic. We should get our children excited – I can see my granddaughter waving a little flag. But we will need the help of their teachers; it's the teachers we need to convince. And then the children will go home and pester their parents.'

The minister of education appeared lost without his private secretary and, as it was apparent that his ministry would be involved in this exercise, he asked his wife to note down the prime minister's words.

'I can already see the children lined up along the main roads, medals pinned to their blazers and proudly waving the new flag,' Minister Mulder said.

'That's the spirit, Minister. We must do everything possible,' the prime minister concurred, 'and I trust with God's help and your hard work this thing will succeed. Now, if the good ladies would be so kind as to excuse us and follow my wife, we gentlemen can continue our discussions in the study.'

A short while later Mr Molineux, with Enoch's help, served the ministers coffee, brandy and cigars while they were seated in the comfortable chairs of the study. Then the prime minister launched into his scheme for placating the natives who were becoming increasingly resistant to the idea of leaving the Commonwealth.

'Over the centuries our forefathers have made many great sacrifices for this country. It is our duty and joy to finally honour this sacrifice by establishing our independence. An important way forward is to encourage the native to understand his own history and place in this land. He should not be denied his own aspirations – which will be realised in areas set aside for his own economic and cultural upliftment.'

Sybrand Schoon unfurled a map of the country. 'This, gentlemen, is how the proposed Bantu republics will fit into the scheme of our new republic. Come closer and have a look. Sceptics will accuse us of fragmenting the country, but our country has its own particular needs. The natives clearly don't want us interfering in their lives – so let us respect their wish for independence and allow them to vote for their own governments in their own homelands, bearing in mind that it is the policy of my government that the native will not own land in any European area. Of course, even with native self-rule we may still have to learn to live with the occasional black spot and the odd fringe dweller. But just think, we all stand to gain.'

His ministers hemmed and hawed while struggling to come to terms with this new idea. Some of the farmers would undoubtedly be disadvantaged when it came to consolidating tribal lands. However, the ministers had implicit faith in their leader, who they believed would never give away too much of their beloved land to the native.

Mr Molinieux sent Enoch off to the drawing room. He found Clara serving coffee and the ladies in very good humour. Christmas plans were being discussed and the subject of children and grandchildren seemed to dominate the conversation. Enoch was not needed and he returned to the study to find the discussions still in progress. A few of the ministers were inspecting the map which the prime minister had pinned to a board, and Enoch could sense that the evening was finally drawing to a close.

'Gentlemen,' the prime minister said, 'life is a challenge. We should all sleep on this matter, but each of you must send me a memo with your thoughts in the morning. It will give me something to think about over Christmas.'

'Let me tell you, sir,' Minister of Bantu Affairs Pienaar said as he and Dr Schoon shook hands in the hall, 'I've got a hang of a Christmas box for you, Mr Prime Minister. Just wait and see.'

Christmas Eve

'Your grandfather doesn't suspect anything, does he?'

'What do you mean?'

'Oh, come on,' Caroline said as she ran her hand through Enoch's hair. 'Whenever I come to look for you, he says you're busy. What on earth has been keeping you so occupied? You haven't been at the pool for ages. People are wondering what's up.'

'I'm fine – and don't worry; Oupa Hans doesn't suspect a thing.'

'You don't think Mfilo saw us in the woods that time?'

'Unless Byron and Augusta Leigh can talk, nobody should ever know.'

'That's just as well,' Caroline said. 'There's nothing Mfilo can say anyway, and Clara's upset because she thinks the butler grassed on her boyfriend to the cops.'

'What do you mean?'

'In plain English, nanny rejects butler for the garden boy and in a fit of jealousy butler betrays the garden boy to the police. Get the plot? And I hear they're not going to let Mfilo out any time soon. Molinieux refused to go and bail him out. I think they sent Zachaeus and your grandfather to see if they could do anything. Which means that we've got ourselves a decent chunk of time.'

'Don't light that thing in the house – only skollies smoke it.'

'Get a life! You could do with a few puffs yourself. Where are you off to now?'

'I'm going up to the house to find out what happened to Mfilo.'

'I've just told you what happened – and there's nothing you can do. Mfilo is definitely in jail and Zachaeus drove your grandfather to Pringle Bay.'

'The prime minister has something urgent to discuss with Oupa. I've got to go and find out about Mfilo. And if you have to, go and smoke that thing outdoors, please. I'll see you just now.'

Enoch raced up the driveway. He was certain that Mr Molinieux had something to do with Mfilo's disappearance. As for Caroline, she was desperate for attention. Alison had warned him to be careful, but he had been taken unawares by what had happened in the woods a few days ago when Caroline had tried to kiss him.

They sat down on a rock, but no sooner had they done so than Caroline threw her arms around his neck and told him that she was not as horrible as everyone made her out to be. Enoch replied that she was beautiful and clever, despite her best efforts to prove otherwise – and that one day she would be quite a catch for some eligible young man. Caroline had then begun to cry and he had placed his arm around her. He had only meant to comfort her, but she had read too much into his gesture.

Now it was Clara who was in tears as she explained to Enoch how the police had broken down the door of their shack on Steenberg Estate well past midnight and had taken Mfilo away, only allowing him to grab a blanket to cover himself. She had no idea where he was being held nor why. Enoch thought that Mr Molinieux might have had a hand in this, although he wanted to discuss his suspicion with Oupa Hans before he said anything to Clara. When he got back to the gate lodge, he discovered Caroline going through his notebook.

'That's private. Oupa Hans doesn't want anyone to read my work.'

'Then why are you writing it? Don't take yourself too seriously, Enoch. I can't understand why your grandfather is being so protective. It's not as though the censors understand a word they read. Your stuff sounds more like a treasure hunt than a book – a kind of Biggles in Africa. Who would ever lose sleep over that kind of thing?'

'Polycarp said he was impressed.'

'Oh, I'm sure he was … with a name like that.'

'He was named after the Bishop of Smyrna.'

Enoch was considering a further response when Caroline dragged him down beside her and when he tried to get up, she pulled him down again.

'For goodness' sake, Enoch – don't be so square. Usually young men flock around me … I take it you've seen a woman's breasts before? Here, let me show you.'

After some time Enoch's awkward fumbling annoyed Caroline and she brought it to an abrupt halt.

'Now was that really such a bore? Obviously, you don't go big on exploring foreign parts …

'And what's this I hear about you going to a new school?'

'I hate the old one – but nothing is certain about St Dominic's,' Enoch replied, providing her with an exhaustive catalogue of his resentments.

'Gosh, sounds more like a concentration camp than a school. No wonder you've got so many hang-ups. Hatherop Castle in Gloucestershire was my last foray into education – total chaos, but I loved it. Never learned a thing there. The old headmistress was practically deaf and had a huge box-like appendage fixed to her backside. One had to sidle up behind her to talk into it. And she wasn't the worst of the bunch. For geography we usually went out riding. And there were always scads of stupid village boys hanging around the place. In the entire history of the school, only one girl ever made it to university – and that was my dear bluestockinged Aunt Alison, which makes her Granddad's favourite, of course.'

Enoch did not know whether or not to believe Caroline. What kind of school would educate girls and not encourage them to go to university? Caroline was difficult and had her peculiar ways, but she had never lied to him before. He decided to ask Alison about it.

'What the girls did learn was how to behave at coming-out parties – misbehave really – and they were skilled at finding husbands, mainly rich, obnoxious, titled gentlemen. Fortunately my aunt didn't marry one of those.'

'And your grandfather?' Enoch ventured, hoping that she would be less reticent than the others had been.

'Top dog at MI5. Ever read Ian Fleming?'

'No …'

'Too lowbrow for you, I imagine – but it's that sort of thing. May I borrow a hairbrush? It's time for me to go. Hope I haven't distracted you too much. You've got plenty of time left to do some of your famous writing before your grandfather gets back. Someone had to take your education in hand. But don't let a little flirtation go to your head; it's just an early Christmas gift.

'By the way, what was it like being a footman the other night?'

'Is that a serious question? I helped at the banquet for Dries's sake – and if you're so interested, why didn't you stay behind to see for yourself?'

'That was another one of Dries's flea-brained ideas. The day he and Aunt Alison actually do something radical …'

'I'll tell you all about it some day.'

Caroline paused for a moment before leaving and kissed Enoch, which led to another awkward moment. 'Who would've believed that old bag in the kitchen capable of such a marvellous act of sabotage – serving sheep's heads at a banquet? She's really gone up in my estimation.'

'Ou Mevrou Jansen didn't mean it like that. Mr Molinieux helped her plan the menu.' Only then did it dawn on Enoch that it might even have been Alison's idea. It was the kind of thing she would do.

'I'm damned sure that it was the old woman's idea. Must dash – Hanneli is probably raring to go by now. I promised to help her arrange the presents under the Christmas tree.'

An hour or so later, on his way back from the clinic, Dries dropped in at the gate lodge to ask whether Enoch knew why Oupa Hans had been summoned to Pringle Bay. Enoch knew of the relationship between Khotso and Dr Schoon, but was under the impression that Dries had a limited idea about what was going on. He was tempted to show Dries parts of the story he had written, but he first had to ask his grandfather's permission. It was bad enough that Caroline had had the audacity to go through his papers. He decided that it was up to Oupa Hans to discuss this matter with Dries.

Even though Enoch knew it to be an inopportune moment, considering Dries's concerns about his father, he asked him a question that had been troubling him for some time – why so many of his friends were in detention or under banning orders while he and Alison did as they pleased without apparent consequences.

'What makes you think that?' Dries said. 'I can do more for my friends being out of prison than I otherwise could. I suppose it's an accident of birth. My father's a powerful man. But the moment he goes, for whatever reason, I go. It's simple. For my family and me there will be consequences. We'll probably end up selling Wepener and leaving for England. That's partly why I want you there.'

'But you can't do that.'

'What do you mean?'

'I promised Ou Mevrou Jansen not to say anything.'

'Enoch, how can she tell you something and keep it secret from me?'

'Because it involves you. She told me because she wanted somebody to know before she died. You can't sell Wepener. It belongs to her. I didn't have the guts to tell you before because you've got a lot of things to worry about.'

'This is a shock … I came to ask you about my father and you tell me about Ou Mevrou Jansen … what an exchange.'

'I just thought somebody should know.'

'Wait a minute … she must've said something to Fanus. I vaguely remember that he once tried telling me about it, but I wouldn't believe him. At the time I was busy and it sounded just like typical old Fanus trying to annoy me and to find reasons for being obnoxious about our parents. I had no reason to believe him. So he died with the secret and as you are the new favourite, Ou Mevrou Jansen told you.

'Don't worry, I'll handle it properly – and thanks for letting me know. This is hardly the time to ask – but do we have time for a quick game, hey, Enoch? I've had quite a day and am desperate for exercise.'

'I have about an hour. Unless I'm expected to help with dinner.'

'Everything is being catered, so there is no need to worry – and I need a game.'

'Great – just give me a minute to change and I'll meet you up at the courts.'

Dries played like a demon. He kept serving onto Enoch's backhand, and whenever Enoch served he managed to return each ball with a stolid determination. It was only in the second set that Enoch gained the upper hand. Just before they commenced a new set, Enoch saw Zachaeus stopping at the gate lodge. He and Oupa Hans had taken along the dogs for the ride and Byron and Augusta Leigh came dashing across the lawn. Enoch managed to shut the gate just in time to keep them off the court. Dries looked at his watch.

'Please don't think of talking to Oupa now, Dries. It's going to be hard enough to get him to the house for dinner. You know how difficult he is. Let's finish this set and get ready for the evening.'

Enoch ran a bath for his grandfather. Oupa Hans complained about being exhausted, although when he saw that Enoch had laid out his clothes, he agreed to go along. Trossie had pressed his suit and had done a good job starching and ironing his shirt. She had even darned Oupa Hans's socks.

'I now consider Schoon officially mad,' Oupa Hans said, shaking his head. 'He's a raving lunatic – a seriously disturbed man. And he's our prime minister. I don't care if you write that down. I did everything I could to stop him taking off for Cofimvaba right away. Fortunately, Witbooi is sick so we couldn't leave. Schoon has no right to spoil Khotso's Christmas, nor mine – and poor Mrs Schoon was in tears.'

'Dries is worried about his father and he wants to talk with Oupa Hans.'

'I've got nothing to say to him about that, my boy. I hope you're wearing the new suit your mama got for you.'

'I've been thinking about it.'

'Don't think. Just wear it. For a shop-bought suit it's quite nice – and you look good in it. Is it the usual Christmas Eve dinner tonight?'

'I'm not sure what we're having. Dries says they've got in a caterer.'

'Sounds odd to me. Imagine getting in strangers to fiddle around with your food. I'm surprised Ou Mevrou Jansen allowed that.'

'Enoch, I am tired – please don't make me sing carols tonight. I'm just going up to the house to be polite.'

Enoch collected the presents he had wrapped. He then went to look for Zachaeus as he thought it best if he drove Oupa Hans to the front door. However, Zachaeus had gone out with the car. Dries offered to collect Oupa instead. A profusion of aromas wafted from the kitchen – curry – not just the usual Malay sort, but proper Indian curry. Enoch thought it a highly unorthodox smell for Christmas Eve. The staff were already gathered around the Christmas tree in the parlour, and Mr Molinieux handed Enoch a glass of champagne when he walked in. Hanneli took Enoch's hand, led him to the tree, and pointed out the presents that bore his name. Alison wore a stunning new dress. He saw Haima's name on one of the gifts, and suddenly it all became clear to him.

A few days earlier he had heard Ou Mevrou Jansen tell Alison that she considered all of God's creatures to be the same and saw no earthly reason why they all could not eat the same food. 'What is wrong with a beautiful goose?' she demanded. 'And how the devil can I go and squeeze the suet out of a Christmas pudding?'

Enoch wondered why this had not alerted him to the fact that someone unusual had been invited to the Christmas Eve party. He could only assume that Zachaeus had driven to Simonstown to collect Haima. And what about Caroline? The prospect of seeing Haima no longer thrilled Enoch as it had done only weeks earlier. However tenuous their budding friendship, Caroline was the first girl who had shown any interest in him, whereas Haima had often snubbed him. And why? It could have been any number of things, the most obvious being that he was not an Indian. Then there was the distinct possibility that she thought him immature. Enoch had a strong feeling that Alison had invited Haima to defuse the 'situation' with Caroline.

Hanneli reached for the presents Enoch held in his hands. 'Can I put these under the tree?' She took them from him before he could reply. 'This big one says Caroline on the card.'

Alison threw her arms around Enoch and kissed him. 'Merry Christmas! I have a wonderful surprise for you …' At that moment Dries and Oupa Hans walked into the parlour and she turned to them. 'Mr Pretorius, how wonderful to see you. I hope you're not too worn out after your tiring day.'

'I wouldn't miss this party for anything, Alison. Good evening, everyone. A merry Christmas. No champagne for me, thank you Mr Molinieux. I'll have a glass of Ou Mevrou Jansen's ginger beer.'

Clara came up behind Enoch and whispered in his ear, 'Has Alison invited Haima?' She seemed quite recovered from her trauma earlier in the day and Enoch wasn't about to mention Mfilo's absence.

'Why do you think there's an Indian chef in the kitchen? He's from the Mount Nelson, nogal. And you must choose one of the two young ladies.'

'What two young ladies?'

'Goodness me, Enoch, you must think I'm blind or something.'

Enoch was overcome with nervousness and he had to place the champagne glass on a table – which was fortunate, as Haima entered the parlour at just that moment, followed by his parents. It would have been the last straw for Mama and Dowa to discover their son drinking champagne, although he believed that they would have had the grace to postpone the reprimand until the following day when he and Oupa Hans were expected at home for lunch.

'So that's Haima ... You've got to go give her a peck on the cheek,' Clara prompted him. 'She's a beautiful girl, Enoch. No wonder you so frightened of her – and how you going to choose between her and Caroline?'

Enoch followed Clara's advice, and for good measure kissed his mother and father as well. Hanneli took an immediate liking to Haima, who was dressed in a gorgeous sari. It was a bit unnerving for him to see her standing there. He had previously only seen her in school uniform. He was breathless. Enoch presented her to Dries and Alison.

'Now we can see why Enoch talks about you so much,' Alison said to her. 'Come and meet the rest of the party.'

Although Haima appeared surprised by such an odd gathering, she carried herself with poise. Enoch was pleased that Hanneli held onto her hand, as it must have made Haima feel more at home.

'Quick, let me show you your present,' Hanneli whispered as Haima bent down to look under the tree. 'It's from Enoch. Mummy said that he's in love.'

At that moment Caroline walked in. She looked stunning in a dark blue cocktail dress. She introduced herself to Enoch's parents and Haima, and then walked across to join Enoch beside the Christmas tree. 'Don't worry about us for now – just devote your attention to that lovely girl.' She then left him to greet the other guests.

'Good thing your mama bought you that suit – we were not expecting to see so many young ladies here tonight.'

'Neither was I, Dowa. It was Alison's surprise to invite Haima. I'm very happy that we are all together on Christmas Eve.'

'Yes, but we can't stay late – we've got the midnight service.'

Mr Molinieux announced that dinner would be ready shortly and showed each one to his place around the table. Only Hanneli's place setting had to be moved, as she insisted on sitting between Haima and Enoch. Mr Molinieux served red grape juice from a decanter to the non-drinkers – and since Enoch was separated from his mother and father by a vast mahogany surface, they could not tell which decanter he held over his glass. Caroline appeared to be on her best behaviour, seated between Enoch's parents.

Enoch had seldom, if ever, seen Mr Molinieux in such good spirits. He pampered Mama and Dowa and was most solicitous of Haima's needs. What surprised him even more was the relaxed attitude he showed towards the rest of the staff. Trossie laughed and chatted, dispensing with her usual gloom.

'Ou Mevrou Jansen says there is no Father Christmas,' Hanneli confided in Haima, before Dowa had ended his blessing. 'She says there's only baby Jesus.'

'I know that,' Haima replied, and to everyone's amazement said, 'I am a Christian.'

'But I thought you were a Brahman,' Enoch exclaimed, having engrossed himself in the Vedas and other obscure texts so as not to appear unprepared were he to be confronted by her father at some point in the future.

'That's a caste designation, not a faith, silly.'

Hanneli shrieked with laughter. 'Haima called Enoch *silly*. Silly Billy.'

Alison smiled at Haima conspiratorially. Enoch could see they would get along well.

'My family's been Orthodox Christian for generations. We worship in our own language according to the Syrian rites.'

'Just as well Polycarp is not with us this evening,' Enoch said, 'otherwise he would've told us about the Syrian rites. He knows all about obscure beliefs.'

'There's nothing obscure about it,' Haima responded.

'Enoch must always have the last word,' Mama said with some embarrassment, 'never satisfied just to listen and learn.'

Hanneli erupted in peals of laughter. Enoch concentrated on the delicious vegetarian fare brought to the table by uniformed waiters. It appeared that the subject of religion, even on Christmas Eve, was best avoided. However, he was looking forward to the further research that awaited him in the library reference room.

Ou Mevrou Jansen said, 'Enoch may be silly, but he is one of the sweetest boys I know.'

This provoked a toast from Alison. 'Here's to the *sweetest boy* we know.'

'Why does Enoch call his papa "Dowa"?' Hanneli asked as they raised their glasses.

Enoch was mortified as this question had often caused him much embarrassment with his friends. He had tried to explain it away by saying that it was the Arabic word for father. That had mollified some of them.

'Why don't you ask Enoch?' Dowa said.

Enoch refused to be drawn on this. Perhaps it was an unwise decision because all eyes were now focused on him as Dowa explained.

'When Enoch was little, he called me Dowa. Don't ask me why – because his mom has always been Mama. No matter how hard we tried, he could never say Papa and in the end we just left it that way. When he was a bit older, we tried again – and I made up a poem to help him. But not even that helped.'

Not to be outdone, Mama spoke up. 'Fred is forever writing his poems,' she said, 'and I'm always worried that he'll influence Enoch. Then I'll never hear the end of it.'

'Tell us the poem, Mr Pretorius,' Hanneli chimed in.

'Let Mr Pretorius enjoy his dinner in peace, my darling,' Alison said. 'And don't forget you're at the table.'

'But Enoch and I sing at the table …'

Dowa needed no further invitation. 'It's only an amusing little thing, Mrs Schoon,' he said before Enoch could prevent him. 'It should take only a minute.'

'By all means, Mr Pretorius. Enoch has always told us that you have an expressive voice.'

A space ship landed on earth to see
how grownups lose their identity,
as soon as they marry and have progeny
they change their names to Mummy and Daddy.
It's true, some do say Mama or Papa,
but they are the toffs and la-di-da.
The Afghan version is a treat,
Mor and Plaar are hard to beat.

The French, as usual, try to be chic
as they dance together, cheek to cheek.
Papa is father, as is the case elsewhere,

while mum is Maman, and no child would dare
to call her by her Christian name –
and leave her without claim to fame.
Mama, Baba, I must confess
make a perfect Zulu address.

While boys have names like Toby and Maximilien
and girls become Flo and Biffy and Gillian –
as soon as they marry they all tend to lose
their names and the freedom to pick and choose.
China has millions of mums and dads
although there are fewer lasses than lads
who cut their teeth on stir-fry, not stew
and grow up to be Dieh and Mamu.
And in India, famed for its breakfast tea,
they call them Mommy- and Daddy-ji.
As to the name, Dowa, I take off my hat
to the young boy who came up with that.

A minute, he had said, but the doggerel ran on for ages, and just as
Enoch was about to try to change the subject, Hanneli cried, 'Please tell
it again, Dowa.'

'No, my darling,' her mother said firmly. 'Allow Mr Pretorius to have
his dinner before it gets cold. After dinner we'll all be singing carols. Mr
Pretorius, that was very charming.'

'I will get Enoch to type it out for you, and then you can read it whenever you want,' Dowa said to Hanneli.

'Thank you, Mr Pretorius – I'll learn it by heart.'

'Come, Hanneli, let's not dawdle,' Ou Mevrou Jansen said, sensing
Enoch's discomfort. 'Mr and Mrs Pretorius have a service to go to – and
we still have carols and the presents.'

Enoch devoted his attention to Haima, but from time to time picked
up fragments of conversation between Dowa and Alison. Only once did
Dowa try to engage him in conversation by asking if Haima was the top
student in their class. When Enoch confirmed this, he proposed a toast
to her continued success.

Not to be outdone, Dries raised his glass. 'Here's to Enoch and his famous book.'

Enoch looked at Oupa Hans and was pleased that he winked.

'To the book.'

'The closed book,' Caroline added.

'What book are we talking about?' Dowa asked.

Enoch was grateful when Oupa replied, 'The Pretorius family history.'

Dries announced that the braai for the staff and their families would be held, as usual, on Boxing Day. Mr Molinieux agreed to be Father Christmas as Oupa Hans was not feeling up to it, and Dries asked Enoch to be at the swimming pool to keep an eye on the children. With the exception of Dowa's performance, it was the happiest Christmas Eve Enoch could remember. The singing resounded throughout the house and Mama held onto Enoch's hand and dabbed at her eyes from time to time.

Hanneli was appointed to hand out the gifts and patiently waited till last to unwrap the presents she had received. Dries showed Enoch how to work his new camera, while Alison helped Haima put on her present: a pair of exquisite earrings, with a matching necklace.

'Enoch has good taste, don't you think?' Alison said as Haima admired herself in a mirror. 'He found them at a dear little antiques shop in Cape Town the other day.'

Enoch had been nowhere near an antiques shop. The jewellery had been a gift to Alison from her father.

'Enoch, you shouldn't have,' Haima whispered. 'This is a beautiful present.'

'Do you like them? I hope you will wear them when we go to the theatre.'

'You mean, if we go. I've only been let out under special dispensation this evening and mainly because Mrs Schoon begged my father to let me come.'

'That's good to know. I'll get her to arrange our dates in future – should you agree.'

'Let me think about it.'

To Enoch's surprise, Haima kissed him on the lips. His feelings were in turmoil. What would he have chosen for Haima had he known that she was expected for Christmas Eve? A box of chocolates. A book perhaps.

'And Caroline, this is for you from Enoch,' Hanneli said as she handed over a large package.

All eyes were on Caroline as she carefully undid the string and removed the wrapping. She withdrew the painting Enoch had worked on and which, apart from Gladys, only Oupa Hans had seen.

'This is a charming landscape, Enoch,' she said as though she really meant it and showed it to the others. 'I had no idea that you painted so well.'

'I'd be careful – the paint is not quite dry.'

Haima's curfew coincided with the midnight service Mama and Dowa were hoping to attend. Dowa was pleased with his new typewriter and fountain pen. With the exception of Oupa Hans and Ou Mevrou Jansen, everyone went out to the car. Haima kissed Enoch and thanked him again for the gift – and added that she was quite fond of him. Enoch thought fondness an emotion more suitable for an aunt or a cousin, possibly a cat, but for now he was consoled by what Haima probably considered a daring endearment.

As Enoch's mother got into the car, she looked at her son with pride. He imagined Zachaeus driving his parents along the Main Road to church, and then continuing all the way to Haima's house in Simonstown. Haima had told him that the wave crests could be seen from her balcony even on the darkest night, and he wondered whether he would ever be standing beside her on that balcony. But for now it was Caroline who stood next to him as they watched the car lights disappearing down the drive. She took his hand and they walked back indoors.

Angel Voices

Earth has many a noble city;
Bethlehem, thou dost all excel:
out of thee the Lord from heaven
came to rule his Israel

— PRUDENTIUS 348–C.413

The late December clouds brought raindrops large as grapes, falling reluctantly and leaving craters in the sand. The drumming on the thatch prompted Dr Schoon to get up from his chair and shut the window. He had been prime minister for almost two years. In the past, as student, lecturer and politician, he had felt secure with the status quo, but now he was worried because so much of the country was in disarray. The unrest in the native locations and reserves had worsened and Dr Schoon had begun to feel control slip from his grasp little by little. It was not that long ago when, as minister of native affairs, he was able to reason with the chiefs and persuade them to cooperate with the native commissioners. Now the direct intervention of the police and defence force had become necessary to curb civil disorder.

The prime minister had even begun to doubt his grasp of the native mind, a mind that after years of study and observation had proved to him to be enigmatic and superstitious, yet pliant and impressionable. He could not avoid thinking that throughout his tenure in Native Affairs he had been tutor to literally millions of people. However, these certainties were being tested in what was rapidly becoming a fast-changing world.

During his last visit to Cofimvaba, Khotso had tried to convince Dr Schoon that the unrest throughout the country was the outcome of an unequal and unjust society. Rather than being a clear and legal demarcation that allowed people to develop along their own lines as determined by the National Party, racial segregation had instead exacerbated the differences between population groups and, Khotso had explained, in time the natives would find increasingly violent means to express their frustration.

Had this argument come from Josias Nkosivile or any other detractor, Dr Schoon would have rejected it immediately, but he had given Khotso's words careful thought. However, to walk a different spoor now would only open the floodgates and he could not allow that to happen. The settling of accounts from time to time in the past had been one thing; now it had become clear to the prime minister that it was his duty to defend the rightful place of his people in this country – the young lions had to be kept securely in their cages.

In response to Khotso's censure, the prime minister had asked himself, 'When a mob is clamouring at your gate would you slip out at the back door to join them in battering down your own front door?' It was obvious that the gateposts had to be strengthened.

Outside in the garden, the bark of the Douglas fir trees darkened in the summer rain and the eucalyptus leaves became waterfalls, funnelling raindrops onto the wet sand. Over the sound of the rain Dr Schoon could hear his wife in the kitchen: the occasional lid being replaced on a saucepan or the muffled clang of the oven door. Mrs Schoon had decided long ago to forego the services of a servant at Pringle Bay and preserve what little privacy and peace she and her husband enjoyed. She also refused to use electricity for cooking at the cottage, preferring the Aga that filled the kitchen with the smell of burning wood whenever she stoked it. It reminded her of how her two boys, the one long dead, had sought the warmth of the kitchen in winter to do their homework at the oak table, rather than at the desks in their bedrooms.

When Dries had returned unexpectedly from London with his young English wife, Arta Schoon had handed Wepener, the family estate, over to him. The beach cottage had now become home to Mrs Schoon. She had never grown accustomed to the official residence in Cape Town and she was reluctant to spend more time there than was necessary. She found Groote Schuur too formal and its attendant servants, gardeners and guards intrusive.

At Pringle Bay she kept the cottage as neat as a pin. She had arranged the pots and pans as well as the Delftware, which she had acquired many years earlier, in a display cabinet. This was her home.

Mrs Schoon was preparing the usual Christmas meal. She had been looking forward to spending Christmas alone with her husband – it would have been the first time in thirty-five years – but then he had so generously invited the children. Mrs Schoon had spent a few pleasant afternoons at Stuttafords choosing Christmas gifts for her family. Dries, Alison and Hanneli were expected at around midday, although the unseasonable rain might delay them. Despite her insistence that Alison's niece come as well, the girl had decided that she would rather spend the day on her own at Wepener.

The refrain 'Sleep in heavenly peace … Slaap in hemelse rus …' descended on the house. Dr Schoon found himself humming along with the tune. He walked into the sitting room to see if perhaps his wife had put on a record or had switched on the wireless while she worked. However, both the gramophone and wireless were off. Voices filled the air. Dr Schoon was certain that he was hearing the voices of angels, deep, resonant and pure. As if he was under a spell, he flung open the study windows, longing to see the heavenly host. He searched the sky, but all he could see was the calm sweep of gulls gliding in the distance. On the beach, however, between the weathered picket fence marking the boundary of their property and the shoreline, he caught sight of his host of angels: hundreds of black men, dressed in suits, white shirts and bow ties. The rain had stopped, as if by their presence they had driven away the clouds.

The prime minister recoiled in disbelief; as he listened, he did not know whether to be outraged at the absence of angels, or thankful for such beautiful song on the lips of natives. He felt ashamed that he had been tricked into believing that angels would descend on his patch of Pringle Bay. As he studied the faces of the choir members, he could clearly see their resentment. He was reminded of the news bulletin about the disturbances in Pondoland he had listened to earlier that morning: 'The rebels cornered in their mountain caves … Refusal to surrender … Smoked out like dogs with tear gas … Cut down by Sten gun fire …' And now it seemed as if the problem had come to haunt him right on his doorstep.

The astonishing sight on the beach and the magnificence of the voices troubled Dr Schoon and stirred up feelings he had successfully suppressed. He struggled with the revulsion that swept over him. It was Christmas, and the day was being robbed of its joy. A grand joke had been played on him.

But his wife had no such conflicting emotions. She tidied her hair and hurried down the gravel path to welcome the singers.

Dr Schoon remembered that, at the close of the banquet he had hosted for his ministers, Pienaar had promised him a hang of a Christmas box in gratitude for his elevation to the ministry of Bantu Affairs. Seeing him standing on the beach, dressed in black, his back towards the house, baton raised, confirmed Dr Schoon's suspicions.

Pienaar turned to see what impression he had made. He knew that the concert he had contrived could not but be pleasing to the prime minister. Pienaar's thick mat of brown hair framed a face on which much careful nurturing had not left a single line of character; however, this deficiency had left plenty of room for ambition, which found expression in his obsequious manner.

'Hey, Minister Pienaar, you so-and-so,' the prime minister exclaimed, trying to kindle some enthusiasm, 'up to your old tricks, hey? Only you could've thought up a Christmas box like this.' Then he leaned over to whisper, 'You know, of course, that you're breaking the law. You think because you're minister you can put the natives on a European beach, hey?' The two men chuckled.

'If you don't watch out, you'll know all about it.'

'Ag, but it's the season for surprises, Mr Prime Minister,' Gawie Pienaar replied.

He was unable to gauge Dr Schoon's real mood. The cheerful look on Mrs Schoon's face, however, allayed his fears.

'Mr Prime Minister is always so serious. Here I bring a bunch of natives to sing for him and he wants to throw the law at me. And I've organised lots of police to keep an eye on them.'

'Come, come now, Pienaar, my young friend. Just look who's serious now. Can't you tell when a person makes a joke? This is a wonderful Christmas present. Look, Mrs Schoon is thrilled. When she was stirring her pots, she thought she was hearing real angels singing. No man – you did the right thing. How can I ever thank you?'

Mrs Schoon's face was indeed glowing with joy. She clapped her hands in pleasure, though a brief frown crossed her face when she realised that she had not removed her apron before dashing from the kitchen. She immediately apologised to the minister for this oversight.

'Come now, don't go make a fuss about an apron,' Dr Schoon said to his wife. 'Tell me, Minister Pienaar, can you get the boys to sing Mrs Schoon's favourite, you know, "Betlehem Ster" …'

The minister of Bantu Affairs raised his baton above the silent heads and brought his charges to attention. Dr Schoon was perturbed by the sight and wondered how much Pienaar had spent on the extravagance: the white shirts, suits and ties and, parked along the gravel road behind the dunes, several large buses from Lombard's Tours. Through the forest of legs he observed that the men were at least wearing their own shoes and sandals, with the odd pair of gumboots in evidence. Pienaar must have scoured the whole of Cape Town to hire so many dress suits. Which men's outfitter in his right mind would take back the suits, Schoon wondered?

Now that the sun had burnt off the clouds and dried the sand to a crust, the men stood on the beach, perspiring, some refusing to sing, although they hid behind others to spare themselves the wrath of the man so recently entrusted with the portfolio of Bantu affairs. The timbre of the voices pleased the prime minister and especially his wife, who could barely conceal her excitement. When the men came to the end of her favourite carol, she whispered to her husband, 'Ag shame, I would have made ginger beer and biscuits – if only I had known these people were coming.'

Minister Pienaar overheard her. 'Now Mrs Schoon mustn't come worry. These poor wretches can't just think that Mrs Schoon can organise an instant feeding scheme. Mrs Schoon should have seen their faces when I gave them each a lucky dip I bought at an Indian shop. The shopkeeper even put in Christmas crackers for their children. And as for drink, these boys got gallons of umqombothi waiting for them when they get back to their locations.'

'Shame, you don't realise that the natives are just like children, Minister Pienaar. They always expect something. When you and the lovely Miss Myburgh get married and have children,' Mrs Schoon remarked, 'you'll understand what I'm talking about. At Christmas every person has got it in his heart to give.' She turned to her husband. He reminded her of the four enormous fish bowls gathering dust in the bottom of their late son's wardrobe. The bowls were filled to overflowing with sixpences Fanus had collected.

'Look, I know what we can do, let's give the natives a handful of six-pences each – finish and klaar. It would be a good way of remembering Fanus this Christmas,' Dr Schoon suggested. 'Anyway, they won't be in circulation for much longer.'

With this gift now decided upon, and seeing no reasonable grounds for protest, Minister Pienaar acquiesced, but he could not avoid feeling that his patience was being tried. The mere act of singing for the prime minister should have been honour enough for these ingrates. The minister neglected to mention that the police had whipped and threatened the men from township streets into waiting buses. He had then felt like a quartermaster, dishing out clothes while they were in transit to Pringle Bay. And he would still have a substantial bill for the dry-cleaning and laundering. Bantu Affairs functioned on a lean budget and had no provision for unanticipated expenditure. Christmas or no Christmas – Minister Pienaar could think of no earthly reason to spoil them.

'Hey, Gawie,' the prime minister said, 'it's nothing but a pleasure for me and Mrs Schoon to do our own special something for your black angels. There isn't any fuss.'

Pienaar, holding the baton under his arm in military style, snapped his fingers at four singers standing in front of him. 'On the double now; I want you to go help the prime minister carry your Christmas box. Jump to it – one, two, three!'

The appointed men broke ranks and followed the path to the back of the cottage where they waited for the prime minister, who had entered by the front door. Dr Schoon could not help noticing the implacable look in the eyes of the men as he handed each one a heavy glass bowl. He shut the kitchen door behind him in an effort to curb the smell of the roasting bird and steaming pudding coming from the stove.

'It's our lunch,' he mumbled, apologetically. 'Your women must also have something nice waiting for you when you get home,' he continued, unaware that the men had not had the opportunity to forewarn their families of their absences.

Indeed, the perception that had emerged in the locations was that the police had taken advantage of the relaxed atmosphere of Christmas and had conducted a massive pass raid. So firmly had that conviction taken hold that ministers in township churches had not neglected to mention in their Christmas sermons the complicity of Lombard's Tours in this devilish scheme – and they vowed that in future those buses would no longer be hired for Sunday school picnics, old-age pensioner outings or for the more lucrative initiation trips to the Transkei.

'You boys ever see so much money?' Sybrand Schoon commented self-consciously as the men carried the bowls past him to the waiting choir. 'There must be at least ten bob for each of you in there.'

'No, Grootbaas Prime Minister,' they replied, 'never seen so much money before, Grootbaas Prime Minister.'

Pienaar drew a line in the sand with his baton and instructed the four to take up positions behind the line, facing the choir. He tapped the chest of a fifth man and instructed him to get the others into a queue and to file past Mrs Schoon.

'Your hands are smaller than mine, Mrs Schoon. You must dip into the bowls for each one – we don't want these boys to fight because one got more than the other.'

'Why don't we use a soup ladle,' Mrs Schoon suggested. 'That would be fair.' The prime minister returned to the kitchen to find a ladle.

'Now listen,' Pienaar said to the man he had appointed as boss boy, 'I want to hear everyone say "thank you" to Nooi Schoon, hey? After that, fall back into line and we will sing a carol or two before we leave.

'Also, while you boys are walking up here, I want you to sing "Away in a Manger", right? Nooi Schoon thinks you are all angels, so I want you to behave like angels and not skelms, do you hear me? Stay in line; there are more than enough sixpences for everyone.' Then turning to the prime minister, he said, 'So, where are the newspapers and their cameras now, hey? This would make a good story for the English papers that say we Afrikaners don't know how to treat the natives. This is one experience these men will never forget.'

Pienaar's reference to the press reminded Dr Schoon about the disturbances in Pondoland. He called him aside. 'Your choir is excellent, but don't forget your duties as minister of Bantu affairs. I would like a full report on the situation in Pondoland with recommendations on what we can do to patch up things there. I'm sorry to keep you in the saddle over Christmas, Gawie – but I'm sure you'll understand that this can't wait. I'd like your report on my desk when I'm back in Cape Town.'

Pienaar had no particular liking for the minister of police, Piet Greyling, and considered him responsible for the massacre. But as he planned to fly out to Pondoland to review the situation, he decided to meet up with some of the chiefs whose friendship he had cultivated. This undertaking enjoyed its own line in his department's budget.

That morning Greyling had telephoned the prime minister to explain the situation. He said that when the rebels had emerged from the caves, the flimsy white vest or handkerchief they had flown from the end of their spears could just as well have been red rags waved at a bull. The police and soldiers had gone berserk.

'They were afraid,' Greyling had said. 'It was dark. My men only wanted to get back to their families for Christmas. Can you blame them, Mr Prime Minister?'

Piet Greyling had been appointed to the only available cabinet post as the members wanted to placate the Afrikaner worker during a time of change and uncertainty. He had begun his working life as a porter and ticket examiner and had advanced through the Railways and Harbours hierarchy. Greyling carried with him the stigma of his class and the peaked cap he had worn every day for twenty years had left a permanent furrow on his brow. The prime minister had had misgivings about Greyling's appointment. Now what better example of the man's gross incompetence was needed? The minister of police had declared a state of emergency on Christmas Eve without consultation, and had asked for the assistance of the minister of defence to deploy troops in a situation that had needed delicate handling.

Pienaar led the choir in a final carol and felt a mounting impatience to get this new task under way. He was already planning to take the wind out of Greyling's faltering sails. As one of the last choristers reached Mrs Schoon, the man executed a theatrical bow; another followed suit, attempting to make his bow even more elaborate. From the corner of his eye Pienaar kept a careful watch for the slightest sign of disrespect, but he need not have worried.

Pringle Bay once more resumed its tranquil atmosphere when the last of the buses departed for Langa and Nyanga. Dr Schoon entered his study to place a trunk call to Pretoria. While waiting to be connected, he gazed out of the window and noticed the footprints on the beach being gradually erased as the tide washed in, and with the seamless grafting of wave upon wave all traces of his visitors soon disappeared. He settled back into his chair and remembered his two boys mimicking sandpipers – racing the edge of an incoming wave and then following it as it receded, to pick playfully at the little crabs, blue bottles and other debris left on the fringes. Their cheerful voices were as clear to him as the earlier carols of the natives. He gave the telephone another vigorous crank.

The aromas of food reached him. Mrs Schoon had prepared roast goose, saffron rice studded with currents, cardamom and cloves, roast potatoes and a brandy-soaked Christmas pudding that had been maturing for almost two months. He wiped his eyes on his handkerchief and thanked God for Hanneli, who had come to fill the void left by the death of his beloved son, Fanus. He cranked the telephone yet again, trying to get the ladies at the Cape Town exchange to respond as he was keen to make his call before Dries and his family arrived.

Dr Schoon was unable to get through to the minister of police; the switchboard at the Union Buildings in Pretoria was not answering. Instead he decided to telephone Khotso, wish him a merry Christmas and confer with him about the situation in Pondoland. About half an hour remained before lunch. He was pleasantly surprised to be put through on his first attempt.

'Khotso, is that you? I want to wish you a merry Christmas, my friend – you and your whole family.'

'Wait a minute – let me put Polycarp on the extension. His Xhosa is now a lot better. To what do I owe this honour, Mr Prime Minister? This is the very first time you have shown concern for the way I spend my Christmas. Thank you, and a merry Christmas to you, the wife and children.

'You think you can risk putting a trunk call through to me on Christmas Day because everyone is at home with their families? Stories are already getting out that people listen in on our conversations. You must be more careful, Mr Prime Minister, before all our secrets get out.'

'I was hoping to stop by at Cofimvaba and see you on our way to the Drakensberg, but it doesn't seem possible. We've been obliged to call an extraordinary session of parliament, so Mrs Schoon and I will not be going to Cathedral Peak after all. But there are a few things we need to talk about. Tell me, how is that jailbird that I sent you getting on?'

'Polycarp is fine. But maybe you should ask him. His parents are now living with us in the compound. They were chucked out of their railway cottage and they are better off here. They told me when Polycarp was small he learned the native dances from the maid and his mother had to beat it out of him. Well, he's getting the right moves back.'

The two men laughed as the prime minister visualised Polycarp with his blazing red hair stomping his eager little legs to unfamiliar rhythms he had learned from his nursemaid.

'So there is some good news, at least,' Dr Schoon said.

'Yes, there is plenty going on here. We all dressed up for the Zionists' nativity procession this morning – some of the children looked like angels and others dressed up as lambs. The whole thing was quite a spectacle – especially for your policemen, who watched from the hills through their binoculars. I hope they enjoyed the show as much as we did.

'You'll probably remember my young assistant, Redemptus; he was here too. These days he has quite a following.'

'Come now, Khotso, we can't be on the telephone all day. All I wanted to tell you was that we will soon have our republic, and the thought has occurred to me that we will consolidate the Bantu homelands too. We will turn the Transkei into its own republic. That means the Bantu will have their own parliaments – I hope you are impressed, my friend.'

Khotso had already heard of this scheme and had grave misgivings about it. Effectively the African would have no say at all in national affairs, and by fobbing them off with tribal independence, the government planned to ensure white supremacy in all but the native reserves. He met the news with silence.

'Hello, hello – Khotso, are you there?'

'Yes, I'm just thinking of how often we are tempted to take our worst fears and try to masquerade them under the banner of progress.'

'My goodness man, Khotso, I know it's Christmas, but you begin to sound like a dominee. You know, it's not easy for me. It's a bit like standing all alone on top of a mountain.'

'Ah, but what a view you must have. Why do you people always have to climb mountains? We only go up the mountains when our cattle go astray.'

'Ag, you never see things my way. Look, Khotso, think of the opportunities independence will offer your people.'

'You are far too ambitious to my way of thinking. You want to change too much at one time.'

'You don't understand, my friend.'

'Surely you didn't call me on this beautiful Christmas Day to talk politics?'

'Khotso, we are too old to argue. Come on, be reasonable. There you are with your wives and children – and me with mine. We have no secrets from each other.'

'Nohlwandle is calling for me. There are many of us at Cofimvaba and we have slaughtered two oxen. I wish you good fortune. Thank you for calling.'

'Please, let's stay in touch – I really need your help with the troubles in Pondoland and with the development of the independent Bantu homelands.'

'Let's not spoil our Christmas. Why don't we talk about this on another day? Goodbye.'

'Goodbye – and thank Polycarp for his help.'

Dr Schoon replaced the telephone and, taking Khotso's advice to enjoy the festivities, banished from his mind what the minister of police had brought to his attention that very morning – the killing of scores of people at Ngquza Hill.

Gerhardus Lubbe

Settling herself comfortably on her grandfather's lap, Hanneli showed him one of the presents she had received for Christmas – an illustrated book of birds with a recording of their calls tucked into the back cover.

'When Papa and Uncle Fanus were boys, they didn't need a book to tell them which bird was which. They could recognise a bird just by looking at it.'

'Tell me about one, Oupa.'

'Your Uncle Fanus used to say the Cape canary has a season ticket because he travels from Rhodesia to the Free State, then to the Cape and on to Natal where all the English people live. And what about the oranjeborssuikerbekkie – can you say that?'

'Oranjeborssuikerbekkie,' Hanneli repeated.

'He's a permanent squatter here in the Cape, with his head always dipped in a protea.'

'But he doesn't live in a protea,' Hanneli protested. 'He can't lay eggs in a protea.'

'Ah, my little princess is quite right. He can't lay eggs at all – his drab little wife does all the work. We used to have the black oystercatchers all over here. Now they are gone.'

'Where did they go, Oupa?'

'Away – perhaps to another country.' Sybrand Schoon thought of the men in their suits arrayed along the beach. That is what they had reminded him of – an army of black oystercatchers.

While Alison and Mrs Schoon were busy setting the table, Dries retired to the bedroom he had occupied as a child and which now served as a study. He wanted to sort through his mother's family papers in the old mahogany desk, as he had decided to take home the original title deeds to Wepener to protect them from the damp sea air. That is what he explained to his mother, who seemed concerned when he asked her for the keys. She was about to say something when her husband brought Hanneli into the dining room.

'Why don't you ask your ouma to tell you about the carol singers who came to visit us this morning,' Dr Schoon said as he led her to the window to point out the spot where the men had stood. 'Hundreds of them – like a whole choir of angels.'

'That must've been quite a sight – a pity we missed it,' said Alison, only half listening as she was trying to make a pyramid of the Christmas crackers on the table.

'Sight and sound …' Dr Schoon said.

'What singers are you talking about, Sybrand?'

'But Arta, my darling, how could you forget something like that? Our unexpected visitors this morning … You are becoming very forgetful.'

'Please tell your oupa he is imagining things, my little sparrow.'

'Arta, those singers Gawie Pienaar brought here – you were handing out all those sixpences to them – you know, Fanus's collection.'

Mrs Schoon laughed and put her arm around her husband's shoulders. She kissed him on the cheek and said, 'Have you been drinking?' She then said to Hanneli, 'Oupa's telling stories … I think the brandy fumes from the pudding are going to his head.'

Hanneli trailed after her grandfather as he went into Fanus's room to look for the fish bowls. Finding them empty, the two went outdoors. The prime minister shut the backdoor and led his granddaughter into the garden. Why did Arta pretend that he had contrived the scene on the beach, he wondered?

'Your ouma is really becoming very forgetful. Now, mind the puddles. Anytime it rains it's a blessing, but rain on Christmas Day is an even greater blessing. Just look at that sunbird over there with green and blue around his throat. It's a kortbeksuikerbekkie. *Shush* … you scared him away.'

Her grandfather's familiarity with birds entranced Hanneli. She grasped his hand and pointed out a red bishop, with its black face and crop, dangling from a reed over the lagoon.

'Now that red bishop,' he explained to Hanneli, 'can fit right into a child's hand. The natives in Zululand also have a name for him – they call him old iHlalanyathi.'

'Ou Mevrou Jansen says we mustn't speak native.'

'And why not? Your oupa used to be the minister of native affairs, so he can talk native whenever he wants. What does Ou Mevrou Jansen know?'

'She knows a lot. And she won't let me eat liquorice strap because it makes my face black.'

'What a silly old woman.'

'Enoch is the *silly* one – his girlfriend said so.'

'Does Enoch have a girlfriend?'

'Oh, yes – he has two and he gave them presents and that makes them his girlfriends.'

'If you say so …'

After a sumptuous lunch they decided that the Christmas pudding would be served at tea as no one, not even Dries, felt like eating anything more. Alison took Hanneli off to have a short nap and both Dr Schoon and his wife decided that a rest would be very welcome. Alison was planning to lie down in Dries's old bedroom; however, he persuaded her to go for a walk along the beach, as he had something to discuss with her.

'If it is a replacement for Molinieux you want to talk about, I'm not interested. I think, for the time being, we can manage quite well without a butler.'

Alison was the one who had recently wanted to get rid of Mr Molinieux.

She remembered the very first time she had spoken to him when she had telephoned from England to interview him; when asked about his experience, he had provided something akin to a police description. She had told him that she would be pleased if he would consider staying on in his old job at Wepener when she and Dries returned. Mr Molinieux's sudden desertion after the Christmas Eve dinner party had come as a shock to everyone.

'We should wait until the right person comes along. Besides, you never know – the old thing might come back,' Alison said.

'I agree – but what I have to say has nothing to do with Molinieux. His behaviour has been so erratic that I was thinking of asking him to leave anyway. He was shouting at everyone all the time.'

'He was perfectly civil at dinner last night – and he especially enjoyed handing out the bonuses to the staff. But I must admit that his recent problems would have driven anyone to distraction. I'm not in the least bit averse to Ou Mevrou Jansen ruling the roost for a while. She seemed quite pleased that Molinieux had vanished, and I'm sure the others will cope perfectly well without him.'

Alison now relished the idea of a walk. The tide was in and they watched the waves crashing against the rocks in the distance, the wind whipping up foam and spray from the crests. They headed towards a cove to shelter from the wind. Dries took off his jacket and spread it on the ground.

'So, tell me, what's so important to have deprived me of my afternoon rest?' Alison wanted to know.

Dries remained silent for a moment. 'It is important. It's about Ou Mevrou Jansen. You know that she's always going on about having been at Wepener since the beginning. Well, that's not entirely true, as the house was built about a hundred and thirty years before she was born. I was poking around in the desk in my room upstairs and found the most extraordinary documents. You won't believe it – but Ou Mevrou Jansen is actually my great-grandmother, and her husband, my great-grandfather Gerhardus Lubbe, left Wepener to her. That is definite – I looked at his last will and testament.'

'What do you mean?' Alison asked. 'That can't be possible – how could you not know about this before?'

'I don't think anyone wanted to know. And if anyone did know, it's the kind of thing that people keep well hidden. No one has looked through those family papers for years – but there is a certificate of marriage which names Gerhardus Lubbe, my great-grandfather, and Hendriena Jansen, and attached to it is his last will and testament.'

'Are you sure that Ou Mevrou Jansen wasn't named after the original Hendriena Jansen?'

'There is no one else in the family with that name. And there's a faded photograph of her as his bride. My great-grandfather looks about as grumpy as all the Lubbes do, but there she is, laughing happily.'

'How absolutely extraordinary. She's a very old woman. Presumably she has the right to sell Wepener at any time.'

'Yes, but she probably had no reason to do that. She must have felt safe behind its walls. And don't forget, we are her family and I will inherit the estate by descent. But isn't it amazing how her marriage has been kept secret for all these years?'

'You know very well why it was concealed, Dries. But surely your mother must know who her grandmother is. Your father would not take too kindly to this discovery ... How absolutely fascinating! And how do you feel about it?'

'It's difficult to say – do we keep quiet or shall we open up a hornet's nest? I'm not at all averse to having Ou Mevrou Jansen as a great-grandmother. She raised us, after all. I mean, she was closer to Fanus and me than our own mother. I remember Fanus used to walk about with his hands in his pockets and Ou Mevrou Jansen would threaten to give him what she called a thorough thrashing. A "bliksemse pakslae" – those words always shocked and amused me. She then sewed up his pockets so that he could not parade around like a "good-for-nothing". Those two were really very close.

'When Fanus's asthma became worse he had to carry around a suitcase stuffed with medicine. Ou Mevrou Jansen helped him through some of his worst attacks. She would place some dagga on a plate and make him inhale the smoke. It was supposed to relax the lungs, and after a bit Fanus could breathe more easily.'

'I know it must be painful, but you've never really told me how Fanus died. Everyone, especially Ou Mevrou Jansen, talks about him as if he were still alive.'

'He had an asthma attack on the rugby field at school. The referee, who knew that Fanus had a weak chest, ran to grab the case with his medicine, but the one he grabbed was filled with schoolbooks. Before he could reach him with the ephedrine, Fanus was dead.'

Alison stroked Dries's head. For a while neither spoke as they listened to the waves and the mewing gulls. Eventually Alison said, 'I think we should speak to Ou Mevrou Jansen before we discuss this with the rest of the family. She may have had reason to keep quiet about her marriage. After all, she's the one who never spoke about it.'

'I think she told Fanus and, much later, confided in Enoch. Apparently she wanted someone to know the truth before she died. This is not the kind of thing Enoch would've kept to himself.'

'Let's get tea over with and get back to Wepener. I can't wait to talk to her. How extraordinary that she should live as a servant in her own house! Molinieux would have had a fit had he known. Just like him to have cleared out in the middle of the night.'

Both Dries and Alison felt a mounting sense of anticipation as they drove up to the front gates of Wepener. Hanneli was fast asleep between them on the back seat.

'A merry Christmas again,' Dries said to Zachaeus. 'I hope you enjoyed your Christmas lunch. And thank you – we won't be needing you again tonight.'

'Thank you, sir,' Zachaeus replied. 'I hope sir and madam also had a happy Christmas. What about Enoch and Oupa Hans? I'll go and get them first before I knock off.'

'Of course – we've had such an exciting day, I'd clean forgotten about them. It would be kind of you to go.'

Dries was not sure how he would approach Ou Mevrou Jansen, but he wanted to raise the matter with her immediately. The lights were still on in her quarters, which meant that she was up. Alison suggested inviting her to the drawing room for a Christmas drink. Caroline's door was shut, and although Dries found the music she was playing disagreeable, it was being played at a tolerable level. Was it possible that Enoch had a civilising effect on her, he wondered?

He knocked at Ou Mevrou Jansen's door.

'It's open,' she said, probably thinking that it was Hanneli come to pay her a call. 'Oh, it's you, Dries. What a nice surprise! It's been a long time since you've come to my room. How are your parents? How was Christmas?'

'We enjoyed the day. Christmas was wonderful. But it would have been much nicer if Oumagrootjie had been with us at Pringle Bay.'

'What are you talking about, my dear?'

'I mean you,' Dries said, taking her hand in his. 'How could you have kept this secret for so long? If only we had known earlier. I don't want to sound melodramatic, but it was like being robbed of the most precious thing.'

'What nonsense are you talking about, Dries? I hope you people weren't drinking too much at Pringle Bay.'

'No, but I made a wonderful discovery – you are my great-grandmother! I want you to put on your best dress and come and join us for a Christmas drink in the drawing room. That's an order!'

'Enoch must have blabbed,' she sighed. 'That child just can't be trusted with a secret.'

Dries kissed Ou Mevrou Jansen on the forehead.

'My boy,' she said, 'you haven't kissed me in a while.'

'That's nonsense. I kiss you all the time. I haven't kept count. Come on,' he said. 'Alison and I will be waiting for you.'

Dries poured a sweet sherry for Ou Mevrou Jansen; both he and Alison drank whiskey. Hanneli had been put to bed earlier. To them there was no question about it – something had changed. Ou Mevrou Jansen's bearing and the look in her eyes, even the way she spoke, showed a transformation.

Alison was the first to speak. 'How did you fall between the cracks at Wepener? How were you forgotten as the mother of your own children?'

'It's such a long story and I don't care to remember it. But some details stand out as if they happened yesterday. During the war, the English billeted Wepener because it was a large house and it belonged to a Boer.'

'But surely he served the colonial government loyally – at least that's what family history says.'

'I don't know exactly why, but the English accused my husband and my son of smuggling arms up to the burghers in the Free State. They came to Wepener and arrested Gerhardus and Willem. Rhodes and my husband didn't see eye to eye – we refused to sell the estate to him, so I wouldn't be surprised if he had something to do with the arrest. He wanted everything hushed up and there wasn't a trial. The English then sent them off to a concentration camp in Ceylon.'

'And then I suppose they took over the house,' Dries said.

'They were officers, mind you, and when they saw my dark skin, they took me for a servant. They kept me on to cook and clean and I've been cooking here ever since. The officers stayed in the house and kept the garden in flowers and vegetables winter and summer. The troops camped on Rondebosch Common – just there where the pine trees are.

'I stayed on because it was my duty to look after Wepener until my husband returned and I thank God that I was able to do that. I was a Coloured woman and they ignored me. When your great-grandfather returned some years later, he was a different man. He hated everyone and we did not live together as husband and wife. He refused to stay in the house and complained that he could smell where the English had slept. He pulled up all the roses and shrubs in the garden that they had planted. My husband accused me of working for the enemy. Two years later he hanged himself in the gatekeeper's lodge. I found him there when I took down his breakfast – toast with bitter marmalade I had made for him the night before. There was no longer room for me in that shrivelled old heart of his.

'Our son, Willem, survived the concentration camp and Gerhardus sent him off to study in Holland, where he married a Dutch woman. When he brought his wife back to Wepener, he refused to recognise me as his mother and kept me on as a cook, just like the English had done. So my life didn't get any better. Because my skin was dark, my own child was ashamed of me and kept me hidden in the kitchen. It didn't take long for everyone to forget about me.

'After my son's death your grandmother went through my cupboards and found my papers, so she discovered who I was. She moved out of the house and went to live at the farm at Verkeerdevlei. Arta was already a young lady of marriageable age by then and she stayed on here. She knows why you never saw your grandmother until the day she was buried. Schoon was up-and-coming and maybe Arta felt that no one would ask any questions if she married a man like him. But I outlived the old generation and God blessed me in both my children, Dries and Fanus. I had the joy of raising you two. And before I forget – Verkeerdevlei belongs to the family as well. The farmer there runs it on a long lease. I set it up so that your mother has the benefit of the farm income for life.'

'But what about you?' Alison asked. 'How did you first come to Wepener?'

'Although I bear my mother's name, I'm the daughter of Chief Sandile of the Xhosas and a Dutch woman he met in the Cape. She returned to Holland after I was born and left me with my father. When I was old enough, he sent me and my half-sister, Emma, from Gcaikaland to the Cape for schooling. She is the famous one, the only daughter that my father acknowledged. I was kept hidden and soon forgotten. We attended St Saviour's Church in Claremont, where I met my future husband – we were in the same catechism class.

'His father was private secretary to Sir George Grey, the governor of the Cape, who knew my father, Chief Sandile. I must have been sixteen or so when Gerhardus Lubbe and I fell in love. When I became pregnant, his father made us get married at Wepener. The priest came here and Gerhardus and I became husband and wife out of the public eye.'

'What a thrilling story,' Alison said, taking Ou Mevrou Jansen's hand. 'Poor you – you've suffered for so many years and yet, you've outlived most of the Lubbes.'

'I don't know if that is good or bad, but I feel so relieved now that everything is in the open. Still, what do you think people would take me for if they saw my old broken-down body on the streets out there? All they'd say is, "Ag, shame, that poor old woman looks like she's been through the mill, charring all her life." And I suppose they would be right.'

'No, they won't,' Dries said. 'I've always thought of Ou Mevrou Jansen as our rock of ages, and surely you've never doubted that. What does it matter what others think?'

'I don't know what to think.'

'Your life is going to change from this moment,' Alison said determinedly. 'However many years you have left with us will be the best part of your life.'

'I've had good times and I've had bad times – but now I'm too old to change.'

Dries was about to say something when Enoch walked into the drawing room and greeted the three. 'I see you're still celebrating. My parents send their best wishes and thanks for a super Christmas Eve. So, what have I missed?'

'There's never much you miss, Enoch. And if there is anything, you'll know soon enough,' Alison replied.

Dries offered Enoch a drink, but he could sense that he was intruding. Ou Mevrou Jansen was all dressed up and Enoch smelled sweet sherry on her breath. He didn't know what to make of it, and bid them all a good night.

The three had by no means exhausted the subject. However, Dries thought it advisable that they sleep on the matter and revisit Ou Mevrou Jansen's strange and tragic history in the coming weeks.

'Any word about Mfilo or Molinieux while we were away?' he asked.

'Nothing,' Ou Mevrou Jansen replied. 'I invited Clara over for lunch, but she wanted to stay at home in case Mfilo showed up. I don't think Mr Molinieux will ever be back, except it feels like he's haunting every room of this blessed house. And Caroline hasn't appeared from her room all day. I offered her something, but she said she wasn't hungry. Maybe I've been too hard on that poor little lost girl.'

Boxing Day

Christmas night was little different from the many others that Sybrand and Arta Schoon had spent together at their Pringle Bay cottage – only this time Dr Schoon lay awake for hours, becoming more and more agitated about the upheaval in Pondoland. As he had promised, Pienaar, the minister of Bantu affairs, had briefed him on the situation by telephone earlier that evening, and was to provide a detailed report on the situation for the prime minister by the end of the following day. However, Schoon had still not devised a clear plan of action for ending the crisis.

The task of apportioning blame for the massacre had fallen to the prime minister. On Christmas morning he had been roused from his bed at dawn to be informed by his minister of police, Greyling, that the provocation by the Pondos had forced him to deploy the police and to seek the cooperation of the army. Those unprecedented steps had left Dr Schoon enraged, and what had made him angrier still had been the way Greyling had tried to shift the blame for the killings from the police onto the army.

To make matters worse, Pienaar had told him that hungry kraal dogs and hyenas had eaten the flesh of the dead and had left the remains of many of the rebels strewn across the veld. Now little could be done to appease the chiefs. Greyling blamed the Pondos for the atrocities, hoping somehow that the gruesome details would eclipse the consequences of his involvement and the fact that it had been his orders that had set Sten guns and rifles against knobkieries and spears.

'If the Pondos were so worried about beasts eating the corpses,' Greyling had said with the instinct of a man well steeped in the lore of the veld, 'why didn't they go and move the bodies of their dead in the first place? It isn't a secret,' he had argued, realising that he had lost the sympathy of the prime minister, 'that if a person leaves anything with blood on it in the open, first flies will come and then animals.'

The prime minister had heard enough. He instructed Greyling to answer questions in parliament after the holiday recess concerning the steps he had taken to quell the Pondo revolt.

That evening the prime minister put through another call to Cofimvaba. He asked Khotso if it would be possible to see him after lunch on the following day. With some reluctance, Khotso agreed. Schoon then telephoned Wepener to thank Dries and Alison for the Christmas presents and to inform Dries that he would send Witbooi over in the early morning to collect Oupa Hans, as they would leave for Cofimvaba at dawn.

That night, to the gentle sound of the waves, the steady rhythm of the water pump in the backyard and its occasional putter when the current faltered, Schoon prayed to his God for guidance. And this time he was determined to exchange his feet of clay for an iron fist. It was only then that he realised that his son would infer from their conversation that he was on his way to see Khotso.

The prime minister stepped outdoors at four o'clock on a brisk Boxing Day morning. Even though it was midsummer and promised to be hot later in the day, his wife insisted that he wear an overcoat, hat and gloves. She stood beside him, holding a picnic basket packed with leftovers from the Christmas lunch.

Witbooi, who had been notified the previous evening, had arrived from Cape Town even earlier that morning with Johannes Pretorius asleep in the front passenger seat. Witbooi nodded his head in greeting to the prime minister and his wife. Mrs Schoon handed the large hamper to him, which he put in the boot of the Daimler. Dr Schoon placed his arm around his wife's shoulders, kissed her on her forehead and suggested she return to bed. With the hum of the car's powerful engine fading, its rear lights disappeared from view as Mrs Schoon shut the cottage door behind her. She crawled into bed fully clothed and wondered what had come over her husband and why he had suddenly decided to go on such a long and tiring journey to Cofimvaba. He needed time to rest and to prepare the speech he was to present to parliament in just a few weeks.

The prime minister was a remarkably austere and practical man. In his professional life he made do with a small staff, comprising a private secretary, two guards and a chauffeur. He was particularly attached to his chauffeur, Daniel Witbooi, a Baster from Rehoboth in South West and, aside from Johannes Pretorius, the only person to have accompanied him on his journeys to Cofimvaba. Witbooi had driven the Daimler for almost fifteen years, virtually since the day Dr Schoon had been appointed minister of native affairs.

Witbooi was a silent man. It was not that he lacked the desire to speak, but he was unable to, as he had no tongue. When he disagreed or tried to show sympathy, he shook his head from side to side, or nodded. The prime minister was grateful for his driver's silence. From the comfort of the back seat, Sybrand Schoon watched the steadily rising sun and the waves threading their way across the bay. The morning still had a chill to it, and though he had earlier removed his overcoat, he drew a black-backed jackal kaross over his knees. The twenty-one pelts that had gone into the making of the kaross still bore the smell of the original inhabitants and reminded him of the many unflattering words associated with their kind – words such as devious, skelm, cunning, shrewd. He felt soothed by the sound of the tyres on the road, the rotting smell of seaweed and salt admitted through the open window and the occasional nod of Witbooi's head. He had not seen Khotso in a while. And now, well on the way to Cofimvaba, all anxiety left him. Johannes Pretorius was still asleep in the front seat.

Mossel Bay came into view; there were a few chokka boats on the way into the harbour and several perlemoen dinghies were scattered across the bay. Dr Schoon craned his neck to look at the Outeniqua Mountains in the distance, but they were driving close to sea level and a thick mist obscured the view. He asked Witbooi to tune the wireless to the morning news. A bulletin on the forthcoming Commonwealth summit in Delhi was followed by Charles Fortune's views on the Springbok side's prospects in the test match against the English. Dr Schoon was not fond of cricket and the bulletin did not hold his attention for long. However, he was pleased to note that the broadcast authorities had implemented instructions for a news blackout on Pondoland. He settled back into the soft leather seat, listened for a few more minutes to the broadcast and soon fell asleep.

The prime minister tossed about on the back seat. Witbooi, noticing his restlessness in the rear-view mirror, brought the car to a halt beside the petrol pumps of the Knysna Shell garage. Alerted by the official number plate and the darkened windows, the pump attendant wiped his hands on the back of his overalls, gave a smart salute and hurried to fill the petrol tank. He could not make out who was sitting in the back.

Schoon woke up and realised that they had already joined the Garden Route. The thought of a steaming cup of coffee and a sandwich had him glance at his watch to find that they were making excellent time. He suggested they stop at one of the Tsitsikamma forest picnic spots. 'You take advantage when I'm asleep, hey?' he said to Witbooi with a laugh. 'You mustn't drive so fast.'

At the picnic spot Witbooi opened the boot and removed the hamper Mrs Schoon had packed. Schoon sat on the kaross spread in the shade. They did not disturb Johannes Pretorius. Mrs Schoon had also made a healthy soup for Witbooi. Three hours later, they made another brief stop on the outskirts of King Williamstown, where they consulted a map together over cups of coffee. The rest of the journey appeared straight-forward. To avoid being recognised, the prime minister asked Witbooi not to pass through Queenstown. At a junction on Route 61 they took the right fork to Cofimvaba, still twenty-five miles away.

'Could you please wake up Mr Pretorius now? He's been asleep for hours.'

Khotso's house finally came into view and Schoon could see a group assembled on the stoep. He looked forward to his reception and, de-spite the seriousness of his visit, to the refreshments he knew would be waiting for him when he, Khotso and Pretorius were safely ensconced behind closed doors.

When the car drew to a halt, Khotso walked up to open the door for him. Schoon perceived that something was amiss as Khotso and some of his wives were dressed in black. Polycarp and two older people, prob-ably his parents, and a young man whom Schoon recognised as Khotso's apprentice, Redemptus, stood in a small group to the side, with a line of Pondo chiefs. The atmosphere was cold and brittle. The prime minister felt as if he had walked into a trap.

'Witbooi, could you wake Mr Pretorius!'

Khotso called Polycarp to his side to interpret. He was distant and would speak only of the sacrilege committed at Ngquza Hill where animals had finished the massacre that the police and army had begun. He told Dr Schoon that, as prime minister, he was responsible for the behaviour of his minister of police and was therefore accountable for the atrocity that had taken place. What was he planning to do and what action had he ordered his ministers to take?

'Khotso, I need to speak to you in private about this. Where is Mr Pretorius?'

'I don't think we have anything further to say to each other, Sybrand.'

'Please, I've come all this way – for old time's sake, just a few minutes.'

Khotso walked ahead of Dr Schoon and asked Polycarp to follow. The prime minister knew that he had little time to ask Khotso for the powerful medicine he needed desperately.

However, the last thing he wanted was for Polycarp to be present when he discussed this with Khotso.

'Polycarp, please go and see what's holding Mr Pretorius, this is important,' Schoon instructed. 'I didn't bring him here to go visiting around the compound.'

While waiting for Mr Pretorius, Dr Schoon had to muddle along in his own rudimentary Xhosa. 'I hear you have something in your safe that will help me.'

'Sybrand, I'm afraid I have nothing in my safe that will be of any use to you.'

'Come, Khotso, people talk about something powerful you've got.'

'What do people know about the secrets in my safe?'

Khotso tried to evade Schoon's pleas, however, a photograph on the wall of Redemptus in his prophet's coat jogged the inyanga's memory. Redemptus's dompas was still in the safe and many people had ascribed magical qualities to it. 'It's true, I have something for you. If you will wait for me here, I will get it ready for you.'

During Khotso's absence the prime minister looked around the study and his eyes were drawn to the mantelpiece. He noticed that Khotso had finished his bust. Schoon went closer to admire it. He thought it a remarkable likeness. Although he did not approve of the stern look the eyes held, he had to remember to congratulate Khotso on his skill. His thoughts were interrupted by an eerie sound of ululation outside.

Khotso returned to the study holding a small, flat leather pouch in his hand. 'Listen to the grief of the women out there! It sounds as if your trusted servant has gone to interpret with the angels. But don't worry; he'll keep your secrets in heaven.'

Polycarp came rushing in with the news. 'Mr Pretorius is dead, Dr Schoon. He has been dead for some time.'

Schoon was so intent on getting hold of the pouch Khotso held in his hand that at first he did not realise the implications of what Khotso and Polycarp had said.

'Hannes Pretorius is dead, Sybrand!'

Only then did it dawn on the prime minister that his interpreter had passed away. 'We must get him back to his family in Cape Town and make sure that nobody hears about this.'

'I will take care of Hannes's body, don't worry. He is one of us. I will take him to his childhood home, and we will bury him on his father's farm in Tarkastad.'

'He is my responsibility,' Schoon insisted. 'I order you to send the body to his family in Cape Town.'

'Your responsibilities are with those who are still alive, Prime Minister. The wrong man is dead. Hannes is just another casualty of your political intrigues. Polycarp, please call Hannes's grandson and let him know what happened. I will arrange for his family to attend the funeral. And I will call Gumede to come and take care of the body.'

Then, turning to the prime minister, he said, 'Speak to the chiefs out there; they have come to see you. Otherwise, I order you to leave the compound immediately.'

Within half an hour of his arrival and with his stubborn refusal to listen to the grievances of the amaPondo chiefs, Schoon got into the Daimler and the grief-stricken Witbooi started the car. Their precipitous departure was accompanied by the mournful ululation of Khotso's wives.

Before they departed Khotso handed Schoon the sealed flat leather pouch on a thong. He ordered him to wear it around his neck at all times.

The Net Closes

Enoch was distressed by his grandfather's death, although the discovery of a hidden side to his parents made him appreciate anew Oupa Hans's last words to him before he had left Wepener in the dark on that Boxing Day morning. Uncomplaining, even though his joints ached and he could barely dress himself, he said to his grandson: 'Life is like a sky full of stars and for each star there is a word, or meaning, but it is written in a language we don't yet understand. Had we spoken that language, we would've been able to read the secrets of the sky. When we die, my boy, we are set free among the stars … Just ask the Bushmen and watch how they inspanned the eland to carry them up through the Milky Way.' Oupa then kissed Enoch and held his hand as he helped him into the car.

His words had caught Enoch by surprise, and it took him some time to appreciate them. As a gardener Oupa Hans usually had a practical sort of way of expressing himself. To him, a mountain was a mountain and a molehill, a molehill. There was no way of making one out of the other. For a man who was passionate about nature, Oupa was indifferent to his grandson's explanation of time zones – and once when Enoch tried to explain to him how it happened that at midday in South Africa it was probably a few hours short of midnight in Australia, he just shook his head.

The night before Oupa Hans's departure for Cofimvaba, he and Enoch were discussing the precarious lives of the few remaining Bushmen. Enoch had asked him whether he knew if anyone had ever gone behind the glass of the museum diorama. Had the poison on their arrows kept its potency, he wondered? The last refuge of these hunter-gatherers appeared to him to have become nothing but dust.

'Even having seen them so many times, the plaster-cast Bushmen appear more lifelike than ever,' Enoch had told him. 'I can't believe that the scars left by the thorns of the acacia trees, or their run-ins with injured prey left such a clear impression in the plaster casts.'

'That's what they look like, my boy, never younger or older since the day they were cast. They neither toil, nor do they reap. Nor do they breathe – each breath we take brings us closer to the end – that is why we die.'

'So, it's better not to breathe?'

'I have often thought that. Sometimes I feel so tired and all I can think of is to blow out my last breath in a thin stream, like cigarette smoke. Breathing is a little bit like love. Every time you think you can do without it, it punches you in the stomach and you start all over again.'

Byron and Augusta Leigh must have known something was amiss. When the sun came up Enoch allowed them into the living room because he felt lonely at the table, but the dogs were spooked by something and ignored him while they went about sniffing at Oupa Hans's scent on the couch and around his unmade bed. Eventually they went outdoors to sit under Oupa's favourite bench in the shade of the vines and to wait for his return.

When Enoch later went to Retreat to take Mr Salie news of his grandfather's death, the tailor cried like a baby. He held onto Enoch, as if the boy could somehow make up for Oupa's absence. When Mochie Salie returned from her shopping at Sammie Ling's Groceries, she insisted that Enoch stay for the promised crayfish curry. However, he had to return to Wepener immediately. The truth was that he had no appetite. Oupa Hans was gone for good and he would never again have the pleasure of listening to him sucking noisily at crayfish claws.

Mr Salie eventually regained his composure. 'And here I was just expecting your oupa to walk in for his last fitting – then without a warning he goes and do this to me. Please take his suit to Cofimvaba,' he said, 'so that he can wear it on his last journey.'

Enoch waited while Mr Salie hemmed the trousers by hand, and then he attempted to pay him.

'No, my young friend, you don't understand – this is for pasella. The last barakat. But if you don't mind … when you go up there to Cofimvaba, do me a favour. Could you please ask Khotso the names for the big Jo'burg race? What am I going to do now that Hannes is gone?

'You know, my father was a harness maker and he always wanted me to have a better life. That's why he called me Idriss for the tailoring. But he also gave me a love for horses. When I was a child, I used to polish the leather for him. There's nothing better than the smell of leather and horses.

'Oh, and I almost forgot – what about paying the rent?'

'Don't worry about it. It's being paid.'

Just before Enoch got to the bus stop he remembered Oupa Hans's last request before he left for Cofimvaba. Oupa had cleared out his pockets and his wallet and had handed him some money. 'Khotso says that Sea Cottage is his favourite to win, and he has never been wrong,' Oupa Hans had said. 'Please give Mr Salie at least ten guineas to put on that horse, just in case I don't get back in time.'

Enoch found the money in his jacket pocket and gave it to Mr Salie as Oupa Hans had asked. Mr Salie handed the money back to him.

'It's bad luck to take money from a dead man and bet it on a horse, Enoch – don't worry, this one is on me. I'll see that you get your oupa's cut.' Then Mr Salie hesitated. 'Before you go – you remember that time you and your grandfather came to the horse races … that morning with the white man …'

'Yes, Mr Molinieux.'

'Whatever his name is – he sold that native out who lived with the Coloured woman, as well as all the grooms at the stables. The police came to arrest Mfilo, even though he had nothing to do with it. He and the grooms are in jail and now there are heavy charges. Watch for it in the newspapers after the holidays. I kept a low profile over there by the Steenberg Estate, so I'm okay for now. But I just wanted you to know that you mustn't keep company with that white lanie. I can tell when someone is rubbish.'

Wepener was in mourning, but Enoch tried to put an end to the gloom by sharing what little he knew about Oupa Hans's life and passed around the photograph album he had stowed away in his trunk. Dowa filled in some of the gaps which Enoch knew nothing about, while Dries filled in others. He was surprised that Dries knew so much about Oupa Hans.

Alison insisted that his body be brought to Wepener for burial. However, she understood when Enoch explained that his great-grandmother, the stout woman with the Xhosa headdress in the faded photograph, had buried his umbilical cord on the farm on the outskirts of Tarkastad and it was right for him to be laid to rest there.

With the exception of Mr Molinieux, everyone was present in the drawing room. Ou Mevrou Jansen suggested that Dries go down to the cellar for a few bottles of champagne. Clara set out twelve glasses and the old woman proposed a toast to the life of Oupa Hans, a man who would have made a garden anywhere on this earth, and in heaven, where he has his work cut out for him.

'To Johannes Frederik Pretorius ... who got there before me,' she said.

'To Johannes Frederik Pretorius.'

Ou Mevrou Jansen kissed Enoch and he smelled the yeast of champagne on her lips. Mama and Dowa had already emptied their glasses, while Khotso's driver, fully rested, was waiting outside in a black Cadillac to drive the Pretorius family to Cofimvaba.

'Before we leave ...' Enoch said. 'I'm not sure how to put it, but I spoke to Mr Salie, Oupa Hans's tailor, this morning and he told me that Mr Molinieux had lodged a false report about illegal horse racing with the police. Mfilo and seven other men were arrested on criminal charges and apparently there will be something in the newspapers after the holidays. Mr Salie doesn't know where they are being held, but he says they are facing serious charges.'

'The blinking two-faced dog!' Clara cried as she dropped her glass on the floor. 'That's why the bugger disappeared.' She burst into tears and Caroline put her arms around her.

EAST LONDON. The Ministry of Police yesterday confirmed the interception of a yellow Volkswagen Kombi, carrying nine Pondo chiefs, on the road north from Cofimvaba. The chiefs were placed under arrest and taken to Umtata for questioning, where they are being held under the Criminal Laws Amendment Act. A police source informed the *Dispatch* that the arrest of the chiefs would have a dramatic impact on reducing the level of unrest and violence in Pondoland, which even with the intervention of the defence force has shown little evidence of abating.

The minister of police, Mr Piet Greyling, is expected to travel to Umtata before the New Year to initiate an enquiry into the confrontation at Ngquza Hill. This usually tranquil area in Pondoland has seen the most sustained level of political violence since the Poqo riots in the Cape and the shootings at Sharpeville in March 1960. At a press conference held before leaving Pretoria, the minister was quoted as saying: 'The native mentality does not allow them to gather for a peaceful demonstration. For them to gather means violence.'

– THE EAST LONDON DAILY DISPATCH

'Piet Lat? Piet Lat Greyling, right?'

'Yes, what do you want?'

'Manie van Wyk. Remember me?' Mr van Wyk removed his railway cap. 'Jirre man, we used to be porters together in Fort Beaufort.'

'What are you people doing here in the devil's kraal?'

'Hey – I can ask you the same question, Piet Lat.'

'Ja, and I would also like to know,' Wilhelmina van Wyk interjected. 'It's not a secret that you and your whole blinking government can't survive without Khotso.'

'Hey, Piet Lat, I always used to complain to you about this wife of mine – she's got a temper and a tongue to go with it. You must watch what you say in front of her. Khotso invited us to come and stay, so we live here now, me and Wilhelmina. Your old Railways and Harbours chucked us out of our cottage at Fort Beaufort and put in a young stationmaster over our heads.'

The minister ignored Mr van Wyk's words. 'And your son, Polycarp, he's here too?'

'You know he's here. Your spies are like a bunch of starving ticks out in the veld, waiting to suck themselves fat with blood. Why don't you ask them?'

Mr van Wyk called them 'gulsige bosluise', voracious bush lice, to show his scorn for the minister and his men. 'My son is Khotso's head teacher and assistant. So we are all present, meneer.'

The Special Branch had interrogated the Pondo chiefs they had arrested on Boxing Day, and the minister of police was convinced that the chiefs had become even more restive since Polycarp's arrival in the Transkei. Greyling was certain that the meddlesome Polycarp had prompted Khotso's refusal to see the prime minister, and his spies had informed him that Khotso had bewitched Dr Schoon's interpreter and then refused to release the man's body into his family's custody.

'I knew all along that Polycarp was behind this mess,' Greyling said to himself, his mind slowly grasping the possibility of blaming the entire Pondo insurrection on Khotso and his head teacher. He enjoyed the thought of holding Khotso responsible, as he considered the inyanga far too big for his boots. He had a good mind to order Khotso to unlock the safe so that he could see if the fabled gold was in there, but Greyling thought better of it because he feared the practice of magic and the muti that might also be hidden in the safe.

He turned to Manie van Wyk. 'We've come to arrest Khotso. Take my advice and clear out. I don't care where you go, but clear off. If we come back and find you and your son still here, we will arrest the whole lot of you. We heard of the fooling around over Christmas, everyone dressed in disguise. I suppose that was Polycarp's idea. Next time we'll lock him up for good.'

'But what has Khotso done, Piet Lat?' Mr van Wyk asked. 'He's a kind man and we hear he's an old friend of the prime minister.'

'Let me be the judge of that. Khotso thinks he's a law unto himself. And I'm here to show him that there's laws for white men and laws for blacks – and all these laws must be obeyed.'

Wilhelmina van Wyk, who had remained silent, interjected, 'Khotso has done more for us than that government of yours. I'm warning you – you'll regret this, Piet Lat. You can't play games with Khotso.'

'Look, Mevrou van Wyk, don't come and threaten me here with witchcraft; just be thankful that we didn't arrest you and your husband also. Remember, you are in no position to threaten the minister of police. I'm taking personal control of this matter and next time I won't be so lenient.'

'I spit on your government …'

'Save your spit, my dierbare Wilhelmina,' said Mr van Wyk, placing his arm around her waist, 'you'll need a proper mouthful when Piet Lat comes around here next time.'

'I'm warning you,' she said. 'Just let me hear you threatening my boy again. Is it not enough that you stole two years of his life?'

Enoch and his parents were exhausted after the long journey from Cape Town when, on their arrival at Cofimvaba, they unwittingly walked into a hornet's nest. Enoch admired the way Mrs van Wyk glared at Minister

Greyling and could sense that she meant every word she said, although it was unclear to him what she could do to protect her only child. Enoch was sure that his own mother would have shown the same kind of tenacity had he been under attack. It seemed to him that everyone was being targeted by the minister of police, whose brutal manner showed that he had no business being in government.

Enoch had the idea that any form of rule should be based on reason and that lust for power, abuse and corruption were a betrayal of the role of a public servant.

'Have all these men come to take me away?' Khotso asked as he surveyed the large police contingent Minister Greyling had brought with him. 'And why should a minister be doing the dirty work of his handlangers? You make me look more important than I am, Mr Greyling. I am a man like you and I don't have the sorcerer's magic to make myself disappear. Unless you think I've got wings and can fly away.'

The minister ignored these remarks and led Khotso to the waiting convoy. The policemen treated Khotso with circumspection, as they were afraid of the witchcraft he might employ against them and their families. Khotso, immaculately dressed, as always, offered no resistance. He knew that Dr Schoon had been provoked when he had left Cofimvaba, but it had never occurred to him that the prime minister would have him arrested. After all, they were old friends and shared too many secrets. He embraced Redemptus, who had stayed on after the Christmas feast. He greeted Enoch and his parents and expressed his regret that he would not be present at Oupa Hans's funeral.

'I leave Polycarp and Redemptus in charge,' he said. 'Please look after my people.'

Andrew Gumede was there, having come south to take care of the funeral arrangements for Oupa Hans. Earlier Enoch had heard him complain to Polycarp about the number of times he had been back and forth to Cofimvaba during the past few months. Enoch's parents stood by helplessly. Oupa Hans was to be buried on the farm at Tarkastad, as Khotso had suggested, the place of his umbilical cord. They had agreed to Khotso's arrangements and were grateful for the inyanga's intervention and hospitality.

Enoch found, to his surprise, that his father was fluent in Xhosa – an inheritance sadly not passed on to him. Despite the tragic circumstances of their visit, he had seen his father in conversation with Khotso the night before and both of them had laughed until the tears streamed down their cheeks. Enoch had not realised that Dowa had a sense of humour, as the serious duty of raising an only son seemed to have deprived him of any joy in life. It was also strange for him to see his mother constantly followed by the youngest of Khotso's progeny as she dished out bags of acid drops and humbugs.

The Lost Sheep

What Enoch had previously thought to be no more than Oupa Hans's fabrications and fantasies about Khotso's life turned out to be true as certain scenes unfolded before his eyes. Khotso was about to be taken away in a police Land Rover while onlookers waited for him to perform an act of magic that would strike down his persecutors and make them disappear. Instead, two lorries came coasting down the drive towards the house, raising a cloud of dust that, for a moment, obliterated Minister Greyling and his men.

Nor were they army lorries as everyone had suspected.

Nohlwandle was the first to speak. 'These farmers have no respect. They are all the same. They pay Khotso pennies and expect their sheep to walk back home for free.'

In a gentle tone Khotso hushed her. His wrists were in handcuffs as he turned to the minister of police and said, 'These men have come for my help.'

'We've got to get a move on, Khotso,' Greyling insisted. 'But I can see these farmers have come a long way. Do your business first and then we go – and don't try any of your tricks.'

Minister Greyling called a young policeman over to remove the handcuffs and stood aside as Khotso welcomed the farmers and enquired about their problems. That was when Enoch realised that Oupa Hans had been telling the truth all along. But Oupa was in his coffin and Enoch had no way of telling him that he now believed him. Khotso took the two farmers and their labourers aside. Both farmers had brought their sons along, presumably curious about the ways of the witchdoctor. One of them, whose lorry bore Grahamstown number plates, had sixteen men in tow. They sat down on grass mats, with Khotso facing the farmer.

'I suppose you've come to see me about the sheep?'

'I have come about the sheep, Khotso.'

'I also know you've come here so I can tell you which of these men have stolen your sheep.'

The farmer jumped up from the bench he and his son were sitting on, shocked that Khotso had so easily divined his problem. 'I have come so that you can tell me which of my labourers has taken my sheep, Khotso.'

'If that is why you came, then I can't help you.'

'But other farmers tell me that Khotso is a man of knowledge.'

'You should know better than to listen to what other people say. Because these labourers are afraid of my powers you brought them here so I can accuse them and they will be afraid and confess to something they didn't do. I will tell you who has stolen your sheep – the man is your neighbour. He drives a blue lorry with a red stripe. That man wants you to blame your labourers for the missing sheep. You know him – he has even sat at your table.'

'I do know such a man, Khotso.'

The labourers and the farmer's son expelled a collective sigh. Khotso had spoken.

'You think bad things about your workers, when all this time you have a greedy neighbour. To make it up to these men, slaughter a sheep tonight and give it to them to make a feast. On your return, you will find that your neighbour has disappeared.'

Khotso dismissed the group and Redemptus led in the next farmer, his son and labourers from Fort Beaufort. Before the second man could say anything, Khotso called his son to him and placed his hands on the boy's head.

'I haven't come about my son, Khotso.'

'Don't worry – I know why you are here.'

The young boy appeared undaunted when he felt Khotso's hands on his head. 'What's this oom doing now, Pa?' he asked in Xhosa.

'I'm blessing you so that you will become a doctor when you are big and will work among my people.'

'You mean my son is not going to be a farmer? We've been farming in our family for over a hundred years.'

'Your boy will be a doctor, my friend. Now, about the sheep ... These men of yours have been sharing your pot. I can see that they've been feasting on what does not belong to them. Redemptus will give you some impepho to burn in your kraals, and you can be sure that the only time they will clip your sheep again will be with the shears.'

'But what are all these policemen doing here, Khotso?' the farmer asked.

'That is Minister Greyling over there who has made no accusations, but he wants to be my jailer.'

'Then what will the people do without you?'

'There is a young man here, Redemptus, he is even better than I am.'

'Do something, Khotso!' The farmer insisted. 'Show them who you are.'

'They are doing this to me because of who I am.'

'Hamba kahle, Khotso. I know you will come back to us.'

'You and your men go well too, my friend. And in a few years I will see your son working among my people.'

The first farmer had already left as he wanted to confront his neighbour before he could make off with the stolen sheep. But as Khotso had warned him, he found the house deserted. The blue lorry with the red stripe was no longer in the shed and there wasn't a sheep to be found on the thief's farm.

A few weeks later the farmer sent a brief article from the *Kokstad Advertiser* to Khotso about a man who had taken his life with a length of hosepipe connected to the exhaust of his lorry. Sixty sheep, the exact number that had disappeared from the farm, were found to be grazing in a nearby field. Nohlwandle opened the letter and read the contents to Polycarp, who later told Enoch about it.

The inyanga turned to Dowa. 'Now listen, Johannes, I have seldom known a man like that father of yours. Not only was he a good servant, but also his mind was never bent by troubles. Tarkastad is the place of his umbilical cord. That's why I kept him here – his body will enrich our soil.'

Even Mama seemed proud of the tribute Khotso paid Dowa's father. She had come close to refusing to marry Oupa Hans's son when her friends protested that he came from a half-baked native family. In the end her heart had prevailed.

Khotso then asked Gumede to inform the native commissioner of his arrest and to see if anything could be done to arrange for his release. There was also the matter of Khotso's marriage, which now had to be postponed. 'Go and see Chief Letlaka and reassure him that the lobola cattle will stay in his kraal. And tell him that even though the marriage date will have to be changed, I already consider our families to be one.'

The inyanga's wives and children were gathered on the stoep to see him off. The Pretorius and Van Wyk families stood by and watched Piet Greyling and his men lead Khotso away. He forbade his wives and children their mournful ululation on his account as he would not be gone forever. Hiding her own anxiety, Nohlwandle consoled members of her large family as the convoy with Khotso and his abductors drove off.

Cape Town appeared to Minister Greyling to be the best location for Khotso's detention as he was well known and feared in the Eastern Cape and not even the most secure prison would have held him there. After the trial he wanted the witchdoctor put away safely on Robben Island as soon as possible and with the least amount of publicity.

Thus far, only two of the detained Pondo chiefs had been helpful to the Special Branch and had been sent back to their clans. They would later be called as State witnesses against Khotso. The others were to be held in solitary confinement in Umtata until they proved more cooperative, or until the situation in Pondoland changed for the better.

As requested, Gumede telephoned Commissioner Brownlee to let him know about Khotso's arrest. At first there was no reply; when he later tried the number, a clerk answered and told Gumede that Special Branch had arrived at the commissioner's office about an hour earlier and taken him away for questioning.

In her discreet way, Nohlwandle took charge of Cofimvaba. She had been shocked by her husband's arrest, not understanding the reason for it, and the subsequent news of Commissioner Brownlee's arrest disturbed her greatly. He was the one person she knew in a position to help.

'I don't believe Schoon is responsible for my husband's arrest,' she said to Polycarp. 'Why don't we try to call him? Surely he has it in his power to release Khotso?'

'That's true – I'm quite sure he could. But I don't think it is the right time to call him just yet. Why don't I speak to his son Dries first and see what he suggests?'

'Could you do that? But what about Greyling's threat against you and your parents? Shouldn't you be making plans to leave?'

'And go where? If you will allow us, we'll stay here. There is nowhere else for the old people to go. And I'm sure they will refuse to move. You heard my mother – you're dealing with a couple of hard-necked Boers who won't take nonsense from anyone, least of all that fool Greyling.'

'I only wish you and your parents would stay. This is the first time Khotso has ever been arrested, and he's not a young man. I am afraid of what might happen to him.'

'I'll do whatever I can to see that he returns to us as soon as possible. If it's any comfort, I was in jail for quite some time and it did me no harm. Anyway, they'll handle Khotso with kid gloves. Didn't you see how terrified they were of him? Don't worry too much.'

As she had not turned to him for advice or comfort, Redemptus realised that Nohlwandle was relying on Polycarp. When later he found her alone, he told her that he had been praying for Khotso. 'Maybe there is a greater purpose in this than we know,' he said. 'We don't know the will of God. Let's wait and see how God will answer our prayers.'

Nohlwandle smiled and took his hands in hers. 'Dear Redemptus, don't be a silly boy; we need more than prayers. What we need is action. Khotso is an old man and this can't be good for him. We'll all praise God once Khotso is safely back here with us again.'

'But Mama, prayer *is* action. There is nothing more powerful than that.'

Dries was alarmed when Polycarp telephoned to tell him of Greyling's arrival at Cofimvaba and the subsequent arrest of Khotso. Dries suspected that Greyling had taken the law into his own hands once again. He could not imagine that his father had ordered the arrest and suggested that Polycarp remain at Cofimvaba, as he was sure that Khotso would return shortly.

Later, when Dries managed to speak to his father on the telephone, Schoon assured him that this was none of his doing and that he would do everything possible to see that Khotso was released as soon as the convoy reached Cape Town. He would personally put Khotso on the next plane back to East London. As for the arrest of Brownlee, the native commissioner, he would find out about this. Dries then arranged with the prime minister's private secretary to meet with his father soon after he had delivered his speech on the following day, as it was not possible for them to meet earlier.

Redemptus realised that he had to leave the Zionists if he were going to be of any use to Khotso. It had come to him very clearly that he should go to Cape Town to see what he could do. Since his arrival at the Apostle's kraal, the furthest Redemptus had travelled was to Cofimvaba, where he had visited Khotso and checked up on his cattle from time to time; and he had been planning to attend Khotso's wedding.

When Redemptus told the Apostle that he wanted to go to the wedding, Zebulon Mtetwa had been furious and at first would not give him permission to go. The Apostle was afraid that Redemptus might leave him. To dissuade him, he told the boy about the dangers of attending a heathen and idolatrous marriage. However, by Christmas some of the Apostle's misgivings about Khotso seemed to have been assuaged, as his entire congregation arrived at Cofimvaba for the celebrations followed by a great feast. But even that measure of seasonal goodwill appeared to have been short-lived.

'You tell me that you want to spread the word in that heathen city of Cape Town. You think the Apostle is an old fool. I know it's Khotso you're after, but he's in the best place for people of his kind. Maybe prison is even too good for him. I warned you that the Lord will deal with him. We serve a jealous God. I wouldn't be surprised if he gets locked up for life!'

This lack of compassion made Redemptus feel an even greater urgency to leave – and he had to do it soon. He was going to ask one of the Zionists to drive him to East London so he could catch the train to Cape Town. But Polycarp stopped him, telling him that he should not interfere as everything possible was being done to secure Khotso's release.

'By the time you get to Cape Town, the old man will already be back here. Just be patient for a few more days. There's nothing to worry about.'

Enoch told Redemptus that he could travel down with them when they returned to Cape Town after the funeral. However, Redemptus was not prepared to wait. So reluctantly Polycarp gave him Dries's name and address as a place where he would be made welcome in Cape Town. Redemptus had about fifty pounds in his pocket, which he had saved from selling a few head of cattle. Although he was determined to leave, he was afraid that he might lose his way in the city among people who had no respect for God. He returned to the Apostle's kraal to collect some clothes and a few possessions. It was Sunday morning, and as he went down to the river to bathe he could hear the drums of the Zionists and the loud exhortations of the believers. Fervent cries rent the air as new initiates were baptised and held under the water to wash away their sins. As he came nearer he found their white tunics blinding in the morning sun and the green crosses stitched on their chests showed up in stark relief. But Redemptus kept his distance and, wading in the river, allowed the water to wash over him.

'You must move on,' the spirits seemed to say, as if to confirm his decision. Suddenly he leaped from the water as though an electrical current had passed through him. He would take the bus to Cape Town early the following morning and see what he could do for Khotso when he got there.

There was a long line of Cadillacs waiting at the compound. Nohlwandle had ordered them so that everyone could attend Oupa Hans's funeral. Enoch handed the new suit to Andrew Gumede.

'Listen here, Enoch, this is a perfectly good suit – I've already dressed your oupa up in his old clothes. A dead man in a brand-new suit? What a waste of a charcoal double-breast and waistcoat. Let me sell this one and send you the money. I'll just keep a small commission.'

Nohlwandle overheard Enoch's protestations and told Gumede not to corrupt the young man. She ordered him to dress Oupa Hans in his new suit immediately. 'And I expect that for each of Khotso's wives, when we go to join the Lord and our ancestors, you will see to it that we go in our wedding gowns. Enoch, you check up on him.'

The Truth Will Out

Ou Mevrou Jansen sat on a tall-backed chair in her room overlooking the garden. She breathed in the cool morning air at the open window. She was not one for drinking tea; on the table beside her stood a glass of ginger beer. When Dries and Fanus were young, they had made fun of her. However, the sting of the ginger beer cleared her throat and settled her stomach.

Ou Mevrou Jansen could see Mfilo over the rise, digging in the garden. Dries had told her that, with the help of a prosecutor and a compliant magistrate, he had arranged Mfilo's release. Bail had been set on the understanding that Mfilo would appear for trial on a range of charges. According to the charge sheet, Mfilo had run an illegal gambling ring in the slums of Steenberg in collusion with the grooms from the Muizenberg stables. The most serious charge against Mfilo was the mutilation of Mrs Oppenheimer's horse, Red Hunter. The owner had been incensed and demanded a thorough investigation and prompt action. However, for the moment Mfilo was free and Ou Mevrou Jansen was pleased for Clara.

The sound of cars and buses reached her from the distant road and the persistent hum of a vacuum cleaner droned somewhere in the house. All these familiar noises, the dogs barking as well as the sounds of industry in the house, had a calming effect on her.

Johannes Pretorius's death had forced her to think again of her own mortality. She wondered if she should ask that her body be taken back to Sandile's kraal for burial. However, she had lived at Wepener almost her entire life and had never even visited Gcaikaland, the place of her father's birth. She decided to ask to be buried alongside her husband in the tiny whitewashed cemetery just beyond the woods.

The house was spotless. Each surface had been dusted and polished. Ou Mevrou Jansen reigned over the house ever since Mr Molinieux had vanished before dawn on Christmas morning. Under cover of darkness he had cleared out his belongings and disappeared without leaving any indication of his whereabouts. The thud of Trossie beating the Persian rugs added to the morning sounds.

Something stirred at the edge of the main lawn and then moved into Ou Mevrou Jansen's field of vision. Considering her advanced age, she could still see quite well. She placed the glass on the floor beside her and loosened her scarf. She saw the dogs running across the lawn with Mfilo in pursuit. One of the dogs carried something in its jaws – and since it was still quite a distance away, Ou Mevrou Jansen could not tell what it was.

Augusta Leigh opened her jaws with a yelp as Mfilo's boot landed on her rump and a turtledove fell onto the border. Ou Mevrou Jansen watched Mfilo rescue the bird. It was still alive and flapped wildly in his hands. He inspected its head, feet and wings and set it free.

The momentous events of the past few days, Dries and Alison's insistence only that morning on redecorating Mr Molinieux's rooms for her so that she could be in the main part of the house, as well as the man's disappearance, had unsettled Ou Mevrou Jansen. The memories she had buried so successfully over the years had been dredged up and had forced her to remember the betrayals and pain she had suffered – not that she had minded being a cook.

Ou Mevrou Jansen fished out a large handkerchief from her apron pocket and wept. 'Fanus's death was God's will. Who am I, Hendriena Jansen, asking God with my tears? And God sent Enoch to comfort me.' She murmured quietly to herself, 'His yoke is easy and His burden is light.'

She went to the kitchen and found Mfilo sitting on the window seat, having a cup of coffee. He was telling Clara how he had followed the dogs around the back of the house and discovered an elaborate trap where Augusta Leigh had found the dove. If only he could find the culprit. He promised Ou Mevrou Jansen that he would keep an eye out for trespassers. The servants were gathered in the kitchen, talking for the most part about Mr Molinieux and his disappearance. Clara blamed herself, but she was elated to have Mfilo back.

Mfilo told her that Mr Molinieux reminded him of his first master, an Englishman, who had treated him worse than a slave.

'When I first work in the garden of that lanie, he tell me to be careful and don't let the fruit get rotten on the trees – and that I must pick the apricots and peaches when they just right because he and madam don't like green fruit. He write in a little book every day about how many peaches there's left on the tree. I didn't steal one peach, but that white lanie always try to catch me out.'

'Just because Mr Molinieux is gone doesn't mean that you can come and talk rubbish,' said Clara. 'You lucky that he even take you on for a job. And you wouldn't be by Wepener now if you didn't get good training. Stop complaining.'

'Mr Pretorius is the one that take me on – not that ou. It's because of Mr Molinieux I'm now in big trouble. I never messed around with horses … I can sit in jail for years.'

'Why don't you jus' go back to the garden and use some of that experience you bragging about, instead of chasing the dogs around? And Mfilo, please leave that trap alone. It's bad luck; I thought you natives knew that. You better wash your hands and say some prayers. We don't want anything more to happen.'

'The bad stuff already happened to me. You upset that Mr Molinieux is gone and didn't marry you,' Mfilo said in a huff.

'Please, you two,' said Ou Mevrou Jansen, 'stop arguing. The child just now walks in here and you two talking nonsense. Haven't we had enough trouble in this house?'

'Now that it's no more Ou Mevrou Jansen, but *Ouma* Jansen, we can't do anything right,' Clara replied indignantly. 'At least Mr Molinieux kept order here.'

'Nonsense, Clara. I really don't know what's got into you. I'm still the same person. I might be changing rooms, but that doesn't make me any different.'

'Now Ou Mevrou Jansen is rich, Ou Mevrou Jansen no more cares what happen to us.'

'Stop your nonsense, child – you are all my family here. And I have always been rich.'

Clara was aware how things had changed, and she knew that no one would ever arrive at her door to announce that she had come into a fortune. She was happy with her job at Wepener, but she could not help wishing that some of the good fortune that had befallen Ou Mevrou

Jansen would come her way. For the old lady to have gone from cook to property owner in a matter of days perplexed Clara. It was one thing calling Europeans by their first names and having them pretend, like Dries and Alison, that everyone was equal, but it was quite another to have an old Coloured women catapulted from the kitchen to the drawing room from one day to the next.

Once the others had left, Clara confided in Ou Mevrou Jansen. 'I was raised to be a servant. It makes me sad to think that there is nothing else to look forward to.'

'Listen, my child, everyone should be raised to be a servant and we should be happy to serve each other. But I know what you mean about being a servant in this darned country. I wish you would leave that Mfilo and find yourself a decent husband. I wouldn't be surprised if he was involved in that racing scandal.'

'He had nothing to do with that. All he ever did was to get the horse manure for our garden.'

'Tell that to the judge.'

'I love him and I don't want to leave him.'

'If that's what you really want, I've been thinking about asking Dries to have the cottage fixed up for you and Mfilo. But it depends on the outcome of the case against him. And then you must get married first.'

'Does Ou Mevrou Jansen really mean it?' Clara jumped up from the table and threw her arms around her. 'But what about Chief Josias?'

'Don't talk about him. Don't even mention his name. I've already spoken about this to Dries and Alison. Alison's being a bit difficult, but will come around to the idea. Enoch can move into my old quarters, but we have to give him plenty of time to adjust – so please don't talk to Mfilo yet.'

'Enoch is adjusting quite good with Caroline – and here I thought he had eyes only for that Haima girl.'

'Don't worry, Caroline will be going back to England in a few weeks.'

Trossie stormed into the kitchen, holding a screaming Hanneli by the hand. 'Instead of wasting your time, you must look after the child, Clara. I was cleaning down by the cottage when she come to look for Oupa Hans and Enoch. The child can just walk out by the gate – and then what?'

'Caroline was keeping an eye on her.'

'Yes, with her head in the pool.'

Ou Mevrou Jansen left the kitchen as she heard the bread van drive up. The long conversation had tired her. She met the driver of the van at the front door every other day with a basket to collect the bread, but the driver practically had to lean on his horn as it took her longer and longer to appear. Alison had suggested that it was time for either Mieta or Trossie to collect the bread; however, Ou Mevrou Jansen declined to relinquish this small and pleasurable duty. She did not mind the girls getting the fish, or running the many other errands that involved going down to the shops on the Main Road. Collecting the bread and milk were her responsibilities and would remain so until she could no longer walk.

When she reached the van, she leaned into the back to inhale the warm aromas. She could distinguish by smell the different kinds of loaves in their trays: the cut loaf, the dark top of the wonder loaf that Enterprise had copied from Duens. She liked its smell of carbolic and molasses, rather than the more robust whole-wheat and brown loaves. The deliveryman handed her the order, enough for two days.

A young native boy, whom she thought to be his assistant, stood near the van. However, when the van drove off he was still standing there.

'Can I help you, young man?'

'I'm looking for Baas Dries Schoon.'

'He isn't here right now and there aren't any spare jobs.'

Mfilo walked up to see what the matter was. The young man appeared glad to see him, 'Hawu, Sawubona Mnumzana.'

'Wenzani, wena mfana? Ufuna ni?'

'I must see Baas Dries. Khotso sent me.'

'I've just told him that Dries isn't here,' Ou Mevrou Jansen interjected.

'Can I wait for the baas?'

'Mfilo, I don't want this boy hanging around getting up to mischief.'

'Ou Mevrou Jansen, he says he's Khotso's apprentice, and he must see Dries. He wants Dries to help Khotso get out of jail.'

'Hubani igama lakho?'

'His name is Redemptus.'

'Who is this Khotso?' Ou Mevrou Jansen demanded to know. 'There is no one here by that name.'

The arrival of the milkman interrupted their conversation. He pushed his bicycle up the rise to the house, scuffing his heavy black boots against the gravel. Ou Mevrou Jansen invited him to the kitchen, as she sometimes did. She told the boy to come along with them so that she could keep an eye on him until Dries got back from the clinic. She rummaged around for an enamel plate and mug for Redemptus and poured them both cups of strong coffee and spread thick slices of fresh bread with butter and jam.

Dries telephoned and asked if dinner could be served at eight, as he was going to be late. Ou Mevrou Jansen was concerned about the boy as it would be dark by then and she advised him to return the following morning. Reluctantly Redemptus left the kitchen and walked back along the drive to the gate.

A tall man weeding the border alongside the path greeted Redemptus in Xhosa. Soon they were deep in conversation. On hearing that the young man had been unable to see Dries and was planning to return to Wepener the following day, Chief Josias suggested he spend the night with him at the gate lodge. Enoch had not returned from his grandfather's funeral and his bed was available. Redemptus was pleased, as he had nowhere to go.

'Enoch is my friend. In Cofimvaba he shared my hut.'

Since Wepener was under constant watch from the road, it was the last place the police would have expected Josias to be. They had searched for him throughout the Peninsula and the southern Karoo. There had been reported sightings of him everywhere. The police had recently found Josias's motorcycle abandoned along the N1 near Worcester.

Dries had arranged for a friend to drive Josias from Worcester back to Cape Town, where he spent two nights in a cave on the lower slopes of Table Mountain. He had then made his way cautiously to Wepener along a hiking trail, walking only at dusk and dawn to avoid hikers. Dries had described the landmarks he was to follow down the mountain to Wepener. The descent had not been easy, but it entailed far less risk of being seen than if he had used the road. He was in a dishevelled state when he reached the estate boundaries, finding his way to the house where an anxious Dries welcomed him with open arms.

Wepener seemed to have become a place of safety for fugitives and for Josias it had become the only place of sanity in the country. While

Josias prepared supper, Redemptus told him about Khotso's arrest and events in Pondoland.

'The prime minister comes to Cofimvaba to listen to the bones, and now Khotso is in jail because the bones don't tell the prime minister what he wants to hear. I always say he must talk to his own ancestors. What do Xhosa ancestors know about his problems? I came here to ask if the prime minister can help Khotso, but Polycarp told me to first go see his son, Baas Dries.'

'I'm not sure what Dries can do,' Josias said, 'but his father is making a big speech in the morning. There's an emergency indaba in parliament where they will talk about Pondoland – so you should go straight there. Look for Schoon's driver Witbooi at the back of the building and tell him that you must speak to Schoon.'

'I know Witbooi; he drives Baas Schoon to Cofimvaba. I've met him, the silent one. I'll try and find him.'

'I'll go and have a word with Dries after dark, and later we'll get Zachaeus to drive you into town. He'll show you how to get there and where to go. And Redemptus, whatever may happen to you, don't ever mention my name or say that you've met me.'

Extraordinary Session of Parliament

Dr Schoon still felt the effects of his long journey to Cofimvaba. He was determined to stamp out any further insurrection in the native areas and townships, especially after the humiliation he had suffered at the hands of the Pondo chiefs. He decided that no questions would be permitted from the benches when Greyling addressed parliament. Dr Schoon knew Greyling to be responsible for the worsening situation, but he could not afford to give the opposition the opportunity to ridicule his minister of police in parliament. After Greyling's address, the Speaker would call on the minister of Bantu affairs, Pienaar, to give an appraisal of the situation in Pondoland, based on the report he had prepared after his visit there on Christmas Day. As Dr Schoon had read the report, he knew that it would go some way to justifying Greyling's actions.

He was also extremely angry about Khotso's arrest and was afraid that this would make matters worse. Here again Piet Greyling had acted in a pig-headed manner. The prime minister was certain that Khotso would not divulge any aspect of their relationship under interrogation, but if details of their friendship got out, he would become the laughing stock of the country and it would hurt his wife deeply. He realised that his last trip to Cofimvaba had been ill-conceived. Special Branch had used the insurrection in Pondoland as an excuse to arrest his old friend and to stir up further trouble among the Pondos. He wondered whether Polycarp would be implicated; the last thing Dr Schoon wanted was to have his involvement in the appointment of Khotso's head teacher made public.

Schoon had spent most of the night reading through the various briefs prepared for him and he had assimilated enough information to present an extemporaneous speech the following day. That was what he did best. A few hours remained before his speech and he did not feel inclined to sit in his office, fending off the inevitable interruptions that he knew would come his way. He decided to stretch his legs, and asked his private secretary to summon his bodyguards to accompany him to the museum at the top of Government Avenue. When the young man asked him why he wished to visit a museum on such a critical morning, the prime minister replied, 'I need an atmosphere of calm.'

The prime minister walked briskly through the Company Gardens. He felt drawn to the Bushman dioramas and had asked his private secretary to have the museum director declare that wing off limits to the public while he was there. Dr Shaw, the world expert on these virtually extinct people, asked whether the prime minister would like her to accompany him. She had helped create the dioramas and was one of only a few Europeans who could speak the Bushman language. His private secretary thanked her for the offer, but told her that Dr Schoon would prefer to look around on his own.

Dr Schoon stood entranced in front of the first diorama, which displayed some lifelike Bushmen engaged in hunting, cooking and skinning animals, and a mother nursing a child. In the background, he saw the finest example of Bushman rock paintings he had ever seen – a glorious frieze of eland which, according to the brass plaque, had been taken piece by piece from a cave in the Maclear district. In the next diorama he saw a group of Bushmen in a cave, one of them painting on a rock surface. Nearby there were other rocks covered with similar paintings. The dioramas ended in a much larger reconstruction of a hearth site in the mouth of a cave. The prime minister marvelled at the lifestyle of these people and the lack of anxiety on their faces.

He felt at home with these plaster-cast Bushmen; they expected nothing from him and allowed him a glimpse into their simple world. Schoon felt a desire to communicate with them. He placed a sixpence into the recorder slot and lifted the earpiece, expecting to hear the staccato clicks of the Bushman tongue. However, as the voices on the tape became audible, he was shocked to hear himself being addressed in Afrikaans.

The prime minister recoiled. The fluency and ease with which the Bushmen spoke his language unnerved him. Clearly upset, he slammed down the receiver. A feeling of nausea crept over him, and the sudden realisation of time passing made him end his visit. Without stopping to thank the museum director, he rushed back to the houses of parliament with his bodyguards following him. He was hurrying down the path through the middle of the Company Gardens when a man leaning against a statue caught his attention. Normally he would not have given him a second glance; but he was no stranger – it was the family's butler.

Cyprian Molinieux's departure from Wepener was not as precipitous as it may have seemed. For some time he had been planning to leave South Africa and return to Scotland. Once he had made the decision, he went about realising it in a practical manner. Having secured a position as a steward aboard the *Pendennis Castle*, he had stowed his belongings on the mailboat that was due to depart for Southampton a few days later. After an absence of forty years, he would be considered a stranger in the country of his birth, but his plan was to make a new life for himself.

Mr Molinieux had even dared to hope that he would find a wife in his ancestral town of Inverness. There would be no more peering over his shoulder or looking into the mirror in fear that he may have been polluted.

For the past few days he had been drifting around Cape Town awaiting the departure of the ship. He was slightly unkempt and very tired, having spent an uncomfortable night on a bench in the Gardens.

Mr Molinieux held the prime minister responsible for the laws that had caused him so much anguish. He was about to return to the ship in dock to have a shave, a shower and a change of clothes in preparation for a visit to the prime minister's residence later in the day. He was certain to be allowed entry to Groote Schuur by the security guards. The man needed to be taught a lesson, but the last thing he had expected was to meet Dr Schoon in the Company Gardens.

That same morning after breakfast Chief Josias looked at Redemptus and decided that the boy was not dressed properly for the task he was about to undertake. His socks were far too bright and the tie he was wearing would draw unwelcome attention. Nor was there any way of telling what people in town would make of his two-tone shoes. He was wearing an ill-fitting suit and his shirt collar had seen better days.

'You're about Enoch's size, aren't you?'

They went through Enoch's wardrobe and chose what Josias considered more suitable attire for the occasion.

'There you are, Redemptus – now nobody can call you a tsotsi.'

'But what will Enoch say?'

'He'll say you look fine.'

About an hour later Zachaeus arrived to take Redemptus to town. He was well known to the security guards at parliament and drove up to the official parking bay. Witbooi was nowhere to be found. As Zachaeus had to get back to Wepener to take Ou Mevrou Jansen to the doctor, he was unable to wait. He told the guard at the gate to let Witbooi know that he had a visitor.

Redemptus was to see Witbooi as soon as he arrived.

Redemptus waited for some time. He was thirsty and indicated to the guard that he would be back in a moment. He wandered through the adjoining gardens in search of a tap. When he had finished drinking and stood up, he caught sight of the prime minister walking in his direction. He recognised Dr Schoon as the man for whom he had thrown the bones at Cofimvaba.

Mr Molinieux saw Dr Schoon almost collide with the elegantly dressed African youth as he hurried back to his office. However, Redemptus was soon forgotten as Mr Molinieux approached the prime minister. Dr Schoon was in a hurry, but he stopped briefly to shake Mr Molinieux's hand and to wish him a happy New Year. 'And congratulations,' he added. 'Your problem has been solved. Your new identity card is in the post.'

Emboldened by this unexpected turn of events, Mr Molinieux did not hear the prime minister's words. He had his hand on a dagger concealed inside his jacket. Before the bodyguards could intervene, he stabbed Dr Schoon several times. As Mr Molinieux plunged the dagger into the prime minister's ribcage, he knew he had achieved his goal as he felt the blade pierce the prime minister's heart. The whole incident took place so quickly that no one in the vicinity realised what had happened. Passers-by may have thought that the stricken man had tripped as Dr Schoon slumped forward and fell to the ground.

Mr Molinieux resisted the attempts of the bodyguards to restrain him, but they were well trained and put their truncheons to good use. The bodyguards dragged him away and flung him into a police van that was parked at the top of Adderley Street. Redemptus, who was still close by, was also arrested and hurled into another van.

Redemptus had only wanted to ask the prime minister to free Khotso. Yet he had found himself in the wrong place at the wrong time and now there was no Gumede to intercede for him. As he was jolted around in the back of the speeding van, Redemptus trembled with fear. He could not shake off the terrible sight of the white man drawing a knife and driving it into the prime minister's chest. It was just as he had seen it in the bones.

When the ambulance attendant turned the prime minister onto his back, his eyes still held a look of surprise. He had been stabbed barely a hundred yards from the entrance to parliament. A labyrinth of pain spread out from his chest and moved across his body, found its way into his arms and legs, and even into the joints of his fingers. However, his mind was still sharp. He attempted to say something, but his jaw would not move, nor would his tongue cooperate though he was desperate to speak.

The words Schoon tried to murmur were lost in the blood that leaked from the side of his mouth. The amulet Khotso had given him on Boxing Day had not protected him. How was it that Arta was not there when he needed her? What was all the shouting, shoving and cursing around him? Where were Dries and his little princess? He tried to raise his hand to remove the cause of the pain, but his entire body was limp. He felt as if it were being taken apart, piece by piece.

Through a haze of delirium, the prime minister saw the chambers of parliament filling with people, the gallery and every available seat. Those who had arrived to hear his speech crowded into the visitors' gallery – even the Speaker's chair had been taken over. All he could see were black faces. Khotso peered at him from his seat on the podium. It was then he realised that it was Khotso's apprentice he had just seen – no doubt sent to cast bad medicine on him.

Around him the stomping of gumboots reverberated in counterpoint to a fearsome chant. The dancers pounded their feet on the floor and Dr Schoon heard the rattles tied above their knees as the dancers began their march through parliament, led by the Gentleman Usher of the Black Rod. The Bushmen from the museum joined the procession, as though life for them had not been frozen in time. However, these images were dispelled as his face contorted into one last grimace of pain. There were doves cooing in the trees and the heavy perfume of frangipani rose on the breeze. The prime minister was rushed to a nearby hospital where the best surgeons struggled in vain to repair the damage Mr Molinieux had inflicted on him.

The Speaker of the House and the minister of defence rushed to Wepener by car, with two motorcycle outriders in front speeding through dense traffic along De Waal Drive. It was their intention to inform Dries of the terrible tragedy that had befallen his father before the news reached him on the wireless – and then to go on to Pringle Bay to break the news to Mrs Schoon.

The two men were in a state of agitation as they rang the doorbell at Wepener several times. 'I thought they had a man to open the door,' the Speaker announced impatiently. Eventually they heard slow footsteps echoing down the hall. Ou Mevrou Jansen opened the door. 'Quick, old woman, this is an emergency. Where is the master of the house?' the Speaker demanded.

'I am the master of the house,' Ou Mevrou Jansen replied.

'We haven't got time to play the fool now. Something terrible has happened. We must speak to your master immediately.'

'I am the rightful owner of this house.'

'Look, old lady, you don't understand. I am the Speaker of parliament and this is the minister of defence. Where is your master?'

'I am the master of Wepener.'

The Speaker pushed past Ou Mevrou Jansen and the two men charged through the house, dashing from room to room, calling for Dries. They finally reached the study where Dries, Alison, Caroline and Enoch were listening to the news bulletin on the wireless. The prime minister had been killed; the police had taken into custody a Coloured man believed to have been employed at the family home, Wepener, as well as his accomplice, an unidentified native youth. They were believed to be members of a clandestine group that had conspired to kill the prime minister.

'We came as quickly as possible to tell you the tragic news, but I'm afraid we are too late,' the Speaker said. 'I bring you the sympathy and heartfelt sorrow of all the members of parliament and of the whole nation; we are all in mourning for this great man. I hope your mother has not heard. Could you break the news to Mrs Schoon?'

'She must know by now,' Dries responded with an ashen face. 'My father asked us all to listen to his speech. Those were his last instructions to us. I will telephone my mother. My wife and I will go directly to Pringle Bay. Please, may we be given an escort? Under no circumstances do I want my grandmother to know about this. I hope you didn't mention it to her when she opened the door.'

'No, it was just an old Coloured woman at the door.'

'That old Coloured woman is my grandmother,' Dries replied impatiently. He took Alison's hand and called for Clara and Hanneli. He asked Enoch to ring for Zachaeus to bring the car around to the front door.

'Enoch, I'd like you to come with us to Pringle Bay, but under the circumstances I think it best if you stay with Ou Mevrou Jansen. Break the news to her gently. And take good care of Caroline. We will bring my mother back to Wepener as soon as she feels strong enough to travel.'

As soon as the Speaker of the House and the minister of defence left the study, Dries told Enoch to go down to the gate lodge and tell Josias what had happened. 'Warn him he must leave. Things are going to get hectic around here and don't forget to take some provisions for him.'

Epilogue

A lone boxing glove encased in plastic hung from a nail on the wall of a shebeen in Gugulethu where Zachaeus took Enoch some weeks after the murder. Enoch was due to leave for St Dominic's at Tsomo the next morning, where he would complete his final school year. After Oupa Hans's funeral, Enoch had asked his parents to meet with Sister Deduch, the head of St Dominic's, and they had finally given their permission for him to attend. Enoch was thrilled at the prospect of being close to Polycarp at Cofimvaba.

Over the years Miss Mgudlandlu, proprietor of the establishment, had convinced her customers that Joe Louis, the world heavyweight champion, had sent her the glove from America. A typed note with an almost illegible inscription from her admirer was displayed on the bar counter for customers who demanded proof of the glove's authenticity.

Miss Mgudlandlu shook Enoch's hand warmly and kissed him. 'I will miss this young man … He was one of my star students. I also knew his oupa well – bless his soul. He used to be a good customer. He first told me you wanted to be a doctor, then you wanted to be an artist. But I hear you are a writer now.'

Miss Mgudlandlu poured their beer into glasses. 'You watch out for the lamp, Enoch. When I close up shop at night, it's the only light I have to work by. Your oupa offered to buy me one of those camping lanterns. He said it would be better for me, but I told him that it was too bright and bad for my eyes.'

On that night, as on so many others, the men admired the glove and, as the drinking progressed, got deeper into conversation about their own fighting prowess. Miss Mgudlandlu kept a strict watch on the glove and would not allow anyone to touch it.

Having agreed about the injustices of the government, the ruminations of the men led them elsewhere – to 1947, or 1948, as none of them could remember the exact date King George VI and his daughters had visited South Africa. The ensuing argument about the year of the royal visit caused deep rifts as each drinker considered his own recollections of the time as being of the utmost importance. Some even cast their minds back to when, as small boys, they stood close to the railway line, barefooted and waving at the royal train as it chugged by.

Others, who knew of the visit only by hearsay, allowed themselves room for invention. The defeat of Field Marshal Jan Smuts at the polls was of significance in their reckonings of the royal visit, as it was by that time that many of the men had first come to hear of Khotso and how he had fixed the 1948 election with his muti, giving the Nationalists a slim majority. According to Miss Mgudlandlu, that was also the year her admirer had defeated Jersey Joe Walcott.

'This one is on the house,' Miss Mgudlandlu said to Enoch. 'Don't listen to these stupid men. They're stuck in the past. Give them a couple of drinks and they can't even find their way back to their pondoks. What on earth does that bladdie King George have to do with us? All he did was put his fat arse on a throne because his brother wasn't man enough to fill it.'

'His brother gave up the Crown for love,' Zachaeus responded.

'Love? My foot. And what do you know about it?'

'I read about it in the papers.'

Compared with the news of the week, however, the 1948 elections and the royal visit paled in significance. Khotso's life sentence for complicity in the murder of the prime minister dominated the headlines. Redemptus, his accomplice, was awaiting trial. His dompas had been found in a pouch around the prime minister's neck. Dr Schoon had worn it as an intelizi to ward off evil. The fact that Redemptus had been arrested in the vicinity of parliament while trying to flee the scene of the crime had provided the State with further evidence of his guilt. He was expected to receive the death penalty.

The shebeen was probably one of the safest places to be as the police had once again gone on a rampage on the streets to show that, despite the death of the prime minister, the government remained in charge. According to rumours making the rounds of the townships, the prime minister had been assassinated because he had offended the witchdoctor Khotso, who had sent his apprentice to Cape Town to remove his protection.

'I heard that the prime minister made long journeys to Cofimvaba to get strong muti,' Miss Mgudlandlu said. 'People say the prime minister didn't show any respect for us natives, but he sure wanted to taste our medicine. White man with the bones. What next?'

'You better shut your trap, Sis Gladys, because jus' now the police come and break down your doors,' one of her customers warned. 'Better not talk about the big man because the walls got ears. Look what happened to Chief Josias – they caught him hiding in a cave and now they going to put him away for life.'

'I'm just telling you what I heard. The walls maybe have ears,' Miss Mgudlandlu replied, 'but that man Schoon can't hear any more because Khotso shut his ears for good.'

Another customer interjected, 'They say it was a Coloured guy who put the assegai into him. I've never seen a Coloured with a spear. It could have been one of those Pondo chiefs.'

'Don't come and talk nonsense,' a fellow drinker replied. 'Anyways, those old Pondos are in the government's pockets. They're not going to do themselves out of a good thing.'

'I heard it was a poor white,' yet another drinker added. However, the man's view was dismissed with scorn.

'I could see it coming,' Miss Mgudlandlu said. 'You remember that day when the prime minister made his big speech on the Parade about this republic thing? He was carrying a dove. He threw the bird up into the air, but it came falling straight down. The white people cheered when he said that the Union Jack must come down and a new flag go up, but he must have known that there was going to be plenty of bad luck.'

With the scraping of a penknife on the bottom of an ancient battery, a customer coaxed the wireless into life for the late news. The new prime minister, Balthazar Byleveld, former minister of justice, was on the air.

'The cabinet will leave no stone unturned to get behind the motive for this cowardly and tragic act. This is not the time for rumours or wild speculation. The security police and the defence force will not rest until each and every subversive element is behind bars. The two main suspects have confessed to their criminal acts and will be dealt with severely; however, the government of South Africa has not ruled out a full enquiry into the tragic death of our late prime minister. As a footnote, I would like to add that, in the heat of the moment, it had been reported in error that a man previously employed at the family home had been involved in the prime minister's murder. Investigators can now definitively report that this was not the case.'

'Ja, nee – I heard that they hide the real killer away because he's one of them and then they come and blame Khotso and the boy,' a patron said in reply to the broadcast.

'Those guys in parliament are so stupid they don't even know that Khotso's muti can hit them straight from Robben Island. He can throw the bones anywhere. Eish, you don't mess with him. And the man can swim – not like Makana, whose magic couldn't keep him on top of the waves.'

Gladys Mgudlandlu placed another beer in front of Enoch. 'Don't let all this get you down, sonny boy. You're a bit older now, and possibly a bit wiser. Maybe you've got your own ideas about this murder thing. Haai man, it must've been bad for Mrs Schoon – how did she take it?'

'She's still in shock,' Enoch replied. 'She's back home now at Wepener. Ou Mevrou Jansen is looking after her.'

'Zachaeus, please give my condolence letter to Dries before they leave for England. Shame, Enoch, I hear your girlfriend is also leaving.'

'How come everyone knows my business?' Enoch asked. 'She told me that she'd be back.'

The patrons stared into their glasses. They were not sure what to make of it all, and were caught between jubilation and mourning. They continued to drink deep into the night. Zachaeus and Enoch returned to Wepener, where Enoch was to spend his last night. He was to leave for Tsomo after breakfast the following morning.

Acknowledgements

With sincere thanks to my wife, Charlotte, for her help and support. My daughters, Makhosazana and Adria, I thank for their patience and devotion. Thanks are due also to my son, Christian Edeani – and Steven Draper for his extraordinary generosity so many years ago. Thank you Barend Toerien for your persistence on my behalf.